THE LOST CODEX

The Works of Alan Jacobson

NOVELS

False Accusations

KAREN VAIL SERIES

The 7th Victim

Crush

Velocity

Inmate 1577

No Way Out

Spectrum

OPSIG TEAM BLACK SERIES

The Hunted

Hard Target

The Lost Codex

SHORT STORIES

"Fatal Twist"

(featuring Karen Vail)

"Double Take"

(featuring Carmine Russo & Ben Dyer)

For up-to-date information on Alan Jacobson's current and future novels, please visit his website, www.AlanJacobson.com.

THE LOST CODEX

AN OPSIG TEAM BLACK NOVEL

ALAN JACOBSON

NEW YORK

Cover design by Jamie Keenan

Book cover text set in Caudex, copyright © 2011 by Hjort Nidudsson

Author photographs: Jill Jacobson (jacket); Corey Jacobson (author bio)

978-1-5040-0363-6

Published in 2015 by Open Road Integrated Media, Inc.
345 Hudson Street
New York, NY 10014
www.openroadmedia.com

For Florence Jacobson

My mother's life changed dramatically the moment her father succumbed to a fatal heart attack at the dinner table. Following that traumatic event, she took on the challenge of raising her younger brother while my grandmother went to work in Manhattan. A dozen years later, during my childhood, whenever there was an issue in our Queens neighborhood, be it a broken streetlight or a problem at our local elementary school, people knew they could rely on my mother to raise hell—and get the problem taken care of. She fought when others yielded. She persisted when others acquiesced. Most importantly, my mother taught me perseverance, a vital trait without which I never would've been able to overcome the obstacles I've encountered in life. While each of my novels could have been dedicated to my mother, my milestone tenth book is for her.

THE LOST CODEX

"At the center of this story is not a diamond, a painting, or a suitcase full of bills, but a book. Some would say it is *the* book: the authoritative copy of a text whose position at the root of more than one civilization has given it bearing on the lives of billions of people, even if they have never read it."

—Matti Friedman, *The Aleppo Codex*

"Just sitting down five minutes drinking a cup of tea with mujahedeen is better than anything I've ever experienced in my whole life . . . I lived in America! I know how it is. You have all the fancy amusement parks, and the restaurants, and the food, and all this crap and the cars and you think you're happy. You're not happy, you're never happy. I was never happy. I was always sad and depressed. Life sucked . . . All you do is work 40, 50, 60 hours a week. [Now] I see paradise and I can smell paradise."

—Moner Mohammed Abu-Salha
American al Qaeda suicide bomber
seconds before blowing himself up

"The history of our race, and each individual's experience, is sown thick with evidences that a truth is not hard to kill, and that a lie told well is immortal."

—Mark Twain

PROLOGUE

Wadi Qumran
One mile Northwest of the Dead Sea
The West Bank, Jordan
August 6, 1953

Eylad Uziel walked carefully over the rough terrain of the Qumran caves. This was Bedouin territory in land governed by Jordan, but he was an Israeli—an unusual if not suicidal proposition. Then again, no one knew his true identity or nationality. Officially, he was the primary translator on the Catholic archaeological team led by Roland de Vaux, a French Dominican priest. Their sprawling, multiyear project was like no other in history: excavating the Dead Sea Scrolls.

Uziel, a soldier during Israel's war of independence and a scholar before that, had been recruited into Mossad, the fledgling security service designed to gather information regarding threats to the state. Given Israel's location, pinned in by hostile countries determined to wipe it off the face of the earth, Mossad's charge was a vital asset during a time of unrest.

But Uziel's assignment was extraordinary. In spring 1947 a Bedouin shepherd had stumbled onto a cave containing ancient scrolls on animal parchment that turned out to be a handwritten copy of the Old Testament, penned thousands of years ago under the threat of the advancing Romans and their conquering marauders. Uziel's job was to blend in with the archaeologists working at the site, take stock of what was discovered, and perform a cursory accounting of its significance. Six years earlier, when the first cave had been discovered, the Bedouins who found the scrolls sold them to private antiquities dealers.

Israel, like the West Bank, was still under British rule at the time and powerless to stop the plundering of what its leaders felt was its legacy: the two-thousand-year-old documents were the earliest recorded portions of the Hebrew Bible ever discovered, copied by an ancient Jewish sect whose members likely believed that they were preparing an archive to preserve their religious and cultural traditions in the event the Romans sacked Jerusalem.

The scrolls belonged in a museum, not on the black market.

Uziel's scholarly work, leading digs and excavating Israel's hidden history in stone fragments, leather parchments, long-buried buildings, coins, and religious artifacts, also entailed providing analysis to the government and its burgeoning national museum, so that the ancient Jewish civilization that populated the Judean land over the centuries could be properly recorded, studied, and brought into historical perspective.

On November 29, 1947—the day of the historic United Nations vote in Queens, New York, that partitioned Palestine and led to the establishment of the state of Israel five months later—Uziel had purchased three scrolls from a Jordanian antiquities dealer.

Examining the manuscripts left him thirsty to see what other parchments had been holed away in that cave—and the adjacent caves that had been excavated in the subsequent years. Not far away sat the ruins of a complex that housed the Essenes, the Jewish sect whose community members were thought to be the scrolls' primary scribes.

Despite Uziel's efforts, and those of other Mossad and government agents, many of the ancient scrolls were still privately held—most notably, by a Palestinian family who had purchased them for a pittance from the Bedouin, who did not know the significance of what they had stumbled upon.

The Vatican had stepped in and taken custody of the rest, and despite requests from numerous Catholic and Jewish scholars, kept them under lock and key, sequestered for some as yet unstated reason.

Uziel made a case to the young Israeli government and national museum that they needed a set of eyes at the dig, overseeing any new discoveries.

Bolstering Uziel's argument, intelligence analysts had heard rumors that Roland de Vaux's deputy, Alberi Michel, was a bigoted, vindictive sort who was a fascist sympathizer and displayed flashes of anti-Semitism. Although Mossad could not verify such allegations, Uziel's mission was approved and conceived in a way that the Israeli government could have eyes on the ground, ensuring that whatever remained of its cultural and historical treasures were not defaced, destroyed, stolen, or sold on the black market.

Uziel wore a straw hat with a wide brim and a white linen shirt, his skin brown from months in the intense sun. Standing on a precipice and looking out at the Qumran landscape, he drew a cotton rag across his brow. There was no breeze and the air was desert dry, despite the proximity of the Dead Sea, which sat off to his left, in plain view on this clear day. Directly in front of him were the undulating burnt sienna and cinnamon colored rocky outcroppings of the hills that sported small openings to the caves which had served as hiding areas for the clay jars that bore the scrolls.

A loud whistle echoed across the divide a few meters away, in the vicinity of Cave 11. Uziel made his way over, navigating the rough terrain and using rope ladders stretched across the stony surfaces.

"I've got something!" one of the men said in French. "Another scroll, a big one."

Uziel quickened his pace. Finds of any magnitude were now few and far between, and witnessing the moment of its unveiling was a once-in-a-lifetime event.

Uziel climbed the rope ladder, slipping twice and nearly taking a header when his toe missed the rung and instead hit a protrusion in the rock face. "What do you got?" he asked in Arabic.

"Look, look!" Michel said. He tossed his whisker brush aside and squared his body in front of the excavated find. "Give me a hand."

There were now three men in the mouth of the cave behind Uziel. He knelt beside Michel and helped him lift the clay vessel from the loosened dirt.

"How do you know there's a scroll in here?"

"There's always a scroll in these pots."

Uziel gave him a look.

"And I peeked."

Uziel laughed—more giddy with excitement than from the comment.

The two men carried the container carefully, the other workers standing aside as if in reverence of its contents. Twenty minutes later, they had the receptacle open and the scroll sitting on a work table that was shielded from the elements.

They put on clean work gloves, then Michel glanced at Uziel. "It's big, like I told you."

"I can see that."

They held their breath as they began to slowly unroll it. After exposing three feet, they paused and Uziel hunched over the parchment. This was why he was here: to read, and translate, the Hebrew or Aramaic.

"Remarkably well preserved," Uziel said. His eyes moved from right to left, line to line, when Michel nudged his left shoulder.

"What is it?" Michel asked. "What's it say?"

Uziel kept reading. "This is . . . it's different."

"Different? How so?"

He carefully unrolled another foot and continued moving across the document. "Extraordinary." He stopped and looked up. "Clear the table, give me more to read."

"Tell me," Michel said, staring at the black ink block letters. "What does it say?"

Uziel soldiered on, his lips moving as he spoke the Hebrew aloud. Ten minutes later, having reached the end, he reached for the chair behind him and sat down heavily.

"I swear it," Michel said. "By the hand of Christ, I will strike you with my walking stick if you don't tell me what it says."

"Christ is an interesting choice of words." He made eye contact and his elation turned to concern. "This could change history, my friend."

PART 1

"Our military and intelligence personnel go face to face with the world's most dangerous men every day. They have risked their lives to capture some of the most brutal terrorists on earth and they have worked day and night to find out what the terrorists know so we can stop new attacks. America owes our brave men and women some things in return; we owe them thanks for saving lives and keeping America safe . . ." —PRESIDENT GEORGE W. BUSH, SEPTEMBER 6, 2006

"Sometimes people don't want to hear the truth because they don't want their illusions to be destroyed." —FRIEDRICH NIETZSCHE

1

14th Street NW
Washington, DC
Present day

The waitress set the glass of Board Meeting brown ale on the table in front of FBI profiler Karen Vail. Vail took a long sip and said, "Notes of dark chocolate and coffee. I've definitely developed a taste for this. It's very . . . stimulating." She winked at her fiancé, DEA special agent Roberto Hernandez.

"You mean like an aphrodisiac?" Robby asked. "Beer?"

Vail leaned close to him, her lips tickling his ear. "When we get home, after I pull your pants off, I'm going to take your—"

Two gunshots echoed off the facades of the neighboring buildings. Vail and Robby pulled their pistols in unison and ran toward the exit of the storefront bar.

"That was nearby," Vail said as she hit the glass door. *So much for a romantic night out.*

"Anything?" Robby asked, swiveling in an arc, eyes scanning the nighttime cityscape.

The vapor from their now-rapid breathing trailed off like apparitions, carried on the breeze that found its way down the collar of Vail's sweater. She had left without pulling on her coat, and the chill made her shiver involuntarily.

A shrill scream off to the right in the vicinity of 14th Street NW sent them sprinting down the block. They turned the corner—and saw a body laid out on the sidewalk, the blood pooled next to it dripping over the edge of the curb.

"Call it in," Vail said as she continued on toward the injured man. She pressed two fingers against his carotid and shook her head. "Let's secure the perimeter, hold the scene for Metro PD."

Robby brought the phone to his ear and craned his neck to find the street signs so he could report their location.

Vail hovered over the body but could not resist the urge to check the identity of the deceased.

C'mon, Karen, let Metro do their jobs. This isn't your case. This isn't your jurisdiction.

She gently patted the man's jacket with the back of her hand, then moved on to his jeans. In his front pocket Vail felt a wallet. She forced two fingers against the denim and extracted the smooth black leather bi-fold. Her heart skipped a beat as she splayed it open and saw an FBI shield. Agent Harlon Filloon.

Whoa. Was he killed because he's a federal agent? Was he working a case? Or is it just a coincidence?

"Robby." Vail held up the credentials so he could see what she had found, then folded them and slid them into her pocket.

He nodded as he finished the call and then reholstered his phone.

"Something's not right." She rose from her crouch and glanced around, her Glock now tight in her grip, following the direction of her gaze.

She moved toward the street corner a few yards away and heard feet slapping against asphalt. *Fleeing suspect?*

Vail pressed her back against the building's masonry wall as Robby headed toward her.

"What's up?"

"Footsteps. Running. Could be nothing."

Glock out in front, chest high, elbows locked against her ribcage, she swung left, around the corner of the edifice—

And saw a man sprinting across Irving Street, approaching a row of brick townhouses. "Hey!"

He turned, their eyes met, and that's when she saw the handgun glint in the amber glow of the streetlight.

"FBI, don't move!"

He twisted his torso and something flew from his hands as he brought up the pistol. But Vail and Robby fired first.

One or both of them scored a direct hit—and a concussive blast blew them both back onto their buttocks, glass and shrapnel flying past, and against, them. Vail shook her head, opened her eyes, and looked up into a fog of detritus floating down toward her. She rolled onto all fours, her hearing diminished. *Robby—*

She swung her gaze around and saw him on a knee, slowly pushing himself upright. "You okay?"

"I think so." He staggered toward her, slipping on shards of glass littering the asphalt.

Car alarms blared as people scurried out of the nearby buildings, running this way and that, trying to escape a formless threat.

As Vail made her way toward the area where the perp was standing when they shot him, she became aware of her phone ringing—and vibrating violently in her pocket.

Vail stopped and brought the handset to her face.

"Agent Vail, this is Director Knox."

A call from the FBI director? On a Saturday night?

"Yes sir," she said as she caught a glimpse of Robby starting to sift through the rubble. "Can you speak louder?" *I just escaped being blown to bits and my hearing's a bit muffled.*

There was a pause, then, "We've got a situation I need you to handle."

"Does it have anything to do with the gunshots? Or the bomb that just went off?"

"Yes. I know you're on site."

Vail looked around, her eyes trying to locate a camera—but she did not see one. "You do?"

Then she remembered the ShotSpotter system installed around the district: hundreds of acoustic sensors designed to capture and instantaneously pinpoint certain sound frequencies, in particular those of gunfire.

"I need you to secure the scene."

Vail jerked her head around as sirens blared in the distance. It was muted, but she definitely knew the unmistakable cry of a law enforcement vehicle. "Metro PD's gonna be here in seconds. Why do you need me to—"

"You are to take control of that scene. Not Metro PD."

"But s—"

"No buts. Listen to me, Agent Vail. You are to take control of that scene on my authority."

"Okay, but—"

"This is the time to follow orders and not ask questions. Can you do that?"

"Of course." *Who am I kidding? Hopefully the director.*

"Harlon Filloon, the downed man, is an agent. You're to protect his identity and keep others—meaning police, medical examiners, forensic personnel—away from his body."

"Yes sir."

"Send Agent Hernandez home. And tell him not to talk with anyone about what he just saw."

"Send him *home*?"

"I don't have time to repeat my orders. Do as you're told. I'll be in touch."

"Yes sir."

"We've dispatched a team that's four minutes out. Let them in. No one else is to enter that scene. No one. Understood?"

"Understood."

"Who was that?" Robby asked as Vail shoved the phone back in her pocket.

"You need to leave," she said, still trying to process what Knox told her—attempting to read between the lines, attempting to understand, attempting to clear her head of the fog induced by the blast. "Go home."

Robby tilted his head. "What the hell are you talking about?"

"I can't say anymore. And you can't either. Not to anyone." She started toward the end of the block, where she had been standing when she pulled the trigger. "Just listen to me. I'll call you as soon as I can."

"What the hell's going on? Why do I need to go home?"

"I don't know. But I've got my orders. And—"

"Your orders are to send me home?"

"Yes. And it'd be best for you to listen."

"Karen—"

"Robby, please. Let me deal with this and we'll sort it out later, okay?"

Jonathan. What are the chances he was on this block at this exact moment when the bomb exploded? C'mon, Karen. Don't be ridiculous. Ridiculous or not, she wanted to be certain her son was safe. "And check in on Jonathan. Make sure he's okay."

"I'm sure he's fine. He's probably at a bar with some friends."

"A bar? What the hell are you—"

"He's in college. That's what college students do."

"Just call him. No—text him, make sure he's okay. Humor me."

"Fine." Robby backed away, then slowly disappeared into the mass of people staring at the destruction—but keeping their distance, afraid to approach.

Vail did not like being rude to Robby, but what else could she do? When the boss of all your bosses ordered you to do something, you did it, right? *Actually, I'd better not answer that.*

As she was taking a quick survey of the area, getting a feel for what she was dealing with and making sure no one approached the scene, a police car pulled up behind her. "Police! Don't move."

You've gotta be kidding me. Vail turned slowly, hands up, and identified herself. "I'm a federal agent. I'm gonna remove my creds," she said, carefully extracting her Bureau ID and then holding it up. "I've taken control of the scene and I need you to clear the area. I'm under orders from FBI Director Douglas Knox. This is a federal investigation, a matter of national security."

The cop clicked on his tactical flashlight and pointed it at her face.

"Turn that goddamn thing off," Vail yelled. "Notify all responding units to establish a larger perimeter and evacuate any restaurants or residences in a two-block radius."

"I don't take orders from you. This is our jurisdiction—"

"Look, I'm just doing as told. You need to do the same. Tell your lieutenant to contact Director Knox's office. Let the brass fight it out."

The officer seemed to think that was a good idea because he pulled his radio and began speaking into it—hopefully conveying what she had said and not requesting reinforcements for dealing with a deranged redhead with stolen FBI creds standing in the middle of a potential crime scene.

While the cop jabbered into his two-way, a couple of large black unmarked cabover vans pulled up, two or three dozen personnel hopping out the back doors dressed in dark tactical coveralls with white luminescent block letters spelling POLICE.

"You Vail?" a man with a square jaw asked as he approached.

"Who are you?"

"The director told me to touch base with you. We'll secure the perimeter. He wants you to start your investigation."

My investigation? "Right."

He seemed satisfied with that response because he turned and headed toward the knot of similarly attired officers who were moving gawkers away from the scene.

A moment later, Vail felt a tap on her shoulder. She turned and saw one of the men holding up a jacket. "You've gotta be freezing."

Must've heard my teeth chattering. "Thanks so much. You're my hero."

The man nodded curtly. As Vail snuggled into the coat, her cell vibrated with a text from Robby:

jonathans fine. hes at a bar. told you.

She dashed off a quick thanks as a red Corvette pulled up. She knew that car, which now bore a personalized plate: BLACK 1.

The vehicle came to an abrupt stop and Hector DeSantos got out of the driver's seat, dressed in a leather jacket and wearing small metal rimmed glasses.

"Hector, what the hell's going on?"

"Nice to see you too. Knox is on his way with some intel. Other than that, you probably know more than I do."

Vail gave him a dubious look. But before she could reply, a DC Fire Chief vehicle—and two engine companies—arrived, their diesel engines and airbrakes making it difficult to speak at normal volume.

They watched as three members of the tactical team approached the commander. A healthy helping of testosterone flew in both directions, Vail catching snippets of the argument. Finally the chief backed away, promising to escalate the matter to higher ranks—after playing his trump card that they were endangering lives by not permitting his men to check gas mains and other flammable infrastructure.

As the commander turned to make his case to his superiors over the radio, a Ford Explorer pulled in behind DeSantos's Corvette. Supervisory Special Agent Aaron Uziel, head of the FBI's Joint Terrorism Task Force for the Washington Metro field office, got out and headed toward them.

"Santa," Uzi said with a fist bump against DeSantos's closed hand. He glanced at Vail, eyes moving head to toe. "Karen. You look very nice. Did we interrupt something?"

"I was out with Robby."

Uzi swiveled. "Where is the big guy?"

"I sent him home." She noticed Uzi's confused expression. "Knox's orders." Vail looked past his shoulder and saw the dozens of men in black outfits now establishing a physical boundary with unmarked sawhorses. *I think I'm starting to see what's going on here.* "A few months ago, I'd be at a loss to explain what's happening."

"And now?" Uzi said.

"Let's start with the fact that Hector's here." She looked at DeSantos, her head tilted ever so slightly, inviting him to jump in.

"And he doesn't get involved in a case unless it's a sensitive matter," Uzi said, glancing at the damaged storefronts and streetscape.

"I'm standing right here," DeSantos said. "You got a question?"

"You have the answers?" Vail asked. "Because, yeah, I've got questions. Like, What's going on? What the hell happened? Who was the guy who got blown to bits?"

"Can't tell you."

Vail narrowed her eyes. "Don't start with me."

"Santa—"

"How about we go get some answers." DeSantos handed booties to Vail and Uzi, then led them down the street and into the epicenter of the blast. Some of the men Vail saw arrive in the black trucks were poring over the wreckage, taking photos and measurements along the periphery and working their way closer to the body. Or what was left of it, which wasn't much.

"Who are these guys?"

"A forensic crew," DeSantos said.

Doesn't look like any forensic crew I've ever seen.

"First impression?" Uzi said. "This was deliberate. And if that's the case, Santa, it needs to be investigated as a terror attack until proven otherwise. As head of the JTTF—"

"That's why you're here, Boychick," DeSantos said, using his nickname for Uzi—Yiddish for buddy.

Uzi glanced at Vail.

"Now you know how I feel," she said.

"Look." DeSantos gathered them together and said, "All I know is that officially this is being investigated as a gas main explosion. Unofficially, yeah, it's a terrorist *event*. And that's why you're here."

"If I'd been properly notified, I could've had my task force—"

"It's sensitive. These guys dressed in black?" He turned to Vail. "They're OPSIG operators."

Vail knew OPSIG stood for Operations Support Intelligence Group—DeSantos's unofficial employer—a black ops unit housed in the basement of the Pentagon that carried out covert, deniable missions around the world.

"Why is this an OPSIG mission?" she asked. "And why am I here?"

"My guess is that you owe Knox for getting your ass out of hot water in London. He needs your expertise and sensibilities on this. You also happened to be first on-scene and he needed someone here he could trust."

I was hoping he wasn't gonna say that. "I'm not a Special Forces operator. I haven't had the training."

"That," DeSantos said, "will come."

Can't wait.

Two bright xenon headlights illuminated them, throwing their shadows across the buildings behind them.

"I think you're about to get some answers," DeSantos said.

The armored black Chevrolet Suburban SUV stopped alongside them and out stepped Douglas Knox, accompanied by two members of the director's protection detail.

"Status?" Knox said, looking at Vail.

"Area secured. Expect calls from DC Metro and Fire."

"Already taken care of."

"May I ask—"

"Sir," said one of the OPSIG agents. "We found something."

They followed the man into the nearest residential apartment building, where the destruction was more pronounced. The odor of cordite was thick and the air was smoky. Using a tactical flashlight, he led them down into a basement room that was stocked with bomb-making materials—and vests in various stages of construction.

"Holy shit," Vail said. "What are we looking at here?"

Knox turned to his protection detail. "Leave us."

"But sir—"

Knox faced the OPSIG operator. "Has this room been cleared? The building?"

"Yes sir."

"We're fine here," Knox said to the agents, who reluctantly left. When the door closed, he continued: "We received intel this morning that there was a high probability of the first-ever suicide bombing on US soil."

Vail felt her stomach tighten. This was not just bad news. It was *horrible* news of the worst kind. Planes hitting skyscrapers resulting in mass murder was traumatic enough. But conventional suicide bombings in a major US city was a whole other kind of terror—one affecting tens of millions of people all day, every day, until the bomber or bombers were caught. The majority of the country's population would be living on edge, waiting for the next explosion to rip through their restaurant, park, or playground.

"We've been working our sources trying to verify that information."

"Why wasn't I told?" Uzi asked.

Vail thought that was a very good question, but was surprised to see Uzi challenge the director so brazenly, particularly in front of others.

"I made a judgment call, Agent Uziel. Which I often do as FBI director." Knox gave him an icy look. "Our source in Turkey, Cüneyt Ekrem, was—"

"Ekrem's unreliable."

"Exactly. And he's failed us multiple times in the past. We only took it seriously because of the implications. The Agency has been unable to verify the intel with even one other source. We intercepted no communication suggesting such an attack was even being planned. Until half an hour ago. My next call was going to be to ASAC Shepard," Knox said, referring to the assistant special agent in charge of the FBI task force, Marshall Shepard. Uzi's boss.

Vail and Uzi exchanged a look—which she was unable to interpret.

"I never made that call because we got a report of an explosion."

"The explosion was the result of my—and Agent Hernandez's—gunfire."

Knox turned to the OPSIG agent. "Was he wearing a suicide vest?"

"Yes sir. That's what exploded."

Knox swung his gaze back to Vail. "Was he planning to detonate?"

She played it back in her head. "I don't think so. I'm guessing that he was trying it out, seeing how well he was able to conceal it under his coat. Hard to say. But Agent Filloon must've seen something that looked suspicious and confronted him. He shot Filloon and tried to get back to his hideout. But Robb—Agent Hernandez—and I engaged him and . . . well, the rest you know."

Knox began pacing, the fingers of his right hand massaging his scalp.

"Was Filloon on duty?" Uzi asked.

"He was," Knox said. "I've had a number of agents mobilized all over the district searching areas, talking with CIs, trying to get verification."

"I should've been notified," Uzi said. "I should've been part of that. With all due respect, sir."

"Noted." Knox stopped and glanced at the workshop table, detonators, circuits, and timers laid out before him. "At least we found him—and his factory."

Vail followed Knox's gaze. "And we're keeping this quiet because . . . ?"

"Because we don't know what we're dealing with yet," Knox said. "And if Metro PD gets involved before we have our ducks lined up, things could get out of hand very quickly. Right now we need to manage the intel, manage the investigation, control who knows what, and when."

Sounds to me like our FBI director is a control freak. Still, he does have a point. His logic is flawed for other reasons, but I'm not the one calling the shots.

"The public needs to know we're under attack," Uzi said. "They could become our eyes, which is particularly important when dealing with suicide bombers. Unfortunately, I know."

Vail understood he was alluding to his time in Israel dealing with the Palestinian intifadas, where suicide attacks in Israeli towns killed scores of civilians in cafés, on school buses, in discos, at wedding ceremonies.

"The president wants to avoid a panic. We can stand here wasting time debating whether or not he's right, but for now those are his orders. Which means those are *your* orders."

Uzi pointed at the laptop at the far end of the room. "Maybe there's something on that comp—"

A phone started ringing. Uzi and DeSantos glanced at each other, then began searching the room.

"Got it," Vail said, holding up the device. "Caller ID, but it's in Arabic. Uzi, don't you speak—"

"Let me see." Uzi took it, looked at Knox, and then reached over to a machine mounted on the table. He examined its steel casing, found a switch—and turned it on. It emitted a low groan and then he answered the call in the bomber's native tongue. He kept his responses short, with a hint of anger and urgency—as best as Vail could tell from his demeanor and tone. She figured the noise from the machine gave him some cover for his voice not matching that of the dead man.

Seconds later, he hung up and pocketed the phone.

"What was that about?" Vail asked.

"We need to go."

"Who was it?" DeSantos asked.

"Our bomber's accomplice. He said he heard about an explosion around here but couldn't get any verification, and wanted to know if everything was okay."

"And you told him?"

"I told him I had a close call, it was nearby, that I wasn't sure it was a good idea to stay here. He said I should go to a safe house they had. They'd regroup and figure out what to do. He gave me the address. Let's move."

"How do you know it's not a trap?" Knox asked.

"We don't. But if it's legit, we may have a lead into one or more of his accomplices."

"Take Team Seven." Knox rapped his knuckles on the door and the OPSIG agent pulled it open. "Tell Team Seven to get ready to roll. Two minutes."

"Yes sir."

"You coming?" Uzi asked Vail as they headed back out to the street.

"Safer here," DeSantos said. "Help them document the scene."

"I don't need you to protect me," Vail said as she matched him stride for stride up the steps. "I'm a federal agent. And I was nearly blown up by a suicide bomber. I'm kinda pissed."

"Revenge?"

"Justice. Besides, have you ever known me to shy away from a fight?"

"I've known you to start a few."

"That's not fair," Vail said. "It's accurate, but not fair."

They emerged into the cold night air, which prickled her skin, awakening her senses as she looked out at the bomber's carnage. "I take it you're coming then?"

"I'm coming."

One of the black cabover trucks pulled up to the curb down the block.

"That's our ride," Uzi said. "Grab a vest and a helmet."

2

The driver of the tactical vehicle negotiated the streets of southeast DC swiftly but discreetly. "We'll drop you two blocks from the target so they don't see a big black truck pull up."

"Roger that," the team commander said over their headsets. He provided some operational details, then said, "We were only able to secure a crude blueprint of the building's interior. A filing by the contractor when it was built. So be careful."

Vail knew that SWAT teams spent days studying floorplans, architectural renderings, and surveillance photos of a facility before infiltrating it. Once you breached the door and stepped inside, you were at a tactical disadvantage to those bad actors inside who either modified the interior or hardened it against attack.

They had no time for reconnaissance, so it came down to getting some idea of the interior's layout and then winging it based on their instincts, training, and best guesses. Your job was to do your best with what you had.

"All I know," the commander said over the comms, "is that the property is a townhouse and part of a public development operated by the DC Housing Authority. There are over two hundred units, one to six bedrooms apiece."

Great. Our tax dollars are paying for the terrorists to live in our country. Gotta love America. We don't discriminate: give us your tired, your poor, your huddled masses, your radicalized terrorists—

"ETA one minute," the driver said.

The men readied themselves, checking weapons and positioning their utility belts.

"Team members will lead," the commander said to DeSantos, "and the three of you will bring up the rear."

Neither DeSantos nor Uzi objected. Vail figured they knew their place because it made sense for a team accustomed to operating together to do their thing and secure the location. She, Uzi, and DeSantos were there for backup, investigative continuity, and support.

They came up 1st Street SW, hung a left on N Street and then a right on Half Street. The truck pulled to an abrupt stop and the rear doors opened. The operators spilled out and deployed swiftly and with relative stealth. Normally law enforcement would've been brought in to evacuate the surrounding buildings, block off neighboring streets, and clear the immediate area of innocents. But there was a substantial risk of tipping off the offenders, and with the onsite mix of suicide bombers and potential explosives, the danger was too great.

Time was of the essence: the element of surprise was all they had.

Had they been deploying in a business district, there would be little likelihood that on a weekend evening many people would be inside the adjacent buildings. But this was a residential neighborhood, densely populated with blocks of three-story brick tenements. "We still have our objectives," the team leader said.

Vail knew those objectives were to apprehend the tangos alive so they could be questioned, in their apartment if possible—and given the location of the target—without discharging their weapons.

She also knew that bombers resided in this building, terrorists who were part of an organization which valued their ends more than the means they employed to achieve them. If a few people had to blow themselves up to make a statement and induce terror, so be it. The man who strapped the bomb to his chest had no regard for the loss of his own life. He was going to a higher place in the afterlife, with a host of virgins who would serve his every need for eternity.

Absurd as that sounded to an unindoctrinated person, these radicals believed it.

Problem is, none of the bombers come back from the dead to tell their buddies it's all a load of bullshit.

The men arrayed themselves in three groups. Using hand signals, DeSantos assigned Vail and Uzi to the two teams he was not shadowing—Alpha and Charlie.

Vail adjusted her vest, which was heavy and uncomfortably tight against her breasts, but she stayed with the group as they snaked through the streets. The building, a block-long two-story masonry structure with an arched entryway, had barred first-floor windows and a PEPCO electrical access panel out front. The commanding officer nodded at the man to his left, who pulled a pair of bolt cutters from his utility belt and removed the lock securing the junction box, then slowly opened the gray metal doors and studied the circuits. A moment later, he signaled a thumbs-up to his CO, who keyed his mic. "Teams, check in."

They each indicated they were in position.

The commander gave a thumbs-up to his breach officer, who in this case was going to use a lock pick rather than a battering ram. The farther they could get inside without the inhabitants realizing anything, the better.

The man removed his kit from the deadbolt mechanism and gave the CO another hand signal.

"Power going out in three, two, one."

The officer brought his hand down and cut the electricity to the building. The illuminated windows went dark and the team moved in, Vail bringing up the rear.

They entered quickly and efficiently, the powerful LED lights mounted to their MP5 submachine guns scouring the darkness. They whispered into their helmet mics, keeping the team informed of the rooms that were cleared.

As they continued toward the back of the apartment, Vail heard a clunk above her. She almost blurted something over the radio but then remembered her microphone was not live; this prevented an accidental transmission that could disrupt the team's rhythm and procedure. Instead, she used a hand signal to notify the closest operator that she sensed movement above her. He did not seem to notice, however, as he moved on, focused on what lay ahead and not on Vail, who was behind him in an area they had cleared, and thus considered safe.

Vail broke ranks and stepped back toward the area where the noise came from. Nothing. Regardless, the team would be heading up to the second story any minute.

As she turned back toward the men ahead of her—who were stacked in line, ascending the stairwell—her light caught the edge of a wall that looked artificial. She stepped closer, keeping the clean Glock .40-caliber handgun she had been issued focused squarely ahead. She turned on the green tactical laser mounted below the barrel and held it at an angle, getting a good look at a wall seam that should not have been there.

There was no external doorknob or other type of pull tag. If this was in fact a faux wall, something was likely concealed behind it.

Vail again looked down the hall at the team—but they had already moved on to the next level. She activated her mic and quietly said, "This is Vail. I've got what looks like a fake door to a hidden space opposite the living room."

"Roger that," the voice whispered back. "Hold tight. We'll double back once we've cleared the second story."

Vail backed up a step, waiting, the pistol still trained on the wall. A creak—and then a clunk.

She ground her jaw. That noise she heard earlier was not from above, but from behind the wall.

Using two fingers from her left hand, she felt along her utility belt and pulled out a long black handcuff key, which she inserted into the crack. She pried it forward, trying to work quietly but getting frustrated that she didn't have a crow bar—which would've popped the damn thing open after one or two pushes.

This is ridiculous. Whoever's in there knows what I'm doing.

Vail finally got enough leverage to grab the edge of what was clearly a door. She pulled it toward her as she simultaneously raised the handgun.

HECTOR DeSANTOS REMAINED IN FORMATION, behind and at the end of the Bravo Team stack, understanding the reason for chain of command but disliking it nonetheless. As a person accustomed to leading, he did not enjoy following. But he had been down this road before as a member of Delta Force. He knew how to take orders. The difference was that in the intervening years he had learned how to take the initiative and evaluate those orders for himself, and then change—or massage—them when the need arose.

If he was confident in his convictions and analysis, and everything turned out well, he could explain it later. It was difficult to argue with success. But not impossible. There were times when he was right—but was reprimanded because he had not carried out his mission as commanded.

The thing was, the people he worked for in OPSIG knew who he was and what they were getting. And he was exceptionally good at his job. Sometimes that was enough to keep him out of trouble. On rare occasions it was not.

DeSantos focused on the men ahead of him. They were stationed at the rear door to the apartment building in case one or more of the tangos decided to leave while Alpha Team was infiltrating from the front.

They monitored the situation on a small LCD screen, taking the feed from Alpha commander's helmet cam. As the operators burst into a room, DeSantos saw movement out of the corner of his eye, fifty feet to his left. "Hey," he shouted. "Hold it right there!"

The man glanced at DeSantos and wisely decided it was smarter to run.

"Tango at nine o'clock."

Two operators joined DeSantos and they headed off in pursuit, running down the six steps and along the concrete retaining wall that fronted small grass lawns. The perp had a decent lead on them, but as they closed the gap—not easy lugging thirty pounds of equipment—an SUV approached. The driver sped up and DeSantos cursed under his breath.

"That better not be what I think it is. Either of you got a clear shot?"

"Got it," said Wickford, the team member to his left, as he ran into the middle of the street and took up a position with his MP5 aimed squarely at the vehicle.

The SUV screeched to a stop and the fleeing tango got in. The truck reversed rapidly, swinging side to side, slamming into the parked cars to its left and right, moving toward the main drag, where it had come from.

"Goddamn," DeSantos said, huffing it down the sidewalk, in senseless foot pursuit of the moving vehicle.

Wickford got off several short bursts, striking the grill and headlights but apparently missing the target.

The SUV swung left at the end of the road, made an abrupt pivot, and headed west on M Street SW. Because OPSIG was black, there was no one to call it into, no dispatcher who could get a cruiser or two to take up pursuit.

DeSantos joined the two operators and immediately engaged Wickford. "What the hell happened? How'd you miss?"

"Mission objective's to take the men alive. I was trying to hit the tires but the asshole was swerving all over the place. As it was, I took a risk."

DeSantos knew Wickford was right, but he still bristled at letting two terrorists slip their net. It was embarrassing. He kicked a rock and watched it bounce along the asphalt.

VAIL SAW THE MAN too late. He slammed the door into her face, knocking her to the floor, then ran past her and out the front.

Vail was on her feet an instant later, headed in the same direction—but moving cautiously in case he was waiting outside to shoot, or stab, her.

She scanned the street, painting the area with her light. The mature trees with their dense trunks and branches and cars lining the curb made it tough to get a clear view of the landscape. As precious seconds passed, she saw nothing.

Then—movement above: in the darkness to her left, against the cloud-patched moonlit sky, she saw a man running along the roof, negotiating its aggressive slope. The apartment compound appeared to be blocks long, consisting of attached rows of homes that ran parallel to one another.

He had a different build from the tango who flattened her on the way out of the house, but nobody would be sprinting across the tops of homes late at night unless he happened to be a criminal trying to evade law enforcement.

"FBI, don't move!"

She had to laugh at that one herself: like this terrorist, who might be a suicide bomber, would suddenly stop, raise his hands above his head and say, "Aw, shucks. Ya got me."

She keyed her mic. "Got a runner, headed north on the rooftops. I'm in pursuit."

"Charlie Team acknowledging. On our way."

That was Uzi's voice, she was sure of it. That was the good news. The bad news was that these townhouses formed the largest blocks of contiguous buildings she had ever seen. But it was easier running on flat ground than a canted roof, so the perp would have to tire before she did—and then she would be waiting for him.

Vail maintained her stride, an accomplishment considering that she was keeping her eye on the perp while simultaneously watching out for broken sidewalk and tree roots—neither was in short supply.

Fifty yards ahead she saw a man running toward her—Uzi, followed by a contingent of operators. The assailant saw them too, and apparently calculating that he would rather grapple with a single woman than a company of armed men, slid down toward the edge of the roof.

Uh, where you think you're going, buddy?

He grabbed the white rain gutter, swung his legs over the side, and hung there, his length stretching down until he dropped and landed with a thud on his feet.

Okay, you made it. Not bad. But now you've gotta deal with me.

"That's far enough," Vail said, leveling her Glock at the man's heart. But she forgot she was dealing with a suicide bomber—or someone affiliated with that mind-set.

He charged her.

Three things flashed through her mind:

1) Shoot the asshole.
2) Don't shoot the asshole because we need to question him.
3) If you draw your gun, you're shooting to kill—a lesson she learned her first year on the job as a patrol cop.

But he hit her full on before she could reason it out.

Vail fisted his shirt and clamped onto it like a Rottweiler, refusing to let go. She twisted hard right as he bulled past her, but kept her hold and bent her knees, bringing her center of gravity to the ground and pulling him down with her.

Before he could squirm away, Vail slammed her pistol against his temple and said, "It's a little different having a gun pressed against your skull. Isn't it, dickhead?"

Uzi came running up and the six other OPSIG men surrounded the prisoner and took control, five submachine guns—with their green lasers—trained on center mass while Uzi applied the handcuffs.

As they led the perp away, Uzi nudged Vail. "Nice job."

"Thanks," Vail said, seating the Glock in its holster.

"Bullshit, that was horrible. What the hell were you thinking, Karen? You drew down on him. You had the guy dead to rights. He was five feet away. And you let him run you over?"

Vail ground her jaw. "We needed to question him, not kill him."

"You don't really want me to respond to that, do you? With all the experience you've had?" He looked her over. "Did you freeze?"

"I told you. We needed him alive so we could sit him down, sweat him. Can't do that if he's got a chest full of .40s."

"Yeah, well, we need *you* alive too. So do Jonathan and Robby."

I hate it when he's right.

"Don't do that again. You were lucky."

"I was not—" Vail stopped herself. "You're right. I was lucky."

Uzi gave her a long look, then nodded.

3

Douglas Knox walked into the briefing room at the Hoover Building, a.k.a. FBI headquarters, or in Fed-speak, FBIHQ. Agents dubbed it the Puzzle Palace because its hallways and doors all looked the same. Getting lost or turned around was a regular occurrence.

An oblong walnut table dominated the space. Water bottles—and nothing else—were set out at each seat. No pads and pens. No laptops or tablets.

Vail instantly knew why. This was a classified meeting and no record of its proceedings would be created. Notes were forbidden. In essence, the gathering never happened—officially or unofficially.

Given what she had just witnessed, with OPSIG operators cloaked in nondescript black tactical uniforms and explicit instructions to keep Metro PD and Fire away, this did not surprise her.

As Knox took a seat at the head of the table, he combed back a lock of gray hair that had fallen across his forehead. To his right sat defense secretary Richard McNamara, and to McNamara's right was CIA director Earl Tasset. At Tasset's elbow was the secretary of Homeland Security, Laurence Bolten.

Across from the men were Vail, DeSantos, and Uzi.

"Hector, give us a sit-rep," Knox said, using operator-speak for situation report.

"We've got one dead tango at the location of the explosion on Irving Street. Bomb-making equipment was found in the nearby building, enough to make several suicide vests, along with materials for constructing corresponding explosives. We don't have an ID on the body yet—or what's left of it—which isn't much."

"Anything of use to us?" Bolten asked. "Papers, manuals—"

"We've got a team standing by, ready to comb the apartment for intel, but our EOD unit is making sure it's clear of booby traps and defusing existing bombs that were in various states of construction."

Glad they're doing that after *we were in there.*

"We have two in custody?" McNamara asked.

"Right." DeSantos leaned forward in his seat and turned to his colleague. "Uzi?"

Using his tongue, Uzi shoved a wood toothpick to the side of his mouth. "While we were doing a once-over of the bomb factory, the deceased perp's cell phone rang. The caller ID was in Arabic. I'm fluent in Arabic, so I answered it." He recounted how they found their way to the apartment in southwest DC and what happened when Alpha Team entered.

"This hidden room," Earl Tasset said. "How many were in there?"

"At the time," Vail said, "I only saw one—but I never had a clear view. When I pulled open the door, the ass—the *perp* charged me and ran out of the house. I pursued, but he managed to escape."

Knox frowned. "So we've got one tango in the wind. Did you get a good look at him?"

Vail struggled to maintain eye contact. "No sir. Average height, five foot nine or five-ten, about a hundred seventy-five, dark hair, darker complexion. In his twenties. No distinguishing marks that I could see. But in all honestly, I engaged him for only a split second before—before he got away."

Knox tilted his head back and sighed.

Hey, no one's more disappointed than I am.

"Another escaped through the adjacent townhouse," DeSantos said, "and it looks like he had a driver waiting. We shot up their car pretty good, but they both escaped. So that'd be *three* in the wind. As far as we know."

"Get a plate on the SUV?"

"Just make and model."

"That's just dandy," Tasset said. "Good work."

Uzi, not a fan of Tasset for personal reasons, tightened a fist on his lap. Vail glanced over, then placed a hand atop his.

"And then?" McNamara asked. "Agent Uziel apprehended the first suspect?"

"Actually, Agent Vail did," Uzi said, pulling his hand away. "Which wasn't easy because he definitely did not want to be captured alive. She put herself at risk to make sure we had an intact suspect to question."

"I'll withhold my applause for now," Tasset said, eyeing Vail. "You did your job. That's why you're on this team."

Actually, I'm on this team because I've got no choice, thank you very much.

"The suspect is being questioned," DeSantos said. "I expect it'll take a while to learn anything useful from him. He's been processed but his prints aren't in any database. I have a request out to Interpol."

"What about the other suspect we captured?" Bolten asked.

"Older, mid-fifties. He hasn't said much. He's missing two fingers on his left hand and the side of his face is scarred over from a bad burn, so I suspect he's the bomb maker and that he's been at it awhile."

Uzi set his water bottle down after taking a gulp. "Based on the clothing and dishes in the apartment, we believe there were four men living and working there."

"So," McNamara said. "What are we doing to find the ones who escaped?"

"Sir," Uzi said. "As head of the JTTF in DC, I'm compelled to recommend that in order to effectively pursue these men, and to investigate this case, I need to assign agents and bring Metro—"

"There is no *case*," Knox said.

"No case?" Uzi glanced around at the people seated at the table. "All due respect, a suicide bomber exploded in the middle of Washington. We found a bomb-making factory with multiple devices in various stages of assembly—this isn't going to be a one-and-done. We need to raise the threat level. The public needs to be notified that we're under attack."

"No," Knox said. "They don't. Not yet."

"Sir. I—"

"Agent Uziel, who is behind the attack?"

"We don't know yet."

"What was the target?"

"We're still inves—"

"Are other attacks planned for the district? For anywhere else in the country?"

"I don't know—"

"That is the point, isn't it? There isn't much we *do* know. We have very few facts. And dozens of questions. The media will have even more. We don't want a panic on our hands, do we?"

Uzi leaned forward in his seat. "Of course not. But we can't keep this a secret."

"The president has asked us to keep it quiet, for now, until we have a better understanding of what's going on."

"We know what's going on. A terrorist cell of suicide bombers has set up shop in DC and we thwarted one attack before they could act. Isn't that the intel you got from our Turk informant, Cüneyt Ekrem?"

"As you said yourself, Ekrem is unreliable. That's why we have to be careful and methodical and keep our eyes and ears open. We need to verify what he told us and not jump to conclusions. At the moment, we have no confirmed intel."

"But—"

"Remember the panic the DC Sniper caused?" Bolten asked.

Uzi sat back. "Of course."

"That's what the president wants to avoid."

"Agent Vail," Knox said, "tell us what you know of suicide bombers."

Vail folded her hands in front of her as she gathered her thoughts. "The study data is all over the place and often conflicting, but the lack of correlation reflects where that research was done, which political and religious ideologies were involved, and which populations were studied. The acts of a bomber in Iraq, for example, are going to be quite different from one operating in Sri Lanka.

"Generally speaking, operationally, the first goal of the bomber is to inflict death and destruction on a specific target. The second goal—which is his overriding motivation and purpose—is to inflict emotional pain and injury on innocents who witness the carnage—and who wait, on edge, for another bomb to go off. Basically, the idea is intimidation, fear and, well, terror.

"That's an important point because the data is more cut and dried regarding the victim population's point of view. The victims are frightened. They're scared. They alter their ways of life. That's why the terrorists are doing it, right? It's not the people they're killing that are affected—they're dead—it's those who live in the community, not knowing when another strike is going to happen—or where."

"Like the DC Sniper," Bolten said.

"Yes. In a sense, suicide bombings are similar to the terror that snipers inflict on their victim populations: you never know where they're going to strike next. And it involves an attack on everyday citizens, who are the victims of a political agenda or revenge against people who have nothing to do with the initial 'offense' or perceived slight supposedly inflicted on the attacker."

"Suicide bombings can be an effective tactic in scoring wins during wartime," Bolten said. "At West Point, we studied the Japanese kamikazes extensively. They had nothing to lose—their objective was to die—so they could be more daring, and penetrate enemy territory more deeply and more effectively, by taking greater risks."

"Right," Vail said. "Along those lines, suicide bombings are also used as an asymmetric tactic to counter a stronger fighting force. An example would be the Palestinian bombers hitting civilian targets in Israel. A vast majority of those attacks came at the hands of Hamas, although some were carried out by its rival, al Humat."

Vail glanced at Uzi and saw his jaw muscles contract—and for good reason: an al Humat operative murdered his wife and daughter.

"There are multiple MOs to their approach," she continued. "The most common is an explosive belt or vest, though two exceptions would be Richard Reid, the shoe bomber on Flight 63, and the attack on the Saudi prince where the bomber placed the explosives inside his body. Car bombs can also be effective—like the Beirut barracks bombing in '83 when a driver plowed his truck into the building. Or boats loaded with explosives, like the USS *Cole* in Aden. I don't have to elaborate on how jets can be flown into buildings. But that's just another form of suicide attack. Less popular tactics involve forcing a driver to crash his bus, like the Palestinians did in Tel Aviv, or driving a car into a crowd of people.

"Given what evidence we've discovered tonight, it looks like they're going the more conventional route—a vest—but since we don't know specifically who we're dealing with, or why they're doing what they're doing, we can't rule out any of these other methods. Because of that, I do support Agent Uziel's recommendation to alert—"

"Noted," Knox said.

Keep your mouth shut, Karen. Just move on.

"Did Ekrem say what group was behind the planned attacks?" Uzi asked.

Knox rose from his chair and began pacing in front of a white board at the head of the room. "I'm reluctant to repeat what he said until we have verification."

"Sir," DeSantos said, "time is obviously critical. If we're going to figure out who's behind this—and stop them before they implement their plan—we need to know what you know. We can cut through the bullshit and figure out if his intel is on target."

Knox stopped and leaned on the back of the leather chair. "Al Humat. Maybe in coordination with Hamas. He wasn't sure. He also suggested Hezbollah played a role, but he wasn't clear on that."

"So," Vail said, "let's assume, until proven otherwise, that Ekrem gave us good info and there's an Islamist angle to the planned bombings. These terrorists were speaking Arabic, so we're in the right ballpark at least. Let's look at this from a behavioral perspective. We know there's a religious element to it, a political element to it, and some good old peer pressure—to help the cause, to do what your friends are doing, to sacrifice oneself for the good of the group."

"Groupthink," Uzi said, moving the toothpick around with his tongue.

"Right. These people are intent on destruction—but they're also motivated by strong religious and political beliefs, as well as their own moral reasoning."

"*Warped* moral reasoning," Earl Tasset said.

"We know that Arab bombers are featured on posters and in videos as martyrs," Uzi said. "There's a financial angle—the bombers' families are well compensated. Hamas has gone on record that depending on who takes responsibility for the attack, Hamas, Islamic Jihad, al Humat, or the Palestinian Authority pays out a lifetime stipend of $400 a month to families of male bombers and $200 per month to families of female bombers."

"Apparently," DeSantos said, "the corporate world isn't the only place women are paid less than men."

The attempt at humor fell flat.

"In the Koran," Uzi continued, "Allah promises martyrs heavenly rewards. We've all heard about the dozens of virgins a male bomber is told he'll get. According to a Palestinian bomber who did not go through with the attack, female bombers are told they'll become the purest and most beautiful form of angel, at the highest level possible in heaven."

"We've been approaching this as if our tangos are all male," McNamara said. "But I do remember some cases involving female suicide bombers. Chechnya, I think."

"Correct," Uzi said. "But they've also been used against civilian populations in Iraq, Pakistan, Afghanistan, Israel, France, Sri Lanka. The best known case out of Iraq was the one where Samira Ahmed Jassim recruited about eighty women for suicide attacks—and sent twenty-eight of them to their deaths."

"Must be one persuasive lady," DeSantos said.

"Not persuasive. Evil. She would arrange for women to be raped, and then convince them to commit suicide attacks as a means to atone for the shame of being raped."

McNamara shook his head. "I remember that."

"If I'm not mistaken," Vail said, "the women who choose to become bombers on their own, their motivation is not political—opposite of their male counterparts. Most common reason is that the women are grieving the loss of family members and they're looking to punish the person they consider responsible."

"Revenge killing," Bolten said.

"Yes. But there are also other female bombers who wanted to martyr themselves for reasons we could never figure out."

"What are the odds women are involved here?" Knox pushed back from the chair and began pacing again. "We may need to adjust our approach. And obviously that expands our dataset quite a bit."

Vail nodded. "It's been a while since I looked at the statistics, but I think women make up about 15 percent of all suicide bombers—at least within groups that use females. Now if we're talking about assassinations by suicide attack, women were responsible for about 65 percent of those. A fifth of them had the objective of assassinating a specific person—compared to only 5 percent for male attackers."

"Meaning?"

Vail lifted her brow. "Well, I think because a woman is more disarming than a man, she's able to get closer to a male target, no matter how well guarded he is. His defenses are down. So when you've got a specific target you want to kill, using a woman for the job is more successful. Bottom line, I don't think we can rule out the use of women as part of this operation. But since we don't know what or who their targets are, and we don't know their motivation, for now we can't say women are or aren't involved. If there's a revenge component or if they're trying to kill a specific person, we have to look at women. Otherwise it'll likely be males."

"Do we have a more specific profile?" Knox asked. "Somewhere to start?"

"I'm not sure we have enough to formulate anything definitive." *Who am I kidding? We definitely don't have enough.*

"Your ass is covered," McNamara said. "We realize you're winging it. We're just looking for some direction based on what we know."

A bead of perspiration broke out across her brow. *So I should make you feel like I'm giving you something useful without sending us off in the wrong direction. Yeah, sure. And for my next trick . . .*

Vail took a sip of water, then set the bottle down. "Broadly speaking, given what we have, we're looking for young adult male bombers, but as I said, we should not be blind to women. Males will be twenty to thirty-five, women will be younger, twenty to thirty. Regardless of gender, they'll be educated, middle-class individuals who may have a connection to a family member who's been killed in either an American action abroad or an Israeli action. The recent war in Gaza is a possibility, but we shouldn't limit ourselves to that. Hamas has been an active terror group for over twenty years and they began suicide attacks in the early 1990s. Al Humat started a few years later, if I remember correctly.

"Some studies suggest the bombers may be depressed or mentally ill individuals. I don't think that's what we're looking at here. This is a sensitive, very daring operation and the planners wouldn't entrust such a difficult operation to an unstable personality.

"I do think we're dealing with a group—that much seems obvious from the crime scenes we visited tonight—and that fits with the intel we got from Ekrem. As Uzi mentioned before, we need to be aware of groupthink mentality. Are you all familiar with that?"

She got a couple of blank stares. "Briefly, it's a situation where members of a group blindly follow the opinions and directions of their leader because they place greater value on gaining consensus and harmony than on the critical analysis of an issue. So if a lot of people are fervently onboard with an approach laid out by their leaders, the others will set aside their personal opinions in favor of acceptance within the group, to keep from being rejected, ostracized, or kicked out. It can be an efficient way of getting things done—but if the group leaders are bad actors, as in this case, you get the situation we've got. Good for them, not so good for us.

"One other thing," Vail said. "This is a group that looks at themselves as the underdogs going up against the big, bad USA: they use these asymmetric terror tactics as a mask to project strength and invincibility."

Knox stopped pacing. "So if I can sum this up, it sounds like you believe Ekrem's info is accurate: al Humat and/or Hamas."

Vail bit the inside of her lip. "Let's say I think Ekrem's info is accurate insofar as it's a group *like* al Humat and/or Hamas. I can't tell you it's specifically those groups or another one like the Islamic State or Islamic Jihad. Then again, a behavioral profile is only designed to tell you the *type* of person or group who committed the crimes. We need conventional forensics and investigative procedures to put an identity to our attackers."

Knox frowned, then took his seat. "Understood."

"Getting back to what Agent Uziel said earlier, sir, we really need to open an official investigation. I can then get full cooperation from my unit. ASAC Gifford—"

"Cannot be apprised of the situation," Bolten said. "Absolutely not."

Tasset leaned forward in his chair. "You're on this team for a reason."

I wish he'd stop saying that.

"And it's got nothing to do with London."

Bullshit. Vail tried to keep a poker face, but her gaze strayed over to Knox. His expression was as impassive as the sandstone columns of the White House.

"Your expertise in behavioral analysis," McNamara added. "It gives OPSIG a dimension we've lacked. You may prefer to confer with the profilers in your unit, but the cases we handle are black. Your group does not exist. The things you do, the missions you carry out, have not happened. Just like in London. That's the way this works. This meeting, in fact, is not happening." He turned to Knox. "I thought you explained all this to her."

Knox did not reply, but Vail wanted to—something like, "I haven't been told a damn thing."

"Do we have a problem, Agent Vail?" McNamara asked.

"No, Mr. Secretary. I don't have a problem." *I've got so many I don't know where to start.*

"Agent Uziel," McNamara said. "You sit on this team for a reason as well. Given your background with Mossad and counterterrorism, is there anything you can add?"

Uzi shoved the toothpick to the left corner of his mouth. "Director Knox mentioned that Ekrem thought Hezbollah might have some involvement in this plot. Around the time the whole thing came to a head with Iran achieving nuclear capability, we intercepted communications indicating that Hezbollah had sleeper cells across the country in dozens of US cities. It sounded like it was a well established network that had been going on for years."

"That's never been verified," Bolten said.

Uzi bobbed his head. "True. But . . . NSA captured a conversation between someone in southern California and a mobile in Mexico. It belonged to one of the Mexican drug cartels: Cortez. We began piecing it together with HUMINT," he said, referring to human intelligence—confidential informants, interrogations, and the like. "We're still working on it but all we've been able to verify is that the cartels and Hezbollah have been working together in some financial capacity."

"That's a long way from sleeper cells in dozens of US cities," McNamara said.

"Call it a working theory. Could be that Hezbollah teaches them how to build tunnels and Cortez pays them for the engineering know-how. Or maybe it's something else. But my instincts as a law enforcement officer tell me that this type of connection makes sense and can't be ignored. It may just be a matter of finding proof. I'll double down and check with my DEA guys on the task force."

"Hector?" Knox said. "Any thoughts on this?"

DeSantos straightened up in his seat. "If we look at a potential threat matrix, if the US went beyond sanctions against Iran and bombed its reactors, and if there were sleeper cells here, their operatives would likely set off bombs here. We'd be under attack within our own borders. The invading army would have been living among us for years."

The room got quiet.

Finally Bolten said, "We need to know if this sleeper theory is rooted in fact—and if it's got anything to do with what happened tonight."

"I can have our CIA and DEA reps on the task force check in with their CIs. But they're gonna ask why. To get it right, they have to have all the facts."

"No," Bolten said. "You can't say anything about tonight. The president made it quite clear."

"Some are going to put it together anyway. But the JTTF is a terrorism task force made up mostly of law enforcement officers. This is what we do. That's our job."

"Your job, your *orders*, are to work this from inside OPSIG. This is bigger than law enforcement. It's a matter of national security and we need to be able to operate without every goddamn blogger commenting on it, crying about privacy intrusions and racial profiling, without journalists bombarding us with questions and hampering our ability to do our work—which is finding these fuckers. You need more help, Secretary McNamara and Director Knox will get you personnel with security clearance."

"I'm not sure that's enough," Uzi said.

"For now, it'll have to be."

4

When Vail walked into her house at 3:30 AM, her chocolate brown Standard Poodle puppy, Hershey, greeted her at the door. He stood up on his back legs and bathed her face with kisses. She gave him a piece of duck jerky and found Robby asleep on the couch, a bag of Trader Joe's spicy flax seed chips on the coffee table perched beside an empty hummus container.

She inched her left buttock onto the edge of the seat cushion beside his thigh and stroked his face. His eyes fluttered open.

"What time is it?" he asked.

"Very late at night or very early in the morning. Depends on your perspective."

He sat up and hung his head. "I was dreaming."

"About me?"

"Of course."

"Right answer. C'mon, let's get you to bed."

Hershey followed them into the bedroom and hopped onto the mattress as Robby stepped up to the adjacent vanity and pulled open his drawer.

"So why did I have to leave? And what the hell is going on?"

Vail had been dreading such a question, which she knew would be among the first he asked. "Look, when you're undercover, you can't talk about the case, right?"

He popped open the cap on the toothpaste. "What's that got to do with this? You don't work undercover."

"I can't say any more."

He stood there, the tube in his right hand and the brush in his left. His brain was not fully awake yet so it was taking him longer to put it together. He set the toothpaste down. "You're telling me you're undercover?"

Vail started removing the makeup she had put on before she and Robby had left for the evening. She glanced at him in the mirror and he seemed to get it: she could not talk about it.

He went back to his teeth, then spit and rinsed his brush. "Is it dangerous?"

Vail thought about that, about her run-in with the terrorist tonight, about what Uzi had said about how she had handled it. "Yes."

Robby set the brush down and looked at her image in the mirror. He apparently decided against commenting.

What can he say? His undercover ops with DEA are dangerous too.

"I don't like it when the shoe's on the other foot."

Vail tossed the cotton cleansing pad in the garbage. "I know."

VAIL ARRIVED at the Behavioral Analysis Unit at 8:30 AM—and found a note on her desk from Lenka, the administrative staff for her boss, Assistant Special Agent in Charge Thomas Gifford.

Rather than lifting the phone, she walked over to Lenka's desk.

"Morning."

"Agent Vail. I left a note—"

Vail held it up. "Found it. Boss wants to see me?"

Lenka nodded.

"He pissed about something?"

Lenka nodded again, then buzzed Gifford and told him Vail was there. "Go on in."

Vail pushed through the door and Gifford motioned her to sit.

"I got a strange call this morning," Gifford said, "from Liz Evanston. Do you know who Liz Evanston is?"

Not even a hello. Yeah, he's pissed all right.

"Your ex-wife?"

"No."

He didn't say any more, so Vail asked, "If this is twenty questions, sir, can I have a pad and pen?"

"She's Director Knox's executive assistant."

She raised both hands, palms up. "You just ruined the game. I had at least another nineteen guesses left."

"She had a message for me. From the director. And it was about you."

"Right. Now I understand why I'm sitting in your office."

"Well, that makes one of us. I was told that you're on special assignment. But when I asked for clarification and details—like how long this assignment would last—she said she didn't know. When I asked if I should reassign your active cases, she said, 'Probably.'" He leaned forward and rested both forearms on his desk. "Now your unit chief and I have the BAU to run, with a lot of cases and very few agents. As hard as it is for me to admit it, you're one of my best analysts. So when you're removed from the equation, I kind of have to know why, and for how long."

"Well, you don't really have to know *why*."

Gifford looked at her.

"I'm just saying. 'Why' isn't releva—"

"Karen," he said through clenched teeth. "What the hell is going on?"

"I can't go into it. But I do need to be excused from my duties for the foreseeable future. I'll be working offsite."

"I'm your ASAC. And that's not an acceptable answer. Where are you getting your orders?"

"I don't think I can say."

Gifford frowned, hiked his brow, then grabbed a file off his desk. "Then no, you can't be excused from your duties."

"But—"

Before she could finish her sentence, Gifford's line buzzed. He hit the intercom. "Lenka, hold my calls."

"It's Director Knox, sir."

Gifford glanced at Vail, as if he was starting to put it together. "Put him through," he said in the direction of the speaker, then lifted the handset. Vail started to rise but Gifford motioned her down. "Mr. Director." He listened for a bit, his face flushing, then looked at Vail again. It was not a pleasant expression. Finally, he said, "Sir, how can I run my unit without—" The jaw muscles in his face tightened. "The good of the country. Yes sir, I understand . . . Yes sir, I will do that . . . No, we'll manage . . . Yes. Thank you, sir."

As Gifford set the handset back in the cradle, Vail slapped her thighs. "Okay, then. We're good?"

Gifford steepled his fingers, his eyes locked with Vail's.

"If it helps, sir, I'm not enjoying this."

"I don't believe you. And it most certainly does not help. What am I supposed to do with all your cases?"

"If I were the ASAC, I'd reass—"

"That was a rhetorical question."

"Right." Vail rose from her seat. She started to leave, then stopped with a hand on the knob. "You have your orders, sir. And I have mine. Neither of us are happy about it. How about we leave it at that?"

Gifford did not reply, so she pulled the door open and left.

5

Lucas Dempsey sat in the back of the black town car, its gray leather soft and pliant against his hand. The thick soundproof glass separating the rear and front seats had a slight green tint, but was otherwise unobtrusive. He glanced down and checked his watch and awaited the arrival of Frederic Prideux.

Like Dempsey, the name Prideux was chosen at random off an online directory of a company's board of directors. It was a nice irony, but in truth he selected Dempsey because it gave the impression of a fighter. And he liked to think of himself in that light.

While his contact knew his true identity, it was safer to use aliases in conversation so the prying ears of the NSA or FBI could not make an easy identification.

But if they were smart, and careful, they would not arouse suspicion.

Prideux approached the vehicle—and was frisked a dozen feet away by Dempsey's personnel before being cleared to approach.

The back door opened and Prideux sat down heavily.

Dempsey, staring straight ahead, said, "What the hell are you people doing?"

Prideux, a slight man whose English was well practiced and near-flawless, tilted his head. "We're doing what's necessary."

"You're working against me. That's not the arrangement. And it's counter-productive, to say the least."

"You move too slowly. And you're restricted in what you can do and when you can do it."

Dempsey laughed—not out of humor but because of his "partner's" audacity.

"Did you or did you not tell me there are limits to what you can do?"

"At times, yes. But we have a plan and we're executing according to that plan. Setting up sleeper cells in DC? Are you out of your mind?"

Prideux snorted. "We're quite sane, I assure you. There is a method to what you perceive as madness."

"Perceive? *Perceive*? Federal agents raided your cell, found bomb-making components and goddamn it, your man blew himself up in the middle of the city!"

"Yes, well, that was unfortunate. But . . ." He shrugged. "So what? We have others that will gladly take his place."

"I'm not worried about losing a man. Or two, or three. I'm worried about the FBI getting close. If they figure out—"

"No, no, no," Prideux said slowly, shaking his head. Calm, cool. "There is no risk here. Remember, we have a man on the inside." He smiled broadly. "Don't we, now?"

Dempsey turned away. He did not feel like the fighter he pretended to be. He felt controlled—when the opposite should have been the case.

"You're moving too slowly," Prideux said. "It's been two years."

"I'm laying the groundwork. It takes time. We discussed this. There are a lot of considerations." He faced Prideux. "You just have to trust me."

"Trust is not the issue. We do trust you. But we want results."

"And I said I'd deliver. I didn't say when because I couldn't. Things are fluid."

"Yes, things are fluid. And that's why we decided to take a more active role."

"A lot of good that did. Your bomb-making factory and safe house are gone."

Prideux turned his entire torso and leaned against the door, facing Dempsey. "Lucas, my friend, do you really think we would go into a war with only one weapon?" He smiled—deviously.

Dempsey was certain the man was studying him, reading his expression. "What do you mean?"

"I mean we're well prepared. I mean we know what we're doing. I mean that you should not worry about us, about our end of things. We have it all under control. Let the FBI think they've scored a major victory."

"You're just making it more difficult. Give me time to sort this out. Let things settle down. Let the media find something else to cover."

Prideux frowned and turned to look out the rear window.

"I thought you people take the long view, the long war. Decades, centuries."

"I don't subscribe to that model. I'm an impatient man. I'm selfish. I want to see this to fruition. I want to taste the olives of my labor."

"You will. But don't fight me."

Prideux laughed. "And why not? We fight everyone else. And we win too. Look at Europe, Lucas. Look at what we're doing. We are taking over. Some may think it's a slow process, but it's happening very quickly. In twenty-five, thirty years Belgium will be ours. Brussels, the headquarters of the European Union and NATO, will be under Sharia law.

"Allah will be the judge and jury of what's permitted and what isn't. There and in the major European cities—Antwerp, Amsterdam, Rotterdam. And my home country, France. It's all going to be under Sharia law very soon."

"Twenty-five years is not soon. Things can happen that derail your plans." Dempsey knew it was a weak shot, a punch without any muscle behind it. Because he knew Prideux was right.

"This is different. We control the process so I can wait. Twenty-five years? Just a matter of time now. Nothing anyone can do to stop it." Prideux chuckled. "Unless non-Muslims start having six kids per couple—which is not going to happen. We will out-reproduce them. We will outnumber them. We will then out-vote them—and vote them out."

"And what is that going to get you?"

"It'll get us Europe. And then we'll move on from there. North America? South America? Maybe both at the same time? Eventually it'll be everything. That is our goal, Lucas. Not just an Islamic state. An Islamic *world*."

Dempsey wondered what he had gotten himself into. Then again, was there really a choice?

"It's all so very simple, Lucas, but they are fools. They don't see what's going on right in front of them, all around them. We even *tell* them what we're going to do. It's not a secret. And still they don't see it! We say it on TV, in interviews, in our mosques, they debate it in their government offices. Their own Members of Parliament warn of it. And still they let it happen. Religious tolerance, the political correctness of this generation only makes it easier, faster." His left eye narrowed. "They have let it happen. Willingly. None of those countries deserve to survive as a nation, as a culture. And they won't."

Dempsey cleared his throat. He felt a sense of anxiety, as if he were Dr. Frankenstein . . . and the monster had just awoken and was about to leave the nest.

Prideux clapped a bony hand on Dempsey's thigh. "Thank you for your time, Lucas. We'll be in touch." He winked, then popped open the door and got out.

6

Uzi set his leather satchel on his desk at the FBI's Washington field office, then headed over to check in with a member of the Joint Terrorism Task Force, Special Agent Hoshi Koh.

Hoshi's desk was a hodge-podge of files, notes, and a variety of tech gadgets: her smartphone, a tablet, a Bluetooth headset, and an external battery pack.

"I'm impressed," Uzi said, taking inventory of the devices.

Hoshi tilted her head and examined his face. "You look tired."

"Late night."

"Another hot date?"

"Not exactly." He stifled a yawn. "Who says hot date anymore?"

"Obviously I do."

"Hey, where do we stand with that wild and crazy theory of Hezbollah collaborating with the Cortez cartel?"

"Soon as I got your email this morning I checked in with DEA. They're running a new informant in San Diego that's shown promise."

"When are we expecting to hear?"

"They're going to get back to us. Any day." Hoshi slipped her glasses on. "Oh—Shepard wants to see you."

Uzi walked into his ASAC's office a minute later. Marshall Shepard leaned his large frame backward in his chair, making the springs creak loudly. "'Bout time you brought your ugly ass into my office. Left that message with Koh an hour ago." He yanked off his glasses. "Take a seat, man. You look tired."

"Jeez, between you and Hoshi, a guy can't have a bad night."

"You hear about that explosion on Irving Street, near 14th? They're calling it a gas main, but I'm not buying it. I called Metro and they said they had no complaint on file. I ran it up the line and the brass wouldn't even take my call, like they were dodging me. You know what I'm sayin'?"

Uzi tried to maintain a neutral expression. "Yeah."

"I want you to look into it. Quietly."

"Quietly, Shep?"

"Yeah, just you and—well, maybe Koh. That's it. Let's find out if there's something fishy going on. I don't know, maybe I've seen too much. Or maybe I'm just paranoid. But I see the CIA's hands in this."

"Really." Uzi grabbed a toothpick from the cup on the desk. "Can't it just be a gas main explosion? They do happen."

Shepard scrunched his dark skin into an animated frown. "I am talking with Aaron Uziel, right? After all that shit that went down with the Armed Revolution Militia, you really think some suspicious shit can't be going down that they're keeping from us?"

Shepard was referring to a case a couple of years ago involving domestic terror attacks aimed at bringing down the US government.

Shepard's desk phone rang. He listened a moment, then said, "Yeah, put him through." He glanced at Uzi and said, "I need to take this, can you—" Before he could finish, the line connected. "Yes sir. This is Shepard."

Uzi rose from his chair to give his ASAC some privacy. But Shepard suddenly rapped his knuckles on the wood desk. Uzi stopped and turned.

"Can you give me details on—" Shepard sat up in his chair. "No, no, of course. I'll make him available. Whatever you need." He hung up the phone and glowered at Uzi.

"What?" Uzi asked. "Who was that?"

"You know damn well who that was. I thought you were my friend."

Uzi took his seat again. "I am, but I've got no idea what you're talking about."

Shepard grumbled something unintelligible under his breath. "You're going to be working a project for the director. And you didn't see fit to inform me?"

"Oh, that." Uzi unwrapped the toothpick and placed it in his mouth. "I'm not supposed to talk about it. It puts me in an awkward position, given our relationship."

"Which relationship are you referring to?" Shepard asked, his eyebrows raised. "That I'm your boss or that I'm your friend?"

"Both." Uzi started rolling the cellophane wrapper between his fingers. "C'mon, Shep, we've been through this before."

Shepard shook his head. "Care to tell me what you're going to be working on?"

"Can't."

Shepard leaned forward, his gaze boring into Uzi's. "This have anything to do with that explosion last night?"

Uzi did not reply—but he did not need to. Shepard was a sharp guy and he knew Uzi very well. A slight twitch in his eye, a dilated pupil—it didn't take much—and Shepard would know the answer.

Shepard slapped the table with a large, thick hand. His brass FBI paper-weight jumped. "Knew it."

"Yeah, well, keep it to yourself. I have a feeling you're going to be brought into this sooner rather than later. I tried to convince—actually, I'd better shut my mouth."

Shepard twisted his full lips, then nodded slowly. "Fine. Go play spy. Or whatever the hell it is you're doing. Keep me posted."

"I can't—"

"Yeah," Shepard said with a dismissive wave of his right hand. "Whatever. Get your ass outta here."

7

Operations Support Intelligence Group
The Pentagon
Arlington, Virginia

Vail was led through the Pentagon's river entrance and down a nondescript corridor to a single elevator door. She was instructed to place her hand over a glass plate and a yellow light ran beneath it. The car arrived seconds later. Her escort dipped his security card, pressed the B button, and said, "Someone will meet you downstairs. You can take it from here."

Gee, you think? "Thanks."

The elevator doors slid apart and revealed a uniformed officer who was tall and broad, with calloused hands and a wind-weathered face. "This way."

He brought her down a tiled corridor to a room at the end of the hall. She saw another panel beside the door and did not need to be told what to do. She placed her palm on it and waited for the sensor to scan her print. The electronic lock buzzed and the man turned and left her, headed back the way they had come.

Inside, she felt like she had walked into a gamer's paradise: wall to wall flat screens, all displaying satellite or real time surveillance images from around the world. A constant flow of cool air swirled around her ankles, keeping the tech equipment well ventilated.

People milled about the large, high-ceilinged room, which was dimly lit and had personnel seated at workstations along the periphery, headsets on and monitors perched at eye level on articulating metal arms.

Uzi and DeSantos were across the way, in a separate glass-walled room that featured an oval conference table. When she walked in, they were talking with Troy Rodman, who was larger than the guy who had led her down the corridor and a shade darker than the rosewood surface peeking through the sheaf of papers scattered across it.

"Agent Rodman," Vail said. "Good to see you again." The last time their paths crossed they were in the back of a van in the outskirts of London, in deep trouble with the British authorities.

"Troy. Or Hot Rod. We're a team. Takes too damn long to communicate when we're on a mission if we're saying Agent this, Agent that."

"Got it." She gestured to the papers. "What are you working on?"

"Compiled a list," Uzi said, "of most likely groups to have the will, wherewithal, and balls to put together an operation like this."

"The balls?"

"Not many have the guts to attack the United States—because we *are* gonna find out who did the deed, sooner or later. And then they're gonna pay for it. A select few are willing to take it on the chin in exchange for the points they score in the initial strikes. It buys them a higher profile, makes recruitment easier."

"It also requires patience," DeSantos added, "and coordination—to gather and purchase the materials, bring in the people with the skill set to build these explosives. Not all of them have the resources and network to make this happen."

"What about Ekrem's intel?" Vail asked.

Uzi grabbed a handful of almonds from a bowl to his right and popped one in his mouth. "We didn't want to get myopic by focusing on what he gave us—especially because we've got no idea if all, or some, or none of his info's legit."

DeSantos pulled a sheet from among the papers containing a scribble of handwritten names and handed it to Vail. She read: al Humat, al Shabaab, al Qaeda, al Qaeda Organization in the Islamic Maghreb, East Turkestan Islamic Movement, Hamas, Hezbollah, Islamic Jihad, ISIL/Islamic State, Islamic Jihad of Yemen— "Lists like this are okay, but we can make ourselves nuts looking at every Tom, Dick, and Harry."

DeSantos snorted. "More like Abdul, Mohammed, and Akbar."

Vail gave him a look that said, "I'm not in the mood." "Point is, we have to focus on the most likely groups."

"Like I said, that *is* the list of most likely groups."

Oh. Lovely. "Look, I know you have doubts about this Ekrem guy, but maybe it makes sense to start there and see if we can eliminate Hamas and al Humat. Then we can move on to the rest on this list."

Uzi nodded. "Makes sense to me."

A trim and curvy woman in khakis with long brunette hair approached with a Bluetooth headset protruding from her ear. "Hector, I've got something you should hear."

DeSantos introduced her as Alexandra "Alex" Rusakov. "On this case?"

"Yeah, NSA sent it over, priority one. They normally don't get to intercepted communications this fast, but because of the potential for impending attacks it was elevated and they—"

"Audio or video?" Uzi asked.

"Audio," Rusakov said.

Vail set down the list. "Let's hear it."

"It's in Arabic. But I've got a translation." She handed over a printed page.

"I'd like to hear the original recording," Uzi said.

"Channel five," Rusakov said as she reached over to the nearest panel and pressed a few keys.

Uzi slipped on a set of headphones and listened as the others consulted the translation.

"What are we reading here?" Vail asked.

"NSA intercepted a cell call from an area in southwest DC to Gaza. They couldn't triangulate because it didn't last long enough. The rest is pretty self-explanatory."

```
DC UNSUB:      Can't reach four of our men. Don't know
               what's going on. Someone posted some-
               thing on Facebook about an explosion on
               Irving Street. That was where Habib was
               working. Couldn't reach him so I called
               Wahi. He didn't know anything about it
               so he called Habib and he answered.
               Habib said the explosion was close but
               he was fine. Wahi told him to come to
               the safe house, but he never made it
               and I haven't been able to reach him.
               I haven't heard from Osman or Tahir
               either, so I don't know what's up with
               them.

Gaza UNSUB:    We'll look into it. If there was a
               problem, they'll go off the grid, keep
               quiet until they think it's safe to
               contact us. Everything may be okay,
               but stay indoors until I contact you.
               Allahu Akbar.

DC UNSUB:      Allahu Akbar.
```

Vail set the paper on the conference table. "No question the guy in DC is one of our offenders." She turned toward Rusakov, two workstations to her left, and said, "Can the NSA give us anything else?"

"They're doubling back to see if they've got other captured conversations that haven't been transcribed yet. There's a backlog of Arabic language recordings."

Vail noticed Uzi was still huddled over the desk, concentrating. She tapped him on a shoulder and he pushed up the headphones. "You're spending an awfully long time listening to a short conversation. Something's bothering you."

He sat down heavily.

"What is it, Boychick?" DeSantos asked.

He ran his tongue from left to right over his bottom lip. "The guy on the phone in Gaza. I think I know that voice."

8

Vail waited for Uzi to elaborate. When he did not, she nudged DeSantos, who shrugged. "Uzi, who is it?"

"If I'm right, he was a senior al Humat operative when I was"—he hesitated, then turned to Rusakov. "Alex, can you give us a minute?"

"Boychick, she's part of OPSIG. She's got full clearance."

Vail examined Uzi's face—she knew he was uncomfortable with more people knowing his secret. It was one thing for Knox to know, and for her, DeSantos, and Rodman to know—he hadn't had the choice when it was disclosed. Adding to that list did not seem like a good idea, and Vail had to agree.

"Alex," Vail said, "I think it'd be best."

Rusakov squinted dissatisfaction, then nodded and backed out of the room.

"Where'd you find her?" Vail said as the glass door clicked shut. "The latest Miss World pageant?"

"She's tougher than you think. Lethal, in fact. Her beauty gets her close to HVTs," DeSantos said, using the military acronym for high value targets. "Go on, Boychick. Who does the voice belong to?"

"When I was in Mossad, this guy was working with Hamas, smuggling rockets and mortars through the Sinai. He designed the network of tunnels they spent years building—sophisticated tunnels with reinforced cement walls, ventilation, electricity. They eventually built hundreds of them crisscrossing Gaza, stretching from the Egyptian border all the way into Israel."

"Like the drug cartels," Vail said, referring to their method of smuggling drugs from Mexico into San Diego.

DeSantos sat up straight. "Like the drug cartels. Ekrem's intel—and NSA's intercept—suggested Hezbollah might be working with the Cortez cartel. What if you're right, Boychick? What if they showed Cortez how to build their tunnels?"

"Then we might have problems." Rodman rose from his chair and walked over to the near wall, where a map of the United States was illuminated on one of the screens. Rodman said, "What if they've built a network of tunnels under the US?"

"It's expensive and time-consuming," Uzi said. He thought a bit, then added, "It's possible to do because they build shafts inside other structures—warehouses, garages, houses—that eventually resurface inside another building on the other side of the border. If they do it well, the presence of equipment and the removal of dirt—and lots of water, because tunnels flood while they're being built—isn't really noticed. Still . . . it's a tremendous amount of work. They'd need a really good reason to do that."

DeSantos joined Rodman at the map. "Like moving one or more dirty bombs around the country without our sensors—which are now in a lot of US cities—picking them up?"

They were quiet while they pondered that. "Before we get too far down this road," Vail said, "let's back up. Uzi, you said you know this guy, the Gaza voice. How about a name, description, some background?"

"Kadir Abu Sahmoud." Uzi rubbed at the stubble on his cheeks. "He's probably about fifty now, bearded, dark complected, about five-nine. He's a violent psychopath. As if that's not bad enough, he's a religious zealot who, like all extremists, interprets the Koran as a violent call to arms. We all know the type."

"Got some stuff here," Rodman said as he scrolled down a page on his laptop. "Comes from a well-to-do Palestinian family. Father a doctor, mother a lawyer. Discovered jihad when he killed a Jewish family in the Golan Heights as they farmed their watermelon patch. He was sixteen years old. With that multiple murder on his resume, he was asked to join Force 17 in Lebanon, as one of Yasser Arafat's personal bodyguards. That was 1981."

Rodman's eyes moved across the screen. "A year later, Arafat's PLO was forced to leave Lebanon—but Sahmoud stayed behind and joined Hezbollah. At nineteen he did some training in Iran under the Revolutionary Guard, where he was recruited by Hamas. He rose through the ranks quickly in the early to mid-1990s when he helped plan drive-by shootings and firebombings in Israel. Then the suicide bombings began, and he was one of the lead planners for the Afula attack, along with the bomb maker, Yahya Ayyash, when a teenager rammed a car packed with explosives into a commuter bus.

"Sahmoud disagreed with Hamas leadership a few years later and formed al Humat with Abu Hassanein, an equally violent former Hamas militant. Their first act was sending a youth into a school with a suicide vest. Fourteen kids were killed, sixty-nine were wounded. Seventeen lost limbs."

"I'm already liking this guy as our prime suspect," DeSantos said.

"I've seen all the general FBI briefings," Vail said, "but I'm far from a Mid-east expert. I know what I read in the papers about Hamas and al—"

"Bottom line," Uzi said, "is that the extremists believe their purpose in life is to fight a holy war to kill the Jews and take over Israel. They don't want a two-state solution. They want a one-state Islamist country."

"And that's the problem with Hamas and al Humat," DeSantos said. "They shoot rockets into Israel knowing Israel has to retaliate. But Hamas uses women and children as human shields to show a large casualty count. Their operations manual explains the strategy and why it's such an important tactic. The Gazans, meanwhile, are caught in the middle, used, abused, intimidated, and harassed. Hamas tells them that this jihad is Allah's will. Instead of focusing on building a future for their people with infrastructure and jobs and commerce, they carry out terrorist attacks using militant violence."

"You said their main purpose is to wage a holy war," Vail said.

"Two groups, similar philosophies. Hamas has three branches: one provides funding for schools and health care, one deals with political and religious mandates. Then there's a terrorism-based military unit that gathers information about Palestinians who've violated Islamic law and others who are informing for Israel. Their Izzedine al Qassam squads carry out the attacks. They're organized into small, covert terror cells that operate independently of each other.

"Al Humat was born from Hamas and shares its religious and political views—violence aimed at destroying Israel and replacing it with an Islamic state. Its virulent hatred of Jews and Judaism is deeply rooted in the anti-Semitic writings of the Muslim Brotherhood—which is where Hamas got its start back in 1987. Hamas is a more militant Palestinian offshoot of the Muslim Brotherhood, and al Humat is a more militant offshoot of Hamas. Al Humat doesn't dabble in politics. Its sole focus is the death and destruction of those who stand in the way of Sharia law."

"Like the US," Vail said.

"Like *all* civilized, democratic, western countries," Uzi said. "Some of its leaders have gone on record saying that democracy is the exact opposite of Sharia law. When they talk about taking over Europe, they talk about converting everything and everyone to Islam. Because no other religion or belief structure can coexist with it."

"That's an important point right there," DeSantos said. "This isn't a regional issue. It's not about what's happening in Israel with Hamas and al Humat and Islamic Jihad and Hezbollah. This battle's being fought in dozens of European cities. The scope is global—because their *plans* are global. And unless something's done, Europe has about thirty years before it starts turning into a group of third world countries. It'll fundamentally change the world.

It's the single biggest threat to democracy in modern times. Sharia law will set back civilized society centuries."

"So that brings us back to Ekrem's intel," Uzi said. "Sounds like he was giving us good information about al Humat's involvement."

Rodman took his seat. "And that brings us back to Kadir Abu Sahmoud."

"Yeah." Uzi swallowed hard. "Sahmoud was the bastard who trained Batula Hakim."

Vail knew—as did DeSantos and Rodman—that al Humat's Batula Hakim was the terrorist who murdered Uzi's wife and daughter eight years ago.

She also knew, without it needing to be stated, that if Sahmoud was in any way involved with the current plot, capturing Sahmoud would be a priority—and it had nothing to do with exacting justice. Knowing DeSantos, such a "capture" order may involve lethal force, as it did with Osama bin Laden.

Rodman glanced at the printed translation. "How sure are you that it was Sahmoud's voice?"

Uzi pondered that for a few seconds, then said, "Not enough to hold up in a court of law. I *think* it is. But I'm not completely sure."

"Let's get a voiceprint analysis," DeSantos said. "Do you think Mossad has a clip of Sahmoud on file?"

"Very likely. I'll look into it."

"The director general is in Washington," DeSantos said, "meeting with Tasset this week."

Uzi's jaw muscles tensed. "I know."

"You could just request a voiceprint through the usual channels within the CIA—"

"Better to go to the horse's mouth. Faster, less bureaucracy. No filters."

"But I'm sensing you don't really want to deal with Aksel," Vail said.

Uzi pulled his gaze away from DeSantos and took a seat. He leaned back and closed his eyes. "It's complicated. Let's just say that Gideon and I didn't always agree on things. Oil and water personalities."

DeSantos tilted his head. When Uzi did not elaborate, DeSantos added, "Among other things."

"Then why don't we just send the request over to Tasset and—"

"No." Uzi was on his feet. "I'll meet with Gideon." He gathered his black leather jacket off the seat back and slung it over his shoulder. "I'll let you know what I find out."

9

Uzi met Mossad director general Gideon Aksel by the Delta security bollards at the west end of Pennsylvania Avenue, across from the Blair House. Because the street fronted the White House, it was under constant surveillance by the Secret Service and Metropolitan police. In fact, two white, blue, and red cruisers were parked in the middle of the roadway at forty-five degree angles to each other, a hundred yards ahead, opposite the White House lawn.

As Uzi approached, the four agents in the foreign dignitary Secret Service detail perked up. He held up his FBI creds and they relaxed—slightly.

"Gideon."

Aksel tilted his head back and peered at Uzi through his glasses. But he did not return the greeting.

"Wearing glasses now, Gideon?"

"I'm getting old. Shit happens."

A grin broke Uzi's face. He surprised himself. Because of all the previous bad blood that existed between these two men, he had been dreading this meet. But it seemed to have gotten off to a nonthreatening start. Perhaps it had something to do with the fact that Uzi had saved Aksel's life a couple of years ago.

"How's your hip?"

Aksel was a stocky man, about five foot eight, but exuded the body type and constitution of a tank—a battle hardened outer shell and something of a mystery inside.

"Just a flesh wound. I was fine."

Uzi didn't know if Aksel was playing off the famed Monty Python line—when the Black Knight had both arms chopped off and claimed it was "just a flesh wound"—or if he merely meant to play down the severity of the injury. Knowing Aksel's toughness and pigheaded steadfastness, Uzi surmised it was likely the latter. At the same time, he knew the injury—a bullet wound to the hip—required surgery and substantial rehabilitation. But the Mossad chief was walking along the White House wrought iron fence and showing no signs of a limp.

"You said you need a favor."

Uzi squinted. "I said I needed some help on a case."

"Same thing."

Uzi did not agree, but he did not want to get into another argument with Aksel. He stopped and faced the man. Behind them stood the front entrance to the White House, the small flower-rimmed fountain in the center of the expansive tree-dotted lawn.

"We captured a recording of two individuals, one here in DC and one in Gaza."

"And you're trying to ID the Gaza caller. You need a voiceprint match."

"Actually, I need a biometric automatic voice analysis. And acoustic and phonetic analyses while you're at it. I have to be sure about this." Uzi handed Aksel a USB thumb drive. "If you know who the other voice is, the DC suspect, that'd be helpful too."

"You could've handled this through the normal CIA-Mossad channels."

"This is very important, Gideon. I didn't want to trust it to lower-level analysts."

Aksel studied Uzi's face a moment, focusing on his eyes. "The explosion near 14th Street. That's what this is about."

Uzi's face sagged—and he immediately realized he had already answered Aksel's question. Then again, he didn't know why he was surprised. Aksel had an uncanny ability to know things very few others knew, to put unrelated events together and to find significant commonalities that led to key intel—or an arrest. Uzi shifted the leather jacket on his shoulders. "I didn't say that."

"Oh, but you did, Uzi. You've always had that weakness."

"Don't start with me, Gideon." He clenched his jaw, let the anger subside, and refocused. "Will you help us ID the voice?"

"Of course."

Uzi glanced at the four men standing nearby. "Can you guys give us a little more space?"

They all seemed to glance at Aksel, who nodded. They backed up a few steps but maintained their formation.

"Have you heard any chatter about a collaboration between Hezbollah and the Mexican drug cartels?"

Aksel's eyes narrowed. "That's one of the reasons why I'm here in Washington. One of our men inside Hezbollah warned us a month ago that he heard a major cartel was making large sum payments into Hezbollah accounts. We've been trying to verify it."

"All that money. In exchange for what?"

"We can speculate, but speculation isn't actionable intelligence. One thing he said is that it sounded like this arrangement had been going on for some time. Years."

Years? Uzi stepped closer and dropped his chin. "Have you heard anything about suicide bombers setting up shop in the US?"

Aksel's face remained impassive, but he looked off into Lafayette Park, beyond Uzi's left shoulder. "That's the second reason for my trip to Washington. Be careful, Uzi, you're coming close to impressing me."

Uzi forced a grin. He was not going to let Aksel goad him into an argument. "When do you think you can get back to me on that recording?"

"I'll have the lab get right on it."

"Oh—whatever you find, the only people authorized are Knox, Tassett, and me. Don't put it through normal channels. Is Roni still there? Can you give it to him?"

Aksel unfurled a handkerchief from his wool overcoat, removed his glasses and huffed on them, then wiped away the smudges. A long moment passed before he set them back on his nose and peered at Uzi with a tilted head. "I thought you gave up covert ops when you left Mossad."

Uzi had no answer to that other than the truth. "So did I, Gideon."

10

Uzi was standing in the Washington field office elevator with Vail and DeSantos when his phone rang.

"Whoa, hang on a sec, Hoshi. I'm in the building on my way up. Can it wait?" He glanced at the floor number. "Thirty seconds."

"What's the deal?" Vail asked as he dropped the phone back in his pocket.

"One of my task force agents. Something urgent."

"How is Hoshi?" DeSantos asked with a wink.

"Why are you looking at me like that? She's fine."

"Yes, she is. Very fine." He held his hands up. "Hey, you know she likes you, Boychick."

The doors slid apart and they followed Uzi through the glass security doors and into the large open room where Hoshi's cubicle was located.

"I remember you," Hoshi said. "DeSantos. Hector."

"Well, I prefer Hector DeSantos. No pauses between the names. But yeah, that's me."

"And I'm Karen Vail, BAU. I don't think we've met."

"Hoshi Koh. I'm Uzi's right-hand man." She glanced at Uzi, then added, "So to speak." Hoshi grabbed a set of headphones and handed them to Uzi. "This call just came through. I took it and started recording as soon as I realized what the guy was talking about. I missed the first ten seconds." She struck a few keys on her computer and Uzi listened, then said, "Okay, stop. Send this to my desktop." He motioned Vail and DeSantos to follow him into his office.

They stepped inside and Vail closed the door. Uzi sat down at his desk and turned on the two speakers. He pressed play and the recording started: ". . . long you think you can pull off this charade about calling it a gas main explosion."

"Sir, I'm not sure I know what you're talking about."

Hoshi's voice.

"You the fucking FBI? The Joint Terrorism Task Force?"

"Yes sir. You said you had information for us on—"

"I want to talk to someone who's in charge."

"You can talk with me. I'm in a position of authority. I'm a supervisory special agent."

"Not good enough. I'm going to call back in twenty minutes. If you don't put me through to someone in charge, you and your FBI are going to be sorry."

The recording stopped.

A knock at the door, and Hoshi appeared. "Assuming he's punctual, he'll be calling in about seven minutes."

"What tipped you off?" Vail asked. "Why'd you start recording?"

"The first thing he said to me was, 'I have information about the bombing last night.'"

"Let's be ready to record when he calls again."

"That sounds like the same voice," Vail said.

"Same voice?" Hoshi asked.

Uzi glanced at DeSantos. "Uh, can you give us a moment, Hoshi?"

She stepped back. "Uh, yeah. Sure."

DeSantos turned to Vail. "No one is—"

"Yeah, yeah. Got it. Sorry."

"Yes," Uzi said. "Same voice. So how do you want to play this?"

"See if we can find out why he's doing this, what his plans are, and who he is."

DeSantos stifled a laugh. "We should just ask him? And you think he's going to tell us?"

"He'll tell us," Vail said. "Maybe not everything, but he'll want us to know who's behind it and why they're doing it. They know we're going to find out sooner or later, so why play games? Remember, they're not afraid of us."

Uzi checked his watch. "They're not afraid of dying, that's for sure."

"Except for the guys in charge," Vail said. "*They* don't want to die. They claim it's because they need to stay alive to play quarterback and continue the cause. But everyone below them is expendable."

The light on Uzi's phone console lit up. He stabbed at the line button.

"He's on," Hoshi said. "I'm recording and running a trace."

"Got it." Uzi pressed the line button. "This is Agent . . . Shepard, special agent in charge of the FBI Joint Terrorism Task Force. Who am I talking with?"

"You're talking with the people responsible for the explosion last night." The voice was accented, confident—almost cocky.

"Do you have a name?"

"Tell me something, Agent Shepard. Does the FBI really think it was a gas main that blew up?"

"You know the answer to that question," Uzi said.

"How many of these are you going to be able to explain away?"

"How many attacks are you planning?"

"Tell you what. Why don't we help you out and go public on al Jazeera and then everyone will know you were hiding the fact you're under attack."

"I'm still waiting for your name. You know we're going to find out sooner or later."

"Then it will be later."

Uzi glanced at Vail. It was a telling look letting her know she got it wrong. "What do you want?"

"You call us terrorists. So it's obvious, isn't it? We want terror. But that's so simplistic. Here's the truth: some of us want to kill the infidels. Some want revenge for how you treat and defile Islam. We don't all agree on what we want—except for one thing: all of us want the Jews out of Palestine. We don't want a two-state solution. We want it all, all the land. Jews will not be allowed to own even one square meter."

Uzi shook his head, threw a quick glance at Vail and DeSantos. "And you think that suicide attacks in the US will help you, how?

"Some of us enjoy killing. And like I said, some want revenge. Me? I like seeing fear, I like seeing the mighty America crumbling, cowering in fear. Like on 9/11. When the towers fell, hundreds of thousands of my people danced in the streets."

Scumbag. I look forward to meeting you someday. In a dark alley.

"I remember," Uzi said. "I watched your celebration on TV."

"And I want to see your talking heads shouting at one another on your stupid news channels. I want to create division in your country. But it's not a fair fight. You're all so brainwashed by your freedoms and democracy that you've got 300 million opinions, all convinced you're right. Your political system is corrupt, bought by lobbyists."

"Sounds like you've got a long list of things you don't like about us."

"What do I want, Agent Shepard of the FBI Joint Terrorism Task Force? I want to expose your country for what it is. I want to destroy your economy. I want to bring you to your knees."

"How about we get together over a beer, talk this out?"

DeSantos and Vail looked at Uzi.

The man laughed. "That would make your job too easy."

"No, seriously. We can meet at your safe house in southwest DC."

There was silence.

"Listen to me, Kadir. Mind if I call you that? We both know how this is going to play out. You're gonna set off some bombs, innocent people are gonna die, and you'll celebrate for killing the nonbelievers. But then we're gonna track you down and send a Hellfire missile crashing into your car. Or your house. So why don't you and I meet and we can settle this, man to man?"

"'Innocent people'? There are no innocent people in America. You are all infidels! And you're going to die for your sins against Allah. You get fat earning your money, stuffing your faces, and flaunting your cars and houses. You're comfortable moving about the streets without a worry. That's going to end. You will be afraid. Afraid to go outside, afraid to be *inside*, not knowing when someone in your market will blow up, when someone in a movie theater will blow up. When a student in school is going to blow himself up, when someone in the subway is going to blow herself up. You call us terrorists. You're right. Because if there's one thing we know well, it's how to terrorize. Remember that."

The line went dead.

Uzi sat down heavily.

"That went exceedingly well," Vail said.

Uzi's head snapped up. "You think so?"

"No."

DeSantos shrugged. "At least we know where we stand with him. He hates us."

Vail rolled her eyes.

"I think it's safe to say we're dealing with Kadir Abu Sahmoud. He was shaken when I called him Kadir."

"I'm going to inform Knox," DeSantos said, pulling out his phone.

Uzi's Lumia rang. He answered it, listened a moment, and said, "Thank you. I appreciate it . . . No, I'm not surprised." Uzi laid it on the desk and sat down heavily. "That was Gideon Aksel. Positive confirmation on the voiceprint. It's Sahmoud. Don't know yet about the other person on the call." Uzi sighed, then said, "Do you think I shouldn't have revealed that we know who he is?"

Vail took a seat opposite Uzi. "I can make a case for handling it both ways. Obviously there are more risks in telling him we know his identity. But there are so many variables in this thing that I don't think there's a right or wrong answer. If he's a psychopath, it won't freak him out. It may've surprised him, but he recovered quickly. A guy like that, you might try to build him up next time, tell him how great he is, how impressed with him you are, how he's been able to set up these cells without our knowledge. Make it real or he'll see through it. He might bite. It'll feed his ego and he'll eventually make a mistake. Can't guarantee it'd work, but you never know."

DeSantos's phone vibrated and he consulted the display. "Knox is on his way over."

"Bottom line," Vail continued, "is that the more we engage him, the more conversations we have with him, the better. We might be able to pull some forensics from something he says, a background noise. It's better than not having any contact with him at all. You've started a relationship with him. That's a positive."

Hoshi knocked, then pushed the door open.

"You get anything?" Uzi asked.

"He used cloud bouncing."

"You're kidding me."

Vail looked at Uzi, then DeSantos, who shrugged. "Cloud bouncing?"

"There are services that route calls and internet to other clouds, removing identity and routing randomly. It's the latest in obfuscation. Good for baddies, bad for goodies."

"So, in English," Vail said, "the trace didn't work."

"Come in, Hoshi." Uzi gestured at the door. "And close it."

It clicked shut. Hoshi scanned their faces, shoulders tense. "What's going on?"

"There are some things I can't tell you. You're just going to have to trust me. Are you okay with that?"

"Did you seriously just ask me if I trust you?"

"Fair enough." Uzi reached into his drawer and pulled out a toothpick, studied it a second and then popped it between his lips. "You heard the phone call so you have an idea of who I was talking to and what's going on. This involves the explosion last night—which I know you already figured out."

"Thanks for giving me some credit."

"Kadir Abu Sahmoud is mixed up in this. As you heard, he's planning attacks on the country."

"So you want me to—"

"I want you to keep it quiet. This is not to be discussed with anyone. Including Shepard and the rest of the task force. Can you do that?"

Hoshi's face scrunched in confusion. "We're the JTTF and Sahmoud is a major terrorist on our Ten Most Wanted who's about to launch suicide bombings on the United States. And you don't want anyone on the task force to know about it? Or our boss?"

"That's right."

Vail had to laugh. "I'm sorry. It sounds just as bad when you say it."

"You're not helping," Uzi said to Vail.

"We'll eventually lift the veil on what's going on," DeSantos said. "We just need some time."

Hoshi thought a moment, then nodded. "Just don't get me fired, okay?"

Uzi gave her what looked to be a strained, almost pained smile. "Of course."

After she left, Vail turned to DeSantos. "Lift the veil? You trying to be funny?"

He shrugged. "Best I had at the moment. It was awkward."

"Whole thing's awkward. She's right—that's why we have a JTTF. We should be using every member on that task force—and dozens more."

"Leave it be," DeSantos said. "If that's what the president wants, that's what we do. We're just soldiers in a bigger war. There's stuff we don't know. There always is."

"Nice digs you got here." Vail glanced around the room. "You said you wanted us to come to your office so you could give us something."

"Right." Uzi rose from his chair and went over to a bookcase against the wall. It was filled with a number of objects including a couple of framed photos of a woman and a young girl.

His slain wife and daughter. A pang of pain struck Vail deep in her stomach.

To the left of the pictures sat a Lucite block encasing what looked like a computer chip and an Intel logo above an inscription recognizing Uzi for his work on the Pentium 4 processor. A bullet-holed canteen lay on its side, a worn olive military canvas pouch covering its bottom half.

Uzi moved a couple of other items aside and revealed a very dangerous-looking knife.

"I know what that is," DeSantos said. "You kept it."

"You told me to put it on my bookshelf."

DeSantos winked. "That I did."

"*I* don't know what it is." Vail looked from DeSantos to Uzi.

"The Tanto I used to kill the piece of shit who murdered Dena and Maya." He handed it to Vail, who hesitated. "Go ahead. I had Tim Meadows get the blood off for me. He used some kind of industrial crime scene cleaner."

"That's okay. I'm good just looking at it."

"Take it," he said, holding it closer in front of her. "It's yours."

"Mine?" Vail reached out and wrapped her fingers around the handle. She had to admit, it was beautifully balanced. It felt powerful.

Uzi took the leather case and slipped it over her head.

"Boychick. You can't give Karen a knife like that without teaching her how to use it."

"Way ahead of you. After London, Cooper and I gave her some private lessons."

"Cooper's the best," DeSantos said. "Do you remember what they taught you?"

Vail turned the knife, examining its edge, the walnut handle and inlaid chrome design. "More or less. I sparred a few times with an instructor at the academy."

DeSantos snorted. "Yeah, well, it's like training drills in the shooting house. You need to become so comfortable with the knife it's like an extension of your arm."

"Very Zen of you, Hector. Who would've thought."

"I'm not joking. Knife fighting is close quarters combat. There's very little room for error. One cut and you're dead. But forget the knife. If you're in close quarters combat, unless you know who you're up against, you don't know his skill level. And the really skilled fighters are so good, they're so lethal, don't even need a knife. Their hands are their weapons."

"Most important thing?" Uzi asked, playing the role of teacher.

"Not getting killed?" Vail said.

DeSantos reached over and took the Tanto from her. "I don't think you should give this to her, Uzi."

"Hey." Vail slapped DeSantos's forearm with the back of her hand. "Don't get all bent out of shape. I know the most important thing: not having it taken from you."

DeSantos bowed his head. "Yes, just like your Glock. Same principle."

Uzi took the Tanto from DeSantos and placed it back in Vail's hand.

Robby is not going to like this. She slipped it into the leather sheath—but because of her anatomy it did not fit as well as it did on Uzi. She would have to wear it elsewhere.

The door opened and a tan-suited Marshall Shepard stepped in. He paused in the entry, eyed Vail, Uzi—and then DeSantos. His gaze lingered on DeSantos.

"Shep. You remember Karen Vail of the BAU and Hector DeSan—"

"Oh, yeah, I remember Mr. DeSantos." His expression twisted into a frown as the two made eye contact. But when his gaze settled on the Tanto around Vail's neck, he tilted his head and said, "Mind explaining what's going on here?"

Vail gestured to the bookshelf. "Uzi was showing us his collection of—"

"Tchotchkes," DeSantos said. He glanced at Uzi and lifted his brow.

Shepard stood there working it through, then folded both arms across his chest. "You people take me for a fool? Uzi, I expected more of you."

DeSantos's phone rumbled again.

"Shep, please. Don't jump to conclusions."

"Let's step back for a second. There's an explosion downtown that no one at DC Metro seems to know anything about. And District Gas has no reports of a gas main explosion. That doesn't add up. You don't seem to be particularly concerned—and we both know with your background, you should be all over this like peanut butter on bread. But you're pretty laid back about it. That doesn't add up, either."

"I can see why you're—"

"Shut up. I'm not done." He cleared his throat. "Sorry to be boring you, Mr. DeSantos. Put the phone away while I'm talking."

DeSantos squinted as he slipped the handset back in his pocket.

"Koh looks like she's on pins and needles," Shepard said, "and when I ask her to check on something for me, she says she's in the middle of something for *you*, Uzi, and she'll get to it ASAP. Excuse me? I say. You're talking to your ASAC. She apologizes, then says to give her a few minutes. So I do that—and when I come back, she says she can't talk about it, that I need to talk to you. Then I walk in here and I see Hector DeSantos, a man who works God knows where, whose cover with the Department of Defense is as shady as a Mulberry tree in the middle of the White House lawn. Oh—and let's not forget the call from the director's office."

"That call," DeSantos said, "should be enough for you to back off."

Shepard took a couple of steps toward DeSantos. "You will address me appropriately, Mr. DeSantos, or you can get the hell out of my building."

DeSantos's right eye twitched.

Defuse this, Karen. Now. Even if playing mediator is not your strength.

"Look," Vail said, raising both hands. "We shouldn't be fighting each other. We all have jobs to do and we're just trying to do them."

"Really?" Shepard said, stepping closer to the circle. "Uzi has a job—working for *me*. You have a job too—but I bet if I call your ASAC, Agent Gifford will tell me you're *not* working for him right now, that the director told him you were on special assignment."

Uzi's phone buzzed. He pulled it from his pocket, glanced at the screen, and said, "Shep, I need to take this." Without waiting for permission, he answered the call. "Yes. Yes sir, Mr. Director." He held out the Lumia toward Shepard, who hesitated, then snatched it up.

"Marshall Shepard." His large lips thinned, his face tightening in anger. "Yes. I understand. I'll be here." He hung up and handed the cell back to Uzi. "He's on his way up to meet with us."

They stood there staring at the floor, the walls, the ceiling, their fingers . . . no one speaking—until the door opened and Douglas Knox entered.

11

Knox stood in the modest-size office, the lines in his face deeper, his complexion grayer than last they saw him.

"Agent Shepard and I will talk privately in a moment," he said, his dark tone mirroring the long look he gave Shepard. "But we need to address the current situation. Brief me on the conversation with Kadir Abu Sahmoud."

I know better than to ask how Knox knew about a conversation that just happened.

Uzi summarized the exchange as Knox began to pace. He absorbed the information in stride, his face expressionless.

"I'd like to recommend we go public with this before they do," Vail said. "We should control the message."

Knox did not reply, but he nodded at DeSantos.

"We bought some time to get a handle on things," DeSantos said, "which I assume was the idea behind being black. We now know what, and who, we're dealing with. Now when we release a statement, we'll sound like we know what's going on. Less chance of a panic."

Knox stopped, considered his comments, and said, "Agent Uziel?"

"Raise the threat level and mobilize the task force. I can have them up to speed in thirty minutes. There was no evidence of nuclear material in the safe house or the bomb-making factory we raided. But given their work in Gaza building tunnels, and Hamas being a proxy for Iran, and Iran having nuclear material, and al Humat residing in the same neighborhood as Hamas . . . I think we should pay close attention to our radiation sensors deployed in major cities. And maybe even get some more of the mobile units on the streets of DC, New York, Chicago, San Francisco, Los Angeles."

Knox resumed pacing. "A lot of connect-the-dots there, Agent Uziel. But I agree. I'll make the case to the president." He stopped, turned, and faced them, then set his gaze on Uzi. "Are we overlooking al Qaeda?"

Uzi thought a moment. "I don't see their fingerprints on this, sir. A few years ago AQ was funding a number of al Humat's activities, but I think they've outgrown that dependence. No, I think for once AQ doesn't have its hands dirty here."

"I agree. But if your assessment changes, I want to know ASAP." He turned to Shepard. "Anything to add?"

Shepard looked like he had plenty to say but kept his mouth shut. "No sir."

Knox rocked back on his heels. "Sounds like we have a plan of action. I'm having a dossier assembled on Sahmoud. You'll have it in half an hour. Assuming the president agrees, you can disseminate it to your task force."

"Anything on the three who escaped when we raided the safe house?" Uzi asked.

"On my way over here I was given the names of two men identified by Interpol based on fingerprints lifted from the townhouse: forty-three-year-old Tahir Aziz, co-conspirator in the Madrid bombing who's been active in recruiting Dutch youths for the war in Syria, and thirty-nine-year-old Esmail Ghazal, who helped plan the Paris Métro bombings in '95."

"So these are seriously bad dudes," DeSantos said. "And we had them."

"I emailed each of you photos Interpol had on file."

They reached for their phones simultaneously. Vail pulled up the pictures and committed them to memory. "Surveillance photos? From when?"

"Ghazal from two years ago and Aziz from six years ago," Knox said. "An important question for DHS to answer is how they got into the US without setting off alarms. Director Bolten is handling that. And I—"

The door swung open and Hoshi stuck her head in. "Sir—sirs, there's been an explosion at Metro Center."

"Casualties?" Vail asked.

"Don't know yet. Comms are down, not all the cameras are operating. Metro PD and first responders are en route and I just dispatched a team."

Uzi, Vail, and DeSantos started for the door.

"Have a car ready for us downstairs," Uzi said. "We're on our way."

12

Vail jumped from Uzi's Tahoe SUV, which he parked on F Street near 12th Street NW. The three of them ran across the wide avenue toward the vertical brown landmark Metro Center Station sign and underneath the open skeletal structure of the office building that rose above the district's second busiest subway station.

People were streaming out, running up the stairs and escalators, fighting amongst one another, pushing forward and climbing over others who had fallen in the surge to evacuate.

Jesus, they're freaking out. Just like Sahmoud said. Just like I *said . . . people afraid of when—and where—the next explosion would come. He'll be looking for news reports and uploaded smartphone videos on YouTube and Facebook.*

"He's probably got one or more guys onsite," Vail said, "filming, gauging our response. You see anyone who's too calm or seems more interested in watching or recording it than getting their butts out of danger, check 'em out."

They struggled to move against the tide, trying to get down into the belly of the station.

It did not take long for them to see the devastation. The previously majestic arching eggshell colored ceilings were charred black. Emergency lights were on but were glary and too few in number. Plenty of them had been damaged and were out of commission.

Large chunks of the brick concourse were lifted up, carved away by the force of the impact. Most tellingly, five cars were derailed, forming a jagged line one in front of another. Dozens of metal ball bearings lay scattered about the wreckage.

A smoky pall hovered in the air above the damaged trains. First responders were setting up Jaws of Life to pry open twisted doors, taking axes to the windows, and helping passengers to safety. The flow of people toward the exits was constant, bottlenecks occurring at the lower platform areas where the masses funneled into the narrow escalators.

Vail stopped along the elevated bridge between tracks and looked out among the commuters, tourists, businesspeople, children . . . searching for the two middle-aged men featured in the photos they had been given.

Wait—is that Ghazal? She leaned forward, saw what appeared to be one of her suspects, and headed toward his location.

She pushed her way down the escalator until she hit the platform. But all she saw was the back of his head, bobbing up and down as he went.

Is that the same guy? Black jacket, dark hair, about five foot ten.

Vail wished she had a radio to alert Uzi and DeSantos—because as she moved in the man's direction, he was headed away from her. And given that he was not near one of the exits, there were fewer people there, allowing him to move faster without running.

Vail fought forward, reached a clearing, and sprinted around broken chunks of concrete, metal, glass, and brick. She lost sight of him for a second—stopped, glanced left, then right—and found him. She tackled him from behind and took him down hard. His shoulder slammed into a canted section of cement and she landed atop him.

But it was not Ghazal.

"What's wrong with you," the man said, pushing at her face with his free hand. "Get the hell off me!"

Vail gathered herself and stood up, glanced around—and saw Ghazal, looking back at her, apparently thinking he had given her the slip.

Not so fast, asshole.

She took off in his direction, pulled her Glock—and then immediately cursed. There was no way she could use her handgun in a crowded Metro station.

"FBI. Stop!" In that fleeting second, she realized she had been reduced to the impotence her unarmed British comrades experienced when chasing a suspect. *Stop! Or I'll yell 'stop' again.*

The only question she had was if Ghazal was carrying. He would not hesitate to fire a weapon in a densely populated area. That would fit well with his goal of death and destruction.

That was a moot point because his only escape route was into the crowd of people still trying to exit the station. If he was going to turn and start shooting, he would have done it already.

But is he wired with explosives?

She remembered the bio Knox had given them—albeit extremely lacking in detail: Aziz and Ghazal were planners, not suicide bombers. They let the young, foolish, disenfranchised followers blow themselves up. These assholes were the "brains"; they did not want to die. They pulled the strings on the *tactics*, not the explosives.

Vail closed the gap and was only about ten feet behind him. She sliced between two men in suits, nearing the end of the escalator.

Gotta get him before he reaches to the top. If he makes it out of the station, we'll lose him.

As he hit the last step, Vail extended her left arm over a woman's shoulder and grabbed Ghazal's collar. He tried to wrestle free but it was difficult in a crowd because he was fighting the bodies all around him in addition to the one behind him, which happened to be yanking him backwards with tremendous determination.

Vail maneuvered her Glock against Ghazal's temple. "FBI," she said loud enough for everyone in the area to hear. "Esmail Ghazal, you're under arrest."

But like a running back in the grasp of two defenders, he kept pushing forward, twisting, squirming. "What are you gonna do? Shoot me?"

"Give me a reason." She dug the pistol's barrel into his skin.

He stopped struggling and she pulled cuffs from her belt. "Down on the ground." Vail followed him to the floor as people streamed around them. She stuck her knee in his back and ratcheted the restraints around his wrists as her Samsung vibrated.

She shifted her weight and, keeping pressure on Ghazal's spine, she reached for her new Bureau-issued Samsung Galaxy. She was still getting used to the larger device and fumbled it, sending it clanking to the floor. Great, Karen. Smash the screen on the shiny new smart phone. Good way to endear myself with my unit chief. She picked it up and was relieved to see it was still in one piece.

Text from Robby.

bombing at metro center

She wrote back:

i know i am there

She was about to reholster the phone when Robby's response buzzed:

so is jonathan

What? Vail's chest tightened, her ribcage constricting as if a cobra was snaking around her torso.

For a split second, her mind went blank. Then: *how the hell am I gonna find him? Is he okay?* He was a student at George Washington University, so naturally he traveled around DC on the Metro. It was one of the advantages of going to college in a city with an extensive mass transit system. And aside from Union Station, Metro Center was the system hub.

She typed back:

where is he

While she awaited the answer—hoping Robby *had* the answer—she visually searched the station's interior, trying to locate her son.

j is ok. tried calling us but only text got
thru. trying to get out of train somewhere

She swung her gaze back over her shoulder. Was he in a derailed car or one that was on another track? Metro shut down all traffic in and out of the station as soon as they got word of the explosion, meaning all nearby trains were immobile.

Vail stood up and pulled on Ghazal's forearm. "C'mon, asshole, get up."

She held up her creds and repeatedly shouted, "FBI, out of my way!" and like Moses, parted the sea of people and made it back down to the platform. Realizing she would have to drag Ghazal through the area of devastation, she thought instead of cuffing him to a fixed metal post or railing—when her phone rang.

Jonathan.

"Mom, I'm okay. I tried calling you before, but the call wouldn't go through. I sent a text—"

"I know, Robby told me. You sure you're okay? Where are you?"

"I'm fine, I'm outside the police blockade they just put up. Near F and 12th."

"Stay right there, I'm coming out of the station."

VAIL EMERGED FROM THE METRO where she, Uzi, and DeSantos had entered before they split up. She saw Uzi standing near his Tahoe, phone pressed against his ear.

She brought her prisoner to him and said, "Ghazal. Hang onto him. I gotta go look into something. Give me a few minutes."

Uzi's brow rose and he shifted his phone to take custody of the handcuffed man. "Hoshi, we've got Ghazal. Call you back."

Vail headed for the police barrier Jonathan had mentioned—and then saw him beside a Metro officer, chatting him up. To his credit, the cop was doing his best to maintain crowd control while keeping Jonathan engaged.

"Sweetie," she said as she hugged him. "When I got Robby's text . . ." She pushed away and held him at arm's length. "I was so worried."

"We were just coming into the station when I felt the car shake. It was like an earthquake or something. It kind of jumped off the tracks but we weren't going very fast. They finally got the doors open and we evacuated."

She hugged him again.

"What happened? What caused the explosion?"

"Can't say. But since *I'm* here with Uzi and Hector DeSantos . . ." She winked. "Figure it out."

His jaw went slack. Before he could ask any more questions, she said, "You going back to class?"

"I—I guess so. Unless they cancel it." *Which they'd definitely do once they figure out what's going on.*

An ambulance screamed down F Street and stopped a few feet ahead of a fire engine.

Jonathan turned to her. "Is there—is there anything I should do? Anywhere I should go? Anywhere I should avoid?"

She wished she had something to tell him. But that was the point with these types of terror attacks: there were no safe places. All she could come up with was, "Avoid crowded, popular areas."

He scrunched his face. "You serious? In DC? How am I supp—"

"I don't know. I—I'm working on it."

Vail gave him a peck on the cheek, then headed back toward Uzi while jotting off a quick text to Robby letting him know she saw Jonathan and that he was safe. As safe as one can be with suicide bombers setting off explosives around town.

"Nice work," Uzi said as she got into the SUV. Ghazal was in the backseat, flexcuffs securing his ankles together and his wrists to the door.

"Where we going?"

Uzi turned over the engine. "To get some answers."

THEY PULLED INTO THE UNDISCLOSED LOCATION that, according to Uzi, was known only to a handful of operatives—and until sixty minutes ago, that exclusive list did not even include himself.

They had injected Ghazal with a mild sedative supplied by Rodman on the side of the road, just outside the district. They blindfolded their prisoner, then with Rodman seated beside him, they drove an hour into a sparsely populated area of Spotsylvania County. During the ride, Vail had an opportunity to read through a dossier Knox and Tasset had assembled on Ghazal and Aziz. It was incomplete, but she hoped it would be helpful.

From the exterior, the building was a nondescript, cheaply constructed tilt-up warehouse with a loading dock in the rear and a faded black-and-white aluminum sign that read, Newman Industries. Uzi pulled the SUV into the parking lot, which was well shielded by hedges, shrubs, and trees.

Inside, however, after passing through a solid steel door, the structure was a highly secured lockdown facility.

Uzi, Vail, and Rodman led their prisoner along a cinderblock lined corridor. DeSantos was waiting at the end, arms folded across his chest.

"I don't like the road we're headed down," Vail said. "Been there. Done that. Didn't enjoy it."

They handed off Ghazal to two stocky men in jeans and sweatshirts, who took him inside an adjacent room.

"What happened in London was extraordinary because of the circumstances," DeSantos said. "We're on US soil here. This is going to be an interrogation, but it's going to be clean."

Vail knew that "clean" was a relative term; she took it to mean that they would only use standard interrogation methods, nothing that would cross the line. That said, with the known threat of imminent attacks hanging over the country, just how aggressive they got depended on how close DeSantos felt they were to the information—and if he felt Ghazal was holding back. She and Uzi were bound by procedure and law. DeSantos was not.

Vail and Uzi walked into the room, where DeSantos had already gotten started. Rodman remained outside to observe.

Their prisoner was seated at a stainless steel table that was bolted to the cement floor, Ghazal's wrists secured to a thick ring in the center of the sparse, metal surface. Two rather conspicuous cameras were mounted on the walls.

"There's no point in denying involvement here," DeSantos was saying as they entered. "We saw you at the safe house. We've got your fingerprints there."

"You know nothing," he said in heavily accented English.

DeSantos laughed. "That's why we're sitting here in this room. Because there are things we don't know. Things we want to know."

"There's also a lot we *do* know," Vail said. "We know about Sahmoud. We've talked to him."

Ghazal's eyes narrowed. That was apparently news to him. Good; keep him guessing. Throwing him off balance increased his unease, made him less sure of himself.

Uzi stepped in front of the table. "Look, asshole. We're not interested in wasting time. Tell us where and when the next attack is gonna be."

Ghazal seemed to consider that for a moment. "I don't know. That's the truth. Sahmoud and—we're given orders two hours in advance. We do what we're told."

"We know you're one of the planners," DeSantos said. "So cut the bullshit of being out of the loop."

"I plan, yes. But they decide when it's gonna be. I always plan for a lot of targets but *they* choose which ones."

"Who else is working with Sahmoud?" Uzi asked.

"No one."

"Bullshit. Who is it?"

"If Sahmoud wants you to know, you'll know. You're not going to get that from me. I don't care what you do to me; this is not something I will tell."

Vail glanced at DeSantos. She could tell by his smirk that he was willing to bet money against Ghazal's last proclamation.

"We've been analyzing the explosives and paraphernalia in your bomb-making factory." Uzi paused, then said, "We also found sniper rifles. That makes us think this isn't a one-dimensional attack."

When did he find out about the sniper rifles? When he was on the phone with Hoshi? Why didn't he tell me?

Ghazal smiled.

Uzi studied his face a moment. "What do you think you're going to get from launching these attacks?"

"We're fighting the enemy. Infidels, nonbelievers. Anyone who is not Muslim. Anyone who does not follow the laws of Allah. Anyone who does not follow Sharia law."

Vail came up alongside Uzi, gently nudged him aside, and took a seat opposite Ghazal. She had an idea. She twisted in the seat and looked at Uzi and DeSantos. "Would you two mind giving me some time?"

They hesitated, but clearly not wanting to break their unified front—and trusting Vail's sensibilities—left the room.

When the door thumped shut, she turned back to Ghazal. "Sharia law is all that matters."

Ghazal nodded.

"Okay," Vail said, "I get that. See, I've studied Islam. There are some wonderful things in the Koran."

Ghazal looked at Vail, a look that said he was unsure of what to make of her, of where she was going. Trying to determine why she was being nice to him.

Truth is, Vail wanted to ram her fist into his nose, then gut his stomach with the Tanto Uzi had given her. This bastard had killed innocent men, women, and children whose only "crime" was being in the wrong place at the wrong time. Well, that and the fact that they did not have the same religious beliefs as him and his ilk.

Vail pushed the animosity from her thoughts. There was no place for it right now. Later, maybe. But not now.

"Was Tahir with you at Metro Center?"

"No. He's busy with other things."

"You were only there to observe, right? To make sure the plan you set out went the way it was supposed to go. And if your martyr did not have the courage to set off his vest, you had the failsafe, the switch, to detonate remotely. Right?"

Ghazal nodded.

"Sahmoud told us about the dirty bomb."

Ghazal's mouth dropped open.

She made a huge guess—and based on Ghazal's raw reaction, she hit pay dirt. "I'm concerned about that," Vail said. "Because we're not talking about a hundred people dead in a Metro station. We're talking about thousands of deaths, if not more. And a significant portion of a city left uninhabitable."

"That is not my concern."

Vail pursed her lips. "Depends on how you look at it. If you're nearby when it goes off, you'll be poisoned too. And your job is to plan the attacks, not be martyred. There are others for that."

Ghazal did not object.

"Were you involved in planning the release of the dirty bomb?"

Ghazal dropped his gaze to the table.

"Esmail, I'm pragmatic. We can't stop the attack. You know that. I know that. But I have a son who's innocent in your jihad—"

"There are no innocents in America."

Vail shook her head disapprovingly. "I know that's the line. I know that's what you're brainwashed into believing. But my son is a believer. He's been asking about converting to Islam. That's why I know about the Koran and the beauty it contains. He and I discuss it almost every night. He's not an infidel."

Sell it, Karen, keep steady eye contact.

Ghazal leaned back and nodded approvingly. "Then he can be a martyr. If he dies for our cause, that is a great honor."

Dammit, you asshole, I need to find a way to reach you. Connect with you.

"You have a daughter," she said, subtly changing tactics. "I know that as a father you're just looking for her to have the good things in life." Truth was, Vail knew that these extremists did not value the lives of their children the same way Americans did. But she was trying to reach Ghazal on a level he was unaccustomed to being talked to. It was bad enough he was being questioned by a woman in power. If she could appeal to him as a mother would appeal to her child, she might, perhaps, be able to access some humane part of him he had buried long ago.

He again looked down at the table. "This has nothing to do with my daughter."

"I'm asking you to spare the life of my son. I would do the same for your daughter. Just tell me where the dirty bomb is being deployed, what city. I understand you don't know when it's going to be set off. But if I know it's going to be in DC, I'll send my son to friends of his in New York City."

Ghazal's eyes rose from the table and met Vail's stare. "That would not be a good idea." He held her gaze.

Vail could not help but swallow deeply.

Holy shit, he just confirmed my suspicions about the dirty bomb and where it's going to be launched.

She refocused. "Thank you. As a parent. I—" She allowed some tears to flow into her eyes. "I thank you for your decency. Is there anything else you can tell me about the dirty bomb? How powerful is it?"

"I told you enough. That question has nothing to do with the safety of your son."

Vail licked her bottom lip. "Fair enough. Are you planning any more attacks here in DC?"

"The odds are in your son's favor. We should leave it at that."

"So no more suicide bombings are planned for DC."

Ghazal shrugged.

What the hell did that mean? Asked and answered? Or, "You said that, not me."

"Because we've captured your cache of explosives?"

He snorted, a contemptuous outburst. "That will not stop us. I think you are smart enough to figure out why."

Yeah, I guess I am. They've got other stashes. Or ways of getting more without us knowing.

"Where are your smuggling tunnels located?"

He kinked his head to the side, a look that said, "Did you really think I'd answer that?"

A knock at the door nearly made her jump.

Vail got up from her seat and walked into the corridor. Uzi was there alongside one of the large men she had seen when they first arrived. Uzi led her into a room across the hall.

As the door clicked closed, DeSantos turned away from the wall of monitors, which showed high resolution color images of Ghazal's face and body from multiple angles. She had only seen two cameras, but apparently there were more embedded in the walls and table. Another screen, where Rodman sat, showed the man's blood pressure and heart rate. Impressive.

"Nice work in there," DeSantos said.

"Have you notified the JTTF in Manhattan?"

"I called my contact at the National Counterterrorism Center," Uzi said. "But there's not much to go on."

DeSantos glanced back at the monitors. "We're not really sure what we've got. They weren't direct admissions."

Vail felt blood rushing to her face. "What are you talking about? He has no motivation to feed us bullshit. He's not giving us locations. He's not telling us when. He was responding to indirect questions, on a level jihadists aren't used to—his defenses are lower. He's talking to a woman in a position of power—which he probably isn't used to, either. I took him out of his element, which, again, is going to lower his defenses. I think on the scale of reliable intel, what he told us is pretty damn good."

Uzi scratched at his temple. "I can't disagree."

"In terms of his body language," DeSantos said, "I think you're right."

Rodman touched the monitor in front of him. "Same here with BP and heart rate."

"But," Uzi said, "is that enough? How actionable is the intel?"

Vail rubbed her forehead. "I need some air." She walked outside, finding her way through the maze, and out the front door. The cold air prickled her cheeks and she took a deep breath, filling her lungs.

They're planning to set off a dirty bomb in New York City. Jesus Christ.

Vail pulled out her Samsung and stared at it. *Don't do this, Karen. Let JTTF do its thing. But without actual proof or verification, will the task force act on it? What if Ghazal was bullshitting me?*

No. It felt legit. Go with your instincts.

She dialed and waited for it to connect.

Carmine Russo answered on the second ring. "You know, when I told you not to be a stranger, I didn't mean you should call me so soon."

"This isn't a social call." Her tone was serious—but then again, this was a serious matter. Russo had been Vail's mentor going back to her early days in law enforcement. Now a captain with the NYPD, she thought he needed to be plugged in.

"Uh oh. What's up? And if you tell me we've got another serial killer in New Yor—"

"We've got a situation. This isn't really in your wheelhouse, but I want to make sure the information makes it to the department ASAP, without delay."

"What information?"

"Did you hear about the gas main explosion in DC last night?"

"No. Why would I hear about that? Any casualties?"

"None you would've heard about."

"Huh?"

"The explosion you didn't hear about was a terrorist cell of al Humat that had set up a bomb-making factory in downtown DC. We stumbled on one of the bomb makers, I shot him and inadvertently set off his vest. An undercover

FBI agent was killed before I got there. We ascertained the location of their safe house, arrested one and at least two got away. Today they set off a suicide bomb in Metro Center."

"I got a text about that," Russo said. "Maybe half an hour ago. No known cause yet."

"Bullshit. It was a terrorist attack. We grabbed up one of the planners, who's got a history of other bombings overseas."

"Fuck."

"Haven't gotten to the good part yet."

"There's a good part?"

"We have reason to believe they're going to set off a dirty bomb in Manhattan."

There was silence, then Russo said, "Still waiting for the good part."

"The good part is that we've got some advance notice. And also that I'm giving you a heads-up instead of waiting for the FBI to run it through their National Joint Terrorism Task Force at the National Counterterrorism Center, who'll send it on to their New York JTTF, who'll then run it up the ladder to 1PP," she said, referring to the brass at One Police Plaza—NYPD headquarters.

"Where's the attack going to be?"

"No idea."

"When?"

"No idea."

"And this is the good news?"

"No, Russo, it's awful news. Whisper in your buddy's ear at the Counterterrorism Unit. Tell him to turn up those sensors you've got, that domain awareness system." A comprehensive security apparatus, the domain awareness system consisted of security cameras deployed around the city in coordination with radiological sensors, nuclear detectors, license plate readers—all processing information in real time and reporting to a central location in Lower Manhattan.

"I'll talk with the commissioner, make sure he's up to speed."

Vail glanced around the countryside—at least, what she could see over the tops of the tall hedges. "Probably best to leave my name out of it."

Russo snorted. "No shit, Karen."

"Gotta go. We're questioning the asshole we caught at the Metro."

"Hey, thanks for the heads-up."

"Good luck—and tell Protch I said hi."

"Tell him yourself." With that, he hung up.

Vail lowered the handset from her ear, wondering if she had done the right thing. *Yes. As a person, it was the right thing. As a law enforcement officer, I broke protocol.*

But lives were at stake. Whatever heat she took—if any—she would sort out later.

She walked back into the building just as Uzi was on his way out.

"Get anything else?"

Uzi pulled his keys out of a pocket. "Let's go. Hector's staying behind."

"You didn't answer me."

He paused with his hand on the doorknob. "No. We didn't get shit."

13

Vail sat across from Robby at dinner. Their home was quiet without Jonathan around—although he was a frequent participant for a home cooked meal when they could coordinate their work and school schedules. Jonathan had pledged the Beta fraternity, which took up a number of his evenings when he was not studying.

Vail's aunt, who lived in a separate part of the house, ate early dinners and went to bed hours before they did. Her presence in the home was hardly detectable.

Robby sliced at his steak, then stabbed a chunk with his fork. "I think you did the right thing. It wasn't according to the book, but this is bigger than the book. It's about saving lives. And since no one knows when this dirty bomb will go off, and exactly where, bureaucracy has no viable place in the equation."

"There's another part to this." Vail took a sip of her Hall Cabernet. "We got some intel that one or more of the Islamic extremist groups might be collaborating in some way with Cortez."

"Cortez." Robby studied her face as he chewed, trying to process the reference. "The drug cartel? The one that—"

"Yes." Vail knew that mere mention brought a personal note to her comment because of Robby's past brush with Carlos Cortez, his men, and their affiliates. "We don't know the details. Some unconfirmed intel from a well placed CI. He's not always been reliable, which is a problem. But so far some of what he's told us has been right on the money." She set down her glass. "Uzi and Hector think it could involve tunnels. And if Hezbollah is involved and they're proxies of—"

"Iran." He chewed on that a moment. "I sat in on a briefing awhile back about Hezbollah, Hamas, al Humat, Islamic State. All the bad actors. Money laundering schemes, stuff like that. Sounds like it might be even worse than I thought." He played with the broccolini on his plate. "Islamic extremists and drug cartels. Murder and mayhem. Never gonna be peace on this planet."

"We need confirmation of the connection." Vail set her glass down.

Robby must have realized the conversation had paused because he suddenly looked up from his plate. "What?"

"We need to know if that intel is reliable. I imagine DEA can find out."

"DEA has agents sitting on Uzi's task force. Why doesn't he ask them?"

"He has. They're working on it. But I don't know how good they are. I know how good *you* are. And if I ask you to look into this, you'll do it and you'll do it well. And fast."

"Did I miss something? Did you just ask me to look into it?"

"I am now."

Robby chewed his steak slowly, appearing to mull the compliment—and the request.

"Problem?"

"No," he said without looking up.

"While you're at it, see if your DEA sources have heard anything about nuclear material being smuggled in from Iran through South America using the drug tunnels that cross into the US."

"Hezbollah is well connected with the leadership in Venezuela."

"That's a start. I need more. I need actionable intelligence."

"I'll check with my ASAC, see if we've got anything."

"Do that and they'll give it to someone else to look into. Or he'll just tell you it's covered by the guys on the JTTF."

Robby swallowed his food, set his fork down, and leaned back in his chair. "Look, I've only been on the job a couple of years. I'm doing well, working my way up. But DEA is pretty strict about its regs, maybe more so than the FBI. And they're really respectful of chain of command. Pushing the envelope may not be such a good idea."

Vail played with her wine glass. "Obviously I don't want you to get in trouble. Forget it."

"You won't be angry?"

Vail thought about Robby's own words, uttered moments ago: this is bigger, more important, than following procedure. It was about saving lives. Still, she did not want to pressure him.

Vail reached over and took his hand. "I don't want you to do anything that'll jeopardize your job. I know how important it is to you, how hard you've worked to get where you are. Uzi's people will come through. If not, I'll get the info some other way."

Robby continued eating, but he appeared to be mulling over what Vail had told him because he was uncharacteristically quiet.

Perhaps he was thinking about his ordeal at the hands of Cortez. Maybe he was using his knowledge of the drug trade to consider the long-term implications of the cartels working with terrorists: criminals and religious extremists in cahoots.

It was hard to know the full impact of such alliances, but one thing was certain: whatever it was, it was not good.

14

National Counterterrorism Center
Liberty Crossing
McLean, Virginia

Vail parked her car in front of the large National Counterterrorism Center complex, which was dominated by a modern butterfly shaped six story glass-and-concrete edifice. Before she opened her door, Robby called.

"Only got a minute," he said. "I found a guy at DEA, in SOD, our Special Operations Division, who'll meet with you, give you a briefing on that thing you asked me to look into."

"You're shitting me."

"I'd enjoy yanking your chain—just to return the favor—but no, I'm serious. Name's Richard Prati. He was scheduled for a DHS CT briefing at the NCTC, so it worked out well. He'll go early to your meeting, then stick around for his."

He briefs the Department of Homeland Security on counterterrorism. Robby scored. And tonight, he may score again.

"Just got off the phone with Uzi. He cleared it with Knox. Sorry you weren't the first to know, but things are moving fast."

"Thanks, honey. I really appreciate it."

"I'm emailing you a quick bio on Prati. And yes, you can make it up to me later."

Vail got out and joined Uzi and DeSantos as they strode along a wide gray, tan, and sand colored cobblestone walkway that led to a plaza formed by the V of the building's two forward-facing wings.

They passed between the vertical cement-and-steel security barriers and beneath the American flag, which hung limp on its pole in the still air.

The NCTC, as it was known in government acronym parlance, was originally established in 2003 as the Terrorist Threat Integration Center, part of a constellation of solutions outlined in a scathing 9/11 Commission report that excoriated the intelligence community. They were tasked with creating and maintaining a database of known and suspected terrorists, and collecting and coordinating terrorism-related material from all sources. Most importantly, they were in charge of sharing the information with the affiliated agencies domestically and overseas and working with the FBI's JTTFs and the Defense Department's combatant commands to ensure a coordinated flow of alerts, data, and trends.

Given the importance of its mission, it was remarkable nothing like the NCTC existed prior to 9/11—and in retrospect it was no wonder that an orchestrated attack could be noted by so many disparate agencies yet stopped by none—solely because each knew nothing of what the other had discovered.

They assembled in the operations center, a massive open space with computer workstations arranged in rows facing an enormous high-definition flat panel screen rivaling those in sports stadiums. Ringing the periphery, on a second story, were meeting rooms and an observation deck that looked down over the floor.

Douglas Knox stood with the CIA's Tasset, Homeland Security's Bolten, the Defense Department's McNamara, and two other men Vail did not recognize.

Knox turned as the trio approached. "Agent Vail, this is the director of National Intelligence, Brandon Lynch."

Vail and Lynch exchanged pleasantries. "Beautiful facility you have here, Mr. Director."

Lynch, a black man dressed in a crisp dark suit, pink shirt, and a three-point folded handkerchief, harrumphed. "In the grand scheme, it's a shame we need to have a place like this. But this is the world we live in." He turned to Uzi. "Agent, good to see you again. And . . . Hector." He gave a stiff nod.

Uh oh, there's a history here. And it's apparently not a good one.

"I don't think we've met," Vail said to the as yet unidentified olive-complected man with a narrow, thinly trimmed beard.

"None of you have met him," Knox said. "This is Mahmoud El-Fahad, CIA."

Vail and DeSantos took turns shaking his hand. Uzi was slower, more reluctant—or more careful. Vail couldn't determine which. Both, perhaps.

"You are . . ." Uzi said.

"Palestinian," Fahad said, apparently understanding what Uzi was asking.

Although Uzi did his best not to react, Vail saw it. His body language was fairly restrained in times of stress—no doubt a learned trait from his days with Mossad. But she knew Uzi well. She saw the tension in his shoulder muscles.

"Great," Lynch said. "Let's go to the briefing room. The president should be there by now."

The president? Had I known I would've worn my pumps. And my black sweater. And my—Jesus, Karen, stop it.

"Go on," Knox said. "We'll be there in a moment." He waited until the men cleared the room, then addressed Uzi. "I am not immune to how this affects you, Agent Uziel. But Fahad understands the terrorist mind-set; he's got contacts here and abroad in the Palestinian community and might be able to get us intel as to who's involved. He's lived in the West Bank and he knows Gaza."

"I understand, sir."

"How much access will Fahad have?" DeSantos asked.

"As much as any of you."

"He's an operative?" Vail asked.

"Fully vetted. Exemplary record. For now, he's a member of the team. One of us."

Uzi scratched at his temple. "Right, but—"

"Enough said, Agent Uziel." Knox's jaw was set. This was clearly not open for debate. "Let's go. We don't want to keep President Nunn waiting."

As they walked, Vail glanced quickly at Richard Prati's bio that Robby had emailed—and came away impressed.

A moment later, they entered the conference room. Like the rest of the facility, it had a modern bent. The walls were a multi-toned blue with a large NCTC seal behind the long ovoid desk, a fixed workstation that featured a maple laminate top, a power strip with computer ports in front of each seat and perforated stainless steel panels on the inside of the oval which featured dramatic floor lighting that looked more appropriate on a *Star Trek* set than in a government counterterrorism center.

Red LED clocks were mounted on the wall displaying the current times for Kabul, Beijing, Baghdad, Taiwan, Tehran, DC, LA, and Chicago, as well as "Zulu."

Vance Nunn was seated at the head of the table, a small LCD display in front of him. Water bottles were set out for each of the attendees and tented name placards faced the president.

Also present were Marshall Shepard and Ward Connerly, the president's chief of staff, as well as the chairman of the Joint Chiefs and a handful of others from the NCTC whom Vail did not know.

Nunn watched as Vail, Uzi, DeSantos, and Knox entered and found their seats. The fifty-three-year-old, heavily jowled chief executive folded his hands in front of himself and made eye contact with the participants. "All the high-tech gadgets money can buy, all the brightest minds in intelligence, two hundred thousand employees, three dozen satellites, drones all over the goddamn Middle East, military bases all over the world, a $40 billion budget. And no one was able to tell me we have sleeper cells on our soil? That we had bomb makers holing up in Washington building explosive vests? How the hell is that possible? Anyone?" He glanced around, but no one answered.

"How many attacks on our homeland are acceptable before we get our acts together?" Connerly asked. His gaze settled on Uzi.

Uzi folded his hands and paused a moment to gather his thoughts. "Mr. President, Mr. Connerly . . . intelligence is an inexact science. We collect information from a variety of sources—HUMINT, satellites, intercepted phone calls and emails, captured hard drives—and so on. We analyze it all and make a best guess as to *what's* going to happen, *where* it's going to happen, and *when.* Sometimes we're right and sometimes we're not. Sometimes we just have blind spots. Despite all our technology, we're still just people left to draw conclusions. And people make mistakes."

Vail watched Nunn's reaction; Uzi was dangerously close to talking down to the president, who should have been aware of that information, given the normal course of his regular briefings. Still, she thought Uzi was justified in pointing out the challenges they faced. If nothing else, it served as a reminder—as well as an answer to the president's question.

"That sounds more like an excuse," Nunn said. "And excuses don't save lives, now, do they?"

"Sir," DeSantos said, "we're dealing with an enemy that adapts. They're increasingly sophisticated and extremely well funded. These groups have people raising money all over the world—including inside the United States. And they've carried out kidnappings to extract ransom in the tens of millions of dollars. Al Qaeda and its member organizations have taken in over $150 million from kidnapping Europeans. Islamic State has *billions* from captured banks and oil fields."

Nunn frowned, then turned to Tasset. "Earl?"

Tasset adjusted his glasses. "I have to agree. We used to be able to check visas, profile by screening for Muslims who've traveled to terrorist hot spots and training camps or who had suspicious family connections. But our enemy nowadays could be our own citizens, naturalized Americans who have passports that go to fight in Syria with Islamic State or al Qaeda or al Humat, then return home and walk among us. Our neighbors, teachers, doctors. They look like us because they *are* us."

"Just like we have undercover operators infiltrating their mosques," Uzi said, "they've infiltrated us. England has the same problem we do, maybe more so because their Muslim population is greater. After cutting their teeth with Islamic State and al Qaeda in Syria or Iraq, British nationals are returning home with perfectly valid passports and setting up terrorist cells. That makes it extremely difficult, if not impossible, to stop."

Nunn shifted forward in his seat and leaned both forearms on the maple desk. "The American people don't want long-winded explanations and political spy babble. They get that from the talking heads on TV. I have to give them answers. I have to give them hope and security. I have to deliver the goods. Which means *you* have to deliver the goods."

Very helpful, sir. Bury your head in the sand. Ignore the facts. There must be a way to fix something if you insist there is.

"Why don't we move on," Lynch said. "We've got some relevant pieces of information to report on." He glanced at McNamara. "Richard, the prisoner. Your people get anything of use?"

McNamara cocked his head. "That'd be Esmail Ghazal. He's given us a few things, most notably a planned dirty bomb attack on New York City, as we discussed last night in our—"

"Yes, yes," Nunn said. "Do you believe him?"

McNamara turned to DeSantos, who answered.

"Mr. President, I was in charge of the interrogation. I believe what we got was reliable. But it was too short on details to be worth much."

Nunn hesitated, made quick eye contact with Tasset, then Knox.

"What about that informant in Turkey?" Nunn asked.

Tasset nodded. "A lot of the info he gave us seems to have panned out. But we've gotten everything from him that we could."

"We're analyzing data every day," Lynch said. "Every hour. Something's bound to break."

Oh, great. We've been reduced to hoping and praying?

Nunn leaned to his left, seemed to be straining to read one of the name placards, then sat back in his chair. "Mr. Shepard, can you add anything?"

Shepard pulled open a manila folder with his thick hands. "Yes. Yes sir. Forensics are in for the four crime scenes: the site of the original explosion on Irving Street; the bomb-making factory and storage site; their safe house that we raided; and the Metro Center station.

"At crime scene two—the bomb factory—we found vests laden with explosives in various stages of completion. One of the engineers, or bomb makers, was shot by Agent Vail and DEA Agent Roberto Hernandez. Their rounds struck the explosives and set them off. Obviously killed the engineer. But based on what our forensics team found there, it appears that four men were living in that safe house."

"Overall, three tangos escaped," Uzi said, in case the president did not do the math.

"Jesus Christ."

"Did the explosives tell us anything?" Bolten asked.

"They did," Knox said. "I suggest we let Mahmoud El-Fahad report on that."

Nunn sat forward, squinted to read Fahad's nameplate. "You work for?"

"CIA, sir. I'm an operations officer, born in the West Bank. I've been stationed there on and off for nine years."

Nunn shot a glance at Tasset and said, "Continue."

"Generally speaking, in terms of delivery method, Hamas uses belts for suicide attacks while al Humat uses vests. As to the explosives themselves, Palestinian engineers use primarily two kinds. They're both effective in accomplishing their goal—death. They're also inexpensive, impossible to track, and relatively easy to obtain. I'm talking about triacetone triperoxide, known as TATP, and TNT. TNT is repurposed from old land mines or smuggled in through the tunnels Hamas has built. These tunnels crisscross most of Gaza and are very sophisticated. Last year Israel destroyed the ones that led into its territory but left a lot of the remaining ones intact when the cease-fire took effect. Hamas and al Humat have since reopened some of the tunnels that were closed off and they remain effective conduits for obtaining bomb supplies, rockets, and other armaments.

"Acetone peroxide is another explosive they use. The chemical may sound familiar because it is—women use it for removing nail polish and bleaching their hair. But using it as an explosive is dangerous. One way of identifying a Palestinian engineer is by injuries from peroxide—burns and missing fingers and hands are common.

"To partially answer your question from before—how can they have assembled all this stuff right under our noses—not only do they use the peroxide because it's cheap and easy to get, but because it can't be detected by bomb-sniffing dogs."

"What about ammonal?" Uzi asked.

Fahad nodded. "It's easier to work with and safer—and it minimizes the amount of peroxide that has to be used."

"We didn't find any ammonal at their factory," Shepard said.

Uzi removed a toothpick from his pocket but did not open it. "They use lightbulbs as detonators, right?"

Fahad's brow rose. "Right."

Lightbulbs? "Uh, can you explain that?"

"The wire is coated with a flammable chemical," Uzi said. "When the bulb is lit, the wire heats and the bomb detonates. Cheap, low-tech, reliable, and undetectable. Is that what they used at Metro Center?"

"No," Fahad said. "That entire attack was different. It packed a much stronger explosive punch, which means it was likely carried onto the train in a large backpack and/or duffel bag, maybe a suitcase. We're still sorting through the wreckage looking for it. To cause that kind of damage, ATF told me it had to be C4, maybe even a combination of different types of explosives and methods—suitcase, vest, and backpack."

"Palestinian bombers typically use shrapnel in their bombs," Uzi said. "Any sign of that?"

"Yes."

Uzi faced the president. "Most of the deaths from suicide attacks come from the shrapnel thrown off during the blast. A favorite method these bomb makers use is to fill the explosives with ball bearings up to seven millimeters in diameter. When these steel balls are used as projectiles, they travel at roughly the same speed as bullets fired from a gun. So it's like being hit by automatic rounds of a submachine gun—several hundred rounds in a split second."

"To sum all this up," Fahad said, "the materials we found in the bomb-making factory that Agents Vail and Hernandez stumbled on had all of these ingredients, confirming our belief that this cell is very likely of Hamas and/or al Humat origin—or they've been trained by these groups."

Uzi waited for the president to ask a question. When he did not, Uzi said, "Since we intercepted communication between the planner in Gaza and the engineer here in DC and the guy in Gaza was the voice of Kadir Abu Sahmoud, and Sahmoud is the co-founder of al Humat, I think it's safe for us to operate under the assumption that al Humat is behind this operation."

"But we don't have positive confirmation that voice was Sahmoud," Lynch said. "Making an assum—"

"We do have positive confirmation."

Knox sat forward. "We do?"

"We do, sir. I gave the recording to Mossad and they did a biometric automatic voice analysis and ran phonetic and acoustic analyses with samples they had of Sahmoud on file. It was a match."

"How come this is the first I'm hearing of this?" Tasset said.

"We also had a conversation with Sahmoud," Vail said. "He and Agent Uziel—posing as ASAC Shepard—spoke yesterday."

"Posing as me?" Shepard asked.

"I couldn't take a chance he'd know my name," Uzi said. "I meant to give you a heads-up in case he called again, but the Metro bombing hit. Things have been moving very quickly."

"Why would he know your name?" Fahad asked.

Uzi squirmed in his seat. "Not important. But I felt it wasn't worth the risk."

Fahad hesitated but apparently decided not to press the point. Instead, he asked, "Did Sahmoud take responsibility for the bombings?"

"We spoke before Metro Center. It was a pretty frank discussion. He launched into the typical Islamic extremist rant." Uzi turned to Vail. "Based on what he said, did you have any doubt that Sahmoud was involved?"

"None."

A red light on the phone in front of the president lit up and blinked. He lifted the receiver and listened a second. "Fine. Send him in." As he hung up, he said, "Richard Prati, Special Agent in Charge of the DEA's Special Operations Division, is going to brief us. This is on your request, Agent Vail?"

"And mine," Uzi said.

Following a knock, the door swung open and a stocky, dark-suited man entered. Vail envisioned a bulldozer—and his demeanor seemed to fit her mental image.

"Agent Prati," Connerly said. "A little advance notice would've been appreciated."

Prati froze in place and looked at the president. "I—I thought—"

"We pulled strings to get him here," Uzi said, "and only got it arranged about an hour ago. We need to hear what he has to say."

Nunn waved Prati to a seat near the other end of the briefing room. "You have five minutes, Agent."

Prati set down his leather briefcase and removed a USB drive. "May I?" he asked, holding it up. "PowerPoint."

"Go on," Lynch said.

While he plugged the device into a port along the top of the briefing table, Vail said, "Agent Prati ran the Special Operations Division in Virginia for nine years, overseeing thirty agencies."

"Brits, Australians, Mexicans, Canadians—we had 'em all." Prati picked up a remote and aimed it at the screen. The word "narcoterrorism" appeared in bold red letters.

"I was asked to address two main issues." Prati directed his remarks to the president. "First off, it's important to give a frame of reference as to what we're dealing with. Narcoterrorism is a problem that keeps escalating—yet the public has no clue. I used to think that was okay because the more the public knows the more the media would be in my face. But now I realize that was wrong. We need people to know because it's ballooning out of control. And it impacts every family in every corner of this country."

Nunn twisted the left corner of his mouth, something between a frown and a chuckle. "A bit over the top, no?"

"No," Prati said flatly, holding the president's gaze.

I like this guy. He's got balls.

"The DEA chief of operations calls these narcoterrorists hybrids—one part terrorist organization and one part global drug trafficking cartel. He specifically called out groups like the Colombian FARC, the Taliban, Hamas and Hezbollah. Obviously, al Humat is now a member of that team too." Prati glanced around the table. "These terror groups are turning to—and in some cases *into*—criminal enterprises to fund their operations."

Prati pressed the remote and a new red and yellow slide appeared: two circles overlapped one another to form an orange center: a Venn diagram showing the intersection of terrorists and criminals. "I don't have to tell you why this is a very, very bad thing. Annual drug trafficking income, worldwide, is over $400 billion. Think about that for a minute. That's billion, not million.

"Used to be, terror groups were interested in one thing: furthering their political cause. They committed violent acts and murdered innocent people who didn't believe as they did. No more." He flipped to another slide showing a complex series of squares and arrows.

"But global terrorist organizations are large, sprawling enterprises nowadays and they need funding to operate. We've done a good job shutting down or limiting many of their traditional funding streams, so the terrorists are turning to criminal activity for money. Drug trafficking generates more cash than any other commodity, so it's an ideal source of revenue for them.

"The drug trafficking money is brought in through Beirut and put into overseas bank accounts, then wired to the US—hundreds of millions of dollars a month—and that's just the money we know about. God only knows what else is going on. But here's the thing: no matter how much it is, that money's dirty."

"Obviously," Vail said, "they launder it somehow."

"Used cars." Prati pressed a button and a red laser dot appeared over one of the boxes in his flow chart. "These groups have set up a vast network of hundreds of US car dealerships that buy millions of used cars and then ship them to west Africa, where they're sold legitimately on the open market. But along the way, a cut of the profit goes to the major terror groups. It's a multi-billion-dollar business."

"Makes sense," DeSantos said. "Several thousand dollars per car, if not more. An easy way to move, and launder, a lot of money very quickly. And no one suspects a thing."

"I was briefed on synthetic drugs last month," Tasset said. "Manufactured in China."

Prati leaned back in his seat. "Yes. They're sold here in grocery stores and minimarts. The proceeds, hundreds of millions of dollars, are then sent to Yemen, where they're distributed to the terror groups. But it doesn't have to be drugs. Money is sent through the legit banking system to China to pay for cigarettes, clothing, shoes, sneakers, toys, computers—all sorts of stuff. The Chinese manufacture these things and ship 'em to South or Central America to get laundered: they're sold through legal businesses to generate clean cash. The money then gets sent to the drug traffickers overseas. Like I said, nothing generates cash as well as illicit drugs."

"You called the terrorist organizations sprawling enterprises," Vail said. "Why do they need so much money? I mean, how much does it cost to build some homemade bombs?"

"It's not just the attack, which, you're right. Doesn't cost a hell of a lot. Take 9/11, their most ambitious operation. It cost a little over half a million. But these terror groups are no longer loose associations of people running around the deserts of the Middle East wreaking havoc and setting off car bombs. They're organizations that fly their operatives from country to country. They run training camps, pay salaries, purchase weapons and ammo, buy buildings, build infrastructure, make fake passports, rent safe houses, pay bribes to key people in government. After 9/11, the CIA estimated that al Qaeda spent $30 million a year just to run their organization. That was a long time ago, so the cost has gone up." He looked at Tasset and got a nod of acknowledgment.

"Terrorism is an expensive business," Knox said, "generating the kind of profits US corporations would envy."

I wonder if the Service Employees Union has cracked al Qaeda.

"So let me get to those two questions you had," Prati said with a glance at Uzi. "Does Hezbollah have sleeper cells in the US?" He folded his hands on the table in front of him. "This has been talked about for years. Back in 2008 when their military leader, Imad Mughniyah, was assassinated in Syria, Hezbollah threatened the west. The FBI—"

"Went nuts trying to track down and keep tabs on sleepers here in the US in case they decided to retaliate," Knox said.

"Thing is, we didn't find a whole lot and they never attacked us."

"They never attacked us," Uzi said, "because they raise too much money from supporters in the US."

Prati shrugged. "Maybe. Bottom line is that we never found actual cells here. But here's where it gets muddy. Remember we talked about the car dealerships? Hundreds of other related businesses and groups have been set up across the US to assist in, and establish, this trade-based money laundering scheme to sell used cars and ship them over to west Africa. But it's all being funded by this criminal money coming in from Lebanon. Anything goes bad—we bomb Iran to take out their reactors, whatever—then they've got these 'operatives' living in the US. American citizens who can take action on their behalf. Are they sleeper cells?"

"It's a matter of semantics," Fahad said. "Whatever you call it, it is what it is."

"That's my point. Has it happened? Not yet. Do we have evidence of an organized sleeper network? Not to my knowledge. But is there one? I'll let you answer that."

Actually, I think al Humat's already done that for us.

"Second question." Prati advanced to the next slide, which showed the international radiation warning symbol. "Are they smuggling nuclear material from Iran through South America into the US through the drug tunnels? Again, we've got no proof. Does that mean it's not happening? Of course not. We just haven't caught anyone doing it. Another thing you gotta consider is that, theoretically, the drug cartels should not want any part of these terror groups."

"Why's that?" DeSantos asked.

"Simple. They got a good thing going. They bring in their product, they monetize it, and there's not a whole lot we can do to stop it. We can narrow the hose and reduce what gets in, but the water still flows. And they make a shitload of money. Why risk it by working with a terrorist group, the most hated entity on earth?"

"Hang on a second," Vail said, raising a hand. "So you're saying they *don't* work together?"

Prati chuckled. "Listen carefully, Agent Vail. I said 'theoretically,' didn't I? Here's how it works. They're not *officially* working together. But it doesn't happen at the leadership level where they formalize a partnership. A jihadist comes up to the guys running a particular tunnel and works a deal with them. They let him bring his stuff through and no one's the wiser. Money changes hands, and bang. The material's moved through the tunnel. Most of the drug activity takes place during the day so they can hide their semis in broad daylight among all the other legitimate trucks on the road. They don't run their operation at night because they'd stick out like a red giraffe."

"Instead of being idle at night," Uzi said, "the tunnel makes them money and the jihadis' product gets across the border. Everyone's happy."

Except us.

"So are they moving nuclear material through the tunnel?" Prati asked. "Why the hell not? These guys that run the tunnels, they don't open the shipping pallets and look inside, I can tell you that. But it doesn't have to come through South America. Everyone's so fixated on Mexico, the southern border. What the hell's wrong with Canada? We're virtually telling these characters to come in from the north—we've got a huge border that's even more porous than the southern border. And yes, before you ask, we have found some huge, very sophisticated drug tunnels coming across from Canada."

The briefing room door opened and a man in casual dress clothing entered. "Excuse me. I have something for you, Director Lynch."

Lynch waved his fingers, motioning him in.

"I'm actually done," Prati said with a glance at his watch. "Unless you have any more questions, I have to brief DHS in ten minutes."

"Thanks for your time," Nunn said. "Any follow-up can be handled through Agent Uziel."

Prati passed Uzi a business card, gathered up his briefcase, and then left the room.

Meanwhile, Lynch accepted, and signed for, a manila folder. As he read the document inside, his brow crested. "We found a fingerprint on a bomb fragment from the first blast. It came back as Qadir Yaseen."

"Yaseen?" Uzi nearly rose out of his seat. "You sure?"

"What is it, Agent?" Knox asked.

"Yaseen is a very skilled bomb maker. He's al Humat's rock star, so to speak. Innovative, creative. Dangerous. Mossad tried taking him out twice and missed both times. If he's involved in this . . ." Uzi's voice trailed off.

"If he's involved in this," DeSantos said, "it's a big operation."

"Right. He doesn't get involved unless it's 'worthy' of his time and effort."

Nunn slapped the table. "Enough of the doom and gloom. Our backs are against the wall. I get it. Everyone in this room gets it. But I want to hear how we're going to get *them*." He turned to Vail. "You're with the BAU. Give us something to go on."

"I have, sir. We understand the mind-set and we're beginning to understand their motivation behind these attacks. I can tell you that like Islamic State, al Humat is not limited to Gaza and strikes against Israel. Hamas, al Humat, Islamic State, al Qaeda, they all have the same kind of charter—basically, they want to create a caliphate that will rule the world. An Islamic world, under their rule. While Hamas's charter talks about world domination, it hasn't moved beyond Israel yet. But al Humat, which cut its teeth in Gaza under Hamas's tutelage, has.

"My sense is that they're spreading their wings, trying to recapture legitimacy in their circles. Having been overshadowed by the younger and more ambitious ISIL, they are, in a sense, taking them on, challenging them for the spotlight. That's why they've done something that ISIL has threatened, but hasn't yet tried: carried out successful attacks on US soil."

"You're saying we're in the middle of a parent/child spat, where one is jealous and acting out, crying out for attention?" Nunn asked.

Vail nodded. "The analogy is odd, perhaps, but the psychology is sound."

"Why do you think this is an issue of attention?" Knox asked.

"The higher profile the attack, the greater the recognition. When ISIL beheaded James Foley, the media played along and gave them what they craved: attention, a world stage. Everyone suddenly knew who Islamic State was, even if they didn't follow the news. That's what al Humat is now after: a way to quickly grow its profile."

"Al Humat is not nearly as well funded as ISIL," Uzi said, "because it's not trying to establish a nation-state and it hasn't assembled a traditional army that can capture strategic resources, like banks and oil fields. But al Humat has no shortage of allies among fellow Islamic groups and Middle Eastern countries. And it's got more than enough money to accomplish its goals."

"Richard," Nunn said. "The Pentagon's plan?"

McNamara tugged on his tie knot. "We're ready to mobilize when and if you give the word, Mr. President. This threat has the potential to move beyond anything we've seen. We need to prepare for everything. And the only way you do that is to take a cold, steely, hard look at it. Make an objective assessment. And get ready."

"I agree," Uzi said.

Shepard nodded.

Nunn pursed his lips. He considered the defense secretary's remarks a moment, then said, "I don't want to overreact here. We need to be measured in our response. Creating a panic in cities across the country will serve no one."

Vail felt her lips moving before she could take a split second to filter her thoughts. "No offense, Mr. President. But I think blowing up a Metro station already did that. In essence, by striking our nation's capital and killing innocent civilians, al Humat has declared war on the United States."

There was silence. No one made eye contact with Vail—or acknowledged her statement—until Knox cleared his throat and said, "Agent Vail." He gave her a look that she could best interpret as, keep your mouth shut.

Nunn, apparently recognizing that her comment demanded a response, leaned forward, his brow hard. "I do not believe, Agent Vail, that anyone has taken responsibility for the attack. Am I wrong?"

Vail shot a quick glance at Knox. *Does he expect me to ignore a direct question?* "No sir. At least, not directly. But Kadir Abu Sahmoud said—"

"Exactly. For now, we monitor and plan." Nunn turned to Knox. "Douglas, the FBI will remain vigilant in its investigation and counterterrorism activities. Richard, the Pentagon will prepare a response plan if and when a response becomes necessary. Key targets, buildings, infrastructure. You know the drill."

"Yes sir," McNamara said. "But if it is al Humat, we're talking about hitting Gaza. And we know the quagmire Israel waded into when it—"

"*If* it is al Humat," Nunn said, before pausing, "*if* that's where they're located, *if* that's where this Sahmoud character is located, that's what we'll go after. You have a problem with that?"

"No sir."

"Good. We'll cross that bridge when the time comes. *If* it comes. For now, we operate defensively." Nunn glanced around, a cursory acknowledgment of the attendees, then said, "Thank you all for your diligence. Keep my office apprised of any developments."

Vail rose from her chair, confused over the president's passive posture regarding al Humat. After the next attack—wherever and whenever that was—he would have to alter his approach. Unfortunately, she had a feeling that time would come sooner rather than later.

15

As they filed out of the conference room, Knox pulled Uzi, Vail, and DeSantos aside.

"I know we've opened this thing up," he said as he led them down an empty corridor. There were numerous doors with biometric locks, but all were closed and no one was within earshot. "You'll be working this case on two levels: first, as terrorism task force members. Second, as off-book OPSIG operators."

"How can we do that?" Vail asked.

Knox nodded, as if acknowledging the issue. "I didn't say it was going to be easy. I just said this is how you're going to operate. You'll know when you have to change hats."

Change hats?

"Hector will guide you. He's adept at navigating the world of covert ops."

They turned to DeSantos, whose face was impassive.

"Hot Rod will be providing support and join you when necessary. But I want this to be a four-man team and Fahad will be your fourth team member."

Uzi's Adam's apple rose and fell conspicuously.

Hold it together, Uzi.

Knox stuck his chin out and studied Uzi's face. "Can you do that?"

Uzi swallowed again. A fine line of perspiration had broken out across his forehead. Knox had spent his career reading—and manipulating—people. Surely he was aware of how this would affect Uzi. Was he purposely spiting Uzi for some reason? Or did he truly feel Fahad would be an important contributor to the team?

In her dealings with Knox, he never struck her as the type of individual who would jeopardize an operator's mission with petty maneuvers. He was calculating and shadowy and powerful and his motives were not always clear, but he was very bright and he understood human nature. The trust he built was based on *mutual* trust.

Or fear and leverage.

Uzi took a breath and shrugged. "Yes sir. No worries."

Knox studied his face with a squinty eye. "Well, there *will* be worries. But if you tell me you can manage this, I'll take you at your word."

With that, he turned and left them standing in the corridor.

VAIL WALKED WITH UZI AND DeSANTOS out to Uzi's car. As soon as the doors closed, Uzi's gaze settled on Mahmoud El-Fahad as he exited the NCTC.

"Boychick, you really have to learn to play well with others."

"Do I have to remind you that my wife and daughter were murdered by a Palestinian?"

"A Palestinian *terrorist*, Uzi," Vail said. "You have to make the distinction."

"I know." He grasped the back of his neck. "I know. But . . ."

"When you lived in Israel, did you have any Palestinian friends?"

The question seemed to jolt Uzi. He sat up straight. "Of course. Good, hardworking people who just wanted to live their lives. Pawns in a political chess match."

Vail lifted her brow. "Then what's the problem?"

Uzi looked out the window and watched as Fahad shook hands with Douglas Knox. "Palestinians are indoctrinated at a young age. Some of it's subtle, some of it's blatant—like their school textbooks. Filled with anti-Semitic and anti-Israel rhetoric, denying Israel's right to exist, presenting the Israeli/Palestinian conflict as a religious battle for Islam—a jihad for Allah, a struggle between Muslims and their enemies. Not to mention the oldie but goodie: the Holocaust never happened."

"Not a recipe for a peaceful coexistence," DeSantos said. "I'll give you that."

"That's not the point. I mean, it is—but this stuff, it's very powerful when you're fed this bullshit at a young age. Look at ISIL—they've done it on a mass scale and turned normal youths into violent, brainwashed jihadists that chop off innocent people's heads. It's a very powerful tactic, imprinted in the brain, incorporated into your belief system, your moral base."

"Of course," Vail said. She could tell Uzi was struggling with this. There was something he wanted to say, but he could not bring himself to come out with it. "But that's got nothing to do with this mission."

Uzi craned his neck back and stared at the car's ceiling. "Fahad is the right age to have been brainwashed by that crap. He grew up under Arafat's rule. The textbooks are a little better now—which is to say they were that much worse back then. How—how can I trust Fahad? On a mission like this, it's *all* about trust. You have to be able to rely on your colleagues implicitly. You can't be charging ahead on a frontal assault while also watching your back. That's what your team members do." He turned to DeSantos. "Santa, tell her."

"She knows. We went through this in London."

Vail leaned away and appraised Uzi. "You should've told Knox you've got a problem."

"Knox? He knows all this. And yet he put Fahad on our team."

"So then he's convinced Fahad won't be a problem."

"Or his skill set and knowledge are so important that he's willing to take the risk. Positives outweigh the negatives."

"Let Hector bring it up. Knox trusts him."

"Happy to do it," DeSantos said.

Uzi chuckled. "Not sure Knox trusts anyone. You know?"

Vail placed a hand on Uzi's shoulder. "No. Just the opposite. I think he trusts us implicitly. He may not give you that impression, but deep down, I really think he does."

"He's got our backs," DeSantos said. "But you haven't known him as long as I have. Even if you're not sold on the trust question, you know he cares deeply about his baby. He created OPSIG."

"Hector's his best operative," Vail said. "He wouldn't be reckless in risking his life if he had doubts about Fahad."

"You think he considers me his best operative?"

Vail elbowed him in the side.

Uzi took a deep, uneven breath. "Okay. But just remember that even the great Douglas Knox isn't perfect. He makes mistakes like the rest of us."

"And if he's wrong about Fahad . . ." DeSantos shrugged. "Well, we'll just have to fix it."

16

Uzi walked into his office and found Hoshi at her desk, an Excel document crammed with tips, thoughts, and suppositions plastered across her spacious LCD screen.

"How's it going?"

Hoshi leaned back and appraised her spreadsheet. "We've got a lot of busy work going on. Not sure any of it will lead anywhere."

"So a typical day at the office."

"A typical day following a terrorist suicide attack. Yeah."

He glanced around, determined no one was nearby, and said, "I want you to check something out for me. Discreetly. Shep can't know."

Hoshi frowned. "Another one of these, 'you can get into major trouble but I'm asking you to do it anyway' type things?"

"No. But Shep won't be happy. Knox won't be happy, either."

"So a typical day at the office."

Uzi had to laugh. "Are you implying that I've asked you to do things like this before?"

"You know I can't say no to you. What do you need?"

"There's an operative with the Agency. Mahmoud El-Fahad. I need whatever you've got on the guy. Classified stuff, shit that's buried behind walls."

Hoshi lowered her voice. "You're asking me to hack classified databases and you don't think that'd bring major trouble if anyone found out?"

"It sounded a bit better when I said it, didn't it?"

"Just a bit. And what do you suspect? You think the guy's a mole?"

"No." Uzi rubbed his forehead. "I don't know. I guess I just want to make sure he's legit, that he can be trusted. He's Palestinian and Batula Hakim was—"

"It's time you let go of that."

Uzi stared at her. Was she right? What was the right amount of time to let something like the brutal murder of your wife and daughter fester? *Was there* a right amount of time? Of course not. But there was a *normal* amount of time. There had to be. If his favorite shrink was still around, he could ask him. But he was not—and Uzi was never one for psychoanalysis, anyway. What he had with Leonard Rudnick was special, a onetime thing. So for now, he would go with his intuition. And at the moment, he felt like he needed to dot all his i's, to make sure everything was as it was supposed to be. Then he could relax.

"Okay."

"What?" He realized he'd been staring at the far wall.

"I said okay, I'll dig around. You need anything else? You were kind of spacing out."

"That's it. I'll be in my office if you find anything."

UZI SETTLED INTO HIS CHAIR and pulled out his Lumia. He put it in encrypted mode and dialed. Gideon Aksel answered.

"I need you to look into something for me."

Aksel laughed. "I don't work for you. In fact, *you* used to work for *me*, remember?"

Uzi buried his face in his right hand. "How could I forget?"

"What is this favor? Which, by the way, will be the second one you've asked for in, what, twenty-four hours?"

Uzi ignored the dig, massaged his eyes. "I need whatever you've got on Mahmoud El-Fahad."

"Name is familiar. Should I know him?"

"As director general of Mossad, I really hope not, Gideon."

Aksel was quiet a long second, then said, "I'll see if there's anything to find."

17

Eastern Market was dominated by a block-long nineteenth-century Neo-Renaissance brick building that sat a quarter mile from the seat of US government. A hundred years ago, it was considered the unofficial town center of Capitol Hill.

Ten feet from the edifice and running its entire length sat a permanent green corrugated metal roofed pavilion where vendors sold their wares, sheltered from the sun and rain. People milled about: men, women, and children, couples young and old purchasing fresh fish and meat, baked goods and various kinds of cheese.

But in the mall's administrative office in a corner of the far-flung facility, things were not as lively: an array of black-and-white security cameras displaying various angles of the retailers' stalls and cafés stared back at Omar Jafar. Jafar reclined in his creaky chair and watched the activity on his monitors.

The job was generally tedious, the most excitement coming from an occasional shoplifter or the equally random elderly individual suffering a heart attack. The majority of the time, he passed his shift watching hordes of people pass the prying eyes of his lenses buying merchandise, eating food, and drinking coffee, beer, or wine.

Jafar leaned forward, the back of his chair springing up and snapping against his torso. He tilted his head and spied a male dressed in a black hoodie carrying a backpack and moving through the crowd, which, in and of itself was not unusual. But the man's demeanor, the wandering nature of his gait, told Jafar that something might not be right. After the mysterious explosion at the Metro station, he had been warned by his boss to keep an extra vigilant eye on customers exhibiting suspicious behavior.

Jafar studied the screen: the "person of interest" was about five foot nine with a dark complexion. Thin, no distinguishable marks that he could see. Watching the man move from one monitor to another as he made his way through the market, Jafar thought back to his security guard training. What information did the police want? Physical description and his reason for suspecting the individual of foul play.

Jafar grabbed his two-way radio and headed out of his office, walking briskly toward the location of his target. He did not want to call the police yet, not until he had a better indication that something was really wrong.

As he approached the two large doors that formed the main entrance to the building, he saw his suspect thirty feet ahead. The man stopped to talk to one of the vendors, then pulled a large brown paper bag from his backpack just as Jafar heard a loud crashing noise off to his right.

Smashing glass—crumpling metal—revving truck engine—

Patrons yelling, diving to the side as an armored vehicle blasted through the doors he had just passed, coming to rest inside the market's entrance.

"What the f—"

Jafar reached for his radio and fumbled for the dial when automatic gunfire burst out. People screamed as bodies fell—

A man's guttural proclamation of "Allahu akbar!" snagged his attention. Jafar swung his head left and saw a masked male wearing military-style gear running toward him, spraying the area with high-powered rounds from some kind of machine gun.

Jafar pushed between a woman and a child and dove to the floor. He clapped both hands over his head and hid—until a massive explosion turned everything black.

18

Vail and Robby walked into Foggy Bottom's Burger Tap & Shake at Pennsylvania Avenue and 23rd Street.

They stood in the back, away from the line, looking over the menu that featured a description of the restaurant's meat: "Throughout the day, we grind on premises a custom blend of three-day aged, naturally raised local harvest beef chuck and brisket."

"My taste buds are moaning," she said, then noticed Robby was looking at her. "No comment please. I'm just plain hungry, okay?" She glanced at her watch. "Where the hell is Jonathan?"

"Late."

She took Robby's hand and squeezed it. "Thanks again for getting us Prati. Still a lot we don't know. But the stuff we do know . . . it's just kind of depressing."

The door opened and Jonathan walked in with rumpled clothing and mussed hair.

"This is how you show up for lunch with me and Robby?"

"I was still sleeping when you called," Jonathan said, bumping a fist with Robby. "Late night."

"Oh yeah?" Robby asked.

"It's Saturday, I knew I could sleep in."

Vail frowned. "One advantage of you going to school so close to home is that we can get together once in a while."

"Some might call that a disadvantage," Jonathan said, his slight chuckle suggesting he was only half joking.

Robby gave him a disapproving shake of the head.

"Just kidding. It's definitely nice to be able to see you guys."

"As long as it doesn't interfere with your college experience."

Jonathan tilted his head. "Well, yeah."

They ordered at the counter and found a booth, then waited for their food to come.

"So are you closer to catching the terrorists?" Jonathan asked.

Vail shushed him as she glanced around. "You know I can't talk about it." Jonathan's face scrunched a bit, tense from concern. "We're making headway. We'll get 'em. Just stay away from public gatherings."

"Police are all over the place. Barricades up on half the streets around campus. Freakin' pain in the ass."

"One of the exciting things about GW is that it puts you at the intersection of politics, law, and power. You can't walk a block or two without hitting a building of significance to the country—or the world. The International Monetary Fund, the White House, Supreme Court, Con—"

"I get it, Mom."

"That makes us a target," Robby said. "More bang for the buck than hitting Kansas or Wyoming, you know?"

As he said that, Vail felt a gust of wind rattle the large glass storefront window to her left. "Did you feel that?"

Robby nodded slowly as he swiveled in his seat and looked out at the people on the sidewalk and across the street in Washington Square Park. Most had stopped and were craning their necks in all directions. A few started to run and—

Vail's Samsung began buzzing. It was a text from Uzi:

> new attack. eastern market. meet me there.
> on my way, im close

Shit, that wasn't a gust of wind, it was blowback from an explosion.

"Gotta go." She rose from the booth.

"Everything okay?" Jonathan asked.

Vail looked at her son. Even if she had thoughts of lying to him, she knew he would know. "Another bomb," she whispered.

Robby started to rise but Vail waved him back down.

"I'll see you later."

VAIL ARRIVED AT THE INTERSECTION of 7th Avenue SE and North Carolina Avenue and pulled her car against the curb in front of Port City Java. Several Metro Police cruisers were lined up along 7th, blocking access to the wide cobblestone road that fronted the market.

But what caught Vail's eye was the carnage before her. The covered pavilion that ran the length of the brick building had been toppled, the steel columns supporting it knocked out from beneath the roof and folded in half as if struck with a baseball bat.

Bodies lay sprawled on the pavement, paramedics and first responders triaging the injured and yelling orders to others in the vicinity. Vail jogged along 7th, headed toward a concentration of police cars, fire engines—and a SWAT van.

She pulled on crime scene booties and moved closer. The double wood doors at the entrance to the market—doors she had passed through many times over the years—were missing, the opening enlarged by what appeared to be an armored truck, the rear of which was partially protruding from the building's interior.

DeSantos, wearing a wool overcoat, was inside talking to a CSU technician. He caught Vail's gaze and waved her in.

She made her way over the chunks of cement and fragmented brick, getting some assistance from another officer who helped her across the debris-laden threshold.

Inside, devastation. The normally bustling marketplace, which featured vendors and restaurants on both sides of a central aisle, was in pieces. Bloody bodies, and parts of others, were strewn across the wreckage—as far as she could see.

"What the hell happened here?" she asked under her breath.

DeSantos apparently heard her because he said, "Just setting off a bomb must be getting boring for them." He handed a piece of the rubble to a nearby technician. "Best we could tell—I only got here about ten minutes ago—they drove up 7th in that armored truck and crashed through the pavilion, mowing down as many people as they could. They swung right into the building, plowed through the entrance. Then they got out."

"How many?"

"Two, best we can tell."

"What happened after they got out of the truck?"

"They started moving through the crowd, firing AK-47s. Two cops saw the truck hit the pavilion, so they were on scene immediately. They came in through the east entrance, drew down, and that's when the jerkoffs detonated their vests."

Vail climbed atop the front bumper of the truck and looked out over the interior. Headed in her direction was Uzi, stopping to render assistance to medics who were administering to some of the fallen victims. The scene looked like a war zone.

"So, what do you make of this?"

Vail turned. "What?"

"Instead of loading explosives into a backpack or suitcase, they used a truck, assault rifles, and suicide vests. I'm not a detective, but I do understand the concept of MO. And they just changed their MO completely."

"Objective was to kill as many as they could. Invoke fear. What better way to do that than by changing the method of attack? You don't know what's coming next. You can't draw a pattern. More terror that way."

"Why hit the market?" asked Uzi, who was approaching.

"We've increased police presence and restricted access to important buildings, made it more difficult for them to go after hard targets. So they chose a soft one."

"Smart."

"Scary smart. They're well organized, prepared, flexible, and as we know, well funded."

Uzi's phone rang. He glanced at the display and said, "I gotta take this."

GIDEON AKSEL'S VOICE WAS TIGHT, concern permeating his tone. "I've got something for you, Uzi, but you're not going to like it."

"I'll be the judge. Tell me what you've got."

"Just so you know, I've verified this. There is no question of its accuracy. None."

"Got it. What'd you find?"

"You wanted info on Mahmoud El-Fahad."

"Anything and everything."

"January '03. The suicide bombing in Haifa."

"The commuter bus?"

"The bomber, he was Fahad's nephew."

Uzi glanced over at Vail and DeSantos, still chatting by the armored truck. "His nephew was a suicide bomber?" Uzi closed his eyes. "Fahad's nephew was a radicalized terrorist?"

"It sounded like this man meant something to you, so I knew you weren't going to like it. But facts are facts."

Uzi found a clearing and sat down on a damaged metal stool that had belonged to a now-destroyed deli. The prone body of a dead security guard was laid out before him. He averted his gaze. "Was Fahad involved?"

"Answer me. This man is important to you, no?"

"In some ways, yeah." He wanted to give Aksel more, but he was already dangerously close to stepping over the line.

"I don't know if he was part of the plot, Uzi. I dug around, talked with the men involved in the investigation. Mossad's got nothing. Shin Bet had nothing on Fahad. Now that could be a good thing—"

"Or it could mean nothing."

"Or it could mean nothing. I can tell you he was there. He saw his nephew blow himself up."

Uzi could not help but cringe. "Anything else in Mossad's file? Did we have any contacts with Fahad?"

"Only one. Nothing of any significance. He was questioned. The interrogators noted that he seemed distraught but he denied any knowledge that it was going down. There was no proof either way, so he was not held. We had no further contact with him. He left the West Bank five months later for the US."

Uzi remembered being told that Fahad had lived in the West Bank and knew Gaza well. "Has he been back?"

"Multiple times. Nothing unusual about his visits."

And he's a CIA operative whose territory included those areas. Uzi rubbed the back of his neck. He turned and saw Vail walking toward him.

"Thanks, Gideon. I'll look into this."

"Why are you asking about him? Any reason for us to be concerned?"

Uzi thought about that a second. "I honestly don't know. He's—and you didn't hear this from me—he's working for us. So he should be fine. But . . ."

"But if his nephew was a suicide bomber, someone he was close to, you just don't know."

"Thanks, Gideon. Gotta go." He disconnected the call as Vail stepped in front of him.

"Everything okay?"

Uzi rose from the stool and took a long look at Vail. He did not know if he should say anything about what he had just learned so he went with how he genuinely felt: "We're under attack and our enemy has been able to do anything they want, whenever they want. No, everything's not okay." In the distance, Uzi caught sight of Fahad approaching.

"There's something else. That call."

"Yeah, that call." He watched as Fahad closed to within twenty feet then stopped and looked at one of the victims sprawled facedown across a vegetable counter: a man wearing a backpack, a brown bag still clutched in his right hand. "Let's go see what our new task force member thinks of what happened here."

VAIL AND UZI CAME UP BEHIND FAHAD, who was examining a deceased sweat-shirted male slumped over a vending stand.

"Mahmoud," Vail said.

He turned, a frown etched into his face. "Call me Mo." He gestured at the body, which showed evidence of multiple bullet entry wounds across its back. "These bastards aren't going to stop unless we stop them."

Kind of like a serial killer.

"This is not like any attack I've seen carried out by Hamas or al Humat," he said. "Completely different methodology."

"Hey. Boychick!"

They turned to see DeSantos walking toward them, negotiating the ruins littering the market's floor.

"We got something." Two Metro police officers brushed past, an injured man wedged between them, his arms draped around their shoulders. "A finger."

"A finger?" Vail asked.

"A severed finger, probably from one of the bombers." DeSantos handed her an evidence bag containing the bloodied digit.

"You're giving me the finger?"

"I think they've already done that," Uzi said.

"No kidding," DeSantos said as he took the bag back. "CSU found it several dozen feet from the remnants of the bomber's vest. When a suicide bomber blows himself up, the direction and location of the explosives sever the head and send it flying clear of the blast."

"Thanks for that image," Vail said.

"In this case," DeSantos continued, "because of the double blast, both their heads were obliterated. This finger may be our only lead in terms of giving us an ID."

"Well if it isn't Aaron Uziel."

They turned to see Tim Meadows, an FBI forensic scientist, approaching from the opposite direction. "Should've known you'd be working this case."

"The worst criminals bring out the best and the brightest the Bureau has to offer," Uzi said. "Except that doesn't explain why you're here."

"I see our agent with the name of a submachine gun is locked and loaded with humor." He turned to DeSantos and eyed him a moment. "No offense, but if you're on the case, that's not a good sign."

DeSantos shrugged. "Guess that depends on how you look at it. I think it's a good thing. Actual work is going to get done."

"And my favorite female shrink," Meadows said, giving Vail a hug. "Or maybe just my favorite female." As he leaned back he seemed to notice Fahad for the first time. "Hmm. I don't think we've met."

"Mahmoud El-Fahad. CIA."

"Guess we're pulling all the cans of alphabet soup off the shelves for this one, eh?" Meadows chuckled.

Alphabet soup was a common slang term to describe the government's acronym and abbreviation nomenclature for its agencies: CIA, FBI, NSA, DoD, among dozens of others.

"We've got a finger," Uzi said gesturing at the evidence bag in DeSantos's hand. "Can you make sure it's processed—"

"ASAP, yeah, I got that. Don't you know that I've come to realize that if you're on a case, it's automatically important?"

Uzi leaned back. "What's gotten into you?"

"I've learned that certain things are not worth fighting. Death. Taxes. Bureaucracy. Aaron Uziel."

"That's some great company, Uzi," Vail said.

Uzi frowned. "Yeah, whatever. When can we get an ID?"

Meadows rocked his head side to side. "How about ten minutes?"

"Don't play with me, Tim."

Meadows took the bag from DeSantos and held it up to the light. "I've got a mobile lab outside. Let me see what I can do."

MEADOWS WAS WRONG: he didn't have an answer for them in ten minutes. He had something for them in eight.

"The digit was intact, so I didn't have to play with it to raise the print. I scanned it, uploaded it, and the computer got a match."

"Can you email it to me?" Uzi asked.

Meadows pulled out his phone, tapped and scrolled and the image of whorls and ridges was on its way.

Uzi forwarded it to Gideon Aksel the second it hit his inbox, with a request for information.

Vail, who had taken a look around the remains of the market, its deceased shoppers and retailers, returned to the group.

"Anything?" Fahad asked.

"Death and destruction," Vail said. "But you knew that already. You?"

"We got a hit on the print."

"An ID? This fast? Tim, you're setting a dangerous precedent."

"I got a hit, not an ID. Sorry to get your hopes up."

"Then I take it back. No precedent. Just disappointment."

"Ouch," Meadows said. "But before you judge me, since our bomber's print was in AFIS, I did some more digging to see if our muskrat's got a record."

DeSantos turned away from an ATF agent he had been conferring with. "Hold on. This *muskrat* got a name?"

"I'm sure he does," Meadows said. "I just don't know what it is. Yet. But he was apparently storing up nuts for a long, cold winter."

Vail looked at Meadows. "Kill the friggin' muskrat. Just tell us what you found."

"Latents from a New York City crime scene matched our bomber's print."

"Homicide?" Vail asked.

"Bank robbery, eighteen months ago."

"From bank robber to suicide bomber?" DeSantos pulled his chin back. "You trying to be funny?"

Meadows held up one of his hands. "I'm only telling you what I know. I didn't say it made sense."

"So what's the connection between the bombing and the bank heist?" Vail asked. "What was stolen?"

Uzi pulled out his phone. "I'll see if Hoshi can set up a conference call with the detective on the case."

"My old stomping grounds," Vail said. "I think we should go there, meet with the guy, talk with the bank administrators, look at who's got accounts there."

"Set it up," Uzi said. "We've all got go bags. Let's meet at the field office in an hour.

19

They arrived in New York City at 6:00 PM, avoiding the typical weekday rush hour traffic.

En route, Knox informed them that Secretary Bolten had convinced the president to raise the threat level and go public with the terrorism connection—something Vail and Uzi felt was long overdue.

Vail also called her buddy Carmine Russo and asked him to track down the detective who handled the bank robbery case. Since it was a shared jurisdiction with the FBI, she also attempted to reach the special agent who spearheaded the investigation, but he had not returned her call.

The detective, Steven Johnson, agreed to meet them over a beer at Reade Street Pub & Kitchen, a favorite watering hole of Feds—and some cops.

As Uzi navigated the streets and drove along the West Side Highway, Vail tensed—a visceral reaction.

"What's up?" he asked.

"Nothing."

"Bullshit."

Vail looked away. "I lost a partner near here a long time ago." She coiled in the front seat, bringing her knees up and grabbing them with her hands.

"Care to talk about it?"

"Car accident. Ironically, we were chasing a van filled with explosives. Sedan came out of nowhere."

Uzi nodded, checking his mirrors before glancing back over at Vail. "All worked out, though, right?"

"My partner died."

"Right. Except for that."

Except for that.

"Then there was 9/11. I was in a high-rise not far from here. A few blocks."

"On 9/11? You never told me that. You were there?"

Vail drew her legs onto the seat, close to her chest. "Not something I want to talk about."

"No shit. Your body language says all I need to know."

Vail mentally appraised herself—and released her grip on her shins, let her feet fall to the floor.

"We're close," DeSantos said.

"And who is this guy we're meeting?" Fahad asked, rubbing his eyes and sitting up in his seat.

"Have a nice beauty nap?" DeSantos asked.

He yawned widely and groaned loudly. "Oh, man. Sorry. Haven't gotten a lot of sleep lately. You take it when you can get it."

"We're meeting with Detective Steven Johnson," Vail said, "out of the 6-6 precinct. He and Special Agent Patrick Tarkenton handled the bank robbery. Haven't been able to reach Tarkenton. We'll see what Johnson can give us."

Fahad ruffled his black hair and rubbed his cheeks with both hands, trying to wake himself up. "I need a coffee."

They found curb space half a block from the Reade Street Pub & Kitchen, then passed under the green awning and entered the restaurant. The place was comfortable and homey, with a model train running on an oval track suspended from the ceiling.

They saw a man meeting the description of Detective Johnson—chocolate brown head shaved bald—and still dressed in a dark suit from his workday. He had taken a table near the bar with his back to the brick wall, which featured a large green and yellow neon sign that read "Reade Street Pub." The place had an unfinished ceiling with exposed ventilation pipes—built decades before such a style was in vogue.

Johnson had taken it upon himself to get a pitcher of Reade Street dark ale for his visitors, which Vail noted almost before she reached the table. Fahad ordered a black coffee.

They all shook hands, Vail and Uzi leading the introductions—with DeSantos and Fahad foregoing mention of their employers. The idea was to give the impression that all of them were with the Bureau. Say CIA or Department of Defense, and some detectives clammed up. As it was, they were not keen on cooperating with Feds. But if an FBI task force had been set up for the robbery, the agreement governing it would have prevented Steve Johnson from even talking to them. One detective famously refused to give his own chief details of a case—and the chief was so pissed off that he tried to have the man transferred to a different precinct for refusing his request.

"You know," Vail said, "I gotta ask, because I see the resemblance. You wouldn't be one of Leslie Johnson's relatives—brother, maybe?"

"Older brother, yeah. You know Lee?"

"We partnered together. I'm ex-NYPD. Haven't talked to her in a year, year and a half. How's she doing?"

"Just passed the sergeant's exam."

"Good for her. Give her a hug for me. And my congrats."

"Thanks for meeting with us," Uzi said. "We're up against the clock."

"You know we're talking about a bank robbery here, right? Nothing too sexy. Or really that important. No one was killed. They came in at night."

"We're looking at the perp for something else." *And that's really all we can say.*

Johnson lifted his brow and harumphed. "You know there was a Fed who worked it too. Guy by the name of Tarkenton, or something like that."

"Patrick Tarkenton. Yeah, I left a message. Anything you can tell us about the robbery?"

"I brought you a copy of our file. You obviously got some juice up top with the brass."

Vail had to keep herself from laughing. *If it's juice, it'd be poisoned.* "I still have a friend or two." *Gotta remember to thank Russo. That's probably why this guy's here, helping out a bunch of Feds after a long shift.* She took the file, splayed it open, and shared it with DeSantos.

"How sophisticated was it?" Uzi asked.

Johnson swallowed a mouthful of beer. "They got a lot of stuff, so I'd say it was *successful.* In my book, that's what matters, not how sophisticated it was."

Fahad dumped a packet of sugar into his coffee. "I'd normally agree with you. But that's not the case here."

"They used bombs." Vail looked up from the file. "They blew the vault mechanism with C4."

"Yeah, that's right," Johnson said. "We looked at that pretty hard because not everyone can get C4. But your lab didn't find anything that could help us trace it. Oh, and they used something else I'd never heard of."

DeSantos pointed to a paragraph of the report. "Triacetone triperoxide. TATP."

Johnson snapped his fingers. "Give that man a cigar."

Vail wiped at her glass with a finger, making a line in the condensation. *That confirms it for me. There's a connection here. But it's not adding up.*

"Our EOD guys said something about TATP being easy to get, but really dangerous to work with. Funny, because I remember thinking, if they can get C4, why use that other stuff?"

"Did you ever figure it out?"

Johnson drained his glass, then set it down and poured another. "They thought they needed the C4 to blow the locking mechanism and the TATP to give it extra power behind the blast. C4's hard to get. Maybe they could only get a small amount."

"What'd they take?"

"Some jewelry, some bonds, some cash. Usual stuff. I mean, the kind of shit people usually put in safe deposit boxes. Nothing stood out, to be honest with you."

"And you never caught 'em?" Uzi asked as his phone vibrated. He stole a look at the display and then pushed his chair back to take the call.

"No. And we got nothing off the security cameras."

"How many were there?" Fahad asked.

"Three inside, one spotter outside. Wore ski masks. Never did any other jobs, least not that we could tell."

Johnson leaned back from the table. "Ah . . . gotta go use the head." He glanced at his watch, then stood up. "Give me a minute, will ya?"

DeSantos watched Johnson move off toward the front of the bar, then turned to Vail. "You look like you're onto something."

Uzi finished his call and swiveled back toward the table.

Vail cocked her head, considering DeSantos's comment. "Maybe. Just trying to reason it out. Think this through with me: they went after the vault, not the safe. There's a lot more cash in the safe. I don't know what the local thrift keeps on hand these days, but it's gotta be a sizable figure. Tens of thousands?"

"Depends on a lot of factors," Uzi said. "That sounds about right. So what?"

"So he's got no idea what's in the safe deposit boxes—it's a wild card. Could be some diamond rings, but maybe not."

"Unless they knew what was in there," Uzi said. "They knew someone who banked there and had a box."

Fahad twirled his glass. "First thing to follow up on tomorrow, when the bank's open."

"Would you like to put a print with a name?" Uzi said with a grin. "Our upstanding citizen is—or *was*—Haddad Sadeq."

Vail gestured at Fahad. "Mean anything to you?"

He thought a moment, then sighed in resignation. "No."

Uzi glanced at Fahad, then said, "Sadeq was an operative for al Humat."

"Where'd you get that?" Fahad asked.

Uzi hesitated, then said, "Not important."

Fahad pushed his chair back and faced Uzi full-on. "Bullshit. It is important."

"A reliable source."

"We're a team, right? Why won't you tell me?"

"Do you reveal all your confidential sources?"

"Of course not. But with this group, we've got to trust one another completely, or it won't work."

Uzi stared hard at Fahad. Vail sensed there was something he wanted to say, but couldn't. Why?

"Boychick, Mo's right."

Uzi clenched his jaw, then said, "Mossad. A guy I know. That's all I can say."

Fahad absorbed this information without any outward reaction.

Vail examined her glass, took a sip. "We're missing an important point. We've got a group of bank robbers that hit a local thrift, the target being its safe deposit boxes. They get jewelry, cash, other shit. But does that make sense?"

"No," Uzi said.

"No. It doesn't. Sadeq was a known operative of al Humat, and al Humat is a terror organization. They're not into robbing banks. It's not their MO. Islamic State, yeah. But not Hamas. Not al Humat. They get their funding other ways."

"Your point?" Fahad asked.

Vail spread her hands. "So there had to be something in that vault that they were really going after. They knew it was there—and I'm willing to bet they got what they came for."

Johnson returned to the table tugging on his belt, readjusting his trousers.

"I'll get the next round," DeSantos said, then went to the bar to get another pitcher.

"You have a list of the victims?" Vail asked, thumbing through the file. "The ones who lost stuff in the theft?"

"I got some. FBI took the lead on all follow-up. There should be something in there," he said, wiggling an index finger at the file. "But safe deposit boxes aren't insurable, and the bank doesn't cover those losses. Most people don't know that. They think it's the safest place they can keep shit, but it's not. I mean, if someone breaks in, there's nothing protecting them."

"So there might not be incentive for someone to report their losses," Vail said.

Johnson thought about that. "Yeah, I guess. But if we're asking them what was stolen, why wouldn't they tell the truth?" Almost as if he realized the answer before he finished asking the question, he said, "Oh."

Yeah, if they've got something illegal in the box, they're certainly not going to tell the police when it's stolen.

DeSantos returned to the table with the pitcher, then filled everyone's glass.

"This case you're working," Johnson said. "Sounds big. Like it's got nothing to do with bank robbery."

Vail raised her glass and clinked it against Johnson's. "Detective, I don't know what you're talking about."

20

The following morning, they met Agent Patrick Tarkenton at the FBI field office at Federal Plaza. Vail had considered Russo's offer to stay at his place in midtown, but the thought of spending any time with Sofia, his wife, made her graciously decline. Instead, she bunked with the rest of the group at a cheap motel in Flushing, near Citi Field and just outside Manhattan.

When they met in the lobby, they had a message from Fahad stating that he would not be joining them but would touch base later.

"That's weird," DeSantos said.

"Maybe he's following up on something. Or maybe he had something to deal with on a case."

Uzi frowned. "Or maybe it's something else."

"Give it a rest," DeSantos said. "You gotta let it go."

They rode the subway into the city and spent half an hour walking through the case with Agent Tarkenton. He retrieved the file and handed it to Vail, who began reading through it.

Tarkenton explained that he did not have much information to offer—nothing more than Johnson had given them—and said that because the reported losses totaled only about $11,500, with no repeat or prior heists matching the robbers' MO, investigation of the theft dropped on their list of priorities.

"Since there are three of you asking questions about a cold case robbery, I assume there's more to it than that. Have they hit another bank?"

"Something a hell of a lot more serious," Uzi said. "The bombing at Eastern Market in DC? We found one of the bombers' fingers there. Print matches the latent you pulled from the bank's vault. Our suspect isn't a bank employee and we doubt he was one of the safe deposit box holders."

Tarkenton absorbed this, then his eyes widened slightly. "You're saying our bank robber is your suicide bomber?"

"Right."

Tarkenton sat back from the conference room table and appraised his colleagues. "Hey, I worked up the case, gave it the attention it deserved at the time. I did my due diligence and I filed my paperwork with headquarters. My squad supervisor signed off."

"And yet," DeSantos said, "here we sit."

Vail closed the file Tarkenton had given her. "Name's Haddad Sadeq, an operative with al Humat."

"You're shitting me." He studied their faces a moment. "I had—I mean, how was I supposed to know?"

Vail pushed the folder across the table toward Tarkenton. "We'll need a full list of the victims, the people whose boxes were broken into."

"Isn't there one in here?" He grabbed the file and started rifling through it. "Must be on the server. I'll get you a printout before you leave."

TWENTY MINUTES LATER, they were sitting in the Pershing Square Central Café, across from Grand Central Station. The increased police presence, a result of the elevated terror alert, was evident with Hercules teams—specially trained Emergency Service Unit cops outfitted in helmets, Kevlar vests, and submachine guns—and critical response vehicles traversing the city's streets.

Vail had eaten in the restaurant a few times, but it had been many years. Nevertheless, the area was filled with memories of the time she spent patrolling New York City streets as a cop, then as a detective . . . and then as a green FBI agent.

A few blocks away sat Bryant Park, where the Hades serial killer had left a victim four years ago. The image of the body—of that case as a whole, which consumed nearly twenty years of her career as a law enforcement officer—still bothered her.

Although the café was wedged beneath the Park Avenue viaduct, it was bright and cheery inside because it had a wall of windows looking out onto Park. At 7:30 AM, the place was buzzing with diners and waiters rushing from table to table, bumping into customers, spilling a bit of milk off a tray, or almost toppling a nearby platter. This morning the restaurant lived up to its motto: "The busiest and best breakfast in New York."

Despite the commotion, Vail, DeSantos, and Uzi were absorbed in their conversation, cups of high octane java by their elbows and a plate of bagels with smoked salmon, capers, and cream cheese in the center of the table.

They each had a list of people whose safe deposit boxes were emptied. Notes were written across Vail's copy. She was scanning the document a fifth time when DeSantos interrupted her thoughts.

"You got that name from Aksel."

Uzi did not look up from the paper. "Yeah. I've been keeping him in the loop. He's given me some valuable intel."

DeSantos bit into his piled-high bagel and spoke while he chewed. "So you two have patched things up?"

Uzi lifted his brow. "I guess. I don't know. We haven't talked about it. Right now it's a relationship of necessity. We've got a situation and we're professionals trying to figure it out."

"Good. I know he means something to you. I know it hurt when you thought he betrayed you."

Uzi turned his attention back to the paper. "Depends on how you look at it. It's complicated."

"I know."

Vail set her pen down. "So I've done an analysis—" She stopped and glanced at them. "Am I interrupting?"

"Go on," DeSantos said.

"I've gone through the names and sorted them by ethnicity. By my estimation, and based on the info Tarkenton had in the database, twenty were Italian, fourteen were Irish, nine were Jewish, five were Greek, four were Hispanic."

"So it's a typical cross-section of New York."

Vail shrugged. "I guess so. But that's not what's important."

"Just means we've got a lot of people to interview."

"It's easier than that," Uzi said. "It's al Humat, right? They're not interested in Italians, or Irish, or Greeks, or Hispanics—"

"Jews," Vail said. She thumbed through the document again, going back to the first page. "Here. We've got one who's a rabbi from Aleppo."

"Syria?" DeSantos asked, scanning the page and finding the name on his list.

"Moved to Brooklyn twenty-five years ago. Another works at a camera store in midtown, and another is a registered nurse at Bellevue—" She stopped and paged backward. "But this has to be it. A former Syrian Jew? And an al Humat operative? I smell a connection. There's something there. This is the guy we've gotta go see first."

Uzi shrugged. "Seems right to—"

Vail's phone rang. She pulled it and found Carmine Russo's caller ID prominently displayed, along with his photo.

"Russo—"

"You still in New York?"

"Yeah. Just getting started."

"Meet me in Times Square."

"Times Square? Are you kidd—"

"Trust me, Karen. It'll be worth your while."

21

They arrived ten minutes later but had to stop two blocks short of the address Russo texted her because of a barricade of NYPD police vans and cruisers. A light rain had begun to fall and the sky had darkened, threatening a storm. It was not cold enough for snow, but the smell of it was in the air.

"You text Mo?" DeSantos asked as they exited their sedan.

"I did," Vail said. "Told him we were on our way, gave him the address. He didn't reply."

Uzi gave DeSantos a concerned look.

"I'm sure he's just following up on some things." DeSantos hesitated, then said, "But it *is* very weird, I'll give you that. Maybe his phone died."

Vail displayed her credentials and pulled up her collar as they headed toward the north area of Times Square. They made their way through the crowd of officers at Broadway and 47th Street, where the humongous billboards flickered, changed colors, blinked, and rolled. The brightly lit Coca-Cola advertisement made Vail feel thirsty.

Ahead of them was an imposing fifteen-foot-tall statue of Father Francis Duffy and the aptly named Duffy Square, which consisted of rising stadium-style seating that canted over the roof of the TKTS discount Broadway box office. On a normal day, a video camera projected live footage of the people seated on the stands onto a large overhead LED screen.

It was not difficult to see where the focus of the crime scene was, as the camera was still transmitting.

"Shut that thing off. C'mon, dumbshit. Can't be that hard to flip a friggin' switch."

It was Captain Carmine Russo, standing inside the crime scene barricade, a dozen feet forward of the imposing statue.

"Russo."

He turned and saw Vail, then pushed past the men in his way. He gave her a hug. She made introductions and Russo shook their hands. "So you're Uzi," he said. "Thanks again for your help with Hades."

"All in a day's work." Uzi gestured toward Duffy Plaza. "What do we got here?"

"We got us a friggin' mess, is what we got. I'm talkin' about the turf battle. FBI wants the scene. JTTF's here, along with agents from the Field Intelligence Group and something called the foreign counterintelligence squad. Never knew you guys had a foreign counterintelligence squad."

"I'll see what I can do about the turf bullshit, but I have a feeling that's gonna be something the commissioner and director are going to need to address."

"I don't see any signs of an explosion," Vail said.

"No explosion." Russo chuckled, then handed out booties. "Follow me. Got somethin' for ya, Uzi."

They walked single file past the statue toward the stairs that rose at a forty-five degree angle. Russo nodded at a couple of cops guarding the crime scene and tinned an FBI agent who seemed bothered by their presence.

Vail saw the problem immediately. About ten steps up, halfway to the top, a woman was reclining face up on the red Plexiglas and rubber surface, a wood-handled knife protruding from her chest.

DeSantos stopped a dozen feet shy of the body. "A woman's been murdered. Why's this relevant to our case?"

Russo glanced over his shoulder but kept moving. "Come see for yourself."

As they gathered around the middle-aged Hispanic female, Vail gestured at a piece of paper pinned to the woman's torso by the knife. "There's a note." She knelt down and kinked her neck to get a clear view. "Oh. Shit."

> For FBI agent "Shepard": You are a liar. We know who you are Aaron Uziel and we have a debt to settle with you. First, a word of advice. There's trouble in the first ward. Don't say we didn't warn you.

"First ward?" Uzi asked.

"Guy's a friggin' riddler," Russo said. "No idea what he's talking about. You?"

Uzi shook his head. "I'll get one of my agents on it, see if there's any place in the country that uses wards—Chicago?"

"I think there are parishes, but—"

"That's a good start," Uzi said as he tapped out a message to Hoshi.

"They killed a woman just to leave you a note?" Russo asked.

"They want to put people on edge," Vail said. "And they're trying to keep us guessing, off balance. That's the reason for the riddle. Inject uncertainty, leave us chasing our tails. And give us a sense that we don't know what's coming next."

DeSantos pivoted and looked at the distant streets, where throngs of people still moved about behind the police barricades. "How can something like this can happen in the middle of such a busy place?"

"Hey, it's Times Square," Russo said. "Tourist sees something weird, he figures it's some kinda performance art and moves along. I mean, there are women parading around wearing nothing but two circles of paint the size of a baseball—"

An FBI agent adjacent to Uzi's right shoulder slumped forward as the crackle of a sniper rifle rang out.

"Shooter!" DeSantos said, then grabbed Vail and started moving down the stairs as he craned his neck in all directions to get a read on where the shots were coming from. "See anything?"

"Came from the east," Uzi said as they headed toward the massive Duffy statue. "Agent was right in front of me, facing west. Entry wound was through his back."

"Hope you're right, Boychick." They moved around to the side of the replica Duffy, using its breadth as a shield.

Russo squeezed in beside them on the edge, keyed his mike, and reported the sniper's suspected location.

"All these Hercules teams and no snipers?"

"The teams make people feel safe," Russo said. "A show of force. But no, we don't deploy snipers unless we get a specific threat. Even if we could put a hundred sharpshooters on buildings in high profile areas of the city, no one wants to live in a police state. And the mayor—"

Another two shots, and a couple of cops, who were trying to get a better angle to locate the gunman, fell to the pavement.

"Body shots," Uzi said, peeking around the edge. "Whoever's up there knows what he's doing."

On Russo's radio command, a number of emergency service unit officers and uniformed cops from the NYPD's substation at the south end of Times Square headed into the surrounding buildings to lock them down and begin a search.

Vail moved to the far end of the statue and craned her neck, stealing a look around its edge, searching the buildings. Raindrops plunked into her eyes and she blinked them away.

"Gotta be a roof," she said. "Windows don't open."

Uzi moved slowly around the edge and then pulled back. "There's only one possible twenty, given the angle of the shots. Above the Sbarro, maybe nine or ten stories up. Otherwise, it's just billboards, lights, and electronic signs—or the angle's all wrong or the building's too high."

Vail and DeSantos inched around the front of the statue and looked at the area Uzi had described.

"I see him," DeSantos said, then ducked back. "You're right."

"Do we have a clear shot?"

"Tough angle, but it's possible."

Where's Russo? Vail texted him the sniper's location. But another rifle blast rang out and a cop who was attempting to cross to the other side of the street went down. *Goddamn. I'm not waiting for Russo's guys to get this asshole.* "Let's take a shot."

"That's not funny," DeSantos said.

Russo's text came back:

esu and hercules en route sit tight

"Hercules is coming to save the day."

"Again, not funny."

"No, the Hercules team. They've only got submachine guns so I'm guessing they're getting rifles and double timing it over here. ESU's coming too," she said, referring to the NYPD's SWAT equivalent. "We don't have time to wait. I say we put this bastard down."

"With handguns?" Uzi asked. "From this range? Against a sniper rifle? Soon as we clear the cover of the statue, he'll pick us off. Just like the others."

"I did something like this with Delta Force," DeSantos said. "He's sighting through his scope. If he's not looking at us when we expose ourselves—which would be a hell of a coincidence—he won't see us till it's too late."

"And if he does happen to be looking our way?"

DeSantos shrugged. "He won't be able to hit all of us. And he may not even hit *any* of us."

"Sounds like an awesome plan," Uzi said, the sarcasm thick as he drew out the word "awesome."

"This can work," Vail said.

Another shot, this time striking a young female pedestrian a block away who had not taken adequate cover. Her torso absorbed the hit, then she fell to the ground in a heap.

Uzi turned away from the downed woman and faced Vail. "Okay. I'm in."

"Who's the best shot?" Vail asked.

Uzi and DeSantos simultaneously said, "Me."

"Men." She shook her head. "Hector, still using that canon?"

"Yep," he said as he attached a sight to his .50-caliber Desert Eagle. "Now outfitted with a Leupold scope."

"Sorry, Uzi. His is bigger."

"Hey, a .50-cal with a scope? All yours, Santa."

"Do me a favor," Vail said, "and get him before he gets us."

DeSantos checked the Leupold, then held his Desert Eagle in both hands between his thighs, pointed at the ground.

"On my mark." Vail peered around the edge. A few seconds later the shooter revealed himself, sighting through his scope for another victim.

"Got him," she said. "Mark!"

DeSantos swung out into the open and squared himself as Vail and Uzi came out firing. Before the cacophony of gunshots ended, the sniper tipped forward over the edge of the building and tumbled face first to the pavement, passing the Broadway billboard ads for *Phantom* and *Wicked*.

It did not take long for him to touch down.

22

They stood over the suspect's prone body, a stream of blood leaking into the street and joining rainwater running off into a nearby sewer. The drizzle persisted and had dampened Vail's hair, making it frizzy. Her hands were starting to freeze.

But she hardly noticed. Rather, the image of the man free falling from the building had dominated her thoughts, bringing back memories of another high profile terror attack she was once involved in.

"Pretty clear what he was after," Uzi said.

The comment drew Vail from her reverie. "What?"

Russo joined them, three Hercules teams alongside him. They fanned out and brought their rifles up, searching the surrounding rooftops through their scopes.

Russo craned his neck to the spot where the sniper had been perched. "Nice shot."

"*Lucky* shot," DeSantos said.

"Shoulda waited."

"Couldn't," Vail said. "Seconds counted. He wasn't stopping till we stopped him."

"You think this was all about me?" Uzi asked.

DeSantos knelt down and carefully moved the shooter's jacket with the back of his hand, searching his pockets. Russo pulled out a glove and handed it to him.

"Maybe," Vail said, "given what's written on that note. But I think there's more to it than that. Like why they didn't set off a bomb. And why they used the murder of that woman to send you a message. And why they chose to do it here."

"Which is?"

"Times Square isn't just a public place, it's high profile."

"High profile doesn't quite cut it," Russo said. "We had a discussion about this in our counterterrorism briefing last month. Based solely on tourists, Times Square is the number *two* attraction in the world behind the Las Vegas Strip. It gets over 130 million visitors a year, a bit more than Disneyland and Disney World. It don't get more high profile than this."

"We got security footage?" DeSantos asked.

"Oh, yeah, plenty a cameras. I'm sure we'll have this goon on film on at least one a them. I'll see what we got." Russo pulled his phone and walked off to make his call.

"You okay?" Vail asked.

"Hmm?" Uzi was staring at the body, then pulled his gaze away. "Yeah, I'm fine. I'm—whenever someone takes a shot at you and kills someone else instead, you feel kind of guilty. Responsible."

"I don't have to tell you that's ridiculous."

"We can't know for sure the sniper was there just for you," DeSantos said. "They had no way of knowing you were even in New York."

Uzi seemed distracted. "Yeah."

"And the message on that note would've been delivered to you whether you were here or not."

"I agree," Vail said. "The sniper was there to pick people off. I don't think they necessarily cared who. Cops, FBI, women, children. You, if you were here. But whether you were here or not, the shooter was going to take his shots. It fits the purpose behind all these attacks: induce terror and fear in the general population, leave them wondering what's coming next. Each one of their attacks has been different in some way or other."

Uzi was silent a moment, then walked up the steps and knelt at the murdered woman's side. "Amsterdam."

Vail and DeSantos, who had followed, looked at each other.

"There a reason why you just said 'Amsterdam,' Boychick?"

"Amsterdam, 2004. Guy by the name of van Gogh was shot in the middle of a crowded square, then a knife was driven through a note into his chest." He gestured at DeSantos. "You've got gloves—check to see if she was shot before she was stabbed."

Russo walked over while DeSantos examined the body.

"Any witnesses?" Vail asked.

"I'm sure there were plenty, but we only managed to get a couple. Conflicting descriptions of the perp, which—"

"Not surprising in stressful times. People don't see what they think they see."

"Exactly. The cameras will give us a better look."

"Either of them say anything about the woman being shot before she was stabbed?"

"No."

"Yes." DeSantos looked up at Russo, shielding his eyes from the rain. "GSW to the chest, just above the stab wound."

Uzi nodded. "So it fits. But what does it mean?"

"It means the sniper may've had an accomplice. He took the shot, woman goes down, his buddy stabs the note to her chest."

"Who was the doer in the Amsterdam case?" Russo asked.

"An Amsterdam native of Moroccan descent, Mohammed Bouyeri. MO was very similar: high profile location, in the middle of a lot of people, dramatically staged with the knife and the note."

"So what's the connection?" Russo asked.

DeSantos rose from his crouch as the medical examiner's vehicle pulled up to the edge of the plaza, in front of the George M. Cohan statue at the southern end of the square.

"Wanna give me that canon for evidence?" Russo asked, gesturing toward the Desert Eagle.

"Nope," DeSantos said as he went about detaching the scope.

"I think we should just let it go," Vail said, looking hard at Russo.

"Tell you what," DeSantos said. "Take it up with Director Knox. He tells me you should get the gun, I'll hand deliver it."

"Knox."

DeSantos shrugged. "All I can say."

"We've gotta follow up on something," Vail said. "Keep us posted on what you find here?"

Russo's brow bunched as he studied her face. "Anything you'd like to tell me? You know, share resources?"

"I'm sure the NYPD will be plugged into everything that's going on," DeSantos said.

Russo gave him a dubious look. "Yeah, right."

23

Vail found the address for Menachem Halevi, the Aleppo rabbi and safe deposit box holder, on the way back to their SUV. He lived in the Borough Park neighborhood of Brooklyn, an Orthodox Jewish enclave bordering its Italian counterpart not far from the Verrazano Bridge.

"That's a little surprising," Uzi said on the ride over. "An Aleppo rabbi would live in Flatbush, on or around Ocean Parkway, not in Borough Park."

"Is that some kind of rule?" Vail asked.

Uzi chuckled. "Borough Park is mostly Hasidim of European background. It's unusual to find Syrian Jews here, but not impossible, I guess."

They parked on 50th Street and walked to the corner at 14th Avenue where they found the seven-story brick apartment building that, by the look of it, dated back at least several decades. Signs above schools and storefront shops bore Hebrew and English lettering.

As they walked through the small courtyard formed by the two wings of the complex, a man in a black overcoat and matching felt hat was coming through the glass doors.

"Hold that," Vail said, showing her FBI credentials.

The religious man averted his eyes, as the Orthodox are inclined to do around women, but stopped and kept the door from closing.

Vail, DeSantos, and Uzi entered the building and proceeded straight ahead to the elevator. Uzi pulled open the steel door and they stepped into the car.

"This is pretty friggin' old," Vail said. "Don't think I've ever seen an elevator like this." A tarnished penny was stuck inside the cross-hatching of the small glass window of the door that swung closed. She thought about taking the stairs instead, but DeSantos shouldered her aside.

"Deal with it. It's a short ride."

A moment later they arrived at the fifth floor. They found the apartment at the end of the hall and pushed the chime. There was a ruckus inside, the sounds of young children playing and roughhousing.

"Good thing today's Sunday," Uzi said. "Saturday, the elevator wouldn't have been working and no one would've answered the door." He apparently noticed DeSantos's inquisitive head tilt, because he said, "The Sabbath."

Vail knocked firmly—the weak "ding-dong" was no match for the yelling kids—and seconds later a man in his forties appeared.

"Yes?"

As Vail studied his face, formal dress, and demeanor, she had a feeling he looked older than he probably was.

"I'm Aaron Uziel, FBI. We're looking for Rabbi Halevi." He held up his credentials for the man to peruse—which he did, with a backward tilt of his head so he could view them through the reading portion of his glasses.

"What does the FBI want with him?"

"We're following up on the bank robbery eighteen months ago. We've got some questions."

The man lifted his brow. "You found him. Come in." Leaving the heavy gauge metal door open, he turned and proceeded into the apartment. Well worn olive carpeting led to a dining table wedged along the left wall. Directly across was a living room of modest size, about a dozen feet wide and fifteen long. Five children, ranging in age from what Vail estimated as three to nine, were running around, slashing at each other with fake swords and jumping off plastic play structures.

"Sorry to bother you on a Sunday," Vail said, "but these questions couldn't wait."

Car horns—loud and long—blared outside on the street.

Halevi sat on a chair near the knot of children. Vail, Uzi, and DeSantos sank into the couch against the long wall. The youngsters seemed unfazed by their visitors and kept playing as if they were not there.

One of the boys stopped suddenly and looked at Vail. In fact, he was staring at her. He pointed and said, "Is that a real gun?"

Vail looked down—and quickly brought her jacket around, covering the protruding handle. "It is. I'm a police officer."

"Police officers protect people," he said. "Can I see your gun?"

"Isaac," Halevi said, "don't bother the nice lady. Go back to playing."

A woman a few years younger than Halevi walked in, wearing what appeared to be a wig, but as with her husband, her style and demeanor gave the impression of someone senior to her true age. "We have guests, Menny?"

"This is my wife, Miriam." He handed her a box of crayons from the coffee table. "They have questions about the robbery. At the bank."

Her forehead rose in surprise. "Can I get you anything to eat or drink?"

The three of them declined and Miriam took a young girl with her into the kitchen. Isaac hopped into his father's lap, his eyes riveted on Vail.

"A year and a half goes by and we don't hear anything, and then suddenly three FBI agents show up with questions. On a Sunday, no less. Something doesn't quite seem right."

"Can't argue with that," DeSantos said, conceding the point. "We think the robbery could be important to another case."

"How can I help?" Halevi asked.

Another boy climbed onto his father's unoccupied leg and started bouncing.

"Shmu, sit still, please."

"We think the robbers were after something very specific," Uzi said. "We're taking an inventory of what was stolen."

"I told the detective and that FBI agent back when it happened. They wrote it all down."

"So some cash, jewelry, a few bonds. That's it?"

"Sounds right. There wasn't much. More sentimental than valuable."

"How much jewelry?"

Halevi shifted his legs and moved the children a bit. "Just a few family heirlooms. A gold ring with some diamonds, an opal broach, and two pendants from my parents. Worst of all, my grandparents' Shabbat candlesticks. It's all I had left from them."

"That it?" DeSantos asked.

"Like I said. It had more meaning to us than value to others. If it was someone looking for something specific that had a lot of value on the open market, I don't think we were the target."

"But you had a large box," Uzi said, "two feet by two and a half feet by six inches. Why would you need such a large box for only a few pieces of jewelry and a couple of candlesticks?"

Halevi swallowed noticeably. "It was the only one they had available at the time. Sometimes these boxes, there are waiting lists."

Uzi nodded, accepting the explanation. But Vail sensed that something was not right. She glanced at DeSantos, who seemed to have similar concerns.

"You sure?" DeSantos asked. "The case we're handling is very important. It's not just a bank robbery. As you noted—quite astutely—there are three federal agents sitting in your living room on a Sunday." He let that hang in the air as the three of them observed the rabbi.

The younger boys went flying into Halevi and he fought to keep himself upright and the other kids balanced on his lap.

"Hey," Isaac said. "Cut it out."

"Please. Raffi, calm down." Halevi swiveled his gaze to Uzi. "If we're done here—"

"No," Vail said. "We're not." She had one card to play, and she decided now was the time—even if it meant revealing sensitive information. "We have reason to believe that al Humat was behind the bank robbery."

"Karen." Uzi's complexion shaded red.

She ignored him and focused on Halevi, whose face now sprouted perspiration that glistened in the light streaming in from the nearby windows.

Car horns blared again outside.

"So, rabbi, let me ask you once more. Why would al Humat target you?"

He leaned back and yelled into the kitchen. "Miriam! Can you take the kids?"

She walked in and clapped her hands. "Come with me, we'll make Play-Doh. Who wants to help?"

They yelled and ran out, leaving Vail and Halevi staring at each other.

"I think we'll go for a walk," Uzi said, elbowing DeSantos—who reluctantly complied.

As they left the apartment, Vail sat back in the couch.

"You need to talk with my father," Halevi said.

"Your father? The owner of the box was Rabbi Halevi. You said you're Rabbi Halevi."

"My father is also Rabbi Halevi." He shrugged. "We're orthodox. This is not unusual. And you didn't say which Rabbi Halevi you wanted to talk with." He rose from the seat and walked into the hallway and turned right. Two minutes later, he returned with an aged man, white bearded and slow of gait, with a dark complexion.

Halevi helped his father to the chair and explained who Vail was and why she was there.

"Rabbi, the case my colleagues and I are working is extremely important. I'm sure you've heard about what's been going on in Washington and what happened today at Times Square. And now three federal agents show up at your door asking about a bank robbery from a year and a half ago. I can't say anymore, but I'm sure you can connect the dots."

"Tell her, Father."

"No," he said with a raspy voice. "This is not something we speak of."

"Father—"

"Rabbi," Vail said firmly. "Let me make something clear. Withholding information in a federal investigation is called obstruction of justice and it's a crime we take very seriously—especially when lives are on the line."

The elderly man craned his stiff neck up to his son, who nodded. "Lives are on the line?"

"They think al Humat was behind the bank robbery," Halevi said.

The man squinted. "I don't understand. Terrorists don't rob banks. Why would they do that? For money? If they wanted money, they'd rob the *bank*, not safe deposit boxes. No?"

"Al Humat gets all the money it needs from its . . . collaboration with other criminal organizations. Robbing a bank in Brooklyn is a high risk act. There had to be something inside that would give them more than money."

"There was." Halevi nudged his father.

The elderly man shook his head. "She would not understand."

"Maybe. But her partner would. Aharon Uziel," he said, using a Hebrew pronunciation of Uzi's first name. He turned to Vail.

She pulled her cell and texted Uzi to come up immediately. He returned less than two minutes later, sans DeSantos.

When he walked in, he seemed surprised to see the elder man. Vail explained who he was and that there was, indeed, something of importance in the pilfered box.

"You said, rabbi, that I would not understand. Because I'm a woman?"

He looked at her a long moment, as if he was determining if he could discuss this with her present. "If I'm going to share this secret with you, please call me Yakov. Good? Yes?"

Vail grinned. "Yes."

"And we need a drink."

Halevi rolled his eyes. "I'll go get something."

24

Do you know much about the Jews of Aleppo? Agent Uziel?"

Uzi pursed his lips. "I know some. There was once a thriving community in Aleppo. Until 1947 or 1948, and then the Syrians turned on them and destroyed the synagogues, their homes. They harassed and killed them."

"Good enough," Yakov said. "The Aleppo Jews had lived in Syria for three thousand years. They were part of the culture, a part of the land. But these men and women had something even more significant: custodianship of one of the most important books in the history of Judaism, perhaps Christianity—and all other religions that arose from Judaism. Do you know what book this is?"

Vail shrugged. "The Bible?"

Yakov's head bobbed up and down. "Emphasis on *the*. The authoritative book, the oldest, most accurate text of the Hebrew Bible."

"So you're talking about an actual book. A rare manuscript." Vail's mind flitted back to her time in London when she dealt with another rare manuscript, one that touched off a rough time in England that nearly got her killed.

"Calling it rare is doing it an injustice," Yakov said. "It's been known as the Crown, the Crown of Aleppo, and the Aleppo Codex. What it *is* is the most important book in history."

"What's so special about it?" Vail turned to Uzi. "Have you heard of it?"

Uzi laughed. "Yes. I even got to see a few pages once at the Israel Museum in Jerusalem, where they keep the Dead Sea Scrolls. I asked to see more, but it's locked away in a vault that requires three keys, a magnetic card, and a six-digit code. It's an ancient manuscript steeped in mystery."

"We'll get to that," Yakov said. "First, you wanted to know what's so special about it. It's one of a kind. But even that's not what makes it so special. There are plenty of ancient manuscripts that are one-offs. To understand its significance you must understand the time, what was going on."

Yakov cleared his raspy throat and leaned forward slightly. He lifted a wrinkled hand and gestured as if delivering a soliloquy. "Around the year 930 CE, Judaism was splintered. Its traditions and teachings had been handed down by oral tradition for millennia, covering everything from how they should relate to one another, how they should treat the land, and most importantly, how they should speak to God."

Halevi walked back in with a tray containing eight glasses, half of which were filled with ice cubes and water and the other four a milky-white liquid. In the center was a clear bottle featuring a green and gold label that contained Hebrew lettering.

"By the time of the First Temple," Yakov said, "they were beginning to write down these oral traditions and laws—which really were their bible, their *manual* for how to live and act. But the Temple was their spiritual, religious, and community center. When it was destroyed by the Babylonians, the Jews scattered. They eventually rebuilt the Temple, but then the Romans destroyed it and the Jews lost their unifying center of life.

"They needed something that could survive the leveling of a building, something that could be taken with them to whatever region or land they found themselves in. Something that couldn't be wiped out by an invading army."

"A book," Uzi said. "Or a Torah."

Halevi handed out the glasses.

Vail took a sip and drew her chin back. *Whoa.* "What is this?"

Uzi laughed. "Arak. A Middle Eastern distilled drink made from grapes and anise seed."

"Interesting," Vail said as she held up her glass. "Continue, rabbi."

Yakov sat back and thought a moment. "In the seventh century, Masoretic linguistic scholars in Israel who stressed the rabbinic teachings began standardizing the variations in the Hebrew language that had developed after the Temple was destroyed. Early in the tenth century, Rabbi Aaron Ben Asher was tasked with taking all this work and writing a reference text that set out Hebrew's vowels and grammatical rules as well as how the prayers were chanted—its cantillation."

"Cantillation?" Vail asked.

"Melodies," Halevi said. "Forgive my father. He's been a teacher all his life. What he's saying is that the scholars were trying to preserve Judaism's tradition, culture, and religion for future generations by standardizing the language and cultural nuances that had developed. They created a system of vowels and melodies, chapter and verse to organize the teachings and make it so anyone could learn the language. Three hundred years later, Ben Asher and the scribes brought it all together in an authoritative reference text—the codex. It was to be something that could culturally and religiously connect the thousands of communities that had fled to different countries."

Yakov set his drink down, stroked his long white beard, then reengaged eye contact with Vail. "Discrepancies in the Torah, ambiguities, differences in interpretation, had to be avoided to keep the religion together, to keep it from splintering. Ben Asher's goal was to create the perfect, *official* text."

Uzi held his glass up to the light that streamed in through the windows. "Not to rush you, rabbi, because I'm enjoying this history lesson. But this case, we're up against the—"

"I'm getting to the point," Yakov said, waving a wrinkled and arthritic hand. "Be patient, my son."

Uzi squirmed on the couch cushion. Vail placed a hand on his knee, telling him that she sensed there was, indeed, a point to Yakov's discourse.

"Animal skins were prepared and special permanent ink was mixed from crushed tree galls, iron sulfate, and black soot. It took Ben Asher and his scholars decades to research the codex and it took the scribes five hundred or so pages to write it. Almost two hundred years later, in July 1099, the Crusaders sacked Jerusalem, murdering thousands and destroying the Jewish quarter, their places of worship, Torahs, and books. One book in particular survived, however. Do I need to tell you which?" He tilted his head at Vail, then Uzi.

Uzi said, "The Aleppo Codex."

"Yes. Except that it wasn't called The Aleppo Codex. Not yet. Even then, the codex's importance was known. The Crusaders captured it, and other holy works, and demanded money. The Jewish community took out a loan from Egypt to pay the ransom—this is all documented in letters archaeologists have found—and that's where the codex remained, in Egypt, until about 150 years later.

"During that time it was used by one of the world's greatest philosophers and physicians, Moses ben Maimon—Maimonides. Maimonides used the codex as one of his main tools for creating the Mishneh Torah, books that provided a simplified description of Jewish law and rituals—a guide used even today."

"Around 1375," Halevi said, "Maimonides' great-great-great-grandson left Egypt and brought Maimonides' library with him—which included the codex. He settled in Aleppo and for safe keeping, placed the codex in a synagogue, locked away in a stone and iron chamber. It was removed only for certain scholars and dignitaries."

"And that's where it stayed until 1947," Uzi said.

Yakov nodded slowly. "Yes. The Aleppo community considered it their divine purpose to safeguard it. They believed the codex was not supposed to leave Aleppo. There's an inscription on the first page that reads, 'Blessed be he who preserves it and cursed be he who steals it, and cursed be he who sells it, and cursed be he who pawns it. It may not be sold and it may not be defiled forever.'

"They took this very seriously. Even when Syrians were turning against the Jews and killing them, burning their synagogues and books, the Aleppo elders refused to move the codex to Jerusalem, where the new country's president wanted to place it in the national museum. In the end, with Aleppo's Jews being smuggled to safety in Israel—the codex was moved, rather circuitously, to Jerusalem."

"But something happened," Halevi said. "Sometime around its arrival in 1958, part of it went missing."

"The first two hundred pages," Yakov said, the glass in his hand. He took a drink, his hand trembling. "The search for those pages went on for twenty-seven years. Problem was, no one knew when they disappeared. Some claimed they were destroyed by the fire that Syrians set in the Aleppo synagogue during the riots. And there were burn marks on the corners of the surviving pages, so it looked like those two hundred pages were lost forever. But scientists later realized that the damage to the pages wasn't carbon from a fire but some kind of mold. Eyewitnesses came forward and said the codex survived the fire and that the pages were lost while being snuck out of Syria."

"We started hearing stories," Halevi said, "of parts of the codex showing up in other countries. Pages, fragments of pages."

Uzi sat up. "A black market. Dealing in antiquities and rare manuscripts."

Those words caused a contraction in Vail's stomach.

Halevi pulled over another chair and sat. "Mossad got involved, the IDF, the court system, even psychics. And then in 1985, they heard that the missing pages were buried in Ein Ata, a village in southern Lebanon. Israel controlled that area at the time, but because it was so unstable, a search party went in under IDF escort. They came up empty. But an Aleppo Jew, Joshua Ashear, the one who tipped them off that the codex might be there, stayed behind with a friend of his. Two days later, they found the pages hidden in a dealer's attic. Not wanting to entrust the pages to anyone but people the man knew, Ashear passed them to an Aleppo rabbi, who transported them to the Aleppo Jewish community in São Paulo, and then on to Panama City. Two years later, they were brought here, to Brooklyn."

Oh shit. That's what was in the safe deposit box.

"I see where this is leading," Uzi said. "You had the pages. That's what the bank robbery was all about."

"How did al Humat know?" Vail said.

"There were rumors for years they were in Brooklyn," Yakov said. "A fragment was found in a rabbi's wallet when he died. His daughter didn't know what it was but when she met with a reporter she talked about seeing me bring a sheaf of pages to their home when she was a child. That innocent comment spread through the community like a contagious disease. It wasn't a secret any longer that I had most of the missing pages." He shrugged. "I thought it was a secret within the Aleppo community. I was wrong.

"We moved to Borough Park, away from the other Aleppo Jews. But it didn't matter. A few weeks later I was approached by a man who said he was an Israeli antiquities dealer. Sometimes you can't tell if they're Jews or Arabs. If they speak Hebrew, know Israel, it's hard to trip them up. I asked some questions, he seemed legitimate . . . but now thinking about it . . . who knows."

"What did he want?"

"He wanted to buy the missing pages for $100 million. I didn't deny having them—I told him I wasn't in a position to sell them. And I might've told him they have no business being bought and sold on a black market. If they went anywhere, they'd go to the Israel Museum, where the other half is kept."

Uzi snorted. "You basically told him you had them."

"I suddenly had visitors from the government, scholars, the Israel Antiquities Authority, journalists from the *New York Times*. Even a man who was writing a book about the codex."

"Forgive me for asking," Vail said, "but why didn't you turn them over to the Israeli government?"

"The pages weren't yours," Uzi said. "They belonged to the Jewish people. It's one of the most important artifacts of our religion—of *all* religions that grew out of the Torah—what some call the Old Testament."

Halevi sank back in his chair. He finished the Arak in his glass and stared into its empty bottom. "The Aleppo community was given the codex for safekeeping. We protected it for six hundred years. We were never supposed to let it out of our sight. And as soon as it left our hands, the most important part of it—the first two hundred pages—were stolen. We're talking about almost the entire Torah, the foundational narrative of the Jewish people. The Five Books of Moses. Genesis all the way to Deuteronomy."

"That doesn't answer my question," Uzi said.

Yakov looked at his son, who nodded vigorously, silently urging him to come clean. But the old man sat there a long moment, staring at the carpet.

The sounds of the children playing in the other room wormed their way into Vail's thoughts. Cars honked outside. And in the back of her mind, an internal clock was going off like an alarm, telling her she needed to figure out how this fit with the terror attacks.

Yakov said, in a voice barely above a whisper, "I was protecting us from ourselves. What's in those pages would make it impossible for Israel to ever have peace with the Palestinians."

25

Uzi sat forward on the couch. "Say what? How could a tenth-century book affect a peace process in the twenty-first century?"

Yakov licked his lips, then took another glass and poured more Arak. He offered the bottle to Uzi and Vail. Both declined.

"The codex consists of beautifully handwritten, perfect Hebrew. Almost 3 million characters, all impeccably drawn on parchment that measures 10 inches by 13 ½ inches, 28 lines to a column, three columns to a page. But . . ." He stopped, took a drink. "There are also tiny notes in the margins. Most of them describe how the Torah should be read. Some point out when a certain word appears for the first time or when a word's not to be spoken aloud, that sort of thing. But a few of the notes are different. They give the location of an ancient structure in Bethlehem. And that could make a peace agreement next to impossible."

"Just a guess here," Vail said, "But this is the part you mentioned earlier that I would not understand."

"I'm not sure *Agent Uziel* fully understands it. But he has an idea, no?"

Uzi nodded. "The geopolitics of the West Bank land are complex."

"There comes a time," Vail said, "when you have to seek peace and accept a two-state solution, even if you have a valid claim to all of the land."

Uzi chuckled. "And therein lies the problem. The two-state solution is a western construct, a foreign concept to Middle Eastern culture. It arose because the west wanted to do something to break the impasse, to solve the problem. The Middle East is such a screwed up region, it's easy to point to Israel, a democratic and moral society, and think, 'Now, *there's* something we can fix. We just need to carve out two countries and make peace.' But if you understand the mind-set of the region, you know that it's largely a problem without a solution."

"And what is this mind-set?" Vail asked.

Uzi held up a hand. "Let's first approach the issue from a western point of view. Two states make sense because Arabs lived on some of that land too, at times, so that'd be a fair compromise. Except that Hamas, Palestinian Islamic Jihad, al Humat, al Qaeda, and ISIL are on Israel's doorstep. To the north and east there's ISIL in Syria, Hezbollah in Lebanon, ISIL and an al Qaeda affiliate near the Golan Heights—and in Iraq. To the south, the Sinai's a terrorist breeding ground. Not to mention a nuclear Iran nine hundred miles away—kind of like the distance from Manhattan to Chicago. All these things need to be dealt with in a negotiated deal.

"Question is, with Iran supplying missiles to its proxies and allies in Hamas, al Humat, and Hezbollah, is a true peace possible? Even if most Palestinians are in favor of the Israel Defense Force pulling out of the West Bank, they know the Palestinian Authority can't control the extremists. Within a year, black-masked Hamas or ISIL fighters will overrun the West Bank, which is smack dab in the middle of Israel. You think Syria's a mess? Just wait. Like I said, it's complicated—but despite all the obstacles, it's worth pursuing. *If* you have a valid partner to negotiate with."

"The codex adds another complication," Yakov said. "Those notes in the margins, they were written eleven centuries ago. Ben Asher and Ben Buya and their scholars weren't concerned about the land claims of the present day—because the dispute didn't exist back then. So you basically have an unadulterated truth about rights to the land. Indisputable fact."

Halevi had gotten fidgety, shifting his weight and pulling on his black beard: visibly uncomfortable. "Father, we have been through this."

Yakov shook his head. "And I disagree with you."

"There is no such thing as truth," Halevi said. "There is no such thing as fact."

Whoa, hold on a second. Vail cocked her head. "As an officer of the law, I can tell you that there absolutely is truth. Facts are just that—truths, events that happened."

"I'm speaking as a rabbi. Philosophically, Agent Vail. Each person believes his view is objective, when in fact it's *subjective* because he approaches a topic or an issue with his own worldview. And his worldview influences his read of documents, of evidence, of history. He considers facts through the lens of his preconceived belief system, and he accepts as true all of those things that reinforce his worldview. He rejects all of those that don't."

"But truth is based on a set of facts that actually happened," Uzi said.

"Ah, but my truth may be different from your truth because I'm telling you what I saw. And what I saw is different from what you saw because I see through my eyes, which means those facts have already been interpreted through my lens—my past experiences, my observations, my beliefs. My filters. So there is no such thing as a singular truth—not even in mathematics. There are too many variables. It's truth according to *me*. Follow?"

"I understand the concept," Vail said. "But it's hard for me to accept given everything I've devoted my life to. Law and order, evidence, testimony."

"Then I've given you something to ponder. The rabbi in me is happy. But here's my point. Take it a step farther and apply these concepts to conflict resolution—in this case, a peace process. Everyone sees the world through his own narrative and doesn't accept the veracity of the other person's narrative. That's what we're dealing with regarding the Palestinians. The Palestinians reject the evidence that the First and Second Temples existed because it doesn't fit their worldview. They believe that Jews have no claim to the land of Israel. And because of that belief, the Palestinians refuse to accept Israel's *right to exist*. This goes, of course, to the heart of the Hamas and al Humat charters. It's all stated there in black and white for anyone to read. It's why Palestinian textbooks teach the children that one day they will kick the Jews out and inhabit all of the land."

"And that brings us back to what I was talking about before," Yakov said. "The notes in the margins of the codex. Some of them make specific mention of King David's palaces. They even note where the kingdom was located."

"And why is this a problem?" Vail asked. "Sounds like a good thing."

Yakov smiled for the first time—wanly. "Because a couple of years ago ruins were discovered that archaeologists believe are from one of David's palaces. There were earthenware storage vessels inside with Hebrew impressions that read, 'To the king.' It's a problem because I know these ruins are what's described in those notes in the codex."

"I'm still not getting it," Vail said.

Halevi said, "These ruins are on Palestinian land in Bethlehem."

"Ah. That explains it." Uzi nodded slowly. "Because Bethlehem is in the West Bank, there's no way the Orthodox ministers in the Israeli government would agree to a peace deal that gives away their ancestors' sacred land, land where one of King David's palaces sits."

"This is why the settlers live in Area C in the West Bank," Halevi said. "There *is* historical record of Jews having lived in the West Bank. Other archaeological finds—buildings, documents, tablets, burial grounds, coins, parchments, Torahs. It's very compelling evidence, if not *conclusive*. And when you put it together with a document written in the tenth century, at a time when there was no land dispute, no reason to lie or manipulate information, you have something that not only directly contradicts the Palestinian worldview but it makes it virtually impossible for Orthodox Jews to give up land that needs to be part of a two-state solution."

"That problem with facts and truths my son mentioned," Yakov said, "which he fixates on . . . When you start to line up multiple instances of disparate, unrelated instances that corroborate and support a set of proposed facts, these facts became less suspect and move toward being a real, verifiable fact. A truth."

"I understand that," Uzi said. "But land swaps would be part of any peace deal to meet security needs. The Israelis and Palestinians could simply swap that Biblically significant land for other land."

"You're not talking about 'just' a palace," Halevi said, "but a kingdom that covered a very large area. The Jews have lived there for thousands of years. That's the problem with the settler movement. I don't disagree with them. But what you said earlier, Agent Vail, that at some point you have to compromise, I agree. There needs to be peace, and if the radical factions can be neutralized and if we can have a legitimate government on the other side that can enforce an agreement, like Egypt and Jordan have, it's best for everyone."

Uzi turned to Vail. "And that brings us to the other obstacle."

"The mind-set of the region that you mentioned."

"Right. The notion of compromise doesn't compute in the Middle East. The unspoken MO is that giving something to your opponent doesn't promote reconciliation with them, it just tells them they can demand more. You give them something, they'll be at your throat for more. Compromise is seen as a weakness. So you don't dare give anything—not an inch. It's the way the Arab world thinks. And since half the Jews in Israel were kicked out of their homes in Muslim countries in the twentieth century, they're intimately familiar with the concept."

"That's ridiculous," Vail said. "It's crazy."

"To you and me, yeah. But in the context of the Middle East, it makes perfect sense. It's the way things are done, the way they *have* been done. But even if you can fight that backward mind-set, you've got another insurmountable obstacle: groups like Hamas, Palestinian Islamic Jihad, and al Humat don't want a peace deal, they want the land. All the land—all of Israel. No matter what *proof* is unearthed, they'll never accept that Jews have lived there for thousands of years."

"The irony," Halevi said, "is that in Islam there are ancient documents that refer to the Temple and talk about King David being in Jerusalem, about Jews living there. These are their own ancient texts. Yet the extremists reject them because they can't accept it. They refuse to accept it."

Vail thought about that a second. "Do they know what they've got? With the codex."

The elder rabbi leaned back in his seat. "Do they know the importance of the codex and its value to the world's religions and, obviously, to Israel? I have no doubt."

"Right," Vail said. "That's why they broke into the vault. That's not what I mean. I'm talking about the notes in the margin."

Yakov pulled on his beard. "I don't think so. They'd have to be able to read and interpret the Hebrew and I just don't think Islamic extremists are interested in reading a holy Jewish text. They'd also have to put it together with the Bethlehem archaeological find, which the government has tried to keep under wraps because of the potential fallout with the Palestinians. The bigger the deal you make about it, the more of an issue it becomes. Negotiations become more difficult, start to look like blackmail."

And they're apparently difficult enough without ancient texts adding complications.

Vail rose from the couch, followed by Uzi. "Thank you." She pulled out her card and handed it to Halevi. "You think of anything else, please let us know."

26

Uzi checked his phone while they descended in the slow-moving elevator.

Vail took a deep breath and kept her gaze on the floor.

"You okay? Oh—your claustrophobia."

"I'm fine. We'll be out of here in a minute." *Or an hour at the rate this thing moves.* "Talk to me, take my mind off it."

"Mo hasn't replied to my texts or phone calls. I tried reaching him before I went back upstairs."

"That's annoying."

"Annoying? How about unprofessional, irresponsible, sus—" The elevator hit the ground floor with a thud and Vail pushed the steel door open.

They walked outside, where DeSantos was waiting in the front courtyard.

"Anything from Mo?" Uzi asked.

"Nothing. Goes straight to voicemail. Anything worthwhile up there?"

"Karen'll fill you in. I've gotta make a call." Uzi headed toward the sidewalk as he pulled up the number. It was answered by Isamu.

"A year, year and a half ago we worked together on the Hades case," Uzi said. "We used the domain awareness system to—"

"I remember," Isamu said. "Your name kind of makes you unforgettable."

Uzi had to laugh. "Listen, I'm in town on a counterterrorism case and I need some help. If I send you a photo of someone, can you run it through the facial rec system and let me know if he's been anywhere in the city? I gotta find him."

"Suspect?"

"A person of interest. Let's just leave it at that."

"Send it over, I'll see what I can do. Facial rec still isn't up and running everywhere, but maybe we'll get a hit."

Uzi thanked him, then stood there thinking before rejoining Vail and DeSantos. Spying on a fellow federal agent was an extreme measure . . . but was it crossing the line? Perhaps. But for Fahad to go dark, without explanation, was potentially problematic considering who he was—and his family history. It could be innocent—but short of injury or emergency, there was no good excuse for his lack of contact in the middle of a major investigation.

"Let's go," DeSantos said with a shove to his shoulder.

The jostling woke Uzi from his fugue. He pulled out his keys as they started toward their car. "Did Karen fill you in?"

"She did."

"Where is she?"

"She went down the block to get us something to eat. Something the rabbi recommended as you were leaving. Rooga—rooga-something. You know, that thing you do with your throat. The 'ch' sound, like you're bringing up sputum.

"Rugalach."

DeSantos pointed at Uzi. "Yeah, that."

"It's a twisted pastry, kind of like a cross between a strudel and a croissant."

"Whatever."

"So what do you think?" Uzi asked. "About what Karen told you."

DeSantos shrugged. "Obviously we need to find these missing pages."

Uzi stopped walking. "It's not obvious to me. The codex is incredibly important in world history, no question. It burns me that a terrorist organization has those pages—but tracking down stolen artifacts is not our job. We've got enough on our plate."

"You're missing the point," DeSantos said, turning and walking backward along the sidewalk, facing Uzi. "Find those codex pages and we'll find Kadir Abu Sahmoud."

"Don't you mean the opposite?" Uzi asked. "Our job is to investigate and find Sahmoud—and when we do, we'll find the codex pages."

"Boychick, you're thinking like an FBI agent."

Uzi stopped walking. "I *am* an FBI agent. I'm in charge of the DC Joint Terrorism Task Force, remember?"

DeSantos closed the gap between them. "Look," he said, keeping his voice low, "right now you're working a case that sits on the border between domestic investigation and black ops. That's why OPSIG is involved."

"I didn't ask for this assignment. I should be doing what I'm supposed to be doing."

"You *are* doing what you're supposed to be doing: helping prevent another attack and catching the bad guy. Does it matter how you do it?"

"I think it does. I gave up the covert ops life."

"And Knox pulled you back in. To pay off a debt."

Uzi clenched his jaw. Years ago he had omitted key information from his original FBI application—but Knox knew the truth all along and he waited patiently until the time was right to call in his chit. It's the way Knox worked—quietly, patiently in the background, picking his spots to swoop in and pounce: leverage his intel, win concessions to make people do what they did not want to do, reveal what they did not want to reveal.

VAIL SAW UZI AND DeSANTOS down the block. She whistled but they did not respond. She continued toward them carrying a clear plastic container filled with pastries.

"These are dangerously delicious. I got chocolate, chocolate, and chocolate. Hope that's okay."

Uzi and DeSantos were staring at each other: silent anger.

I leave for five minutes and the men forget how to play nicely together. "I sense some tension." She studied their faces a moment, then said, "Let me guess. You guys disagree on what we should do next."

"Yeah," DeSantos said, his jaw fixed. "Uzi thinks we should go after Sahmoud and forget about the codex. That's the 'FBI thing' to do."

Vail nodded slowly. "Well, I'm FBI. And I'm gonna give you my opinion. Right now, there is only one thing we can do—and that's investigate and follow the leads. And our only lead is this lone fingerprint and the stolen codex pages. We've got a lot of little puzzle pieces with nothing tangible connecting them. But these codex pages, we know who has them and—"

"Do we?" Uzi asked.

"Yeah. It's reasonable to assume that something this important is being held by the top dog. That's Sahmoud. Follow the trail and it'll lead us to him."

Uzi shook his head. "I've got nothing better, so I'm on board. For now. But if we get a more substantial lead—like something dealing with the actual terror attacks—then *that's* where we put our energies."

"Fine," DeSantos said.

"Fine," Uzi echoed as he resumed walking toward their car.

27

Vail's phone buzzed as she turned onto the Brooklyn Queens Expressway, headed back to Manhattan. She handed it to Uzi, who was riding shotgun.

"Text from Russo. He wants to know if we're still in town."

Vail merged to the right lane. "Does he have something for us?"

"I'll ask." As soon as Uzi sent off the message, DeSantos's phone rang—and seconds later, Vail's vibrated.

Uzi consulted the display. "Russo said to meet him at Centre Street in front of city hall—if we can get through. They've closed down all the streets in a three-block radius. The bridge traffic is being diverted."

"We'll get as close as we can and walk if we have to. Did he say what it's about?"

"Apparently," DeSantos said, hanging up, "our case. That was Knox. He doesn't have any details but the FBI's now on-scene. He's waiting for an update. And he's on his way."

"That can't be good." Vail accelerated and moved into the far left lane. "Text Mo, give him the address and tell him to meet us there."

"If it'll do any good," Uzi said. "He's ignored us all day."

"I got it," DeSantos said as he started tapping on his phone.

Uzi started to hand her back the Samsung when it vibrated yet again. He glanced at the display and said, "It's Tim Meadows."

"Answer it."

He put the phone on speaker.

"Hey, Karen. I found something that's gonna make you very happy."

"Hi Tim," Uzi said. "What do you got?"

"Uh—I thought I called Karen."

"You did. She's driving."

"Oh, you law abiding citizens you. So I lifted fingerprints from the Eastern Market crime scene. You know the perps crashed into the building with the armored car and then got out and started firing their AK-47s, right? Well, they sprayed the place pretty well before blowing themselves up. I had our techs collect every single shell casing. We just got through testing all of them. The heat of the firing destroys DNA, so that was a dead end. And the heat burned off the body oils we usually need to lift a print so we used gun bluing and found 159 prints. Of the ones where we were able to get a significant number of points, we got matches on all of them."

"Meaning?" DeSantos asked.

"Meaning the same two guys loaded all the magazines. The prints weren't from bystanders who picked up the casings and tossed 'em down."

Vail moved into the middle lane, then leaned closer to the phone. "Did we get a hit?"

"How about, 'Nice work, Tim. Not many techs could've lifted those prints.' You really have to know what you're doing with gun bluing or you screw it up—the whole cartridge would've turned black. And we did it 159 times."

"Yeah, yeah, yeah," Uzi said. "If I wasn't holding the phone and if Karen wasn't driving we'd give you a round of applause." Vail and Uzi shared a grin. They enjoyed yanking Meadows's chain. "So that hit—yes or no?"

"No. I can work miracles but I can't create data where it's not. The perps are not in AFIS."

"Email the prints to me. I'll have Hoshi send them to Interpol. I'll get them over to Mossad too."

"And Tim," Vail said, "You're the best. You know we love you."

"And we love giving you a hard time," Uzi added.

"Yeah, well, the feeling's mutual." Meadows waited a beat, then added, "The part about giving you a hard time."

Their next call was to Knox. They were not on a secure line so they refrained from discussing names.

"The lab lifted two sets of latents off the spent shell casings at our most recent crime scene in your neighborhood," DeSantos said from the backseat.

"Do we have IDs?"

"Nothing in AFIS," Uzi said. "We're checking elsewhere."

Vail signaled to exit the expressway and merged into the adjacent lane. "There's something else we need you to look into." She summarized the salient points of what the rabbis had told her regarding the Aleppo Codex. "We've got some disagreement as to whether or not we should pursue this and how it might or might not be related to the offender who's calling the shots."

"Understood," Knox said. "I'll look into this and see what I can find out. There are some things going on behind the scenes and I have a feeling this could be related. I'll keep you posted."

Uzi hung up and turned around in his seat to face DeSantos. “Not sure I like that—‘things going on behind the scenes’?”

DeSantos snorted. “There are always things going on behind the scenes. We just don’t always find out about them.”

28

Vail exited onto the Brooklyn Bridge, a 130-year-old neo-Gothic span that was the first steel-wire suspension bridge ever built. The brown bolt-and-steel structure that connected the borough to Manhattan was majestic and internationally recognizable.

"I've always liked the Brooklyn Bridge," Vail said. "You know that a woman played a major role in its construction."

DeSantos glanced out the side window at the Manhattan Bridge. "Yeah, right."

"Seriously. The engineer got injured while they were building it and couldn't leave his apartment. So he taught his wife the complex mathematics involved in bridge building and she supervised construction for ten—"

"I see something." DeSantos pointed. "Up ahead."

Yeah. I see something too. Red taillights. Traffic.

Vail thought of exiting at Park Row South but changed her mind and continued on to Centre Street. "I'll get as close to the police barricade as possible."

But before they could approach, the flow of cars along the two lane road slowed—and then stopped.

Uzi sat forward in his seat and bobbed his head side to side. "There it is."

Vail saw it too. A knot of first responder vehicles was visible up ahead, their flashing lights flickering through the barren trees. "Whatever it is, it looks pretty major. They've got that huge emergency response vehicle there."

They made it to the forty-story Manhattan Municipal Building, one of the largest and most picturesque government buildings in the world. Above its tall, columned facade, engravings in the stone trumpeted the city's three names and the years that it began using those monikers: New Amsterdam, 1625; New York, 1664; and Manhattan.

Vail nosed the car up to the barricade near the secured entrance to the arched cobblestone driveway, where a deserted guard booth stood.

They got out and started toward the NYPD vehicles when a cop emerged from behind a cruiser and yelled at them to stop.

"FBI," Uzi called back and held his creds high above his head as they wove between the cars and walked toward the wall of police vehicles ahead of them.

They made their way past the various officers and federal agents who lined the street.

"Russo here?" Vail asked, her credentials now folded inside out and protruding from the pocket of her jacket.

"Don't know a Russo," the tall black man said.

"Captain, NYPD."

"Yeah. Still don't know him. Lotta brass onsite."

Vail lifted her Samsung and started to text him when she heard her name called. Russo was weaving his way through the crowd of personnel.

"Good thing your red hair is easy to spot in a crowd."

"Yeah, it's like a beacon. Lucky me. Good thing I don't do undercover work." *Oh, wait, I do.*

"So what do we got?" Uzi asked.

"One of our mobile radiological sensors tripped going over the bridge. We traced it using the domain awareness system to an overnight delivery truck. Had a team pull it over and ESU got the driver out with a bit of a fight. Wish I could show you but Hazmat's got control of the scene. They think it's contained but they're taking readings as—"

Russo's phone buzzed. He answered, listened a second, then said, "Be right there." He reholstered his phone and waved them forward. "We're clear. No leakage of the material. It's safe to approach."

Russo led the way along Centre Street, past the massive columns of the municipal building, to the secured area.

"What'd he have in the truck?" DeSantos asked.

"Strontium, forty kilocuries."

"Whoa. So they really *were* gonna set off a radiological bomb."

Vail elbowed his side. "Did you question my interrogation skills?"

DeSantos shrugged. "We had doubts. No offense."

"We?"

"Me and others."

Uzi sheepishly looked away.

"Offense taken."

"Because of that phone call," Russo said, "what you told me, I had them turn on all the sensors in the city, double the number of sweeps."

Uzi turned to Vail. "You told him what we got from Ghazal?"

"The president hadn't yet raised the alert. And even if he had, I doubt they'd be thinking dirty bomb. Calling Russo was the right thing to do."

"The right thing to do was to have my office tell the JTTF in New York and have them deploy what they felt was necessary."

"My way was faster," Vail said. "And it worked, so don't give me shit."

Russo snorted. "Still haven't heard nothin' from the JTTF about a potential dirty bomb. Just sayin.'"

Uzi's face shaded red. Vail was certain he was angry with the head of the city's JTTF, not Russo.

"I'll look into it," Uzi said.

"Yeah, you do that. Meantime, like I said. Thanks, *Karen*. All those serial killers you chase? Ain't nothing compared to the number of lives you saved on this case."

Uzi sighed in concession, then looked out into the sea of uniformed personnel. "What was his target, do we know?"

"No idea. We haven't had access to the truck. Now that we're clear, CSU can start digging in," Russo said, referring to the department's Crime Scene Unit.

"Check out the GPS. And the driver's phone. And any emails on his smart—"

"Karen. We got it."

"Right. Sorry."

Russo turned to a nearby detective. "Get a search warrant for the GPS and cell phone."

"How's the driver?" DeSantos asked.

"He's had better days." Russo must've seen DeSantos's furrowed brow because he added, "Asshole's dead."

They arrived at the vehicle, which was swarming with uniformed and Hazmat-suited personnel.

Twenty minutes later, Vail made out the commissioner and mayor, several captains, chiefs—there was no shortage of brass. Russo was part of the gathering. The group conferred for a couple of minutes, then Russo joined Vail, Uzi, and DeSantos.

"So?" Vail asked.

"So they were going to release a dirty bomb inside the Freedom tower. Beyond the symbolism, twenty thousand people would've been killed—in the tower alone. If the bomb detonated on any of the middle or upper floors, the cloud would've hovered over the city, probably even into Jersey."

"Holy shit," Uzi said.

"Nothing holy about it," Russo said. "Pat yourself on the back, Karen. Because that's what I feel like doing right now. If you hadn't told me they were planning this, I doubt we would've stopped it."

DeSantos's phone buzzed and he consulted the display.

"I'm gonna finish up here." Russo checked his watch, then started backing away. "I learn any more, like an ID on the driver, I'll let you know."

Vail nodded at DeSantos's phone. "Anything?"

"Knox will be here in about forty minutes."

UZI'S LUMIA RANG. He recognized the number and excused himself, walking down the street a bit.

"Isamu, what have you got for me?"

"Your person of interest. He met with a Middle Eastern–looking guy on Canal Street. I was able to ID the guy as Amer Madari. He doesn't have a record, but he has been to some hot spots the past two years. Pakistan, Syria, and Gaza."

"Meaning?"

"Meaning he's been to Pakistan, Syria, and Gaza the past two years. I'm not trying to be funny. That's about all we can say. We know those areas are rife with terror groups and terror activity, but we don't know enough of who this guy is to know what it means."

Uzi sighed. "You're right. Thanks for the call. You find out anything else, let me know."

"You want me to keep following this guy?"

That was a good question. Uzi closed his eyes. If Madari turned out to be a terrorist, he would kick himself for not taking action. Then again, Fahad was a CIA operative. Maybe his meets with people who have made trips to hotbeds of terror could be explained. But maybe not. "Tell you what, switch to Madari and let me know if he meets with anyone we should know about."

"Sure thing."

Uzi thanked him and texted Rodman, asking him to look into Amer Madari. He did not explain, merely labeling him as a person of interest. He then took a few minutes to think before rejoining Vail and DeSantos.

One thing was certain: his interest was piqued. The question was, at what point did he have something worth discussing with Vail and DeSantos? Or even Knox?

29

When Vail rejoined Uzi and DeSantos, Knox had arrived and was getting a briefing from police commissioner Brendan Carrig. It did not take long before the discussion got animated, at which point Knox stalked off to meet with the director and an assistant director of the FBI's New York field office.

When he finished and gathered with Vail, Uzi, and DeSantos, his jaw was set, his eyes narrowed. "Where are we on this thing? Anywhere?"

Uzi shifted his feet. "Slow progress. It's hard to know exactly what we know and what we don't know, but we've got a lot of pieces."

"We got a few more pieces this morning," Vail said, "from the rabbis."

Knox glanced around, then led them down the street to an area with fewer officers around. "I looked into that. There's something you three need to understand. And this is not to go anywhere—Where's Fahad?"

"Good question," DeSantos said. "He's been AWOL all day. Hasn't answered any of our texts or calls."

Knox absorbed that, then moved on. "This is extremely sensitive. What the rabbis told you about the codex is true. The fact that Sahmoud has those pages has tremendous relevance to what's going on."

"What *is* going on?" Uzi asked.

Knox gave another look around. It was starting to make Vail paranoid.

"As we speak, there are covert peace negotiations going on in Cairo between the Israelis and Palestinians. Very sensitive. We've been through this before, so you know the deal. The president wants it done. He's putting everything he has behind it."

"That's nothing new in peace negotiations," DeSantos said. "Sometimes they're done outside the public eye so things don't get sabotaged by the media, or by politics. Whatever."

"There's a difference this time," Knox said. He shot a glance around them and inched closer. "According to highly placed sources—so even *I* can't confirm it—the Palestinians are holding two items over Israel's head. One is the codex. The other . . ." He looked at their faces then settled on Uzi's. "The other is something best explained by your father."

Uzi swallowed hard. "My father?"

An agent came up to Knox from behind. "Sir, excuse me for interrupting. Commissioner Carrig wants another word with you. He seemed a little put off."

"He did, did he? Why don't you tell him—" Knox forced a chuckle. "No, I'll do it myself. Thanks." He backed away and pointed at Uzi. "Your father, Agent Uziel."

Vail appraised Uzi, then shoved her hands into her back pockets. "So you going to tell us what the problem is?"

"What problem?"

"You looked like you wanted to crawl under a rock when Knox mentioned your dad."

Uzi turned away. "You know how it is. Family. We've all got our shit."

DeSantos shook his head. "That may be, but that's not what's going on here. You respected your dad. You had a good relationship with him. You looked up to him."

Uzi took a deep breath. "Orders are orders. Let's go."

As they turned toward their car, a glass window beside Uzi's shoulder shattered and the unmistakable crack of a rifle echoed off the tall buildings.

"Down!" DeSantos yelled, dragging both Uzi and Vail lower with fistfuls of their jackets. He pulled them behind an NYPD cruiser parked at an angle by the curb.

They had their handguns out—as did the nearby officers and federal agents in the area.

"Anything?" Uzi called out.

Various replies—all indicating that no one had eyes on the shooter.

Vail snuck a peek over the top of the sedan. "Any idea which direction it came from?"

Uzi came around the edge of the car to get a look at the shattered windshield then craned his neck toward the buildings. "Gotta be in front of us, two o'clock."

DeSantos was taking his time, scanning the rooftops. In the background, Vail heard men yelling, calling out orders.

"Not likely the municipal building or city hall—security's too tight and I'm sure they've been checking rooftops. Not saying a sniper can't get in, but if we're looking at most likely scenarios . . ."

"I don't see anyone," Uzi said. "One shot. He had his shot, took it, and missed. He's gone."

DeSantos straightened up tentatively, eyeing the vicinity. "I agree."

The calls of "all clear" were heard as the law enforcement officers of multiple agencies moved back into the streets, some heading for the neighboring buildings to close off the exits and execute a thorough search.

Good luck with that. The municipal building alone is a block long and forty stories tall.

The three of them continued to scan the rooftops as they talked.

"Is it a stretch to think I was the target again?" Uzi said.

DeSantos holstered his handgun. "I was thinking the same thing. If we're right, it's safe to say they were serious about the threat they pinned to that woman's chest."

Vail leaned back against the nearby car. "Can't say for sure the bullet had your name on it, but it's the most obvious. Especially after what happened in Times Square."

Uzi pulled a toothpick from his jacket pocket and ripped it from its cellophane wrap. "Let's get out of here, go visit my father. See if we can get some answers."

AS THEY HEADED BACK TO UZI'S TAHOE, he could not shake the thought that, once again, only one person knew for sure that he was en route to the crime scene. Well, two: Knox and Mahmoud El-Fahad. Could Fahad have tipped both snipers that Uzi was going to be onsite?

As he mulled this disturbing thought, he pulled out his key fob and hit the unlock button.

The SUV exploded skyward, blowing glass and metal and rubber in all directions.

The three of them hit the pavement nearly simultaneously, instinctively covering their heads with their hands in an almost useless gesture.

Car alarms blared in all directions as men and women came running toward them.

"They're seriously pissed at you, Boychick."

"Ya think?" Uzi pushed himself up and yawned twice, trying to restore his hearing.

"Don't take this the wrong way," Vail said, pulling on her ears, "but maybe you should go back to DC, lock yourself in your house and not come out till we catch these bastards."

Uzi dusted off his leather coat. "Not gonna happen." He looked around. "But we are going to need a new ride."

30

They arrived at the home of Roey Uziel just after 4:00 PM. They had borrowed a Chevy Suburban from the New York field office motor pool then headed toward Roey's residence.

Despite their repeated questions about what had caused Uzi's relationship with his father to deteriorate, Uzi refused to discuss it—nor did he want to call ahead to see if his dad was at home. Vail knew the two things were related—but she did not need her detective skills to reach that conclusion.

As they pulled in front of Roey's apartment house in Greenwich Village, Uzi shoved the gear lever into park and sat back in the seat. "After Dena and Maya were killed, I withdrew from everyone and everything. It was a really tough time. You know that. But I didn't even talk to my father. I should have, but I didn't. I couldn't talk to anyone."

He turned away and stared out the driver's window. "Anyway, I never returned any of his phone calls. He came to my house once and I was home but didn't let him in. I'm pretty sure he knew I was there. Time passed and I never contacted him. He tried once or twice a year later, but by the time I was able to talk about it, I was embarrassed that I hadn't wanted anything to do with him. I can't explain it." He glanced at Vail. "I'm sure you can. If I'd had the chance, I probably would've eventually discussed it with Dr. Rudnick." Uzi popped open the door.

"We all make mistakes," Vail said. "But he's your father. He'll forgive you. You two just need to talk it out."

Uzi seemed to think about that as they walked toward the apartment building entrance.

They climbed five slate steps to a weathered wood door that had been repainted dozens of times during the past several decades.

Uzi led them to a narrow hallway with two doors at the end, where a small window stood above a radiator that piped out warm air. Vail held her fingers over the heat and felt the blood return. *I need to put gloves in my go bag.*

Uzi faced the door to the left and balled his hand into a fist, as if ready to strike its surface. But he just stood there.

"This the place?" DeSantos finally asked.

"Yeah."

DeSantos glanced at Vail, then reached out and knocked firmly.

"I was gonna get around to it."

"We don't have all day, Boychick." There was a sharp, loud bark, but otherwise no suggestion of movement inside the apartment.

"Your dad have a dog?" Vail asked.

Uzi shrugged. "Don't know."

A few seconds later, Uzi rapped his knuckles against the wood. "Dad," he said, dipping his chin, as if out of embarrassment, "open up. It's Aaron."

The door opposite swung open, revealing a woman in her late sixties, some sagging of the face but an otherwise bright complexion and a friendly smile. She was wearing a spandex running suit.

"Roey's not home."

Uzi turned. "You know my dad?"

She stepped into the hall. "You must be Aaron."

"My dad's mentioned me?"

"No. I heard you yell your name." She must have noticed Uzi's shoulders slump slightly—Vail did—because she said, "Just kidding. Of course he's talked about you. He's very proud of you."

Uzi just stood there, staring at her.

"Nice to hear," Vail said, filling the void.

"But you really should come around more. Or call. He hasn't heard from you in years."

Clearly this woman is a good friend of Roey's. "Do you know when he'll be back?" Realizing that it might be odd that she was asking the question rather than Uzi, Vail extended her hand. "Karen Vail. Uzi—Aaron's friend."

"Helen Goldschmidt." She pulled her door closed and sorted out the wires of her iPod. "Roey works lunchtimes at the food bank a few blocks away then goes over to Washington Square Park to play chess with Sal." She turned to Uzi and frowned. "If you were in touch with him instead of ignoring him, you'd know that, Aaron. He needs you."

With that, Helen stuck the headphones in her ears and strode off down the hall.

"Well," Vail said, "that was pleasant."

DeSantos gently slapped Uzi in the chest. "I assume we're going to Washington Square Park."

Uzi was looking down the now-vacant hallway. "Huh? Yeah. Okay."

"We can handle this," Vail said, "if you'd rather not see him."

"No, no. I'm good."

Yeah, I can tell.

THEY WALKED TWO BLOCKS TO THE PARK, which was best known for the imposing marble arch that served as a gateway to the nearly ten acre parcel.

"Looks like the Arc de Triomphe," DeSantos said.

Vail laughed. "That's because it was *designed* to look like it."

They walked beneath the structure, a sculpture of George Washington adorning both piers.

"Ever been there?"

"Nope. But Robby and I have talked about Paris for our honeymoon."

"Too clichéd, if you ask me."

Vail touched his forearm. "Actually, I wasn't."

"Ow."

Vail noted that Uzi was quiet, scanning the park, presumably looking for his father. He stopped and studied the fountain ahead of him, which was spewing water a few dozen feet into the air. Tourists were gathered around the periphery taking photos. In the warm weather kids would be in the surrounding pond, playing and finding refuge from the oppressive humidity.

Uzi turned left and led them down a paved path alongside the barren trees and a row of benches. He headed toward a brass statue on a stone pedestal and stopped twenty feet short of two men seated at a folding table, a chess board between them. Only a queen and two bishops remained.

They stood there a moment, Vail and DeSantos slightly behind Uzi's right shoulder, until Roey Uziel leaned forward, moved his queen, and said, "Checkmate."

Roey, wearing a full facial grin, sat back and caught sight of Uzi. His smile faded instantly, his lips parting in surprise.

The other man—presumably Sal—turned and saw the three of them standing there. It was clear to Vail that Sal did not know who they were, but identified them as law enforcement. "Everything okay?" he said to Roey.

"Yeah. This is my—it's nothing, it's all good. But would you mind if I left you to pack everything up?"

Roey walked toward his son, who just stood there, voiceless and stiff.

"Mr. Uziel, I'm Karen Vail and this is Hector DeSantos. We're friends of Aaron's."

He sidestepped Uzi and shook their hands. "Has my son lost his tongue? You know, I haven't heard from him in seven years. A lot can happen to a person. And I'd never know."

Vail wanted to nudge Uzi, shove him, stick him with a stun gun—something to get him talking.

Roey turned to face Uzi. "Have you lost your ability to speak?"

"We're here on business."

"I can see that," Roey said. "I'm a pretty perceptive guy."

"We've got some questions."

Jesus, Uzi. You're making this painful for all of us.

"So do I," Roey said, his gaze steady, fixed on Uzi's.

"Yeah, well, I don't have to answer yours. But federal law says you have to answer mine."

"All right," Vail said. "Enough. Father and son, I realize you've had a disagreement over something. That's your business. But for now, we need to put aside whatever problem you have with each other and get to why we're here."

"We need your help," DeSantos said.

Roey's eyes narrowed. "You FBI?"

"Department of Defense. Karen's FBI."

Roey nodded slowly. "Why don't we head back to my place. I assume this is something that requires some discretion."

Perceptive guy indeed. "That'd be a good idea."

"Aaron, that sit well with you?"

Uzi licked his lips. "Yeah."

As they walked out of the park and toward the arch, Roey said, "You been okay? Healthy?"

Uzi nodded.

"How's your head? Mental stuff, I mean."

"Better." Uzi glanced at Vail. "I'm doing okay."

"I heard you were with the FBI."

"He runs the Bureau's DC Joint Terrorism Task Force," Vail said.

"Where'd you hear I was with the FBI?" Uzi asked.

Roey continued walking a few steps before answering. "I googled you. There was an article two or three years ago about you working the case of the vice president's helicopter—Marine Two. The crash. That was your case, no?"

"Me and about three hundred others."

"Yes, it was his case," Vail said.

Uzi gave her a look.

They reached the apartment building and climbed the stairs.

"So, how well do you know Helen?" Uzi asked.

Roey paused before he passed through the door. Without turning around, he said, "We're dating."

"Serious?"

"Yeah. Kind of."

"Hey, Boychick. She could end up being your stepmother. Not bad."

Vail elbowed DeSantos.

Roey entered his apartment and tossed his keys on the bureau to his right. The place was well kept. Ahead on a large wall in the living room there were two dozen frames: photos that showed a younger Uzi, a woman that was undoubtedly his mother and one who looked to be a sister—slightly junior to Uzi—and a dark haired, handsome Roey, from years past. Vail saw the resemblance: square jaw, olive complexion, penetrating eyes.

Vail's gaze settled on an 11x14 photo of Uzi and his wife and daughter. They were laughing, seated at a picnic table. She pulled her eyes away from it and noticed that Uzi was fixated on the same picture.

DeSantos saw it too, because he nudged Uzi and said, "We've got some things to square away."

Uzi faced them, his eyes glazed with tears, and nodded. "Dad, we're working a sensitive case that we're told relates to something you know about."

"Coffee?" He asked as he stepped into the adjacent kitchen.

They all accepted.

Roey reached into the cabinet and pulled out a coffee maker. "Who told you I know something?"

Uzi scratched his head. "Well, this may sound strange, but the FBI director." He exchanged a look with Vail and DeSantos then faced his father and chuckled slightly. "Like I said."

Roey stopped, a coffee scoop in his right hand, and considered this a moment. "Okay."

Uzi cricked his neck. "What do you mean, 'okay'? I just told you the FBI director doesn't just have knowledge about you, but he knows that you know something."

"Yes," Roey said with a nod. "I understand the conversation, Uzi."

"Well *I* don't understand. Why would the FBI director know anything at all about you?"

Roey dug into the Starbucks Arabica bag. The rich aroma of freshly ground coffee filled the room. "That's a story with a longer explanation. And I believe one of you said your case was time sensitive."

"Actually," Vail said, "we didn't."

"But it's true, isn't it. Hmm?"

"Yes."

Roey dumped the heaping scoops into the machine. "I make it strong. Is that okay?"

"Dad," Uzi said a bit too firmly, "we don't care about the coffee. Get to the point."

"They used to say coffee was bad for you. But turns out, it's actually good for you."

"Dad—"

"My point, Aaron, is that things aren't always what they seem."

DeSantos stepped closer to the kitchen. "Care to explain that, Mr. Uziel?"

"Call me Roey. And I think it speaks for itself. Doing what you do, Hector, I don't need to explain that to you, now, do I?"

Something tells me we're going to find out, anyway.

Uzi's eyes were narrowed, studying his father. "Dad, what's going on here?"

Roey lifted his chin and whistled. A compact, powerfully built seal-and-white Boston Terrier ran into the room. "Good boy, Benny. Sit." The dog sat.

"When did you get a dog?"

"Tell me something, Uzi. Did I ever do anything wrong to you? To hurt you?"

Uzi looked at Roey out of the corner of his eyes. "No. Why?"

Roey stopped, his finger paused over the coffeemaker's start button. "I want to know why you stopped talking to me. Why you wouldn't take my calls, why you made believe you weren't home when I stopped by to see you."

"That's not why I'm here."

"You want your answers, I want mine. I don't see you for seven years, then suddenly you show up. I want to know if I'm responsible."

Uzi looked away, looked for the nearest dining room chair, and sat down. The others followed suit.

Benny grabbed a tennis ball and leaped into Uzi's lap. He began absent-mindedly stroking the dog's smooth hair. "It was all me. After Dena and Maya . . . were killed, I felt responsible. It . . . it was complicated. I stopped, well, pretty much everything. I stopped living. My heart was beating but my world ended. I didn't want to talk to anyone."

"That was a mistake. And I would've told you that if you'd let me. But you didn't let me."

"I was embarrassed. I—when I was finally able to deal with their deaths, when I began putting my life back together and started my job at the FBI, I dove in and gave it everything I had. It became my entire life, prevented me from thinking about it. Because when I did . . ." He waved a hand. "I felt bad that I'd cut you off. I didn't stop to think that you were in pain too. I'm sorry. In retrospect I handled it very badly, I know that. But at the time, it was all I could do to get through the days."

Roey leaned back against the countertop. "I accept your apology. And you're right, I was in pain too. I loved that little girl. And Dena, she was like my own daughter. The hole it created, I know it's nothing like what you went through, but . . ." He frowned. "*That's* when I got Benny. To fill the void."

The coffeemaker gurgled and java started to flow into the glass pot.

"Anyway, I realize the reason you're here wasn't for us to get right, but I'm glad you're here, whatever it is that brought us back together." He removed four mugs from the cupboard. "Actually I think I know why the director sent you. It involves a rare archaeological find?"

DeSantos and Uzi looked at each other.

Knox wouldn't have sent us here to discuss the codex. Is there another rare archaeological find involved in this?

Roey removed a sugar bowl from a cabinet. "I've only got xylitol, if that's okay. It's all natural—made from tree bark. No artificial chemicals. Tastes as good as cane sugar. Good for the teeth. Will that work for you?"

"Dad," Uzi said, impatience permeating his tone.

Benny jumped off Uzi's lap and went over to DeSantos, who grabbed the tennis ball and played tug of war with him.

Roey set about pouring the coffee. "I haven't discussed the scroll with anyone in many years. Honestly, I hoped it would just go away."

"Scroll?" Vail asked. "What scroll?"

"Director Knox only told us we need to talk to you about something. You seem to know what it is."

Roey hesitated, then handed out the mugs. He pulled over a chair and joined them at the table. "Agent Vail, do you know who Uzi's grandfather was?"

Vail turned to Uzi, who shrugged. "He never mentioned him. He just told me he lived in Israel."

"My father," Roey said, "was Eylad. A Mossad agent. He worked—"

"Wait, what?" Uzi leaned forward. "What the hell are you talking about? Zayde wasn't Mossad," Uzi said, using the Yiddish term for grandfather. "He was a scholar, a professor—" He stopped himself and sat back in his seat.

Clearly Uzi had not known about his grandfather's activities as a spy—but he surely understood why he had been kept in the dark: spies did not share such information with their families. Many never spoke of it even after getting out of the business.

"Sounds like it runs in the family," DeSantos said. He lifted the tennis ball to shoulder height—and Benny maintained his grip. The dog was now a foot off the floor, but he was not relinquishing his toy.

Uzi did not notice. His mouth was open and his gaze had not moved from his father. "Was he a *kidon*?" he asked, using the term for assassin.

"No. Well, to be fair, I don't know the things he did. I asked him a few times, but he never wanted to talk about it. Too dangerous. I only know about one case. But it's a big one."

"And that's the one the director sent us here for," DeSantos said, letting Benny drop a short distance to the floor.

"That's the one. My father worked as a Hebrew and Aramaic translator on the archaeological team that excavated the Dead Sea Scrolls."

The Dead Sea Scrolls?

"At the time, back in the early 1950s, the Qumran caves and nearby Essene ruins sat on land controlled by Jordan. The scrolls are thought to have been written by the Essenes, an ancient Jewish sect that settled outside Jerusalem to escape the Roman persecution. There are a number of interpretations as to why the Essenes were there and why they wrote the scrolls, so I'm telling you the one that my father felt made the most sense based on what he learned. The Essene scribes produced hundreds of scrolls, many of which were copies of one another. They contain the Hebrew Bible, so it's likely the multiple copies allowed the people who lived in Qumran the ability to pray together. Basically, it was like having prayer books for your congregation."

"But some weren't prayer books," Uzi said.

"Right. There were also biblical texts, biblical commentaries, and religious books that were later excluded from the Hebrew Bible when the scholars wrote the Aleppo Codex." He stopped and his eyes flicked from one to the other. "Do any of you know about the codex?"

DeSantos laughed. "We *all* do."

Roey eyed them again, then continued. "Some of the scrolls are manuals of the beliefs and practices of the Essenes, who were freethinkers. Ultimately, nine hundred documents were found. Archaeologists found a large room amongst the ruins that they believe was devoted solely to scroll writing."

"Nine hundred documents," Vail said with a shake of her head. "They were very prolific."

"Some experts think they wrote down all their customs and beliefs because they feared Rome would one day sack Judea—which, of course, happened—and they didn't want their culture to die alongside them. That's why they hid them in clay jars inside caves. Others think the Essenes planned to return when it was safe and retrieve their holy scrolls."

Roey reached into a cabinet and removed a strip of duck jerky, then tossed it to Benny, who dropped his ball and scooped up the treat.

"My father was sent there to observe the excavation process, to make sure rare pieces of ancient history didn't disappear. I mean, there wasn't anything like this ever discovered in the history of mankind. And there still hasn't been, seventy years later. Those scrolls, written two thousand years ago, are our earliest written record of the basis of the Abrahamic religions, including Judaism, Christianity, and Islam—they can all be traced back to those core beliefs. The scrolls told how things were done. The same things you and I do today, Aaron, are written in these documents.

"Unfortunately, a number of important scrolls were found before my father joined the archaeological team. But he was there on August 6, 1953, when a very special find was made. Inside a clay pot, like they were all stored, they found an intact scroll. It was exceptionally well preserved. When they unwrapped the linen covering, no one had touched that document in over two thousand years.

"Your zayde and a French archaeologist named Alberi Michel unrolled the scroll a few feet at a time while he read it from start to finish. He knew then that he'd found something very important. At the same time, he knew it was very dangerous. But he didn't know what to do about it. If it'd only been him there, he would've smuggled it to the National Museum and let them decide how to handle it. But Michel worked for Roland de Vaux, who was in charge of the excavation. The scroll could not just disappear. Michel might've suspected my father, and they might've discovered who he really was—a Mossad operative."

"His cover would've been blown."

"Exactly right, Hector. Since it was my father's job to write a formal translation of the entire scroll, that's what he did. He gave it to Michel that night. The next morning, the scroll—and Michel—were gone."

Vail picked up the tennis ball and tossed it to Benny. "Gone. As in he left? He stole the scroll?"

"Yes, Karen, he stole the scroll, and the translation. But," Roey said, lifting a hand and waving an index finger, "my father had made a handwritten copy of the translation. This he turned over to his boss at Mossad a few days later when he was certain Michel was not returning."

"Did they ever find him?" Uzi asked. "Or the scroll?"

"Six weeks later, Michel turned up in Egypt. He claimed he had been ambushed and beaten."

"The scroll?" DeSantos asked. "Wait, let me guess: whoever attacked him took it. Right?"

"Right."

"What was his reason for stealing it? To sell it on the black market?"

Roey chuckled. "That certainly would've been believable. And he would've gotten a good sum of money for it, even back then before scholars knew what they had in the scrolls. Only a small fraction of them were made public. I think about 80 percent were kept hidden away by the Vatican for thirty to forty years. Christian and Jewish scholars kept asking to study them, but the answer was always no."

Vail splayed her hands. "So where was Michel taking it?"

Roey shrugged. "He said he was hand delivering it to the Vatican because of what was contained inside. He didn't want anyone to see what was written there."

"Which was?" DeSantos asked.

Roey took a drink. He looked down and swirled his mug. "It's still dangerous, all these decades later. Is it that important? Will what's written in that ancient scroll really affect your case?"

"Knox seemed to think it would," Uzi said.

Vail cradled her cup to warm her hands. "How can we answer that question if we don't know what it says?"

"Why do you think it's so dangerous?" DeSantos asked.

Roey took another drink. "Because, Hector, it has the power to change religion as we know it."

31

I know what you're thinking," Roey said. "How could a document thousands of years old impact what people believe today?"

Actually, we already know the answer to that.

"It's *because* it was written so long ago that it has the power to influence the present day. Remember, this was before Christianity, before Islam." Roey sighed. "I'm not a religious scholar, so I only know what I learned in talking with other experts a long time ago. To grasp its significance, you have to understand that many academics believe that Qumran, and the Essenes, gave birth to Christianity.

"The Essenes were freethinkers. Some think they were rebels who were looking for new ways to practice their faith. Because of what's written in the religious commentary of certain scrolls, some scholars believe that Jesus was one of the Essenes, or that he had visited them and shared his beliefs. Remember, Jesus was Jewish—a student of the Pharisees, a precursor to what we now call rabbis."

Vail finished her coffee and set the mug down. "So you're saying that the Qumran community was where the divergence occurred between Judaism and Christianity. Since they recorded Jesus's teachings, it was the birth of Christianity."

Benny put his front paws on Vail's knees and growled softly, daring her to snatch the ball from his mouth.

"You find this very exciting," DeSantos said.

"I'm not very religious," she said, "but yeah."

"There are those who believe that Qumran is where the core Christian beliefs were born," Roey said, "its early beginnings, the formation of those newer principles that became the foundation for Christianity years later. And there's considerable support for that."

"Then what's the problem?" Vail asked.

"There was a very large scroll that Israel obtained in 1948 during the War of Independence. It was the most intact scroll discovered to date and they named it the Temple Scroll because it talked about daily life in the First Temple, the one that was destroyed by the Babylonians—how the sacrifices were made, what the structure looked like, its dimensions and layout, how it was used, and so on. Well, the scroll that was stolen by Alberi Michel? My father called it the Jesus Scroll. Know why?"

"Because it's all about Jesus."

"Right, Karen. But not in the way you think. Here's an example." He craned his head toward the ceiling as he tried to recall the text. "Ah, hell. Hang on a minute." He walked out of the room and returned with a leather notebook bound on the side by leather strings. Roey carefully opened it and turned a couple of pages.

"Here: 'We will establish a manner of living for the whole, so that all may benefit from those around us. We will visit the ill of health, care for the ones whose bellies are not full. We are sent by the Anointed One to heal the sick, by our King to serve the poor, by the Prophet to proclaim hope.' And then there's this: 'Miriam, the Anointed One, assembled the spices and oils for anointing the sick. Joel, the prophet among us, encouraged us to remember Elohim's promises. Saul, whom the citizens of Jerusalem called the King of the Jews because of his knowledge of the Law, leads us with authority and discipline.'

"And maybe the most important passage: 'For the benefit of all, these three will be known as one to whom believers from all walks can follow, and we shall call this person Yesu the Messiah, who represents the anointed one, the king, and the prophet."

Vail, Uzi, and DeSantos were quiet.

Roey added, "There was no distinct J in the alphabet until the Middle Ages. The J was a Y and Yesu, which means savior, was later interpreted as 'Jesus.' Just like Jerusalem was, or is, Yerushalayim."

Vail struggled to process what Roey had just read. *I think I've got it. And I see the problem.* "You're saying that the Jesus Scroll talks about Jesus being a composite character, not an actual person."

"Right. The scholars, priests, and rabbis I spoke with—and it was a very carefully selected group for obvious reasons—felt we were witnessing the creation of a new way of thought, with the intention that it can be used to garner support amongst the Essenes as an offshoot to traditional Judaism. They weren't aiming to create a new religion per se, but were trying to formulate their concepts into something with a slightly different way of life, and then making it simple so others could grasp its directives, ideas, and conventions.

"One thing that a couple of the experts brought up was that scripture contains no true reference to the formal discussion of planned communities or even the concepts of communities. They lived in communities and they functioned as communities at that time and later on because it was commanded that they do so by God, Moses, judges, kings, prophets, Jesus, the Holy Spirit. But the descriptions of communal living came from outsiders. So in that sense this is a departure from all the other writings we found in the Qumran caves."

"I see the problem," Vail said. "If this scroll is legit and dates to the same—"

"My father was there when it was discovered, when it was removed from the cave. He took it from the clay jar with his own hands, he unwrapped it from the linen."

"Only way to know for sure," Uzi said, "is to let science do the talking. Carbon—"

"If they ever find it, I'm sure every single test known to modern science will be run."

"So," DeSantos said, "the takeaway here is that there was no Jesus."

"It's not a new concept," Roey said. "It's been theorized, according to what I was told. But this is proof. As close to proof as you can get. Back before the religion was founded, before anyone could judge it. Pure witness to the thoughts and plannings of a person or a group of people who wanted to put down in writing something that they hoped would resonate with others."

Benny got tired of waiting for Vail to play so he brought his ball back to DeSantos, who again grabbed it and lifted the dog off the ground.

"Why keep this secret?" Uzi said. "Why haven't you gone public with Zayde's translation—with his story? It's of great historical, archaeological, and religious importance."

Roey examined the inside of his empty mug. He rose and poured himself another cup, then did the same for the others. "Ask yourself this, Aaron: will it change anything?"

"Absolutely."

"I mean in positive ways. There are those who'll have their beliefs shaken. It could destroy their lives, shake them to their core."

"Oh, come on."

"Wait a minute," DeSantos said as he lowered Benny to the ground and played tug of war with the ball. "I'm no expert, but my sister likes to dig into scriptures and I've gotten stuck in a few debates with her. One thing she's pointed out is that the authors of the gospels of Matthew, Mark, and Luke wrote to different audiences and painted different pictures of the person of Jesus—depending on what they wanted their audiences to understand. Seems to me that suggests Jesus wasn't just one person, but a combination of people with diverse personalities who could appeal to many types of people by being different to each of them."

"I don't know much of the New Testament," Uzi said, "but we don't have to look at this as just a religious concept. Isn't each of us really a composite—husband, father, law enforcement officer, brother, son, friend?"

"That's true," Roey said. "But the problem is you *can't* strip out the religious aspect. This goes to the heart of Christianity. Jesus is the central figure. If you 'prove' that he never existed, it could shake people's belief structure."

"I agree with your dad," Vail said. "Faith is a deeply personal thing. It gives some the will to survive, a purpose, a focus in life. To others, organized religion is a community. What good would come of harming the very thing these people believe in?"

"Not to mention the political damage to the Vatican," Roey said. "It's taken centuries to repair the relations between the Church and Judaism. The Church has apologized for declaring that the Jews killed Jesus. That was huge. And that's just one example." He shook his head. "No, the scroll's best left hidden away."

Uzi considered that a moment. "You're being judge and jury, Dad. I think you need to make it available and let the scholars and religious sages draw the proper conclusions. For the people, the followers, if their faith is strong, a document can't shake their beliefs."

"But it can, Aaron. Religion is a very powerful thing, my boy. Trust me: the scroll's best left 'undiscovered.'"

"Well," DeSantos said, "that's the problem."

"Why?" Roey looked at each of them. "You found it? You found the scroll?"

"It's been found, yes. But we don't have it. Someone else does."

Roey waited, but no one volunteered additional information. "Well? Who's got it?"

Uzi turned to DeSantos, who shook his head, warning him off.

Vail jumped in. "We can't say. For now, let's just say we don't control them and what they do with the scroll."

Roey's face flushed.

"What's wrong?" Vail asked.

"Someone came by last week asking about the scroll—the translation, actually."

Vail, Uzi, and DeSantos glanced at each other.

"Who was it?" Uzi asked.

"Someone I knew many years ago. When you were a young boy."

"And why would this person ask about something he doesn't even know exists?"

"Because he does know it exists. He's known about it for decades."

"Who is it?"

Roey took another drink, then stared into the mug as he considered the question a moment. "Gideon Aksel."

32

Gideon?" Uzi asked. "How the hell does a retired family physician know the director general of Mossad?"

Uzi struggled to put it together. Then he thought of what his father had said: things were not what they appeared to be.

"You were a Mossad agent," Vail said. "Just like your father. Just like your son. Am I right?"

Uzi's head swung to Vail—and back to his father—so fast that he heard the joints crack in his neck.

"Dad?"

Roey lifted his mug. Uzi grabbed his wrist. "Dad, answer her."

"He doesn't have to, Boychick. Knox knows your dad, your dad knows Aksel. Your grandpops and father were Mossad. For you . . ." He shrugged. "Seems preordained."

"It wasn't like that," Roey said.

Uzi let go of his arm. "It had nothing to do with my father, Santa. I applied, they rejected me. It was Rafi Eitan who—"

"No." Roey leaned back in his seat. "I was the one who killed your application. I didn't want my son having the type of life I lived, the type of life my father lived. It wasn't good for a family. Your mother—well, she was the one who made me see it. She asked me to make it so they wouldn't take you."

Uzi had applied but never got a response—which meant they were not interested. It wasn't until Rafi Eitan, a legendary Mossad operative, pulled strings. That's when Uzi got the call that started his career in spy work. Or so he thought.

Roey grabbed another slice of jerky and tossed it to Benny. "You were exceptionally bright, Aaron, and loved technology. Your mother and I wanted you to pursue that. But if we'd come out and told you that, you never would've listened. This way, you made the decision for yourself."

"With some 'help' from you and Mom. You manipulated me."

"All parents manipulate their children—to eat healthy, to do their homework, to be kind to others—"

"This is different. I was an adult."

Roey nodded slowly. "I know. I told your mother it was wrong. You were happy at Intel, but I knew you still had that burning desire, the same burning desire I had so many years before. Unless I removed that hold I'd placed on your name, you wouldn't get anywhere, and I knew it wasn't something you could accept. So I called Gideon."

"You knew Gideon?"

"I worked under him early in his career. We've stayed in touch."

"Are you still working for them?"

"You know I can't answer that."

As Uzi sat there, a horrible thought occurred to him: if his father had not paved his way into Mossad, Dena and Maya would still be alive.

He rose from his chair and clasped the back of his neck.

Uzi willed himself to stop thinking like that. He had an important case. People were depending on him. He had to focus, push it aside.

"Boychick, you okay?"

"He's wondering, Hector, if he should disown me," Roey said. "If I'd left well enough alone, if I hadn't removed that barrier, he never would've gotten into Mossad and his wife and daughter wouldn't have been murdered."

"Uzi," Vail said.

"He'll be fine," Roey said. "He just needs a minute."

Uzi turned to Roey, a hollow, emotionless look on his face, and said, "We've got a case to work." He stood up and pushed in his chair. "Thanks for your help. And the coffee."

Vail and DeSantos glanced at one another, then followed Uzi toward the front door.

"Thank you," Vail said.

"Aaron, wait. When will I see you again?"

Uzi stopped, his hand gripping the knob. He did not turn around—and did not answer. He pulled the door open and walked out.

33

Outside, they walked to their car in silence. DeSantos was on the phone, following a dozen feet behind them.

Walking by Uzi's side, Vail looked over at him and saw that his brow was hard, his jaw set. He was either angry or concentrating—she could not tell which.

"You can't blame your father."

"I know," he said, keeping his gaze straight ahead.

"Hey, hang on a second." She took hold of his leather jacket and gave a tug. He stopped and reluctantly turned to face her.

"Life is full of these 'what if' alternate realities, Uzi. If only I'd taken the earlier train. If only I'd caught that killer a day sooner, if only I'd seen the car run the red light, if only I'd fired my Glock a millisecond sooner. There's no end to these scenarios. You can go nuts—literally—trying to live life like that. What happened, happened. Your father did what he thought was right for you at the time, trying to make you happy. He had no way of knowing the consequences."

"I know. It's just—I thought I was over it, you know? I thought I'd come to terms with it. Then something like this happens—" He held up a hand. "I'll get past it. It'll scab over again. Meantime, we've got a job to do."

DeSantos came up from behind them. "That was Knox. He knew Gideon paid Roey a visit. And obviously he knew the scroll existed—but he didn't know who had it until he found out the codex was being held hostage." DeSantos glanced at each of them, then said, "Everything okay?"

"He's working through what Roey told him about Dena and Maya."

"I'm good," Uzi said. "Reopened an old wound is all. Did Knox give us anything useful?"

"Just an order: find the documents."

Uzi's phone rang. He glanced at the display and backed away. "Gotta take this." He tossed DeSantos the car keys. "Be right there."

◆ ◆ ◆

UZI ANSWERED THE CALL when he was comfortably out of range of Vail and DeSantos. He felt bad not including them in his fishing expedition on Mahmoud El-Fahad. But until he had more concrete information one way or the other, he felt it best not to accuse their missing team member of anything improper.

"Hot Rod, talk to me."

"So you're right, Amer Madari has a suspicious history of travel to terror hotbeds. But I couldn't find anything indicating he's been radicalized. No bank transfers, no questionable business dealings, no known associates who have terror backgrounds, no trips to terror camps, no Facebook posts showing a tendency toward extremist thinking."

"So you've got zip."

"Basically, he looks clean as far as I can see. That doesn't mean he is, it just means I can't see anything that would raise a red flag."

"Is he too clean?"

Rodman paused a moment. "Interesting question. I'll keep that in mind as I poke around."

"Anything turns up, let me know."

"What's up with this guy? What are you looking for?"

Uzi nearly shared his concerns with Rodman but held back. "He's working with someone I'm keeping an eye on. If he's bad, the guy I'm watching could be a problem too."

He thanked Rodman and rejoined Vail and DeSantos in the car.

"All good?" DeSantos asked.

All good—maybe that was the problem. "Yeah, let's get going."

Vail turned over the engine. "Got some good news and some bad news. Which you want first?"

"Give me the good."

"Heard from Mo."

"Really," Uzi said. "Where's he been?"

"Didn't say. But he's on his way to meet us."

"And that happens to be the bad news," DeSantos said. "We're meeting him at Maguire Air Force Base."

"Why is that bad news?"

"Because we're going to London."

Uzi turned to Vail. "But we're banned from England. We can't go to London."

Vail yanked the gear shift into drive. "That, Uzi, is why it's the bad news."

34

They arrived at New Jersey's McGuire Air Force Base, also known as "Joint Base McGuire-Dix-Lakehurst" an hour and twenty minutes later, using lights and siren and riding the shoulder of the turnpike when possible.

Vail and Uzi stood outside the PX, a Walmart-size store that sold everything a soldier and his family would need. They went on a quick shopping spree, buying three days' worth of toiletry essentials, underwear and socks, 5.11 tactical pants and belts, locking plastic ties, and canvas duffels to carry it all in. DeSantos used his Department of Defense credentials to make the purchase.

He joined them outside and tossed them their khaki-colored bags. An extra one sat on the ground at their feet in preparation for Fahad's arrival.

They turned in unison at the chopping noise of helicopter rotors off to their left. An FBI Black Hawk hovered, then dropped in place to a gentle landing in a field a couple hundred yards in the distance.

Moments later, Douglas Knox joined them at the periphery of the parking lot.

"You obviously can't fly a commercial jet into Heathrow," Knox said as he used his right hand to brush his hair back into place. "A C-17 Globemaster III is fueled and ready to go."

"Going back to London," Uzi said with a shake of his head. "That a good idea?"

"Since it came from me, Agent Uziel, yes, I do think it's a good idea."

"With all due respect," Vail said, "Given our history, I didn't think any of us would be setting foot in the UK any time in the near future." *More like never.*

"We were operating under the same assumption. But circumstances demanded that we reexamine that." Knox glanced around. "Where's Fahad?"

"Supposedly en route," Vail said. "Should've been here already."

DeSantos checked his watch. "You were saying that circumstances demanded our involvement."

"Qadir Yaseen, al Humat's master engineer, the one likely responsible for all the bombings so far, is in London. Tahir Aziz, one of the men who escaped from the safe house, is with him."

"Why not alert MI5?" Vail asked.

Knox frowned. "Aden Buck and I are not exactly on good terms. He took a great deal of heat when I had to clean up the mess you three created. He resisted calls for his resignation, so he came out whole—but not without a considerable loss of political capital, which left him vulnerable and open to criticism by those in the government who smell blood. They know he's down so they think they can push him around. Bottom line, I did tell Buck we had intel indicating that Yaseen and Aziz had entered the UK."

"Then what's the problem?" DeSantos asked.

"He said they could not verify that our intel is accurate. In fact, he virtually denied either man is on UK soil. And we know he's wrong. We've got strong confirmation. CIA is backing us up, as is the NSA."

"But MI5 isn't acting on the intel."

"No. And here's the problem: Yaseen is too important an asset for us to lose. If he were somewhere in Afghanistan, Pakistan, Yemen, we'd locate him and take him out with a drone and a Hellfire. Can't do that in the UK."

"Which might be why he's there," Vail said.

Knox tilted his chin back. "We think he's there to oversee another attack."

"I guess that shouldn't be a surprise."

"Isn't that England's problem?" DeSantos asked. "If they're not going to act on confirmed intel, that's their choice."

Knox swung both arms behind his back. "Theoretically, yes. But England's our closest ally and a strike against the UK is a strike against us. So we're going to help them—even if they don't want it. And in spite of the animosity their MI5 director general harbors against us."

"Why us?" Vail asked. "The risk of us being seen—and ID'd—is very high."

"Because we have contacts there," DeSantos said.

Knox nodded. "I assume that's still the situation?" He made eye contact with each of them. "Or is that a poor assumption?"

"To my knowledge," Vail said, "nothing's changed. But if Buck doesn't want his agents cooperating with us, our sources may not want to risk their careers." *Like we'd be doing.*

"Then let's make sure Aden Buck doesn't know you're in country. That's a good idea, anyway."

"So no contact with Buck whatsoever," Uzi said.

"None. You have a problem, you're on your own. You can't call me. You can't call Buck. You can't call the embassy. This is a deniable op. Your presence on UK soil can't come back at the US."

Uh, wait a minute. When exactly did I sign up for this?

"Agent Vail?" Knox was looking directly at her. "You have a problem?"

Vail glanced at DeSantos, whose expression said, "Keep your mouth shut." "Honestly, sir, if I've got a choice, I'd rather not—"

"You don't have a choice. Simply put, Agent Vail, when you got your asses in hot water and I risked everything to clear your names—or at least to the extent possible—you signed an unofficial contract with me. This is an assignment you cannot refuse."

Before Vail could object—and she was thinking about it—DeSantos intervened. He lifted Vail's hand and gestured toward the engagement ring.

"You can't take that with you."

Knox extended a hand.

She looked at Knox and hesitated. *Well, shit, if I can't trust the director of the FBI . . .* She stood there a moment, her right hand grasping the ring. *C'mon, Karen, you think about it any longer, it's gonna look weird.* She finally pulled it off and handed it to Knox. She suddenly felt naked.

"What's our objective?" Uzi asked. "Assuming we locate Yaseen, how are we going to get him out of the UK?"

"In a body bag. Your orders are to eliminate him. We've had enough of his handiwork. After you make a positive ID, leave his rotting corpse in the UK—or even better, drop it on Buck's doorstep." He shook his head. "Asshole."

"Why not go above his head?" Vail asked, massaging her bare finger.

"That'd have to be handled diplomatically. Secretary McNamara did not feel that going directly to the interior minister was the right move. He'd be more inclined to trust Buck's assessment than ours. And if we want to have any hope of cooperating with MI5 in the future, going over the director general's head is a sure way to put a deep frost on our relationship for years to come. Even if Yaseen never set off a bomb in the UK, if he succeeded in screwing up relations between the FBI and MI5, he'd have hit the jackpot."

An alarm beeped on Knox's phone. He silenced it then said, "Are we clear? Any questions?"

Yeah. How do I unenlist?

It was DeSantos who replied that they were good.

Speak for yourself, Hector.

"When you've completed your mission, proceed to the Royal Air Base, where the C-17 will be fueled and ready to go."

"No Osprey this time, eh?" Uzi asked.

Knox's face broadened slightly. "That's funny."

No, it's not.

Knox handed DeSantos a small satchel, then turned and headed back toward the Black Hawk.

"A word of advice," DeSantos said as he watched Knox walk off. "The C-17's an impressive plane, an engineering marvel and a jewel on the battlefield in terms of moving heavy machinery and troops around. But not so much for creature comforts when nature calls."

Vail cricked her neck. "Come again?"

"You urinate out a little chute along the fuselage. No privacy. Go now or forever hold your pee." He winked, then bent down and gathered up his duffel as a Humvee pulled up in front of the PX.

Vail decided to take DeSantos's advice and started back toward the PX to use the facilities when the Humvee's door opened. Out stepped Mahmoud El-Fahad.

AT THE SIGHT OF FAHAD HEADING IN THEIR DIRECTION, Uzi was conflicted. He desperately wanted more information before confronting the man on his whereabouts and his meet with Amer Madari. But they were about to embark on a dangerous mission, one that required complete trust in your team members. It was now or never.

They met halfway and Uzi handed Fahad his duffel. As they walked back to the Humvee, DeSantos gave him a rundown of their mission based on the information Knox had provided.

By the time he finished, they arrived at the flight line, where the Boeing C-17 Globemaster III was waiting, engines hot. The exterior was painted a matte gray, with the tail call sign emblazoned with "McGuire" in yellow letters on a blue background. The cargo plane was massive, with four jet engines and several sets of wheels beneath the fuselage.

They climbed up the rear ramp and took a look around. The cargo hold was a no-frills shell with wires snaking along the ceiling, levers and coiled cargo straps in open cubbies along the cabin wall, and a nonskid metal floor. While it had a utilitarian look, this plane was relatively new and well maintained.

They pulled down the nylon sidewall seats that lined the periphery of the cabin. Uzi and Vail sat next to each other, while DeSantos and Fahad took positions opposite them on the other side of the fuselage. A tank sat strapped down in the middle, forward of their location, with pallets of crates secured in the center of the hold.

"I booked business class," Vail said. "Where the hell's my cheese plate?"

"Ring the call button," DeSantos said.

"Mo," Uzi shouted across the hold, "you owe us an explanation."

"An explanation. For what?"

Uzi snorted. "For going off the grid. We tried reaching you throughout the day. You didn't reply."

"I didn't think it was important."

DeSantos twisted in his seat to face Fahad. "How would you know?"

Uzi tilted his head. "Where were you?"

"In the city, following up on some things."

They waited, but Fahad busied himself with tightening his harness and did not elaborate.

"Secure yourselves," the loadmaster yelled in from the open tail. "Closing up shop. Oh—the parachutes are in those kit bags up against the bulkhead. We'll be dropping you thirty miles due east of London."

"Wait," Vail said. "What?"

The man laughed. "Relax, just givin' you shit. The disposable earplugs are in that box by your feet. See you across the pond."

DeSantos waved acknowledgment and the large ramp started rising, the exterior light disappearing as the metal door closed with a low groan that sounded like a garbage truck picking up a trash bin.

"How do you know Amer Madari?" Uzi asked above the din.

Vail turned to Uzi. "Who's Amer Madari?"

"Yeah," Fahad said. "Who's Amer—Madari, you said?"

"Don't bullshit me," Uzi said firmly. "I know you met with him this morning." He was talking to be heard over the ambient noise, but his demeanor, and perhaps his tone, made it sound as if he was angry and shouting.

"And how would you know that?"

"Amer Madari," Uzi said, turning to Vail but speaking so that DeSantos could hear him, "has been to Pakistan, Syria, and Gaza the past couple of years."

DeSantos was staring at Uzi, but Uzi could not make out his expression: He could tell he was not pleased. But was he angry that Uzi had been spying on his team member or was he angry that Uzi had not mentioned it earlier? Or both?

"Why were you meeting with him?"

"I'm CIA, Uzi. Sometimes we go dark to follow up on leads. I'm on this team because I'm Palestinian, because I'm trusted in the Arab community, because I have *contacts* in the community. Some of those are going to be suspect, some are going to have records, some may even have a history in terrorism. It's no different than you meeting with a confidential informant who uses drugs or who's committed a felony or who's—"

"Blown stuff up?"

"Yeah. Even someone who's blown stuff up."

"And what about your nephew?"

Fahad's face blanched. The rattle and the rocking motion of the fuselage, as the plane gained speed and rolled along the runway, made his head bob left and right.

"Your nephew," Uzi said, "the suicide bomber who blew up a school bus full of innocent children in Haifa in 2003."

DeSantos leaned forward, his chest straining against the seat restraint. "What the hell are you talking about?" He pulled his gaze away from Uzi and faced Fahad. "What's he talking about?"

Fahad bit his bottom lip. He closed his eyes but did not answer DeSantos's question.

"Answer me, or so help me God, I will have this plane turned around—"

"It's true," Fahad said. "I don't know how you found out about it, but it's true."

DeSantos, Uzi, and Vail shared a concerned look.

"You didn't think this was important for us to know?" Vail asked.

"Yeah," Fahad said, "I could imagine how well that would go over. The Palestinian, the guy you don't trust to begin with, had a nephew who was a suicide bomber, a radical. You really don't understand why I didn't say anything?"

"How the hell did you get into the CIA?" DeSantos asked.

Uzi chuckled. "I know the answer to that. Tasset gave you the chance to prove yourself. And he had something on you, so when the shit hits the fan, you owe him. Big. You'll support him, do whatever he needs you to do, because you have no choice. He's got a secret on you. Am I right?"

Fahad nodded.

"After we texted you to meet us at the crime scene, did you tip the sniper that I'd be at city hall this afternoon?"

"No—why would I do that?"

"Did you or anyone else you know, or anyone you're affiliated with, plant the bomb in my car?"

"What bomb?"

"Answer the question."

"Are you out of your mind?"

"No," Uzi said. "I'm lucky to be alive. So forgive me for asking tough questions you don't want to hear."

"I had nothing to do with that. Nothing." He shook his head. "Look, I understand this doesn't look good. But when I saw my nephew get on that bus and blow himself up, something snapped inside me. I knew he had these crazy ideas but I never thought he'd do something so stupid. But for me, it had the opposite effect. I didn't channel his anger. I realized it was a stupid, ill-advised idea. That's when I came to the US and started a new life, got into the CIA."

"Tasset knew who you were."

"I told him. And I told him I wanted no part of it. Not only did I not want any part of it, I wanted to help find others like my nephew before they had the chance to kill other innocent people." He made eye contact with each of them. "You have to believe me."

"It wouldn't be an issue," DeSantos said, "if you'd told us up front. Or—if you'd just been in touch with us, told us what you were doing—or at very least, that you had a meet or two. But going dark for a good chunk of the day . . . that doesn't work when you're on this team. We rely on each other to be there for each other. No secrets." He glanced at Uzi, then turned back to Fahad. "For now, we'll accept your story—and your explanation. We're headed into enemy territory, for lack of a better term. We all need to be on the same page. And that means we tell each other where we'll be, and when, who we're meeting with, and if we learn new info."

Fahad leaned back and took a deep breath. "Fine. I get it. I'm not used to this. I work alone or with a handler. I'm not a team player."

"Wrong," Vail said. "You *are* a team player. Starting right now."

He sucked on his front teeth a moment, then nodded. "Okay."

The whine of the engines increased and the front of the large plane rose. A second later they felt the lift and they were airborne.

Uzi leaned close to Vail's ear. "How did the assholes know I'd be there?"

"Be where?"

"City hall. The crime scene, the sniper. The guy who planted the bomb in my car."

"You're thinking Mo tipped them after getting our text to meet us there?"

Uzi shrugged. "I don't know what to think. But maybe I'm too close. What's your impartial, rational opinion?"

"I'm your friend, so I'm not sure I'm impartial. I've got a roomful of people back at the BAU who wouldn't use the word 'rational' to describe me. That said, here's what I think. It could be as simple as the perps planted the radiological bomb. They knew we were in the city investigating, so when the truck was discovered, they knew we—you—would be there at the scene. No hidden agendas, no moles."

Uzi sat back and considered her analysis.

"Yes? No?"

"I have to admit," he shouted, "that was a pretty impartial explanation. And definitely rational."

"Would you mind engraving that on a plaque and hanging it on my office door?"

"Only if your boss is okay with it. He tends to yell at me whenever he sees me."

"Same here."

They both laughed.

"You know he's going to be my father-in-law."

They both laughed again. “Makes for fun Thanksgiving and Christmas dinners, I guess.”

As the fuselage jostled against the turbulence, Uzi could not help but wonder if Vail was right. Or if something more sinister was at work.

“These seats suck,” Vail said over the din.

Uzi let his head roll left, closer to her ear. “You should’ve asked the guy about your cheese plate while you had the chance.”

PART 2

"You will invade the Arabian Peninsula, and Allah will enable you to conquer it. You will then invade Persia, and Allah will enable you to conquer it. You will then invade Rome, and Allah will enable you to conquer it."

—Islamic tradition based on the Prophet Muhammad's teachings

"It will be the end of freedom of democracy and submission to God. We don't believe in democracy. As soon as they have authority, Muslims should implement Sharia. This is what we're trying to teach people . . . Eventually the whole world will be governed by Sharia and Muslims will have authority over China, Russia, USA, etc. This is the promise of Allah."

—Anjem Choudary, Islamist preacher
"In His Own Words," by Soeren Kern
Gatestone Institute, September 30, 2014

"They claim to do this in the name of Islam; that is nonsense, Islam is a religion of peace. They are not Muslims, they are monsters."

—David Cameron, Prime Minister, UK

35

Royal Air Force Mildenhall
United States Air Force, 100th Air Refueling Wing
Suffolk, England

They slept on the plane, adhering to the special forces mantra of taking sleep where you could get it, when you could get it. Vail thought it would be impossible to nod off given the environment, but the drone of the engines had a hypnotic effect, and without flight attendants or passengers squeezing by and bumping her shoulder or ill-timed pilot announcements, she caught a few hours before she felt the deceleration and descent toward the British countryside.

When the ramp lowered, the chill, damp air blew in. They powered up their throwaway phones that Knox had provided. They had a message waiting for them: Twitter was abuzz with exchanges between al Humat members and Americans.

"Can't say I've seen this before," Vail said. "Listen to this one: 'We're in your neighborhoods, your cities, your schools. You're not safe anywhere. #alahuakbar.'"

"And the two-part reply," Uzi said. "Don't mistake our @president's weakness as a weakness of #Americans. US is as strong as its people and we are bound and determined to find you, make you pay. #Americathebeautiful.'"

"Here's another," DeSantos added: "'We're going to track you down and take you out, you POS. #askBinLaden.'" As he shoved the phone into his pocket, he nodded at Fahad. "You got a problem with this?"

"Should I?"

"It's your own people who are launching these attacks. Our job is to take them down."

"My people are not terrorists. Al Humat, Hamas, Islamic Jihad . . . they're killers disguised as religious crusaders. Truth is, they're a cancer that's made it impossible for my people to get their fair shake. So no, I've got no problem. Otherwise I wouldn't be here, would I?"

Vail nodded. "Can't say I blame the Americans who tweeted those threats. They're angry. I feel the same way."

"Difference is," Fahad said, "the four of us are in a position to do something about it."

Uzi pushed himself up off the makeshift seat. "So let's go do something about it."

THEY WERE DRIVEN TO THE BASE PERIMETER and given the keys to an unmarked sedan that could not be traced back to anyone—including the United States government.

With Vail driving, Fahad opened his jacket and pulled out four small oblong cases. "I brought us each a gift. Courtesy of the CIA."

DeSantos opened his and held up a pair of eyeglasses. "You trying to tell me something?"

"For defeating the ubiquitous CCTV cameras in and around London."

"Nice thought," Uzi said. "But glasses don't work. The facial recognition software basically ignores them."

"These aren't regular eyeglasses. Granted, they're experimental—but the concept is that the lenses contain built-in one-way prisms that fool the cameras' biometric algorithms. They make the distance between the eyes appear larger, or smaller, than they really are. The technology is pretty simple, really, and is based on existing lens refraction optical tech that's been around for decades. Only instead of correcting eye muscle coordination from the inside out, it works on the cameras in the reverse, from the outside in."

"But it's experimental," Vail said. "Meaning we're guinea pigs."

"Pretty much."

"Great. Glad we've got that out of the way." She took her glasses and slid them onto her face. "How do I look?"

"Very sexy," DeSantos said. "Good frames on you. I think you should keep them. Robby'll like 'em. Speaking of which, did you tell him where you were going?"

Vail looked at DeSantos in the rearview mirror. "You know the answer to that question."

DeSantos grinned. "Indeed I do."

She had told him she was going away for a few days but could not say where she was headed—just that she would be going dark and would be in touch if possible. He knew the deal and accepted it, though he was clearly not happy about it.

"So what's the plan?" Vail asked. "I assume our orders were in that satchel Knox handed you."

"NSA captured the cell numbers of both Aziz and Yaseen. Wasn't easy, but we're talking about the NSA. They're very good. We'll get to see just how good they are because when either of them gets a call, NSA will triangulate and get us a location. If the yahoos don't get a call, NSA will send out signals to ping the phones and get us a twenty. We'll then go there and try to find the assholes before they leave."

It was 1:00 AM when they reached the outskirts of London.

Vail pushed the glasses up her nose, suddenly conscious of the potential for security cameras—both police and private—everywhere and anywhere.

Uzi sat up and stretched, then looked out the side window to get a bearing on where they were. "Let's find a dark residential street. Without CCTV feeds."

"First," DeSantos said, "we've got another car to pick up. Divide up our assets. In case a couple of us get caught, we won't jeopardize the entire mission."

"Kind of like putting all your eggs in the same sedan?" Vail asked.

"I don't think that's the saying. But that's the concept."

Vail drove to the location of the waiting vehicle, left by a CIA asset, and dropped off DeSantos and Fahad before continuing on, looking for a location that met Uzi's requirements.

Twenty minutes later, three blocks from DeSantos's car, they pulled to the curb in a poorly lit neighborhood that did not seem to have any visible cameras. They removed their seat belts and stretched out . . . until a minute later, when Uzi's phone vibrated.

"Start the car," he said as he manipulated the phone to get the address. He read it off to Vail as he plugged it into his phone's GPS. She pulled away from the curb, taking care not to burn the tires.

"Where we headed and how far?"

"It's a bar," he said. "One of the oldest in London. I've eaten there a couple times over the years. The Lamb & Flag in Covent Garden. About ten minutes. Turn right up ahead."

They arrived nine minutes later and parked a block away; DeSantos and Fahad followed suit, approaching from a different direction.

Vail and Uzi headed toward the pub together, holding hands. Behaving like a couple going for a drink after a show was a reasonable cover and looked natural.

Fahad had no history in the country so he was at less risk than the others. Regardless, being seen in public—and potentially on camera—was a gamble for all of them.

Vail and Uzi headed down the narrow, cobblestone Rose Street that led to the front entrance to the pub. The area was relatively quiet, with only the low rumble of chatter from a number of patrons standing outside the bar, drinking at the ledges designed for overflow customers—a popular feature of many London drinking establishments.

As they neared the building, Vail saw a sandblasted circular Lamb & Flag logo in the top glass panel of the door as well as a couple of signs that caught her eye: a laminated no smoking placard and the more disturbing red posting: "These premises are protected by CCTV."

CCTV? In a bar? No wonder we were screwed last time we were in London.

Shortly after lifting off in the C-17, DeSantos had distributed photos of their two wanted men to review—and then commit to memory—before he destroyed the pictures. They had a fairly good sense of what Yaseen and Aziz looked like. The question was, were they still there? Or did one of them merely make a call outside on the corner before getting in a cab?

Vail reseated the glasses on her face. She felt naked—like walking through an airport full body scanner—with no true way of covering up. There was nothing she could do but hope that MI5 and the Met did not retain their biometric data. She did not know how extensive Knox's effort was in getting Aden Buck to purge their system, but she hoped it was substantial—and successful. If not, she, Uzi, and DeSantos were in for a rough time.

They sat down at the bar. The interior was charming, with wide plank wood floors and handcrafted chairs that were worn and nicked from decades of use. A shelf above the counter suspended by polished brass columns was filled with clean beer mugs, something Vail had not seen before. It was a cool effect.

Vail ordered a Butcombe Bitter and Uzi a Fuller's Wild River. They took their glasses to a side booth to get a better angle of the area. An order of fish and chips for Vail and a sausage in French bread sandwich for Uzi arrived ten minutes later, and they quickly dug in, not knowing when they were going to see their targets—or be called away to another location.

As Vail chewed her second bite, her phone buzzed. She rooted it out and grabbed a peek. It was DeSantos telling her that they had a good view of the upstairs bar; they had cleared the restroom and neither man was present. She set the handset aside and took another nibble of her fish. "Nothing on the second floor."

"So they were here and didn't stay long," Uzi said. He snatched up a fry and glanced at his watch. The patrons were thinning out. "At some point we're gonna have to get out of here. Fewer people, more we stand out."

Vail agreed and sent a text back to DeSantos suggesting they get going soon.

But they didn't have to wait long, because moments later her phone buzzed again: They had another hit, and because of the time—closing in on 2:00 AM—this one had more potential as being a place where the men would be remaining for a while, possibly even where they would be settling in for the night.

They returned to their car and Uzi plugged the address into his phone's GPS. The flat was in Greenwich, a decent drive away. "Looks like a half hour," Uzi said. "I'm gonna recon the area while we're en route." He pulled a laptop from his satchel and inserted a device into a side port.

"Where'd you get that?" Vail asked, glancing over at the computer.

"In the PX. I configured it on the flight over."

I was configuring something else. The inside of my eyelids.

"What's that thing you plugged into it?"

"A satellite internet transceiver."

"What do you need that for?"

"Uh, the internet? Ever hear of it?"

Vail gave him a look.

"I figured we'd be on the move, so we can't steal a nearby wireless signal. We needed something that can transmit and receive. The key is connecting to a server that takes satellite downlink and connects to the internet. It goes from my laptop to the satellite, from the satellite downlink to a server, a server to the internet. Got it?"

"I . . . yeah, of course." *Not a word. Well, that's not true. I understood "internet."* "How is that going to help us?" she asked as she negotiated a curve.

"I'll get a view of the area, what's around, what things we have to be careful of, that type of thing. Less suspicious than two cars driving around looking like we're looking for someone."

"And what about that laptop?" She gestured at the screen. "What if—god forbid—we're caught?"

Uzi was striking the keys, logging into the server. "I've got a strong password on the BIOS and the drive's encrypted with Bit Locker. And I've added some other goodies. They won't be able to crack it."

"I've heard of that Foot Locker thing."

He glanced at her. "Uh huh."

Vail watched as Uzi played with the trackpad, zooming and virtually walking down various streets.

"So Greenwich is an interesting place. You've heard of the term Greenwich mean time? Or Zulu time?" He got a nod from Vail, so he continued. "It originated here. I seem to remember a street where the meridians meet and the corner store is named 'The first shop in the world,' or something like that, because it's at longitude of zero-zero-zero."

"I'll pass. Sounds gimmicky."

"I wouldn't take you there anyway. It's only for intelligent people. Its meridian significance is lost on common folk."

"Good thing I'm driving or I'd kick you in the balls. Oh, wait, we're in England. I'd kick you in the bollocks."

By the time they reached Greenwich, a light rain had begun falling, shifting the overall mood from bleak to bleaker.

"Weather's interfering with my signal. But I got what I needed—I took a look around the area where the cell call came from. There are several buildings we need to check out."

Unfortunately, he explained, it was a densely populated neighborhood and the location data provided by the NSA was not as specific as they needed.

"One of the blocks consists of professional and white collar workers in the service, IT, and financial sectors. It's possible the tangos are blending in, using them as a cover, but I doubt it. The other area is a little lower rent district, so to speak, so that'd be my best guess. I told Santa and Mo to take the upscale townhomes. We'll take the middle-class apartment building, take a look around, get a lay of the land, make an educated analysis and pick our spots, then stake out the most promising flats."

"Not quite a needle in a haystack, but . . ."

"The idea will be to narrow the possibilities down by a process of elimination. But if we can't, we'll be stuck looking for that needle."

THEY ARRIVED AT THE APARTMENT BUILDING on a court just off Dartmouth Hill, a four-story series of three conjoined brick buildings. DeSantos and Fahad were parked a couple of blocks away.

"Multiple exits," Uzi said as Vail pulled into the small parking lot. "Those green doors at ten o'clock, eleven, twelve, and one. See?"

"Not really. We need to turn on the wipers. But if we do that—"

"It'll draw attention to the car. And it'll look odd that all the cars in the lot have rain-covered windshields except for ours."

"Yeah, yeah, yeah," she said, leaning forward and struggling to see out the window.

He pulled out his phone, put it on speaker, and waited the two rings until it was answered. "Santa. Status?"

"It's raining."

"No shit."

"Parked at the end of the block. These are like townhouses. Gotta be twenty units along this street alone. Hard to keep an eye on all of them. Lots of cars in driveways, but there are garages for just about every unit. To do this right we really need two cars, one at each end of the long block."

"I know," Uzi said. "But this is what we've got, so we'll make it work. We'll watch in shifts. Karen's got the first one here."

"I do?" she asked, tearing her gaze away from the apartment building.

"Mo's taking ours," DeSantos said. "Have a good nap. Out."

Uzi moved his seat back to a fifty degree angle and shifted his body to get comfortable. He folded his arms and closed his eyes. "Wake me if you see anything."

Assuming I don't fall asleep.

36

Yo, Karen! Wake up. Karen."

Vail felt a hard shove, then a poke. "Huh? What?" She sat up and opened her eyes. *Still dark. What the hell time is it?* She found the dashboard clock: 4:30 AM. *I've only been sleeping twenty-five minutes?*

"They're on the move. Start the car."

Uzi's phone buzzed. He answered it as Vail cranked the engine.

"Hold on," Uzi said, grabbing her right forearm. He listened a moment, then said, "Shut it. We're going in."

Her eyes burned and she felt like her head weighed fifty pounds. *More like a hundred. Just want to go back to sleep.*

"Going in?"

"Santa and Mo are coming around to follow them. We're gonna check out their flat."

"Can you do that? I need some sleep."

Uzi peered out the rain-streaked window, watched two men on foot as they walked about thirty feet from their car and headed toward Dartmouth Hill. Back into the phone: "Okay, I see you coming up the street, headlights off, right? . . . You got them? They're leaving the parking lot right now—" He peered out the corner of his right eye, attempting not to turn his head in their direction. "Cool. They're all yours. Going in. Let you know what we find."

Vail pulled her exhausted body out of the seat and gently closed her car door. The prickle of cold raindrops made her shiver. She tightened the muffler around her neck. "Why the hell are they on the move at 4:30 in the morning?"

"You're not really expecting an answer, right?" He pulled out his lock pick kit and had the exterior door opened in four seconds. They stepped inside and climbed the steps.

"How do we know which is their flat?"

"I saw a light come on in the room fronting the parking lot on the fourth floor. We should be able to figure it out based on that."

They reached the last landing, Vail's legs feeling more like lead than flesh and bones. She stifled a yawn but a low groan escaped her throat.

"Wake up and get ready," Uzi whispered as they headed down the dimly lit hall. "That's the flat right there." He nodded toward door a dozen feet away.

They walked up to it and Vail pressed her ear against the metal. She shook her head no.

Still, they exercised caution. They had their weapons in hand now, untraceable handguns provided by Knox—the Glock L131A1, a British version similar to the models they used in the Bureau—and, most importantly, not found in the United States.

None of them carried American identification; they were traveling on Canadian passports—a favorite trick of Mossad.

Uzi did his thing with the lock and Vail quietly opened the door, moving slowly with the barrel of her pistol leading the way.

The place was dark. Her eyes were adjusted to the low light so she was able to get a decent idea of the flat's layout. Had there been someone sitting still in the corner, however, she never would have seen him.

They silently closed the door behind them. Splitting up, they cleared the rooms and reconvened a moment later in the kitchen. The flat was sparse, a fully furnished rental by the looks of it, with two or three men occupying the residence.

"What are we looking for?" Vail asked in hushed voice. There was no one there, but it was the middle of the night and they did not know how well sound traveled between the units.

"Anything and everything. But if you see a computer, let me know."

"Desktop in the bedroom at the end of the hall."

"Show me."

Vail led him to it, and he reholstered his weapon. "You're on point. Someone comes in that door—"

"I'll be sure to tell him how atrocious the furniture is, that the place needs a woman's touch."

"Stay alert and don't nod off. We have no idea if anyone else lives here and is on his way home from the local pub this very minute."

Shit. Good point.

Uzi woke the computer and the logon screen asked for the password. "Crap. This is gonna take a little longer than I'd hoped."

37

DeSantos was riding shotgun, leaning forward, peering into the dreary darkness. It had stopped raining but the streets were shiny and their tires made unwanted whooshing noise as they drove.

"Oh Jesus," DeSantos said. "A traffic circle?"

"Bloody useless if you ask me. It's a tiny intersection. What's the point? More work than just a simple four-way stop sign."

The vehicle turned, avoiding the roundabout. "Stay with him," DeSantos said. "It's your lucky day. Left turns in the UK don't go through the stupid circle." He glanced at Fahad. "Did you say 'bloody'?"

"Trying to get into the vernacular," Fahad said. "If you think like the locals, better chance your cover stays intact."

"You're schooling me in undercover work?"

Fahad picked up speed a bit and turned as directed, following the car onto Wat Tyler Road. "I don't like this, Hector. It's not well lit, but it's the middle of the night and there are no cars out. Except theirs. And ours."

"Just stay with them. If they make us, we'll deal with it."

DeSantos fired up his phone's GPS and started following along on the screen, using his left hand as a shield to keep the light from illuminating their interior. "Coming up on Shooters Hill Road." He looked up just in time to see the vehicle ahead of them accelerate and hang a sharp right.

"Time to deal with it. They made us."

"I can see that, Mo. Stay with them. And put our goddamn lights on. No point in trying to do a high speed pursuit without being able to see where we're going."

Fahad did as suggested and said, "They're in a Fiat. We should be able to make up some ground."

As predicted, they closed the gap. The perps swung left onto Hyde Vale, a curving residential street with tall brick apartment buildings on the left and a wooded, hilly landscape to their right.

The Fiat hit a speed bump well in excess of the safe rate of travel for the road and they lost control, skidding on the slick asphalt and slamming into a blue panel van on the right before bouncing off it and careening into a station wagon.

"Whoa! Slow down, slow down," DeSantos yelled. A man jumped out of the back door of the Fiat and took off on foot up the hill into the blind of trees. The sedan then sped off, down Hyde Vale.

"Shit," Fahad said as he brought the sedan to a stop. "I'll take the guy, you follow the car."

Fahad got out and DeSantos slid behind the wheel, shoved the shift into first and went in pursuit of the Fiat. In the rearview mirror, he saw Fahad sprint after his man before disappearing into the pitch darkness of the trees.

As they sped down the curving road, the area turned more residential, the buildings mostly single brick-and-stone homes set back off Hyde Vale with lawns and landscaping out front.

DeSantos drove hard and caught up to the Fiat—which had a flat left rear tire.

He rolled down the window, then reached into his jacket and pulled out his Glock. One advantage of driving in the UK was that with the steering wheel on the opposite side of the car, his right hand was free to shoot.

He leaned out, lined up the tritium sights, and squeezed the trigger. One shot at a time to minimize noise and attention. After firing three rounds, he realized he was succeeding in nothing but generating calls to the Met—something they definitely did not want.

The driver of the Fiat was a persistent little twat because he kept going, turning right onto Royal Hill and swerving through the business district—book shops, pubs, apartments, and more pubs—as a light or two snapped on in response to the ruckus the sedan was making as its backside scraped along the pavement.

DeSantos was trying to make out the layout of the road ahead, hoping to find a stretch that would be wide enough for him to come up alongside the Fiat and force it against the curb.

As he passed Burney Street to his right, Royal Hill opened up into a two lane road. But before DeSantos could accelerate, the Fiat hung a right onto a main drag, in what looked like a commercial district. A strip mall—or London's equivalent—was ahead and he passed a storefront with bold orange and blue signage that read, "ISIS Greenwich Education."

DeSantos laughed—this was probably not a good time to be in business with a company named "ISIS" anything.

The moment of levity vanished as DeSantos passed an HSBC bank branch and decided it was now or never. He had no idea where this joker was headed, and he did not want to be led into an ambush.

He accelerated and veered left to come around, but the Fiat countered by swerving into the center of the road.

DeSantos reached into his jacket again and pulled out the Glock. "Enough." There were few, if any, homes in this area so the risk of a witness or collateral damage was minimal.

With the third round he hit his target—the Fiat's right rear tire—and the car slapped down fully against the pavement, sparks emanating from the metal bumper like firecrackers exploding against a dark night sky.

The front doors opened and out spilled two men. They turned and fired on DeSantos, who ducked beneath the dash as he slammed on the brakes. The windshield shattered and rained fine granules of safety glass across his hair and lap.

He got out and initiated foot pursuit. They turned left in front of the Mitre Hotel, then passed O'Sullivan's Bar—and in the reflection of the dark windows, DeSantos caught the image of one of them running with a cell phone pressed against his face.

Warning bells sounded in DeSantos's head. He had no backup and he had no idea where they were leading him. But there was nothing he could do.

They jumped a low wrought iron fence and seemed to be heading back the way they had come, through a lawn in front of what looked like a church, then back onto the main drag, Greenwich High Road, and through town. These two guys were unfortunately fast and they kept DeSantos—a runner himself—at a safe distance.

They passed the Greenwich Market, a narrow cobblestone alley, where DeSantos saw signs for the Cutty Sark schooner.

He knew there was a rail line somewhere nearby, which could create complications. There were no trains running at this time of the morning but a station, with its myriad tunnels and passageways, could serve as its own means of escape.

They turned right onto Thames Street—and again his internal alarm tripped.

The men had led him into a construction site, which looked to be extensive. They disappeared into the darkness headed along a makeshift sidewalk that was off to the far right of the project.

DeSantos slowed, removed his Glock, and continued after them. He had not traveled all the way to the UK, chasing a well-known bomb maker, only to break off pursuit when he was close to apprehending him and his accomplice—even if the safer play was to pull back. And if one of the men ahead of him was in fact Qadir Yaseen, then the man with him was likely Tahir Aziz or someone of equal significance.

Still, he could not shake the bad feeling that this was not a random chase, that they had an escape route planned. And either DeSantos was being led to a convenient place for them to execute him out of view of a surveillance camera, or they had someone waiting to whisk them off to safety.

He pushed on, his feet crunching the dirt-strewn concrete of the sidewalk, when he felt a stiff breeze ruffle his hair. The smell of water hit his nostrils . . . and that's when he realized where he was: the Thames was dead ahead. Was that their objective?

As he pondered that, he saw signs for the Greenwich Pier—and the sky-blue pipework and aquamarine of the manmade jetty that projected three dozen feet into the river.

The two men were now sprinting for the pier—and off to the left, DeSantos heard an outboard engine moving quickly. And with it, he presumed, a small boat of some sort.

If that were the case, this would be his only opportunity. The men hit the gangway and ran down the incline, which dipped twenty degrees toward the water's surface. Pulling up to the perpendicular dock—and barely visible in the darkness—was a Zodiac or some other kind of RIB, or rigid inflatable boat.

It slowed as it approached the pier and the men timed it well, as they reached the mooring platform a moment before their getaway vehicle pulled up. There was no way DeSantos would reach them in time.

They jogged along the wharf's edge and hopped into the back of the Zodiac, its engines cut back to an idle.

With no other boats anchored nearby that DeSantos could use for pursuit, there was only one thing he could do: he pulled up and leveled his Glock.

38

Anything?" Vail asked in a low voice.

Uzi clacked away at the keys, stopped, waited, and then started typing again. "No. I'll get it, I think. Question is when. You find anything?"

"Place is pretty clean for a bunch of bachelors."

Uzi glanced up. "Find anything that resembles ancient scriptures? Like the missing Aleppo Codex pages or the Jesus Scroll?"

"Wouldn't that be nice. No, the place is kind of barren, actually. A few Korans, prayer rugs. Some porn magazines."

"You're kidding."

"Nope."

"Anything good?"

Vail gave him a look.

"Right." Uzi turned his attention back to the screen. "I saw you emailing someone. Nothing personal, right?"

"Actually, I was sexting Robby. What do you think I am, a black ops rookie?"

"If the shoe fits."

"I was posting to Facebook. A photo I took of Hector on the C-17." She winked at Uzi. "Yes, I'm kidding. But Hector's very smart, you know that?"

"I've worked with him a really long time, on and off for a dozen years or so. Of course I know. You're suddenly realizing that?"

"I'm not 'suddenly realizing it.' But I did just realize why he bought makeup for me and stuck it in my duffel."

Uzi went back to the keyboard. "Because he wants you to look hot on our op."

She play slapped him in the back of the head. "You're saying I need makeup to look hot?"

"Don't repeat that to Robby," he said with a chuckle. "The powder and brush are for lifting latent prints."

She stood up straight. "Yeah. I thought that was good, resourceful thinking on the fly."

"You don't think it was a bit sexist? That he put the makeup in *your* duffel?" A grin broke his face, but he kept focused on the monitor.

"Not at all. If we were stopped and searched, it made perfect sense. Last I checked you guys are as straight as it gets and wouldn't be caught dead wearing makeup."

"If we were stopped and searched, makeup in a man's luggage would be the least of our problems. We'd be in the shit because of the Glocks. We're in England, remember?"

How could I forget?

"He also bought me clear packaging tape, which I used to lift a bunch of prints. I dusted and photographed them, then emailed them to Tim Meadows. That's why I was on the phone. And yes, I deleted the email and the photos afterward with that ShredderApp."

"You're learning, very good." Uzi hit a key, waited, then pumped a fist. "Got it. I'm in."

THE SHOTS ECHOED on the flat waters of the Thames.

But more importantly, despite the dim light, they were on target and must have struck the inflatable portion of the Zodiac. It veered right toward the shoreline and DeSantos took off in a sprint around the timber and glass buildings on the promenade that fronted the pier and the foot path that paralleled the Thames.

He came upon a complex of large, regal, limestone-columned buildings—the Trinity Laban Conservatoire and the Old Royal Naval College.

Passing the line of trees, he glanced at the river to his left. In the cloud-obscured moonlight, he saw the RIB, its outboard engine still running, heading toward the shore.

He hopped over the wrought iron fence and crossed the strip of grass and slipped between the benches that were normally populated with people watching the maritime traffic on the Thames.

DeSantos climbed another railing and landed in the coarse sand of the river's edge. As he drew his Glock, he realized that the Zodiac had caught on something because it was stuck about a dozen feet away, its engine still running. More disturbingly, he did not see anyone in it.

How can that be? He saw them get in and pull away from the dock.

DeSantos looked around: no one was in the vicinity. He removed his cell phone and set it down beside the pistol on the beach. He patted down his pants to make sure he did not have anything else that would be damaged by the water, then drew his Boker Recurve knife and waded into the cold Thames.

After his last experience in the river, he had learned that the temperature was around sixty-five—not dangerous but certainly uncomfortable in the winter. Of greater concern was the water quality—severe bacterial infections like leptospirosis were common, and dangerous. He was taking a significant risk by wading in, but as he so often had told himself over the years when he found himself in do-or-die situations, he had done worse things in his career.

As he waded toward the Zodiac, he realized it was not a RIB but an IBS, also known as "inflatable boat–small," which sported a rigid rollup deck. Both were military grade vessels used by Special Forces operators, not undertrained terrorist suicide bombers. They were dealing with a different breed here: dangerous, well funded mercenaries who had a sense of what they were doing.

By the time he reached the Zodiac, he was hip deep in the filthy water.

He carefully peered inside—and saw a single body laid out in the floor of the boat. The man was not moving and he had no weapon in his hands. DeSantos flipped the knife closed and clipped it to his shirt, then pulled himself into the inflatable. He cut the engine, which he noticed was a 55-horsepower outboard, and glanced around: no sign of where the others might have gone. They had not left anything of use behind.

But he had to deal with the body—fast, before law enforcement responded. The Metropolitan Police had a marine division with stations strategically located along the Thames. Where the closest one was, he had no idea.

Was it better that they found the dead tango? Would Buck then take Knox's warning more seriously? Or was it worse because DeSantos's forensics were all over the crime scene, thus telling Buck he's in London and severely handicapping their ability to carry out their mission?

As he parsed the scenarios of what would happen if they found the corpse, he became aware of the ticking clock in his head.

They were on UK soil to take care of business—and at this point, involvement from Scotland Yard or MI5 could hamper their ability to do their job. No, this body had to be disposed of . . . or at least the discovery delayed as long as possible.

There was no pulse but there was a rather gruesome head wound. He patted down the man, removed his billfold and a mobile, then shoved the former into his own pocket and used the camera to take photos of the tango's face. One thing was certain: he was not Yaseen or Aziz.

After wiping off the phone's screen, he pressed the deceased's fingers against the glass. He was not sure they could lift a clear latent off it, but it was the best he could do under the circumstances. He huffed on the surface and was able to see a print. Whether it was good enough to run through a database for comparison remained to be seen.

He looked around at the swiftly moving but smooth Thames water, wondering what happened to the other men that had to have been in the Zodiac.

Did they bail when he had started shooting? They had to be in the water. Dead? Or did they escape to the shore on the other side of the river?

Given all the gunshots, he was running low on time and high on risk. DeSantos put the mobile in his shirt pocket, then lowered himself back into the cold water. He felt around the boat's exterior and found the source of entanglement. He removed the Boker and sliced away the fibrous mesh that had snagged the bow, freeing the Zodiac. He used the discarded strips of netting to secure the man's wrists and ankles to the aluminum deck's tie down hooks.

DeSantos had used these IBSs on a number of missions, so he was intimately familiar with what kept them afloat—and what made them sink. Using short, quick strokes he stabbed the inflatable's neoprene fabric in multiple places, making sure to hit each of the air chambers. Combined with the weight of the motor, it would put the boat, and the corpse, below the surface.

That done, he started up the outboard. The strong smell of diesel irritated his nose and he brought his forearm up to fight back a sneeze.

The roar of the engine in the quiet morning hours was like a jackhammer on a country road: people tended to take notice. He set the throttle at a low speed and watched the damaged Zodiac head back down the Thames. If he was lucky, it would sail a decent distance before it went under—and go deep enough not to be discovered when river traffic started in two or three hours.

The four of them should be gone from the area by then, and if they were successful in avoiding the surveillance cameras it would take time to sort out who was involved in this morning's activities.

DeSantos waded back toward the shore. His body shivering from the cold, his legs feeling like they weighed twenty pounds apiece, he headed toward the place where he had left his phone and Glock.

But before he reached them, he saw movement out of the corner of his right eye. He felt a sharp pain in his head as something fast and hard struck him broadside.

39

Uzi studied the screen. "Do you see a thumb drive anywhere? Or an external hard drive?"

Vail searched the bedroom, where the offenders had set up a makeshift office. "I've got my COFFE device, but that's only got like a gig of space on it."

"It'll have to do."

Vail pulled out the drive and handed it over. "You should run the program too."

"Roger that."

The COFFE was a program developed by Microsoft to aid law enforcement cyber units in the capture of temporary, cached files that disappear when a computer is powered off. The captured data often yield traces that a criminal does not realize get left behind when they open documents, visit websites, and transact business.

She pulled out her phone and tried calling DeSantos, but it went to voicemail. Fahad was next—but he did not pick up, either.

"They're not answering," Vail said.

"Just busy chasing bad guys," Uzi said as he copied files onto the USB drive. "I'm sure they're fine."

DeSANTOS WENT DOWN HARD and tasted the sandy silt at the river's edge. A blow to his ribs hurt like hell and he recoiled instinctively—but knew he needed to get up—now, while he still could.

He rolled away from the attacker, his intercostal muscles in spasm and dammit, he probably had a fractured rib.

For now, his sole concern was disabling the assailant who meant to kill him.

Despite the darkness—he could only make out the vague form of a large man in dark clothes in front of him—he was able to hear just fine.

And the sound of a round being chambered got DeSantos's attention.

But that gave DeSantos one bit of vital information about his adversary: he was not a professional—and he was not law enforcement or military, either. Any of those would not have to prepare their weapon. It would be ready to fire. Just like his was.

He rolled two more times and got to his feet—but not before scooping up his Glock. The problem of not being able to see was a two-way street—and it gave DeSantos an extra second to level his handgun and fire.

The shot was exceedingly loud, echoing off the berm to his right and reverberating off the open waters of the Thames to his left. DeSantos dropped to a knee and fired again, and the hulking silhouette of the man crumpled to a ball on the sand.

DeSantos approached slowly, circling his prey, ensuring that the man was truly incapacitated and not merely luring him closer to get a high percentage shot.

But his aggressor was still, and blood was seeping into the porous surface of the beach.

He approached, stepped on the man's wrist, and pulled away his weapon. DeSantos shoved it into his waistband and put his knee atop the man's chest. He was still breathing.

"Who are you?"

The perp spit at him.

DeSantos wiped his cheek with a sleeve. "What's your name?"

Silence.

"Fine. Have it your way." DeSantos put the barrel of his Glock to the right eye socket of the man's forehead. "Last chance. You have five seconds. Four . . . three . . . two . . . one." The man tried to spit again—so DeSantos pulled the trigger.

He rocked backward off the assailant's body and patted him down, finding nothing other than a cell phone. He turned it on and took a photo of the man's face. It was a good likeness, other than the blown-out orbit.

He wiped off the screen and went through the same procedure of pressing the man's fingers against the glass. He tried to catch the stray moonlight to see if it had worked, but it was too dark.

DeSantos gently placed the handset in his pocket and blew air out of his mouth. His head ached from getting clocked and his ribs were sore from getting kicked. He had a problem—what to do with the body so that it would not be discovered for a while.

The best answer was to weight it down with rocks and set it in the Thames. Like the disabled boat, it would hopefully find the bottom of the river.

He gathered up as many stones as he could find and shoved them into the perp's pockets. He wiped off the handgun and slid it inside the man's jeans. It probably was not enough to overcome the buoyancy.

He gathered up his phone and dusted off the sand, then called Fahad. There was no answer so he tried Vail. She answered on the first ring.

"Hey, I need you to pick me up about, I don't know, maybe a hundred yards, maybe two hundred yards from the pier. Due east, along the shoreline. And bring something heavy."

"Something heavy?"

"Yeah. Like some bricks. I need to weigh down a body so it sinks."

"Jesus. I don't want to know, do I?"

"You do. But not now. Hurry. And bring me a bath towel from the flat and a change of dry clothes from my duffel."

"Be there ASAP."

"Faster than ASAP. I may have fired my weapon once or twice. Or five times. Someone might've heard."

"Terrific."

"And tell Uzi to be careful. One tango might've gotten away."

VAIL ARRIVED FOUR MINUTES LATER. She drove the car as close as she could to DeSantos's approximate twenty, but there were no roads that went to the waterline. She headed down Eastney Street, parked at the dead end, and ran the last hundred yards or so. The duffel across her shoulder flapped against her back as her feet struck the pavement.

When she got to an area that she felt might be near DeSantos, she called him on his cell and he directed her to his location. She saw the body lying on the sand and cursed under her breath.

"What'd you bring?"

"Found some bricks in the back, by the dumpster. I brought as many as I could fit in the bag. Hope it's enough. I've never done this before."

"I have."

Vail shook her head. "Life with you is never boring, Hector."

They prepared the body and then DeSantos handed over the phones and Glock to Vail. He dragged the body out into the Thames as far as he could reach—a bit farther than he had gone when he retrieved the Zodiac—and let go. At first the corpse remained on the surface, but with his help it took on water and eventually settled below the waterline.

When he got back he was shivering. Vail helped him undress and towel off, then slip on the fresh clothing she had brought.

"I won't tell anyone," she said.

"What?" he asked as he dried his feet. "That you saw me naked?" He turned to her and gestured with his right hand. "Okay, now it's your turn."

"For what?"

"I showed you mine. Now you show me yours. Then we'll be sworn to secrecy."

"Yeah. Not happening." *But I did enjoy the show.*

"Seriously. You think getting undressed in front of you bothers me?" He balled up the towel and shoved it into the duffel with the other wet clothes. "I've got a lot more to worry about. *We've* got a lot more to worry about. I gave up modesty a long time ago. C'mon, let's get back to the car."

WHEN THEY ARRIVED AT THE FLAT they hoped—and expected—to find Fahad waiting for them. But he was not there. DeSantos tried his phone—and though he still did not answer, he texted back:

on way be there soon

DeSantos related that to Uzi and Vail. He felt gross and thought he smelled like river water. He desperately wanted to shower but did not want to leave trace DNA behind in the flat.

"At some point one or both of those bodies are going to surface and they'll find this apartment," DeSantos said. "We need to make sure there's nothing that points to us."

Another text:

coming up the stairs
let me in
three light knocks

He showed the display to Vail and she made her way to the door. They heard a light shuffle of footsteps in the hall, followed by the gentle rapping Fahad had mentioned.

Vail pulled open the door and he stepped in, looking slightly disheveled, but no worse for the pursuit of his man, certainly compared to what DeSantos had endured.

"Where's your guy?" Uzi asked, still at the desk, working the keyboard.

"Got away."

DeSantos advanced on him. "You're shitting me. I chased one of the assholes into the goddamn Thames. You were on foot. How the hell does a guy like that get away from you? You're a highly trained operative."

Vail looked like she was going to jump to Fahad's defense—but stopped. DeSantos figured she wanted to see how he handled the questioning. More importantly, she probably wanted to know if he was worthy of her support.

"It happens," Fahad said. "I had him for a good three hundred yards, but it was dark and he went into a blind, and I lost him among the trees."

"That was, what? An hour and a half ago? Where the hell were you all this time?"

Fahad squinted. "What's your problem?"

"Just trying to account for your time."

"Santa," Uzi said, still focused on his work. "Calm down. And lower your voice."

DeSantos glanced at his watch and turned away, waving a hand in the process. "We'll deal with this later. The one that got away may circle back. And if he does, and we're still here, he'll know we've got their stuff—"

"And their plans," Uzi said, studying the screen.

"You should've called Karen and Uzi, warned them. As soon as you lost the guy. What if he came back here and they had no idea he was on the way?"

"If it was me," Fahad said with a shrug, "no way would I come back. You gotta consider the flat compromised."

"Depends," DeSantos said, "on what he left behind and how important it is. Remember, risk is not an issue for them. A lot of these guys are suicide bombers."

Fahad's jaw tightened. "I don't need reminding, Hector."

"I think you do. Because we can't afford fuckups. And so far I'm not too impressed with your performance. If we're going to trust our lives to—"

"Another time," Vail said. "We need to get our shit together and get out."

DeSantos shook his head in disgust. The sun was beginning its rise, the sky brightening—which meant they did not have much time.

"You two go take positions outside, one out front, one out back. You see the asshole come back, let us know." DeSantos gave Fahad a hard look. "Think you can do that?"

Fahad stared back but did not answer.

"Karen, anything that doesn't look kosher, ring us."

"Right." They left as Uzi continued clacking away at the keys. "Quick and dirty sit-rep?"

"Two got away, two dead. Did the best to dispose of the bodies but like I said, they're going to be found. Matter of time." He pulled out the phones. "But I got photos and prints. You?"

"Hacked the PC. Close to decrypting some of their documents. I have a feeling we'll get some good intel."

DeSantos went about printing the latents on the phone screens, then sent the data to Meadows along with the images of the two deceased men. He had no idea if they would get a hit, but he asked Meadows to check with Interpol as well. He hoped they were in the system somewhere, for *something* illegal.

When dealing with foreign countries, the results were less certain. In some places, bribes were paid; in others, police work was inconsistent.

DeSantos packed his duffel and went through the flat, removing signs of their presence. "How much longer?"

"Got one decrypted. Reading it now—" Uzi leaned in close to the screen and cursed. "They're planning something all right. On MI5, with osmium tetroxide."

"What?" DeSantos came up beside him. "Osmium tetroxide isn't stable. MI5 got wind of an attack several years ago. It never got off the ground because the stuff was very expensive and they couldn't find a way of stabilizing the chemical."

"Looks like they solved that problem. And unless we do something about it—" Uzi checked his watch—"they're going to launch an assault on MI5 HQ in fifty-nine minutes—just after everyone's arrived for work."

"Can you decrypt the rest on the fly?"

"Yeah."

"Good. Pack up whatever shit you need. We're outta here in two minutes, no more."

DeSantos pulled his phone and texted Vail and Fahad, told them to meet at their cars in three minutes, and he'd brief them en route to their destination.

"Destination?" Vail messaged back.

DeSantos ignored it as he gathered up his duffel, gave a final wipe-down to Uzi's keyboard, and shut the lights. They walked out the door ten seconds later.

40

We've got fifty-five minutes," Vail said as she fastened her seatbelt. "But do we have a plan?"

Uzi tapped away at his laptop keyboard. "The plan is to prevent the attack on MI5."

"And how are we going to do that?"

"Haven't gotten that far."

A moment later, DeSantos pulled up alongside their car. "Follow me."

"And do what?"

"We'll figure it out on the way." He rolled up his window and headed off down the road.

Vail followed a safe distance behind. "I think we should call Buck."

Uzi leaned closer to the screen. "Can't. You heard what Knox said."

She ruminated on that a bit. Buck was not a likely ally, but faced with intel of an imminent attack on the security service's headquarters, he would have to take action, right? Maybe not. He had not listened when Knox told him he had credible information that Qadir Yaseen and Tahir Aziz were on UK soil. Or had he? Perhaps he did check it out and could not verify Knox's claims. *What would Knox have done if the situation were reversed?*

"I think we should tell him."

Uzi shrugged a shoulder, still pecking away at his laptop. "Call Santa, make your case."

Vail dialed DeSantos, no longer concerned about driving while holding her phone. She got through her first sentence before he cut her off.

"Too risky. If our intel is bad, we're really in the shit. Do I have to remind you what happened last time we were here? We may not get out of the UK again without serious prison time—not to mention their new terrorism laws. Can't take the chance."

"There are a shitload of people working in those buildings. If it's a legitimate threat, we can't just let the attack go down without doing something."

"We will do something. I just haven't figured out what yet."

"What about Reid and Carter?" She was referring to two MI5 agents, Clive Reid and Ethan Carter, who partnered with Vail and DeSantos when they were on an island, literally and figuratively, on the run from law enforcement.

There was silence. She figured DeSantos was working it through, weighing the potential problems—she could think of a few herself—against other options, which, likely, included doing nothing.

"Obviously, since you're suggesting it," he said, "you feel pretty confident they won't try to screw us over. I mean, I got to know them, but you knew them a lot better."

"I know Reid and yeah, I think he's a standup guy. He knows what we were up against, that we were trying to do the right thing."

Uzi looked up from his keyboard. "No one can guarantee the actions of another. You sure about this?"

Am I sure? If I tell them no—which would be the truth—they'll back off. But I can't sit by and not do something. She glanced at the clock: forty-three minutes left.

"Yes."

"Fine," DeSantos said. "You still have Reid's number?"

"I can get it." She hung up and turned to Uzi. Can you get me a phone number?" She told him which Metropolitan Police station she needed to call—the one that Vail temporarily worked out of when she first met Reid. A moment later, he was reading her the string of digits.

She rang through and got a duty clerk who sounded as bored as he probably was. Doing her best to speak in a regional British accent—but saying as little as possible because she knew the more words she spoke the greater the risk her faux dialect would be laid bare. "I need to reach Inspector Reid. Problem with his nephew Brant. He's in a spot of trouble. I'm the headmistress here and he said I should call his uncle, a copper by the name of Reid." She chuckled. "He said he's a detective chief inspector. As if I believe that."

The clerk cleared his throat. "Well, right that, he is. Can you wait while I put the ring up on hold?"

Uh, I have no idea what you said. "Of course."

"He's in the building, I think. Just started his shift."

"That I can."

Uzi gave her a look. Clearly, he was not as impressed with Vail's efforts as she was.

A moment later, the muffling of a phone receiver, a muted, "What? I don't—" He stopped, then into the handset, said: "This is DCI Reid. Who's this?"

"Reid, it's your old buddy, the one you can never seem to face straight on. You always see me in *profile*. Know what I mean?" She didn't want to say any more over an open line.

"What are you—hang on a second, let me get some privacy," he said, pronouncing it with a short "i." After the sound of a door opening and closing, he continued. "Where are you? I thought—well, I thought I'd never hear from you again."

"That makes two of us. But let's just say it was necessary. And I've got something you should know about. Do you trust me?"

"Well that's as stupid a question as I've been asked since—well, since you were here last time."

"Thanks for the vote of confidence. Listen, we've come across some intel—"

"We? You're not alone?"

"We've come across some intel in a . . ." She did not want to use the term "terrorist" in case the Brits' GCHQ, or government communications headquarters, was monitoring calls and sifting for key words. "A tango's flat. Believe me when I tell you this is credible information. My friend hacked the subject's computer. There's an attack planned on MI5 headquarters in—"

"What kind of attack?"

"We're still decrypting files we found on the hard drive—" She turned to Uzi—"You find anything else?"

"Blueprints for the building, but I'm having to decrypt each document separately. Key thing you've got to know is that they're planning to use osmium tetroxide."

Vail put the phone on speaker. "What's osmium—osmium hydroxide?"

"Osmium *tet*roxide," Uzi said. "An extremely poisonous chemical. Even small concentrations gets into the airways, it'll destroy the lungs. It's got a chlorine-like odor, but you wouldn't think it's deadly and wouldn't even know you've been infected until hours later when you suddenly can't breathe and start coughing up blood. And die. The stuff is so caustic it has to be stored in glass because it eats through plastic."

"They were going to use it against us ten years ago in the tube," Reid said. "We had a snitch, found their stash before it went anywhere. Some of our chemical weapons blokes didn't think it would've worked because it's unstable and because the blast would've dispersed the toxin before it could be inhaled."

"Even if true," Vail said, "ten years is a long time. They may've found a better way to deliver it. Are you willing to take the chance it won't work?"

Reid groaned. "No."

"Here's the bad news." Vail found the dashboard clock and hoped it was accurate. "Whatever they're planning, it's going down in thirty-five minutes."

"Shite."

"My thoughts exactly. We're on our way—but honestly, we have no plan for when we get there. What about CO19?"

"If this were a preplanned infiltration, a specialist firearms officer unit would go in. But yeh, I can get CO19 there and the hazardous materials division. Maybe an SAS antiterrorist team too, but that'll take longer because they go through COBRA, the crisis management command center. There just isn't time."

They heard Reid giving orders to what sounded like a nearby colleague.

"Hang on a sec," Uzi said. "Reid—it's not MI5, it's Two Marsham Street. That's the Home Office, isn't it?"

"Home Office, yes. But there's also a block of residential flats, shops, and restaurants there."

"Yeah, but that's not the target." Uzi struck several keys and then turned to Vail. "The government, that's what they're after. There's an analysis of the building, how and why the release of osmium tetroxide gas was the best method to use for the most casualties—without anyone suspecting a thing."

Vail looked at the screen. "It's in Arabic."

"No shit. I can see that."

"I mean, how good are your language skills? Are you sure of what you're reading?"

"I'm pretty sure."

Vail looked at him.

"*Very* sure. Look, I'm telling you. That's what it says here."

"Did you hear that?" Vail asked Reid.

"Got it."

"This is obviously written by a chemist. I don't understand most of it—I mean, I get some of it, but . . . they're talking about using osmate salts and osmium trichloride hydrate to oxidize it to osmium, and tertiary amines to cause a ligand acceleration—"

"You made your point," Vail said. "About your Arabic skills."

Uzi looked up. "Sounds like they know what they're doing. This attack is a legit threat."

"So the Home Office is the target?" Reid asked.

"Best I can tell, yeah. There are several more docs here that I have to crack. But from what I've read, they begged off Thames House in favor of the Home Office."

Vail followed DeSantos's car as it turned left onto a wide road. "Remind me what's in the Home Office?"

"Lots of *people*," Reid said, huffing a bit. He was no doubt on the move while they were talking. "Immigration, passport office, DNA database, surveillance office, police national database, lots of research labs for biometrics, chemical profiling of illicit drugs, counterterrorism—"

"I get it," Vail said. "It's an important government law enforcement building and it'll be a huge blow if they kill a lot of people in those departments."

"I'm begging off," Reid said. "I need my phone to make some calls. And then I've gotta figure out how I know about this. Because they're going to ask."

Vail shrugged. "Anonymous tip. It's true, right? We never gave you our names."

Reid chuckled. "I've missed you guys. Life's been rather mundane."

"Not anymore."

"Right. Wish me luck. We're gonna need a bushel of it."

Vail disconnected the call. "Okay, so if you were doing this, how and where?"

Uzi sat back in his seat and thought a moment. "There are a number of options. It could be something low-tech or fairly sophisticated. If they've got inside help, it'd be more toward the sophisticated end of the spectrum, like releasing it in the ventilation system. If not, maybe a truck bomb that can be driven through a wall and then detonated. We know they're not afraid to die. Given their MO, that scenario is more likely than not. But there could be a dozen other approaches, just as effective if not more so."

"But one of the docs said something about the chemical being the best to use because no one would suspect a thing."

"Right. So you're saying no bomb." He stopped working the keyboard and thought a moment. "An insidious release. Ventilation ducts."

Vail handed her phone to Uzi. "Text that to Reid. Tell him what we think and why."

But just as he began typing, Vail's phone rang.

"It's Reid," Uzi said as he pressed a button.

"Put him on speaker."

Uzi hunted for the right key and then pressed it. "Reid? Just about to send you a text."

"Hold that. We just got an order to evacuate Thames House."

"I know what I read," Uzi said. "That plan was changed. It's the Home Office."

"You said you hadn't finished opening all the documents. Maybe it was changed back. Or someone senior superseded the change."

"We can sit here and guess," Vail said, "but that's not going to get us anywhere."

"Who gave the order to evacuate? Based on what?"

"Anonymous tip came in to the service."

Uzi returned to attacking the keys, but stopped abruptly and looked up.

"No. That anonymous call is a ruse. Don't evacuate. There's a sniper, he's gonna pick people off as soon as they leave the building."

"A sniper? Are you sure about this?" Reid asked.

"No, I'm not sure. I'm—I'm just trying to take what we know and put it together, try to think like them. In New York, they drew us to a crime scene where they'd stabbed a woman in the middle of Times Square. As soon as we got there, we were right in the middle of the plaza when a sniper opened fire on us."

"But who's the target?" Vail asked. "Anyone and everyone who works for the security service?"

"Could be Buck," Reid said. "The director general pushed hard for the new counterterrorism legislation. He said some bloody inflammatory things during his testimony before Parliament, not exactly challenging the terrorists, but fairly close. The PM was miffed, almost cost Buck his job. But it could've made the bloke a target. For that matter, same goes for the Home Office. They were closely involved in that legislation."

"Secure both buildings," Vail said. "They could be going after one or both. We think they're rigging the Home Office's ventilation system."

"And from what I can see online," Uzi said, viewing what looked like commercial property listings, "there's about 500,000 square feet in that building. It's huge. That's a lot of dead people in a very short time."

Reid sighed audibly. "You sure about this?"

"Stop asking that," Uzi said. "We're sure of very little of this. You're getting our best guess."

"If I had time, I'd run it up the ladder, cover my arse."

Vail slapped the steering wheel. "The Clive Reid I know does what he thinks is right and doesn't worry about the consequences."

"So what you're saying is that yeh want me to stake my career on a guess. And yeh want me to take it to my guvnor and my guvnor's guvnor and yeh want me to dae all this—and safely evacuate two massive buildings in twenty-five minutes."

"That sums it up pretty well," Uzi said.

"You know your accent gets more pronounced when you're stressed?"

"Shite."

Vail genuinely felt sorry for him. And she hoped to god they were right. "Good luck, *Mr. Phelps*."

41

By the time Vail and Uzi arrived at the Home Office, the clouds had broken enough to allow the sun to stream through. That would make surveillance easier in some respects, more difficult in others.

DeSantos switched places with Uzi, who continued on with Fahad to Thames House. The buildings were close—blocks from one another—but this was MI5's ballgame. Their role as covert operatives, DeSantos explained, was to observe from a distance for any unusual activity—and capture Yaseen or Aziz, or both.

Defined more specifically, "unusual activity" consisted of a terrorist with a sniper rifle or several glass bottles of osmium tetroxide.

"You're not serious."

"Stranger things have happened," DeSantos said. "But no, these guys are smart—and skilled. I don't think they're as dumb as the idiot serial killers you chase, the ones who get pulled over for a busted taillight with a body in the trunk."

"If you think my job's so easy, why don't you try doing it for a month?"

"I'd be too bored."

"Another time, I'd take that personally." She turned right and glanced around the street. "I don't think we should even be here. We've done our duty. All we needed to do was the right thing—and that was to notify the British authorities. The Security Service is now doing what they're supposed to be doing."

"So you want to leave."

"I think that's what I just said." Vail found a spot to park the car and pulled to the curb. "We're not welcome in this country. No, that's not true. It's worse than that. We're considered *enemies* of the country. If we're caught, we're in deep trouble. This area, with a ton of government buildings around, blocks from MI5 headquarters no less, is filled with surveillance cameras. *Police* cameras. Not private cameras that the Met has to jump through hoops to access."

DeSantos nodded slowly, as if seriously considering Vail's comments.

She kept her gaze on his face but his eyes were scanning the streetscape. "So why aren't we leaving if you agree?"

"Because I don't agree. We're after Qadir Yaseen and Tahir Aziz. We know from visiting their flat and hacking their computer files that they're hitting one or both of these buildings. If our mission is to secure these two bastards—and the documents their organization's holding—why would we leave?"

Dammit. I can't argue with that.

Her lack of an answer apparently gave DeSantos all he needed because he nodded and said, "That's what I'm talking about."

"What are the probabilities that senior guys like Yaseen and Aziz are going to be executing this attack? Wouldn't they have underlings doing it?"

DeSantos shrugged. "Don't know enough to say. This isn't a serial killer case where if you guess wrong, another two or three or five people die. If we guess wrong, thousands will die. In some cases, hundreds of thousands."

"That's the second time you dissed my unit."

"Not disrespect. Simple mathematics. The scale is just different."

She stepped onto the curb. "Where we headed?"

"There's a Caffè Nero around the block, right opposite the building. One of us can hang out there and keep an eye on that entry point. The other can go around the other side and try to look inconspicuous."

"I'll take the coffee shop."

"Figured you would."

"You realize this is a needle in a haystack thing."

"Let's say you're right," he said as they headed toward the café. "That means fewer important people will be inside pulling the strings, releasing the toxin. You're the leader of the op, wouldn't you be nearby to make sure all goes according to plan?"

"Too risky."

"You're thinking like a cop chasing a killer who doesn't want to die. These guys don't care. Success is what matters. I think they're going to be nearby quarterbacking the op."

Vail parsed that as they walked. "Maybe you're right."

"We may get nothing. Or we may get our men."

VAIL SPENT LONGER THAN SHE WANTED inside the café ordering. In reality it was only about twenty seconds, but she felt intense pressure to get back out, to get eyes on the target. She loosened her navy muffler, the warmth inside the store causing her to perspire.

She checked her watch: nine minutes.

Her flat white was ready and she carried the "takeaway" cup outside to the small patio out front. There was one vacant table and she sat down in a chrome and wicker seat. Two blue Caffè Nero banner signs stretched between metal stanchions, separating the sidewalk from the small inlaid glass-block piazza.

The Home Office building across the narrow street in front of her was divided into two distinct sections. On the left was a near-all glass modern structure, architecturally pleasing with a large curving corner. The right portion, connected to its adjacent cousin by a multistory glass bridge, was its design opposite: flat, rectangular, and fronted by metal framework that in itself was ugly but when taken in its totality gave off an artsy sensibility. It was topped along its roof by large rainbow colored glass panels: blue, white, and orange hues were dominant. The edifice was best considered an attractive sum of disparate parts.

Her eyes roamed the exterior as people moved about, many dressed well and moving purposefully toward the building's entrance, about to start their workday. Time check: six minutes. Assuming the terrorists were punctual. Assuming Uzi's Arabic was not flawed. Assuming they had the target right.

Reid had to have contacted his superiors by now. How long does it take to issue an emergency evacuation order?

Vail realized that the Met or MI5 needed to verify both anonymous tips—their legitimate evacuation warning to escape osmium tetroxide inhalation and thus save lives; and the ruse, designed to lure the workers to their deaths.

Vail became aware of a man seated two tables to her right. He had a newspaper open and he was holding it up, but he was not reading it—a ploy for staring straight ahead.

At the building.

He could have been admiring the architecture, just as Vail had done a moment ago, but his body language looked different. She glanced in his direction, noticing that he had looked at his watch repeatedly in the space of a minute.

Just then an intermittent buzzer emanated from inside the building. And then Vail's cell vibrated. She looked over at the man. His neck stiffened and he sat forward, his eyes darting left and right, taking in the situation as he pulled out his phone.

Vail lifted her Samsung and read:

> fire alarm going off. bad feeling.
> looking for snipers. you got anything

She tapped back to Uzi:

> strange buzzer going off.
> eyes on potential suspect

DeSantos:

> look sharp. whatevers going down
> it will be now

It was clear the tangos's anonymous call did not have its desired effect—a forced evacuation of MI5's Thames House—so Yaseen, Aziz, and company switched to a contingency plan to get the people out in the open.

Someone setting off the fire alarm meant an insider. At MI5's headquarters? Shit, if they've got a mole in the British Security Service, why can't we have one in the FBI? Or the CIA?

As that thought caused a cramp in her stomach, sirens in the distance pulled Vail's focus back to the Home Office. People were starting to file out of the building, some running. But this buzzer was not a fire alarm. Maybe it signaled the workforce to evacuate quickly due to an imminent and dangerous incident as part of a crisis management plan. Many large buildings, corporations, and government agencies drew up such procedures in the wake of 9/11.

She texted Uzi, DeSantos, and Fahad and described the suspect—a man in his forties of possible Middle Eastern descent. Hard to tell, since she did not want to let her gaze linger too long.

Seconds later, the man rose from his seat, folded the newspaper, and left it on the table alongside the coffee he barely tasted. Either he's MI5—one of Reid's colleagues who was alerted to the threat and doing what she was doing—or he was a threat, an accomplice to what was going down.

Stay or follow?

Vail waited a moment, occasionally glancing to her right to keep tabs on him. She rose and went over to his table and rifled through the newspaper: nothing written on it, no coded messages on a note buried within. A Caffè Nero receipt. Paid cash. His coffee cup had the name "Ryan" on the side.

So, Ryan, what are you up to?

She started down the street. He had a thirty yard lead on her, a safe distance that protected her from being spotted.

He turned right almost immediately, into what looked like an alley. Vail passed the Romney House apartment building and hesitated, concerned about pursuing him down a narrow lane where there would likely be only the two of them. But she did not know what lay beyond. He could disappear into a building and that would be that.

No choice. Follow him.

Vail hung a right onto what was at best a pedestrian way, with entrances to the apartment buildings that lined both sides. A street sign indicated it was Bennett's Yard. She didn't know who Bennett was and she was not sure about calling it a yard, but it was modern, the brick new and the mortar perfectly pointed.

Ryan was making his way down the path at a good clip, but it kicked left a bit and he disappeared from view for a second. Vail texted the group:

> headed down bennetts yard, away from
> home office. suspect in view. name
> might be ryan. doesnt look irish

She thought of pulling her Glock—or her Tanto—but remembered she was an illegal alien in England and did not want to get flagged on a surveillance camera with a weapon. It was the fastest way to get surrounded by CO19, the Met's "gun squad," a scaled-down version of SWAT that circulated the city looking for trouble. She also hoped to avoid the tactical Trojan trucks that deployed a team of armed officers as well as the three-person police units that patrolled in speedy BMW sedans, always at the ready and never far away from trouble.

Ryan passed the building's parking garage on the left and emerged on Tufton, another residential road with apartments on both sides. He hung a right and then a quick left onto Dean Trench Street.

He suddenly glanced over his shoulder and saw Vail, made eye contact, and then took off on a run.

Shit, shit, shit.

Vail followed, no longer concerned about preserving her cover.

Fortunately, she was a little faster than Ryan because she was closing the gap.

They emerged on a circular street—ironically called Smith's Square—featuring a large majestic building directly ahead, which looked like a church with a columned bell tower.

Text from Fahad:

> shots fired uzi was right sniper somewhere

Followed immediately by another message, from DeSantos:

> karen status re your suspect

She glanced down and read the display, but couldn't reply. A fleeting thought flashed through her mind: had they evacuated the building in time? If it was a gas released into the ventilation system, with a delayed onset of symptoms, it would be impossible to gauge the fallout until later. The employees would be walking dead—without knowing it.

Ryan, or whatever his name was, was onsite to monitor the osmium tetroxide's release. Instead, what he witnessed was the building's evacuation—which might have meant the attack was ineffective . . . or perhaps he knew it came too late.

I should've taken him when I had the chance, when he was just sitting there. What's done is done. Focus on the here and now.

But focusing was not something that would have helped her. Because as she emerged on Smith's Square, a pipe swung out toward her face from behind the edge of the building.

42

Vail ducked at the last second and avoided the blow.

She followed with a backhanded chop to Ryan's throat. He stumbled sideways toward a pay bicycle rack and fell, both hands gripping the front of his neck. It would do no good, of course, but it was a reflex.

Vail pulled a flexcuff from her pocket and strapped it around Ryan's wrists. She pulled them tight, then yanked him onto his back to face her. Her jacket got stuck on the handle of the Glock, and she quickly freed the coat, pulling it around and zipping it, covering the weapon.

"So, Ryan, you and I are gonna have a little chat. I'm Xena the Warrior Princess. Who are you?"

He shook his head, trying to regain his voice. "None of your business," he said, clearly finding it.

"It is my business. Because I think you and your buddies just released osmium tetroxide gas inside the Home Office."

His eyes narrowed: a look of genuine surprise. And he clearly knew what the toxin was. "Who are you?"

"I told you. But the question was, 'Who are you?'"

He did not respond.

"Is Ryan your real name?"

He snorted. "About as real as Xena."

"Didn't think so. What is it?"

"If you know it's not my real name, you know I'm not gonna tell you shit. To use an American idiom."

His speech was clear, his English neutral: not multicultural London English. In fact, not a British accent at all. Not practiced. Natural.

A siren groaned in the near distance: it was only a couple of blocks away. *Crap. Please don't come near here.*

Two bobbies appeared ahead, along the traffic circle, wearing their traditional navy top hats with the prominent silver badge. The scene must have looked odd, with a woman hassling a handcuffed man—and Vail not looking the part of a British police officer.

"What's the problem here?" one of the cops asked.

Normally she would laugh and tell them to go away, since the bobbies famously were not armed. What could they do, yell at her? Scold her? Ask her nicely to stand down?

"She's yampy," Ryan yelled—with a perfect British accent. "And she's got a gun!"

The bobbies pulled side arms—which looked like X-26 Tasers.

Oh, shit. When did they start carrying those?

As if that was not a bad enough development, a white BMW sedan with orange and blue striping screeched around the corner to her right, a block away.

CO19, the armed response vehicle that Reid called in. Lovely. That plan certainly backfired.

Ryan seemed to grasp its significance. But Vail was at a loss of what to do. If the unit stopped, she would not be going up against a Taser. They'd be locked and loaded. With lead projectiles.

And then the worst case scenario presented itself: the BMW pulled to a stop and three men jumped out.

Vail pulled Ryan upright and stood slightly behind him. "Stop right there!"

The CO19 officers did as instructed. But they also had Glock17 pistols pointed at her.

"Help me," Ryan said again. "She tied me up, she's demanding money. I'm just a software developer for the Home Office, border division."

Fuck. What do I do? I can't tell them my name or why I'm here or why I have this guy in cuffs. Or that it was actually my *idea to call in CO19.*

Or why I'm carrying a gun and a lethal knife. Shit, shit, shit.

"Back away from your hostage," one of the Kevlar-vested CO19 officers said, his weapon trained squarely on Vail, a black tactical helmet obscuring part of his face.

How the hell did this happen? "I'm the good guy," she wanted to shout.

That was only partially true. She was on foreign soil on an unsanctioned mission, with a rap sheet in the UK that included the murder of a government official. If they figured that part out, her finch was cooked.

Hector . . . Uzi . . . where are you when I need you?

The cops were still a half block away, a long line of blue bike rentals between her and Ryan and the officers.

"Uh, this man is a terrorist," she stammered. "He just launched an attack on the Home Office. Osmium tetroxide. Check it out, you'll see I'm telling you the truth."

"And how would you know that?" one of the officers asked.

If I told you that, buddy, I'd have to kill you. Crap, I'm starting to think like Hector. "Check with MI5," she said. "Agent Clive Reid."

One of the bobbies cocked his head, then looked at his partner.

Oh, shit. I just blew Reid's cover. My god, can this get any worse?

Reid was an MI5 agent embedded with Scotland Yard—that is, until now.

Vail started sweating. Her face was slick, her underarms hemorrhaging perspiration.

"I'm Officer Manning," the lead CO19 man said. "What's your name?"

Xena the Warrior Princess. "You can call me Al."

"Al," Manning repeated.

Thank god he didn't get the Paul Simon reference.

"Are you armed, Al?"

Only with wit and wisdom. But, apparently, sometimes not both.

"Answer me, Al. Weapons? And I'm not talking about diamonds on the bottoms of your shoes."

Ooops, guess he did get it.

"One more time. Are you armed?"

Well, there's my Glock. And my Tanto. "You're focusing on the wrong problem. This man here's a liar and a terrorist." *Will diversion work?*

"We'll sort it out, no worries, *Al*." Manning took a step toward her.

"That's far enough."

She immediately realized that was a stupid statement. She had no weapon trained on them—or her "hostage." Why shouldn't they advance on her?

Vail could not continue holding them off. Stalling was not going to work with these highly trained officers. And they were clearly more concerned with her than with Ryan. She would be asked to provide identification any moment now, and then they would approach and pat her down, and, well, that would not be a good thing.

"This man is a terrorist with al Humat. He's responsible for the attacks in the US and just now on the Home Office and Thames House."

"And how do yeh know that?" Manning asked, his tone firmer, angrier. "Who are yeh?"

This is the point where I turn and run. What happens to Ryan, or whatever the hell his name is, is no longer my main concern. She would do no one any good by getting arrested in the UK. Now associated in some capacity with terrorism, she would be handled differently and interrogated more vigorously. They would eventually discover her true identity, despite the covert nature of the op.

So Vail did the only thing she could. She spun and took off, back the way she had come, pulling out her Samsung as she went.

Behind her: Yelling. Running footsteps. Cursing.

She pushed the countermeasure glasses up on her sweaty nose and waited for the call to connect. *C'mon, Hector, answer the damn—*

"Being pursued by CO19, get the car, meet me in front of Caffè Ne—"

"But you've got the keys."

Are you kidding me? "Hotwire the car, call Uzi. Do something. If they catch me—" She realized DeSantos had clicked off.

Vail ran back into Bennett's Yard and saw the parking garage she had passed earlier. She unwound her muffler as she approached and tossed it to her right, just past the entrance. If they followed her into the alley, they'd see her article of clothing and—hopefully—think she had turned in.

Because the alley was hooked, they would not get a clear view of her, so at least one or more of them would have to pursue the scarf lead in case she had a vehicle inside and was attempting to escape by car.

Vail ran through the curved lane, emerging on Marsham. Metropolitan Police cars lined the curb space in front of the Home Office and bobbies were milling about the entrances. Fire trucks and ambulances were onsite as well, blocking portions of the narrow road.

The commotion would only help her. Regardless, she did not have much time before the officers who continued pursuit down Bennett would be upon her.

She turned and headed back toward Caffè Nero, looking for a recessed doorway—or some other crevice where she could hide.

As she approached the coffee shop, Uzi came speeding up to the curb ahead of her, at the far corner—Romney Street—going against the one-way traffic.

Vail sprinted toward the vehicle and he popped open the door as she heard, "Stop!" along with several footsteps behind her. She jumped into the passenger seat, slamming the top of her head against the window frame. She grabbed the armrest as Uzi hung a hard left and burned rubber, leaving the pursuing officers behind.

He made another quick turn onto Horseferry and then again onto Regency, where he pulled abruptly to the side of the road. He wiped down the wheel, gearshift, and door with a handkerchief, then handed it to Vail, who did the same. Just as she finished, DeSantos and Fahad drove up.

Vail and Uzi swung their duffels out of the trunk and then got into DeSantos's car. He drove away and put as much distance as he could between them and the crime scenes in the shortest amount of time without running traffic lights or drawing undue attention.

"Keep your head down," Fahad said to Vail.

She leaned forward and dropped her face between her knees and wondered how long it would take before she could feel confident that they were in the clear.

Vail dug out her phone and, keeping low, dialed Reid. He did not answer on the first attempt, but he picked up on the second.

"Things are a little busy, can I ring yeh back?"

"Would love to stick around but—well, you know how it goes. Before we leave, there are things you should know."

"Get on with it then."

"First—what happened? Did we call it right?"

"Give yourselves a pat on the rump. At Thames there was a sniper but he never got the chance to take a shot. One of our own had him in his sights and almost took him down."

"Who was it?"

"Don't rightly know. He got away."

Are you serious?

"Yeah, go ahead and say it: it was an arse fucking screw-up on our part."

"Surveillance video?"

"Being reviewed from multiple cameras. Don't have anything on the roof but they're checking to see if we got a few frames of him on his way up or on the street on the way to the job. If he's a professional, we won't be so lucky."

"And the Home Office?"

"Not looking as good. Took longer to convince them osmium tetroxide was a viable threat. I got it done but not everyone got out in time. Not sure yet how many were infected. But I got preliminary confirmation from our onsite hazardous materials people. You were right."

"A case where I wish we were wrong."

There was shouting in the background, then Reid's voice, muffled slightly by a finger over the microphone: "Deploy the robot and check it out. I'll be right there." To Vail, he said, "You said there are things I need to know?"

"You may have an infiltrator at MI5." When she explained her reasoning, there was silence. "Reid, you there?"

"Yeah, yeah, I'm here. We'll look into it. Take a while to do it right, but I'll let you know if we find anything. What else?"

Vail closed her eyes. She did not want to have to tell him this, but she had no choice. "I, uh, I may've blown your cover."

"I'm up to my arse in a major investigation. No offense, but this is not the time for a joke."

I wish I were joking.

"You are joking, right?"

"I'm really, really sorry. I—I can't go into it on the phone but just know that if I could take it back I would."

"Are yeh sure? I need to know the specifics."

She explained it as best she could without implicating herself as being the woman at Smith's Square who had escaped from CO19.

"I'll see what I can find out. Damage control."

"I'm sorry."

"What's the saying? Shite happens?"

"It's an American thing. And it's just plain old shit. Shit happens."

"You Americans want to take credit for everything, eh?"

"Take care of yourself, Reid. And give Carter my regards."

MINUTES AFTER VAIL HUNG UP WITH REID, when they had gotten outside the city limits and entered the motorway, she sat up and stretched out the kinks in her neck.

"Where are we headed?"

DeSantos, who was driving, looked at her in the rearview mirror. "Right now, back to RAF Mildenhall. Then we'll reassess, connect with Knox, and figure out a plan of action."

Uzi was seated to her left in the backseat, working his laptop keyboard, for the most part silent, clearly intent on decrypting the remaining documents. "Uh—holy shit."

DeSantos glanced in the rearview mirror. "That's a bit vague, Boychick. Can you be more specific? Find something?"

Uzi continued to stare at the screen. "Get Knox on the phone."

Vail pulled out her cell and started dialing. A moment later, she had the director on the line. "On speaker, Uzi."

"Sir, I've found something you need to act on immediately. I've got a captured document that outlines a small-scale repeat of the 9/11 attacks. A single jet."

Vail watched as his eyes moved across, and down, the screen. It was in Arabic, so all she could do was wait.

"Go on," Knox said.

"I'm translating the Arabic," Uzi said. "Looks like it's going down today—tonight—wait, New York is how many hours behind us? Five? Shit, it's going down—" Uzi's head whipped up. "Now."

"Details," Knox said, urgency in his voice. "Give me something. A jet? That's all you've got?"

"Freedom Tower, commercial airliner," Uzi said, skimming the document. "Refers to someone by name of Haydar. That's it. If we've lost contact with any flight, or if anything out of the ordinary is—"

"You're sure of this intel?" Knox asked, the rapid clacking sound of a keyboard apparent over the phone's speaker.

"We're not on a secure line, sir."

"No time. Give me what you've got."

"I'm reading encrypted documents we stole from a PC in the Greenwich cell's flat. Yes, I believe it's reliable intel."

"I'll look into it."

Knox clicked off and the four of them glanced at one another. Uzi turned back to his laptop and continued working.

Vail sat there, staring ahead, numb. Images of the planes hitting the Twin Towers played in her mind. She had seen it firsthand. Now, thousands of miles away, she had only her imagination as she pictured what was going down. She shut her eyes tight. *Not again. How could it be happening again?*

"The dirty bomb wasn't enough?" DeSantos said.

Vail shook the memories from her thoughts. "Maybe this World Trade Center thing is a contingency plan, in case the dirty bomb attack failed—which it did. The tower's a prime target, for obvious reasons."

A minute later, Uzi broke the silence. "Paris."

"What about Paris?" Fahad said.

"That's where these assholes are going. Which means that's where we're going."

"What'd you find?" DeSantos asked.

"Instructions issued by someone in command. They're not named, but they directed all fighters to report to a specific address in Paris after the London operation. I think it's safe to assume that the two incidents we just witnessed were the London op."

"Unless we hear otherwise," DeSantos said, slowing slightly on the motorway to keep his speed at the limit.

"Do you think they're gonna be able to stop that plane?" Vail asked.

DeSantos glanced at her in the mirror but returned his gaze to the road without answering.

"Got something," Uzi said, his fingers suddenly stilled. "A reference to two manuscripts, one of which was transferred to the Louvre for safekeeping while awaiting transport."

"What manuscripts?" Fahad asked.

He gave the document another read before answering. "Doesn't say. And it doesn't say where it's going after it leaves the Louvre."

"When are they scheduled to leave?" Vail asked.

"That's not in here, either. I've got a couple more files to work on, so maybe we'll get lucky."

"I don't believe in luck," Vail said.

"You may not believe in it, but you'd better hope we have some. The good kind."

◆ ◆ ◆

THE VIDEOCONFERENCING ROOM at Mildenhall turned out to be a small office in an older hangar. They filed in, shut the door and locked it, then got ready to call Knox on an encrypted video line.

"How secure is this?" Uzi asked.

"Military grade," said the major who ushered them inside. "We installed our own SIP proxy, and with a VPN and a variety of SIP clients, we made our own platform."

Uzi nodded. "Firewall? Is auto answer OFF?"

"Of course. No one's gonna tap in."

"You use AES 256 or AES 512 crypto?"

"Five twelve," the major said. "And yeah, we've got the high speed hardware to handle it."

Uzi shrugged. "Cool. Let's do this."

"You really understood that?" DeSantos asked.

"Didn't you?" Uzi asked, knowing that DeSantos had no clue what the man had said.

"All I care is that it works. Get Knox on the screen."

"Thanks, Major," Uzi said, then waited for him to leave. He clicked "Start secure communication" and moments later Douglas Knox's face appeared on the large LED flat panel mounted on the wall.

"We found the jet. They're using some kind of spoof on their transponder but satellites located it. A red-eye out of LAX. Since you were the ones to key us in on this, I'm patching you in." He gestured to Rodman, who was seated to his right. A wide-angle view filled the screen.

"What are we seeing?" Uzi asked.

"We scrambled F-22s," Rodman said. "This is the pilot's forward camera."

On the left, the nose of a jumbo jet was barely visible. In the distance, the brilliant white lights and red spire of One World Trade Center was outlined against a dark but brightening sky.

Vail's stomach churned. Her heartrate increased. And she struggled to get air into her lungs.

"We're attempting to establish contact, but the two men flying the plane are not the pilots."

The F-22 pulled back and the full fuselage was visible.

"How many aboard?" Uzi asked.

"It's a 757," Rodman said, "with 199 passengers and crew."

So 199 versus—how many are in the building this time of morning? Restaurant workers, maintenance and security personnel, tenants burning the midnight oil to meet deadlines. Five hundred? A thousand?

"Has the president given the order to shoot it down?" DeSantos asked.

"If necessary, yes. The military's taken over the operation."

"It's not about the number of lives," Vail said. "It's symbolic. Demoralizing to destroy what we fought so long and hard to rebuild."

"They're not gonna destroy anything," DeSantos said, his right hand fisted.

Uzi leaned forward. "Plane's over the Hudson River. If they're going to do it, now's the—"

Before he could finish, the bright flare of a missile launch filled the screen. A second later, the projectile struck the jet's body. It erupted in flames, small shrapnel flying toward the camera. The 757 veered left, then right, then the nose pointed toward the sky and the burning fuselage plunged toward the water.

The camera showed a black and deep blue sky, the F-22 continuing on its straight-ahead path, zooming past the World Trade Center to the west.

Vail, Uzi, DeSantos, and Fahad continued to stare at the screen.

Vail felt intense relief—but had to fight back tears. "What did we just do? I mean, there was no choice, but—I mean, two hundred innocent people . . ."

The screen flickered and Knox was visible once again, a somber expression on his face. "I'll keep you updated. It'll probably be several days before we know how they pulled it off. I doubt it'll be anything extravagant. We all know security on air travel is an illusion."

None of them spoke.

The normally unflappable FBI director turned away from the webcam, took a deep breath, and composed himself. "Right before you called me about the plane, we got reports of an incident in Westminster. You know anything about that?"

"We were there," DeSantos said, "warned MI5 of the intel we pulled from a laptop we found in a flat in Greenwich. But there wasn't enough ti—"

"What do you mean you warned MI5? Not Buck—"

"We utilized Karen's contact, Clive Reid. We helped minimize the impact of the attack."

Knox frowned: he still was not pleased but he could not complain. "Some sort of chemical weapon. Sounds like they're going to be looking at hundreds of casualties. Won't know for a few hours, but it's not going to be a good report."

"They used osmium tetroxide," Uzi said.

"Osmium tetroxide?" Knox's jaw dropped as he processed that. "We'd discussed that a number of times over the years but our chemists told us it was not feasible."

Time to hire new chemists.

"They aerosolized it in the ventilation system," Uzi said. "That's why they won't have an accurate casualty count for a few hours. There's a latency period."

Knox clenched his jaw. "Status on your two targets, Yaseen and Aziz?"

"We believe they were living in that flat," DeSantos said, "but we've got a forensic guy looking over latents we lifted. We engaged three tangos as they left the building. Two were killed, two escaped."

"Are the two dead bodies going to cause a problem?"

Vail turned to DeSantos, who answered. "Just a matter of time. I don't think it'll be traced back to me—or us—but it's impossible to say."

"I'll monitor it on my end. What about Yaseen and Aziz?"

DeSantos glanced at Uzi, then said, "Paris."

"Paris," Knox repeated. "Something I should know?"

"Another one of the encrypted documents I got off that laptop," Uzi said. "It directed all their fighters to an address in Paris after the London operation."

Knox sat back in his chair. "Mr. Fahad, you haven't said a word. Anything to add?"

He pursed his lips and shook his head. "No sir."

Vail's phone vibrated. She rooted it out of her jacket pocket and read the message. *Bingo.*

"Something you'd like to share, Agent Vail?"

"Text from Clive Reid. There was a sniper on the roof of a building near MI5's headquarters. We warned them about that, so they were prepared. The shooter escaped but the Met captured the guy's face on a camera before the attack—including an accomplice. Man carrying the rifle case is—" she consulted the Samsung—"Samir Mohammed al Razi. Other one is Rahmatullah Nasrullah."

Knox leaned closer to the camera. "Say again?"

Vail checked her device and repeated the names.

Knox's right eye narrowed. He swiveled a few degrees in his chair and started working the computer to the left of his desk. He looked up, exposing the deep furrows in his face. "As you all know, President Nunn has made closing Guantanamo Bay a major goal of his administration. Today he's going to announce a plan to transfer all remaining detainees to the US by overriding a congressional ban that specifically prohibits doing just that."

"How many are left?" Vail asked.

"Two years ago we released six hundred, leaving 149. Seventy-nine have been approved for transfer but nothing's happened because there were problems repatriating them. Thirty-seven are going to remain in detention without trial."

"Too dangerous to release but not enough evidence to try them," Uzi said.

"Correct." Knox reached to his right and glanced at a document. "As of right now, twenty-three are going to be prosecuted by a military commission. Five of them orchestrated the September 11 attack. But the big fight is over closing the place down. Of the men already released, seventy-four have gone back to battle as enemy combatants against us."

"I thought it was sixty-one," Uzi said.

DeSantos shook his head. "Classified Pentagon report prepared by the Defense Intelligence Agency. OPSIG was briefed on it two or three years ago. It was never released publicly. Seventy-four."

"Let me guess," Vail said. "Samir Mohammed al Razi and Rahmatullah Nasrullah are two of the men we released."

Knox's lips tightened. "Nasrullah escaped during transfer to the US. The first and only transfer attempted."

"And now the president wants to try moving dozens," DeSantos said.

"What about al Razi?" Vail asked.

"He was among the first wave we set free."

"There's government efficiency for you. Capturing them once wasn't good enough. We have to bring them in twice."

"No," Knox said, his face stern. "This is not an arrest situation. This is a capture and/or kill scenario. Emphasis on the latter. I'm sending you photos of both men. As far as I'm concerned, we gave the assholes a chance at a new life by releasing them. They chose to take up the fight again and blow innocent people up. They give you any kind of violent resistance, they get the death penalty."

And since these guys have no problem dying for the cause, they're not likely to put their hands over their heads and get down on their knees.

"What do we know about al Razi and Nasrullah?" Vail asked.

"Nasrullah was a fighter who was rounded up in an operation that netted us two al Qaeda leaders. He wasn't directly implicated so they didn't have enough to hold him and when they were looking for the least risky to release, he was added to the list. Al Razi's a different story. He's a US-trained sniper we used to fight the mujahideen in Afghanistan twenty years ago."

"That explains why he was the one to take out the MI5 agents as they evacuated the building," Uzi said.

DeSantos chuckled. "He could be the one who took the shots at you outside the municipal building in New York."

Uzi tipped his chin back. "Then I need to return the favor."

Knox faced the camera straight on. "Well, Agent Uziel, I suggest you and your team put yourselves in a position to get that chance. I want these sons of bitches. All of them."

43

Two hours later, they boarded the C-17. Uzi, Fahad, and DeSantos had used the time to plan, check facts, review maps, and connect with colleagues in the States to confirm intel.

Vail touched base with Robby. He was asleep but she decided to wake him since she did not know when she would have access to a secure connection. Their conversation was a bit one-sided, since there was not much she was permitted to tell him.

"We're making progress. That's all I can say."

"After all that's happened—not to mention what you asked me to look into—I've got a sense of what you're working on. And I just want you to know that I'm proud of you." He stared at the screen a moment. "I love you. Be careful, okay?"

Vail blew him a kiss. "Always."

They boarded the Globemaster via the ramp, along with the crew chief—but this time the tank and other cargo that had been secured to the middle of the fuselage was gone. The interior looked a good deal larger—though much darker, since all the lights were off except for a few strategically placed green fluorescents.

The engines roared loudly as the plane began moving down the runway. Fahad was busy with a piece of equipment on the far side across from them.

"Same deal?" Vail yelled above the din as she flipped the seat down, sank into the canvas, and sorted out her restraint.

"Same deal," DeSantos said as he sat to her left. "Except we're going to do things a bit differently."

"How so?" She found the clasp, but in the dim illumination she had difficulty locating the female junction to snap it home. "Can we turn some lights on?"

"White lights are a no-no at night."

"To prevent us from being seen?"

"To preserve our night vision," Uzi said as he tossed a duffle in her lap. "Refresh my memory. Have you ever jumped out of a plane?"

"I went skydiving once. Before—" Vail stopped herself and studied the thick roll straddling her thighs. "I went once."

"Good," Uzi said. "Then this will be second nature to you."

She squinted, not quite hearing him clearly. "What will be second nature?" she shouted.

"What we're about to do."

Uh, no. Not me. "It was a long time ago. I was scared out of my mind."

DeSantos adjusted his belt as the plane continued down the runway. "Did you do it tandem? Attached to someone?"

"It wasn't solo, I can tell you that much." She moved her knees to flatten her feet on the floor and shifted the weight of the duffle kit bag on her lap. "This wouldn't happen to be what I think it is, is it?"

"If you're thinking parachute, then yes."

"You guys," she said with a grin.

Uzi cocked his head at an angle. "We're not joking."

She studied DeSantos's face, then Uzi's, and realized they were serious. *Keep calm. Don't let them see you lose your bladder.*

"You rappelled out of a helicopter," DeSantos said. "Back in Vegas. You were awesome. If you did that, you can do this."

"Do you remember anything about the time you jumped?" Uzi asked.

"I was a teenager. I went with a friend and her father for her birthday."

"I mean about the jump."

I couldn't stop shaking. I almost peed in my pants. There's that.

"We're not looking to scare you. There's just no other viable way out of England."

"I'm not scared." *I'm going to scream.* "So how will this work?" she asked, attempting to keep her voice steady, using the need to talk loudly as a means to force the words from her throat.

"You sure?" DeSantos said. "You look a bit, well, clammy."

"I'm fine."

"It's simple," Uzi said as the plane lifted off the runway. "The C-17 will drop us at relatively high altitude near the French border. We'll land in an area far enough away from a population center. We've got someone there who'll pick us up in his car and dispose of the parachutes."

"Simple," Vail said.

Uzi pursed his lips and nodded. "Yeah. Simple."

"Are you out of your minds? I jumped out of a plane once, twenty-five years ago. I haven't strapped a parachute on my back since then. And you want me to jump out of the back of this beast and land in another country—illegally, I might add—without getting caught?"

"It sounds a lot worse when you say it." Uzi raised a hand, silencing her before she could object. "But here's the thing: you'll be attached to one of us the whole time. We'll deploy the ripcord."

"That's putting my life in your hands."

Uzi nodded slowly. "Pretty much. So all those bad things you said about me over the years? Now would be a good time to apolog—"

"How fast will we be falling?"

Uzi waved a hand. "Not very fast."

"About 120 miles per hour," DeSantos said.

Vail gave Uzi a look. "Yeah, not very fast at all."

He shrugged. "It'll only be a couple of minutes. Once the wind starts whipping past your face, blowing back your hair, you're really gonna enjoy it. It's a huge rush. It won't really feel like you're falling. More like someone turned on a big fan and stuck it in front of your face."

"Looking down at the landscape at night," DeSantos said, "it's pretty cool. We won't see a city, but the night lights are something you'll always remember."

Something tells me that's not the only thing I'll always remember.

"Can't we just drive across the border?"

"Karen," DeSantos said. "Be real." He must have seen her angry look because he said, "Okay, fine. It's a reasonable question. Answer is no, we can't. We're illegal, and even though we have fake passports we're taking a risk the authorities have been alerted to three men and a woman matching our descriptions who were seen near a terrorist attack in the heart of London that killed hundreds of people."

Uzi shifted his torso to face Vail. "The US doesn't have an airbase in France. Can't drive across. Can't take Eurail because there's a major passport check. Can't take a commercial flight because we're sure to be flagged."

"We *can* fly into Germany," DeSantos said. "The Stuttgart Army Airfield in Filderstadt. Then we try to cross over into France. But even with the Schengen agreement, if we use our forged EU passports, there's a border check. It's usually pretty quick, depending on how busy the border is at the moment. But it's a risk."

Uzi checked his watch. "One of us gets snagged, we're all toast."

"So," DeSantos said, "we fly over the top and drop in unnoticed."

"*Hopefully* drop in unnoticed," Fahad added from across the plane.

DeSantos gave Fahad a disapproving look. "This'll be a routine, overt flight over France like the Air Force does several times a month, following the flight plan they've filed. They won't suspect anything. The plane will be on radar—no problem with that—and once we jump, radar won't pick us up. Visually, no one's gonna see us till we're a hundred feet, or less, off the ground." He turned to Vail. "I've worked lots of drop zones when guys are coming in at night. I knew they're in the air and under canopy, but I couldn't see them until they were close to touching down. We've got a high moon so we won't silhouette ourselves to anyone who may be looking our way."

Vail shook her head. "What other things do I need to know about a mission like this? Now would be a good time to tell me."

"You're right," Uzi said. "It would. But missions like this, we've got no idea what the terrorists are up to or when they're going to strike—or how. So we've gotta be flexible and be ready for anything, improvise on the fly. Think outside the box."

Vail smiled wanly. "Boxes can be claustrophobic. I avoid them at all costs."

AT THE APPOINTED TIME, Fahad signaled Uzi and DeSantos that it was time to prepare for the jump. They rose from their seats and donned their parachutes.

"We're going to make this easy on you," Uzi said, motioning Vail up. "We're flying low enough that we won't need oxygen. It'll be a tandem freefall jump from a little under 13,000 feet. You'll be rigged up to Hector. You just hook up to him and fall with us. He'll do all the work and deploy the chute." He examined her face and said, "Are you with me?"

Vail shook her head. "I'm sorry."

"Did you hear what I said?"

"Everything up until you said, 'free fall' and '13,000 feet.'"

Uzi studied her eyes, no doubt trying to determine if she was attempting to be funny or if she was genuinely scared. He must have settled on the former because he did not repeat it.

DeSantos clipped a cleat to her harness, then helped her strap it securely around her thighs and torso. "I remember this contraption. Didn't like it then." DeSantos tightened the straps around her upper thighs. "And I don't like it now. That's a little snug, Hector."

"Sorry." He gave her leg a squeeze. "Good muscle tone. You been working out?"

"Kick boxing." She winked. "Remember that. Next time you try to cop a feel."

"Noted." He tugged on the thick ballistic nylon to test it, then nodded approval. "Ready?"

The crew chief walked over to a panel on the side of the plane, pressed a button and pulled a switch. As the ramp began to lower, a rush of freezing cold air slapped Vail in the face.

Fahad came up alongside them and twisted his wrist to get a look at his watch. "We'll be over the DZ in thirty seconds."

"Roger that." DeSantos turned his attention to a device attached to his chest.

"What's that?" Vail asked.

"GPS. I'm punching in the landing zone grid. Once we're out under the chute this baby'll fly us there, making course corrections as needed—left turn, right turn, and so on. At this altitude, it's all about the GPS."

"There we go," Fahad shouted and gestured out the opening.

Vail watched as the landscape below came into view.

"That's the English Channel down there." He was pointing at the body of water that fed into the Atlantic Ocean.

I'd like to channel something else . . . Superman, maybe?

DeSantos checked their attachment. "You and I are going to dive off the ramp. Once we're in free fall, hold your arms out at your sides to help us fly and keep stable, okay?"

"Can you stop saying, 'free fall'?"

"That's what it's called. We could've done a static line jump, where the parachute's static line is attached to the anchor line cable that's hooked up inside the C-17. As you fall out, the parachute deploys automatically. Problem is a static line typically has to be low altitude, hundreds of feet. Much bigger chance of us being seen." He examined her face. "You okay?"

"I'm fine. Just remind me to stop getting into airplanes with you guys. It always ends up with me doing stupid shit like this." She looked out at the lights below and felt her heart rate increase, her breathing get shallow. *Stop it, Karen. You can do this. Nothing to it—Hector's gonna do all the work.*

He tapped her arm and they moved to the now-gaping opening in the plane's rear, stepping close to the edge. The movement of the plane against the darkening landscape and dense cloud cover was disorienting, and Vail stuck her hand out to steady herself.

DeSantos leaned over, studying the landscape. He motioned to Uzi, holding his index finger and thumb close together. Uzi responded with a thumbs-up.

A green light appeared above them and DeSantos looked at it, then clasped Vail's fingers in his hand.

He waited a beat then nodded to her and they dove forward, into the icy darkness of French airspace.

44

The sensation matched what DeSantos and Uzi had described: like she was dropped into a wind tunnel. They kept moving through the chilled air at a good clip, flat and stable with the drogue chute deployed until DeSantos pulled the rip cord and opened their main chute. They slowed and glided toward the ground.

Vail looked down and saw a blinking red light from somewhere below. It appeared as if DeSantos or the GPS was steering them right for it, and she surmised the beacon was emanating from the person who would be collecting them and driving them to their destination.

A moment later they did a standup landing and touched down onto firm, low cut, perfectly manicured turf. It was a comfortable landing, followed seconds later by Uzi and then Fahad.

Piece of cake.

They quickly gathered up the chute and stuffed it into the backpack, then unhooked the harnesses and balled them up. If someone crossed their path they would look like lost hikers.

"Golf course?" Vail asked, swiveling her head in all directions as they walked due east.

"Golf de Dieppe Pourville in Seine-Maritime," Fahad said. "Upper Normandy. France."

"You speak French?"

"I was stationed here for a couple of years. I had to learn French as part of my assignment."

"That might come in handy," she said. "What's the plan?"

DeSantos checked his GPS and corrected their direction to a northwest bearing. "Back at the base, while you were talking dirty with your fiancé, Uzi and I were plotting things out. We've got two mission objectives in France: first is the flat they mentioned in that document we found on the computer in

London. We need to locate it, infiltrate it, and hopefully engage one or more of our most wanted men."

"Second?"

"Find the document in the Louvre and see if it's what we've been ordered to recover."

"If it *is* in the Louvre, what then?"

"Then we ask to see it and verify it's the one we're looking for."

"And how do we verify it?"

"We've been given some parameters. Basically, if we have reasonable suspicion, we'll make a request of the museum archivist or curator for evaluation."

"I've also got a backup option for verification," Uzi said, "just in case we need it."

"The CIA has set up a cover for you," Fahad said.

"For me? When were you going to tell me about this?"

"Now."

Smartass.

"You have a background in art history."

"Not the same as rare manuscripts."

"Close enough," Fahad said. "You'll be the person sent to the Louvre to examine the document based on a prior conversation you had with someone here who happens to be on holiday now. They won't know what you're talking about, of course, because this is all bullshit."

No kidding.

"If he's above board," Fahad said, "it won't be an issue. He can check out your credentials, which the Agency has constructed during the past few hours. You're a pretty impressive executive with the Museum of Middle Eastern Affairs in Washington."

DeSantos pulled out a night vision monocle and peered into the darkness. "If he's colluding with al Humat, or a front group, he'll hedge and deny."

"And then what?"

"I see him." DeSantos stuck the GPS device in his jacket pocket and gestured ahead.

"Hector, then what?"

"Then, we think outside that box you're so fond of avoiding."

45

They met up with their contact, a CIA operative by the name of Claude, who dumped their stuff into the trunk of his Peugeot. He chauffeured them with an occasional comment in French to Fahad, who was seated in the front. Vail was sandwiched between the large bodies of Uzi and DeSantos for the two-hour drive.

Heeding their own rule of getting sleep when possible, they curled up against one another and grabbed some fitful shuteye.

They were jolted awake by a traffic light somewhere in downtown Paris. Claude pulled to the curb and met a man who emptied the trunk, then filled it with four bulging dark-colored rucksacks.

"What's going on?" Vail asked as she rubbed her eyes, trying to clear the dried goop from the corners.

Uzi swiveled his torso as best he could in the tight quarters. "Claude is exchanging cargo with another operative who's going to dispose of our American-issue parachutes. And he brought us backpacks filled with a couple changes of clothes and a Dopp Kit."

"And how do you know this?"

Uzi turned back to face Vail. Instead, he met DeSantos's gaze. "She continues to question us."

"When do you think she'll finally get the fact that we're just *really* good?"

Claude returned and pulled the shift into drive. As they reentered the avenue, Fahad again started conversing in French. Five minutes later, Claude turned onto Rue du Champ de Mars and parked.

"These are your accommodations," Claude said in French-accented English. He gestured to the hotel a few doors down and across the street.

It was a well maintained six-story building with a small but welcoming entrance, which featured a frosted glass sign that read, Relais Bosquet. A black wrought iron canopy and slate tile sidewalk gave it a classy look.

"That black Smart car and brown Citroën in front of it are yours," Claude said as he handed over two sets of keys. "You need anything else?"

"We're good," DeSantos said. "Thanks for the ride."

"I did the easy part."

Yeah, tell me about it.

"Beware," Claude said. He turned to Vail, his penetrating gaze locked on her eyes, and said, "The police and soldiers are everywhere."

Shouldn't we be more worried about the assholes who are trying to blow us up? Vail looked at Uzi, then back at Claude. "Right. Thanks for the tip."

DeSantos pulled himself forward in the seat. "We'll go in pairs. Karen and I will hang out here for a bit."

Uzi and Fahad got out and retrieved their backpacks from the trunk, then headed across the street.

"So I noticed you arranged for us to sleep together again."

DeSantos consulted his watch and kept his gaze there as he answered. "Yes, I did, my dear. You got a problem with that?"

"I don't." She paused, then said, "But Robby might."

A few moments later, after another check of his watch, DeSantos popped open his door. "Our turn."

They got their gear from the back and started across the street.

"Claude's a bit creepy," Vail said.

"Is that any way to talk about a man who risked his life to help you out of a jam?"

"His eyes are strange. Not like a serial killer's, but kind of . . . empty." Vail took in the hotel's entrance as she stepped onto the curb. "Nice place."

"What we need it for, it's more than adequate."

They walked into the lobby, which had a warm, cozy feel. The registration desk was painted ivory like the rest of the earth-toned lounge, which opened into a sitting area with upholstered couches and easy chairs. Large windows looked out onto the Rue du Champ de Mars.

They were attended to by a thin Frenchman who spoke intelligible English. He checked them in, gave them a password for wireless internet access, and told them that breakfast would be served in the adjacent dining room.

They headed down the glass-walled hallway to the narrow staircase and proceeded up to the third floor. Vail used her key card and opened their door to yellow comforters, yellow walls, and red, green, and yellow floral curtains, with a matching headboard.

"I see the prevailing color theme here." Vail tossed her backpack onto the closest mattress. "How best to describe this room? Small? Cozy? Tiny?"

"Efficient use of space," DeSantos said absentmindedly as he examined the lamps, sconces, drawers, and LCD television looking for, presumably, covert cameras and listening devices. He turned and leaned his buttocks against the bureau. "Two beds."

"Other than stating the obvious, you sound disappointed."

"I enjoyed sleeping with you in London. Even if you did threaten me with that imaginary line in the sand bullshit."

"Same goes here. If you value your manhood, you'll stay on your bed. Remember, Uzi gave me that Tanto. Although I did read somewhere they can now grow penises in the lab. I guess that's something."

DeSantos scrunched his face. "Sensitive subject. Don't joke about things like that." He checked his watch then parted the curtains and looked out the window. "We'll grab dinner then walk through the mission again."

DeSantos unzipped his backpack and rummaged through the contents, then hung up the shirts. Vail followed suit, and a moment later they left for the Café Central a block or so from the Relais Bosquet on Rue du Champ de Mars. It was a charming eatery with white tile and red brick walls, and unfinished wood plank floors. Cigarette smoke wafting in from the covered outside patio bothered DeSantos, but the dessert pastries more than made up for it.

Uzi and Fahad ate at a nearby table but did not converse with them or otherwise make eye contact. They exchanged a few texts as to their plans for the morning and agreed to be on the road by 9:00 AM.

Vail and DeSantos would go to the Louvre while Uzi and Fahad would track down the location of the flat mentioned in the encrypted documents.

Back in their room, Vail washed up and got her kit ready for the morning.

"My bed," she said, pointing to the one closest to the window. "And that's yours. Just so we're clear."

"If I forget when I get up to pee during the night and accidently find myself snuggled up to you, wake me before reaching for the knife, okay?"

She looked at him.

"Just sayin'. It could happen."

Vail fluffed her pillow then pulled back the sheets. "If you value your package—and future relations with your wife—you will not make that mistake."

46

"The Smart cars may be economical, but they're tiny as hell. And claustrophobic."

"If we'd thought of it before," DeSantos said, "we could've taken the Citroën."

"This thing looks like it got stuck in a vise and accidentally compressed."

"Welcome to Europe. Narrow streets, tight spaces, small cars."

He navigated the roads like a native, taking Avenue Bosquet to Rue Saint-Dominique. Vail watched the French storefront shops, restaurants, and cafés pass by. A guide led about two dozen tourists on Segways across the street in front of them while they sat at a red light.

"Looks like fun."

"Great way to see a city. Better than bikes. And you can cover a lot more ground."

As they crossed the Seine River via the Pont de la Concorde bridge, Vail realized she needed to focus on her assignment, get into the mind-set. For a short time, she was essentially going undercover.

"We'll be there in five minutes. You ready, Katherine Vega?"

"That's *Miss* Vega to you. And yeah, I'm ready."

They parked the car blocks away and hiked toward the Louvre. The sky had turned threatening, the clouds getting darker, the air cooler. It was starting to drizzle.

They walked through Jardin des Tuilieries, a sprawling 450-year-old public park and gardens that abutted the Louvre with statues, decomposed granite paths, mature trees, acres of deep green grass, and a large central fountain.

As they passed under Arc de Triomphe du Carrousel, a six-story triumphal arch commemorating Napoleon's military victories, they saw hundreds of people massed in the Cour Napoleon, the Courtyard of Napoleon. In the center of the square stood the iconic seventy-foot glass Pyramide du Louvre that served as the main entrance to the museum complex. Tourists were snapping photos, a few climbing atop a short stone light post and taking forced-perspective pictures where they pretended to be holding the pyramid by its apex. The modern structure sat in stark contrast to the classical baroque design of the surrounding buildings.

DeSantos gestured at the long line waiting to enter the base of the glass structure. "There's an alternate way in that won't be nearly as crowded."

They descended into the Carrousel du Louvre mall, which featured cafés and gift shops, including a Starbucks and an Apple Store. They passed through the narrow high-ceilinged limestone-walled corridor that was lined with vendors on both sides, as they headed toward the expansive Hall Napoleon, a cavernous atrium that featured an inverted glass pyramid, a mirror image of the one above, pointing down into the gallery.

DeSantos led her past two curving staircases that led to and from street level—the pyramid base where the tourists had been waiting to enter.

As they made their way toward the museum, Vail locked on six police officers congregated in the center of the large lobby. She nudged DeSantos.

"It's the largest museum in the world. What did you expect?"

"A walk in the park?"

"We did that on the way over here." She adjusted her faux glasses and ascended the escalator to the "Control des tickets" booth at the Sully entrance. They paid with the euros Claude and his team had supplied and were handed two large vouchers that read "Musee," along with the date and time of arrival.

Vail took a moment to glance at a foldout map that clearly delineated how massive the Louvre was—652,000 square feet containing 380,000 objects.

They split up, DeSantos hanging back and pretending to view the nearby exhibit while Vail proceeded to the office of the curator in charge of Middle Eastern antiquities, a thin, suited man who seemed surprised to be called to the front desk.

"Can I help you?"

"I'm Katherine Vega."

He squinted lack of understanding, but politely replied, "I'm Pierre DuPont."

"I know. Thanks for agreeing to help us."

He tilted his head. "Help?" He said it as if he had just tasted bitter lemon. "I'm sorry, Miss—"

"Vega. I was told you'd be expecting me."

"Well, I assure you I was not. Now, if you'll excuse—"

"Wait a minute," she said. "I came all the way from the United States—Washington, DC—I'm the Middle Eastern artifacts curator with the Smithsonian International Gallery." She dug into her pocket and found the packet of business cards that had been placed in her backpack by the order of the CIA station chief, along with her clothing and identification documents.

DuPont took the card, frowning as he examined it. Without looking at her he said, "And what is it that you're here for?"

"As my office told your office when we called two weeks ago, we're looking for a rare Middle Eastern artifact from the tenth century. A man of your stature surely knows of it." She waited for him to meet her gaze. "It's a Hebrew text that runs about two hundred pages."

DuPont blinked then lifted his brow and shook his head. He handed Vail back her business card—which she did not mind taking—and said, "I'm sorry. We don't have anything like that."

She laughed. "Surely you must've just forgotten. It's known as the Aleppo Codex, or the Crown of Aleppo, or just the Crown. It arrived about three months ago." She was extrapolating based on information Uzi had told her he had retrieved from the laptop. "My assistant discussed this with your staff."

"And who'd she speak with?"

"It's *he*. And I don't remember who Jason spoke with. I didn't think it was important. I never expected the Louvre, of all the institutions in the world, to give us a problem."

"I can't show you what we don't have, Miss Vega."

"That's a shame, because one of our major benefactors was considering a sizable donation to your efforts to purchase the Teschen Table." According to the backgrounder the Agency had prepared for her, it was one of the world's most unique pieces of furniture, an eighteenth-century masterpiece. "I'm told you came up short earlier this year to raise a million euros."

"Yes, well, that effort is ongoing—"

"And the donor I'm talking about is prepared to make a €150,000 contribution."

DuPont tugged at the knot of his tie, looked up at the ceiling, and then said, "I'm very sorry, Miss Vega, but the document you are looking for is not here."

"But one matching its description is. I want to examine it. The Smithsonian sent me quite a distance based on representations your staff made—"

"Unfortunately, that document is being restored in our lab and unavailable for viewing at the moment. I don't believe it's the codex you're looking for. But the one in our lab is in good hands, I assure you."

She snorted. "With all due respect, Mr. DuPont, given your recent history of art restoration, you'll forgive me if I don't trust your assurances."

DuPont's face shaded red.

"It's no secret that da Vinci's *Virgin and Child with Saint Anne* restoration went horribly wrong—"

"That is patently not true!"

"Mr. DuPont," Vail said, keeping her voice calm and even, "I'm not going to debate that with you. I haven't seen it, so I'm merely going by what I read in the news. But I *am* intimately familiar with the restoration process. I'm not looking to photograph or even handle the manuscript without following proper protocols. In fact, a conservator can handle it. No harm would come to it. I just wish to examine and authenticate it."

That last part is actually true. Now, what happens after that . . .

DuPont's face returned to normal flesh tones. He took a breath and thinned his lips. "The restorers are doing just that. And despite your assertions to the contrary, our staff is among the finest in the world. So—"

"I have my instructions. I can't leave without seeing that document. And I give you my word that I'll make a strong recommendation to Mr. Buffett that he make that donation for the Teschen Table."

"*Warren* Buffet?"

"I did not say that." Vail maintained a poker face. "In fact, I've already said more than I should."

DuPont pressed his lips together, a look of frustration. "My instructions are that no one is to examine that document. I'm not even supposed to acknowledge that we have it on premises."

"Whose decision was that?"

"The director of ancient documents, Lutfi Raboud."

Sounds like a Muslim name. Stop it, Karen. Not all Muslims are extremists. This is France, with a large Muslim population. It's very possible he's a perfectly legit museum officer.

"It's out of my hands," DuPont said. "When a painting or antiquity is brought to the basement laboratory for examination, conservation or restoration, it's administratively transferred to another department. The Center for Document Restoration. I get regular updates on its progress but I'm not involved in the process unless there's a question or my input is otherwise required. It is indeed unfortunate that you had to travel all this way for nothing. And I apologize if my assistants were uninformed or in any way misled you. Believe me, the Louvre would like to cooperate in any way possible. But there's nothing I can do."

"Can I speak with Mr. Raboud?"

DuPont audibly sighed. He was getting tired of dealing with Vail and—she hoped—was willing to pawn her off to the person she needed to meet . . . and evaluate behaviorally.

"Come with me."

He led the way out of his office and down the hall to a service elevator. He pressed B1 and the car descended. Seconds later they emerged in a tiled corridor leading to glass doors that opened into a modern, state-of-the-art restoration facility.

DuPont pressed four numerals into a keypad and an electronic lock clicked. Vail memorized the sequence.

"We have a number of restoration workshops in the Louvre, depending on the medium being cleaned and repaired. Our statuary restorations are done in a very large room. It's low-tech, naturally lit with a skylight in the ceiling. The technicians work on wood surfaces that sit atop sawhorses—very different from what you see here."

For a second Vail lost herself, marveling at the tools and instruments she wished she could have spent hours playing with. When she was in college studying art history, never in her dreams did she see herself in the bowels of the Louvre, staring at priceless antiquities.

She reminded herself why she was here and glanced around to get an idea of what type of security measures they had in place.

Vail was sure they were stringent—but, then again, it was best not to assume. One would have thought the White House had surveillance cameras installed all along its periphery—but that did not happen until recently when a gunman took a rifle and buried several rounds into a window where the First Lady was napping. The bulletproof glass prevented injury—but the Secret Service was unaware of the attack and had no "eyes" on the periphery, allowing the sniper to escape. It was but one example of a facility that should have been one of the most secure in the world, yet was woefully under protected.

She saw cameras in the hallway but nothing—as yet—inside the lab.

"Please wait here," DuPont said. "I'll go retrieve Mr. Raboud."

"While you're doing that, I need to use the restroom. Can you point me in the direction?"

"I will escort you. I can't allow you to wander around here unattended. I'm sure you understand."

"Absolutely."

He led her past a number of men and women who were bent over workstations lit indirectly with full-spectrum bulbs, some of whom were peering through high-powered microscopes or jeweler's loupes strapped to their foreheads.

DuPont stopped opposite two doors in a corner of the facility and gestured at the one on the left. Vail proceeded in and made a quick assessment: it was a fairly basic facility with a single sink, two stalls, and a ventilation duct about six feet off the ground. She stood on her toes and tried to get a look inside but was a couple of inches short.

She waited a few seconds, then flushed the toilet and washed her hands.

DuPont was waiting outside with another man.

"This is Lufti Raboud, the Louvre's director of ancient documents." He was a bald, thick man of about forty with a clean-shaven, pock-marked face from childhood chicken pox, by Vail's guess. He wore a black suit and white tie, looking formal and official.

"A pleasure," Vail said. "I've come all the way from Washington to examine the Aleppo Codex. But apparently there's been a bit of a snafu and I need your authorization to see it."

Raboud's face was as expressionless as that of a stone statue. "We are not in possession of that document. I'm sorry you've come so far. This was, indeed, a miscommunication. Was it our fau—"

"I know you have it here," Vail said. "Mr. DuPont and I have already been through the charade."

DuPont lifted an index finger. "That's not exactly what I—"

"So let's save us both a little time. Just let me do my job. I only need ten minutes, at most, with the codex. Whatever safeguards you insist upon will be fine with me."

"I cannot let you see that which we do not have. I apologize if Mr. DuPont led you to believe otherwise." He forced a smile. "Now, mademoiselle, I have a meeting I'm late for." He nodded at DuPont—a stiff, unpleasant gesture—and turned to leave.

"You're a skilled liar, Mr. Raboud. Does it come naturally or did you have to learn it?"

Raboud spun and faced her. His face now showed some character: it flushed in anger.

"Whatever your reason for denying that you have the codex doesn't concern me. Those are administrative matters. I'm solely interested in verifying the art and establishing the document's place in history."

Raboud chewed on that a moment, tapping his right oxford dress shoe. Then he took a step forward and bit his lower lip, apparently still deciding how to respond. "We had a document that some thought was the codex. Because of its controversial nature, we did not want it known that it was in our possession. It would've created difficulties with the Israelis, the Americans, even the Vatican. I was relieved, to say the least, when it turned out not to be the codex. Either way, it's no longer here. We did some minor cleaning and sent it on its way."

Vail studied his face. "Sent it where?"

"That, Miss Vega, was not my concern. And, I might venture to state, neither is it yours."

"Do you have a business card? In case I have any other questions? I appreciate your honesty and apologize for my rudeness."

Raboud ran a tongue across his lips, clearly considering the request. Then he reached into his suit coat and pulled out a sterling silver case. He handed her the card with a bow of his head. "Again, it's a shame you wasted your time."

Vail broke a smile. "I'm in France, in the world's greatest museum. It's not all bad."

Raboud shared the grin—though Vail could tell it was not genuine. "Indeed. Stay the day, enjoy yourself. If any of my staff can be of service, please let Mr. DuPont know." He nodded again at DuPont—a dutiful gesture—and then walked out.

47

Uzi and Fahad sat in the Citroën watching the entrance to a building that one of Fahad's contacts had directed him to. The woman was friends with a seamstress who stitched together material, elastic loops, pockets, and Velcro enclosures for "utility vests" that bore a curious resemblance to those that suicide bombers used to strap explosives to their body.

Although the woman had suspicions, she claimed not to know their true use. Regardless, her brother delivered the finished products in boxes to a particular address in the south—where Uzi and Fahad were now parked. It was in the general area of Paris that was alluded to in the encrypted documents, so Uzi felt there was a decent chance the intel was solid.

They were in the Montmartre district, known for its history as an artist colony where the likes of Claude Monet, Salvador Dali, Pablo Picasso, and Vincent van Gogh had studios. Blocks away, up on the summit of a steep hill, was the domed Basilica of the Sacré Cœur, a landmark visible from many parts of the city.

The cobblestone roadway inclined fairly aggressively ahead of them, with a few businesses and bars on both sides of the Rue Muller and apartment buildings above. The area was fairly well maintained, though it was clear the neighborhood had seen its share of crime. First-floor windows were barred and occasional graffiti adorned the buildings.

Their car was parked at the curb, among many that lined the street.

"So your nephew was a suicide bomber," Uzi said. "That must've been tough."

Fahad pulled his gaze off the building for a moment. His eyes scanned Uzi's face. "Harder than you can know." He turned back to their target. "I didn't agree with his methods, even though I understood what he was feeling. He got taken in by the rhetoric and became frustrated, wanted to do something about it. But the people he fell in with, they were using him. They knew it. I knew it. But Akil was young and naive. He didn't get it. And he wouldn't listen to me."

"I'm sorry he took his own life. I'm sorry he killed innocent children. I wish there was a way to work all this out. But there aren't any easy solutions. This business with the Aleppo Codex and the Jesus Scroll only makes matters worse. As if it needed anything to make it worse."

"That's for damn sure."

"Where do you stand on all this?"

"You mean the peace talks? The two-state solution? Jerusalem? Refugee status? Or whether or not a Palestinian state should be allowed to have an airport and military capabilities?"

Uzi laughed. "I just mean . . . well, where do you stand on the land issue? Are you in the camp that believes Jews never lived in Israel, that the Palestinians should have all the land and kick the Jews out?"

Fahad shook his head. "Look, I'm a reasonable guy. I know the Jews have lived in Israel for what, four thousand years? I'm not an idiot. I don't believe that by repeatedly denying something it'll eventually become the truth. There are ancient Islamic texts that talk about the Jews living in Jerusalem. I've seen them, so I'd be a fool to make believe those documents don't exist."

"There's a but."

"There is a 'but.' Arabs did live in Palestine. We had homes there that we abandoned during the war. That's why the UN declared two separate states back in 1947, one for the Jews and one for the Arabs. We have legitimate claims to the land."

"All the land?"

He thought a moment. "Compromise and conciliation don't go over well there."

"I don't think those words are even in their dictionaries."

They laughed, but Fahad's tone faded to one of introspection. "We should've accepted partition. No negotiation, no compromise needed. We would've had our state and you would've had yours. And a lot of young men would never have died in suicide bombings. A lot of death and destruction would've been avoided. But we've been our own worst enemy. We had a leadership vacuum, got some bad advice."

"You talking about Arafat?"

"He tops my list but he's not the only one." Fahad shook his head. "Things could've been so different with better leaders, smarter leaders, people with a vision. I'm very frustrated for my people." He went silent, staring ahead at the building they were surveilling. "We call the armistice agreement that divided the land al Naqba, the catastrophe. Difference is, I think of it as a catastrophe because of what we could have had. Instead of accepting the agreement, the Arab nations declared war. We lost and got decades of problems. We have to take some responsibility."

"One could say your leaders are still at war to have it all."

Fahad nodded absently. "I wish I could disagree with you."

"Some of my people are wrapped up in that same fight." They sat there a moment in thought. "It's a shame more Palestinians don't recognize Israel for all the good it's done. Forget the technology and medical advancements it's brought the world. Forget that it's the first to send help when an earthquake or tsunami or some other catastrophe hits somewhere. No other Middle Eastern country goes to the lengths that Israel does to protect human rights or practice social justice. No Middle Eastern country offers women equal rights—except Israel, where women have the same rights as men."

"Muslim countries in the Middle East aren't concerned with equality between men and women the way the West is."

"No, I guess not. But isn't it ironic that the Arabs living in Israel are treated better than Arabs anywhere else in the region? Israel's the only country in the Middle East where you're free to practice your religion, worship your God. And despite all the crap that's gone on with Gaza, Israel still donates tens of millions of dollars in humanitarian aid to Palestinians—and opens its hospitals to any Palestinian in need. Even terrorists, as bizarre as that sounds." He looked at Fahad. "Doesn't any of that count?"

Fahad shrugged. "For my people, to the men in charge, the land is the only thing that counts. None of the other things you mentioned matters to them."

"It should. It's important."

Fahad chuckled disdainfully. "They are blinded by their single-minded fixation. Their resistance."

"You really think things would've been different? Wouldn't the extremists have followed the same plan of action?"

Fahad stared out the window, considering the question. Finally he said, "Would we be in the same place we are now? I honestly don't know. But yeah, it's possible."

"Let's hope that one day the Hamases, al Humats, al Qaedas, and Islamic States of the world will go away, that the extremes on both sides will find common ground and see the benefit of working together. Of living together in peace where each side recognizes the legitimacy of the other."

"I share that hope. But after all you've seen? You really believe that can happen?"

Uzi considered the question. "A friend of mine, a peace negotiator during the Oslo talks, a vocal supporter of Palestinians having their own country, used to say, 'You never know. Anything can happen.'"

"*Used to* say?"

"He was killed in a suicide bombing."

Fahad looked at him.

"No, I'm not kidding." Uzi took one last glance around the street. "It's quiet. I think we're safe to take a poke around. If everything looks good, we can break into the flat and go hunting."

Fahad checked his Glock, then pulled his jacket around to cover the handle. "Let's do it."

Uzi grabbed Fahad's arm. "I'm sorry. For how I acted after we met, not trusting you with Amer Madari."

"Hey, I'm not only your sworn enemy but I'm CIA—no one trusts us." He winked. "Apology accepted."

UZI ENTERED THE BUILDING FIRST, followed two minutes later by Fahad. They proceeded separately up to the flat, Uzi by stairs and Fahad by elevator. They both wore their eyeglasses and baseball hats in case there were cameras.

When Uzi and Fahad met down the hall from the apartment, Fahad said that he had not seen any surveillance devices.

"I didn't either. What about the dark blue minivan down the block?"

"Couldn't get a read on who was inside. Looked like two men but there was too much reflection off the glass."

"That's about what I got too. Could be trouble. But we're here, let's go as far as we can. You're up. Go knock."

Fahad would be the "face" of this phase of the operation because he was of the same nationality and could more easily pass for a nonthreatening presence.

He balled his fist and rapped on the wood door. After waiting a long minute, he tried again—but got the same response.

"Hey, it's me, open up," he said in Arabic. A moment later he signaled Uzi down the hall.

Uzi removed a small toolkit from his pocket and proceeded to jimmy the lock. A few seconds later, they were inside. They split up and began searching the flat, which looked like the one in Greenwich: sparse furnishings, a computer, and the detritus of bachelors living in close quarters: the acrid smell of Turkish cigarettes lingered in the air and dirty clothing littered the bedrooms, where bare mattresses sat on worn wood plank floors.

They reconvened in the den five minutes later.

"I've got a desktop," Uzi said, "which means if we want to pull anything off it I have to do it here."

"Can you copy the data and take it with us?"

"I can try." He sat down on a folding chair at the makeshift desk, a coffee table with a couple of thick phone books piled on top of one another to bring the monitor up to eye level. A webcam was attached to a nineteen-inch widescreen LCD.

Fahad checked the time. "I'm gonna stand watch in the hall. I see or hear something, I'll knock twice. It's a small building so I probably won't be able to give you more than a few seconds' notice."

"Understood," Uzi said as he tapped away at the keyboard.

"Think you can you be done in five minutes?"

"If it's a simple drag and drop, yeah. If they've got things encrypted, no way." Uzi looked up. "You're worried about that minivan."

"I'm naturally paranoid."

"If there's one thing I learned a long time ago, Mo, it's that a little paranoia can be an operative's best friend." Uzi glanced at the clock in the computer's system tray. "Give me ten minutes. I'll grab what I can, then we'll get out of here."

UZI HAD BEEN AT IT FOR SEVEN MINUTES, keeping one eye on the time as he worked to decrypt the data. It was as he had feared: if the cell in Greenwich secured their documents it was likely al Humat's standard operating procedure. It made sense: they were a sophisticated organization, disciplined, intelligent, well organized.

He was perspiring profusely, decrypting on the fly and loading the data onto his flash drive as he went, when something caught his eye. He pulled his phone and dialed Richard Prati.

"I don't have a lot of time so just shut up and listen."

"I'm listening," Prati said.

"They're bringing nuclear material in, but they're not using a tunnel. They're coming across the Atlantic, then going down the St. Lawrence River between Canada and the US. About 125 miles southwest of Montreal—near Hill Island—they'll be offloading it onto a truck and crossing into the US on Interstate 81 which runs south through upstate New York, New Jersey, and Philadelphia. They could be taking it into Jersey or Philly but I'm betting they're gonna take another shot at Manhattan."

"I'll run with this," Prati said. "You know when it's going down?"

"No. If I find anything else I'll let you know."

Uzi hung up and flicked his eyes to the system tray's clock. He had less than a minute before he had to leave. As he dragged several more documents onto his drive, an email hit the inbox. It was in Arabic, so he did a quick translation.

> Meet me at noon, roof of the Arc de Triomphe. Don't be late.
> I have new orders for you from KAS.

It was not signed, and the email address was merely a string of numbers at Gmail. KAS. Uzi searched his memory—who the hell was KAS?

And then it hit him: Kadir Abu Sahmoud.

Uzi looked again at the time: noon was twenty-one minutes from now. What to do? He had promised he would be out of there in ten minutes—which was smart regardless of whether or not he had made a commitment to leave.

The decision was clear: take what he had, shut down, and get over to the Arc de Triomphe.

He and Fahad could return and finish going through the files later, assuming it was safe. But the ability to intercept a message from Sahmoud—and potentially capture one of his lieutenants—was now the priority.

He pulled out his USB flash drive and powered off the PC. Seconds later he stepped out into the hallway.

Fahad was not there.

48

Vail joined DeSantos in the Denon wing on the first floor—Room 6, known simply as "the Mona Lisa Room."

Vail had texted him when she left the document restoration laboratory and he suggested this location as an innocuous place to rendezvous: it was crowded and one of the busiest exhibits in the museum, not to mention the most famous.

Vail entered the large, high-ceilinged space. There was an echo of hushed voices off the tall, flat, patterned gold walls. Aside from two rows of framed Renaissance paintings hanging by chains from channels in the walls, the room felt bare.

A crowd of a couple hundred people was concentrated in front of one modestly sized work, however, that hung alone—the *Mona Lisa.*

Arms extended up from the masses, digicams and cell phones aimed at the painting, almost as if she were conducting a press conference and the cameras were microphones recording every word. Off to the right and left were large red and black signs warning people that pickpockets operated in this room: while you studied the famed portrait, criminal elements emptied your person and pockets of euros, watches, jewelry—anything of value. They did not discriminate.

"They had to close the place down yesterday," DeSantos said. "Because of the pickpockets. The workers went on a one-day strike to protest. They were being threatened. Apparently the gypsies operate in gangs now and they've gotten violent, even threatening the security guards. Leave them alone or they know where you live and they'll go after your family."

"You're shitting me."

"Nope. While I was waiting, a young couple told me they'd planned to come yesterday, got here, and were turned away. They had to rearrange their trip to come back today." He nodded toward the left portion of the crowd.

"The guy in black, the woman in gray. Watch him get the wallet out of that tourist's pocket."

Vail saw their methodology: they worked in a group, an attractive female pushing up against the mark while the male crowded him from behind. She engaged the victim, apologizing or making some comment about how packed it was—while her accomplice removed the booty with practiced skill.

Vail set a hand on her concealed Glock and took a step forward—but DeSantos grabbed her arm.

"You're not a cop here, *Katherine Vega*. Let it go."

Vail growled, then stepped back—but did not take her eyes off the perpetrator.

"Find anything out?"

DeSantos's question refocused her. "Yeah. The curator was under 'orders' to deny that they had it."

"He just told you that?"

"Kind of. I can be persuasive when I need to be."

DeSantos lifted his brow. "Go on."

"I ended up speaking with the director of ancient documents, Lufti Raboud. Seems as if the order to deny their possession of the codex came from him. I sent his prints to Tim Meadows."

"How'd you do that?"

"I got his business card. I went into the ladies' room, dusted it, and emailed it to Tim. Because of the time difference it may be a while before we get something."

"Nicely done."

"I could tell Raboud was lying and I called him on it. He came clean and said they did have a document they thought was the codex but it turned out not to be the case."

"Shit."

"Not exactly. I'm pretty sure that was a load of crap too. He said that when they determined it wasn't the codex, he was relieved because of the controversy surrounding it."

"Okay."

"No, not okay. The Louvre's director of ancient documents relieved he didn't have the ability to examine, to touch, one of the most important manuscripts of all time? I'm not buying it."

DeSantos bobbed his head. "Good point."

"He's either an imposter, a sleeper operative, or he's on al Humat's payroll."

"Our focus is the codex."

"He said the document that they did have was cleaned and sent away."

DeSantos nodded slowly, then said, "You don't believe him."

"Assuming it's real, and assuming it did need some restoration, which is certainly reasonable, I may know where it is."

"And where's that?"

"In the restoration workshop. Pretty cool lab in the basement."

"Then we should have a look around," DeSantos said as he scanned the large room. "They're open late, till 9:00 or 10:00. We can't just sit here and wait for it to close."

"You're right. Why pass the time actually enjoying one of the finest collections of art in the world?"

"Given your background in art history, I can see why that's appealing to you. Ain't happenin'."

"Knew you were going to say that."

"Coming back later in the same day would look suspicious if anyone happens to notice." He turned his body to face both Vail and the *Mona Lisa*. "So we have to make something happen."

"Knew you were going to say that too." A few seconds later, she said, "We could set off the fire alarm."

DeSantos scanned the room. "Don't see any. Not sure how that works in a museum anyway. Can't be hooked up to sprinklers. The art would be damaged or destroyed. Must be heat sensors and smoke detectors. We don't smoke, so unless you can spontaneously generate intense heat, we have to find another way."

"You always tell me I'm hot."

"Hot enough to trigger *my* sensors. But not hot enough to trigger the heat sensors. I've got another option. The gypsies."

"I think they prefer the term Roma."

"Fine. The Roma."

"You want to pay them to break in and steal it for us?"

"That's not a bad idea. Problem is we'd never get it back from them. No, we use them as a diversion."

"I'm listening."

"I'm thinking."

Five minutes later, he had the seed of a plan: they would observe the behavior of the Roma pickpockets and then select one to approach with an offer: they would pay him €500 to cause a distraction significant enough to draw security to the area. It was likely they had compatriots in other areas of the museum, so if they coordinated the disturbance, security—and those monitoring whatever surveillance cameras the Louvre had—would be drawn to respond. When they were done, assuming they performed as agreed, DeSantos would meet his contact outside and give him another €500.

"I'm not sure I like this."

"I'm not crazy about it either. But it's the best I can come up with that won't put our asses on the line or our faces on camera. The Roma are used to brushes with the guards—and because of what happened yesterday, I'm sure the guards are on edge about it. The response should be bigger than usual."

Vail hesitated.

"You got a better idea?"

"No."

"How sure are you that Raboud was lying?"

How sure am I? Good question. She took a moment to replay the conversation, reconsider his body language. "Sixty-forty. Maybe seventy-thirty."

DeSantos considered that. "We're here. The codex may or may not be here. I say we go for it."

Of course you would.

"You have doubts?"

She leaned close to him. "We're in a foreign country on forged passports, about to break into the Louvre's document restoration lab and steal an invaluable ancient artifact that may or not be there. With no valid exit strategy. And we're relying on a criminal enterprise to help us." She shrugged. "What's there to doubt? Sounds like a flawless plan."

"Good, then we're in agreement."

She gave DeSantos a look but it did not deter him.

"Let's take some time to pick the right guy to go after."

"And how do you know who's Roma and who's a tourist?"

"The tourists come and go. They look, they gawk, they shoot photos, and then move on. The thieves move in, do their thing, and then shuffle over to another area."

"How do you know this?"

"I've been watching. Very little gets by me, *Katherine*."

"I could provide plenty of examples, but what would be the point?"

"You realize you just said that out loud."

"No I didn't."

DeSantos shook his head in disappointment. "Are you with me or not?"

"Do you really have to ask?"

"I was being courteous. Now go take a position on the far side and observe. Be discreet."

"Thanks for the advice. I was going to make it really obvious."

They wandered off and watched the area for ten minutes before DeSantos rejoined her. "I've got our candidate. Give me €500." He held out his right hand and she peeled off the bills. "Hang back here."

He walked over to a male who appeared to be in his early twenties and whispered in his ear. He listened a moment then nodded. DeSantos shook hands with the man—the handoff of the money—and walked back to Vail.

"We're good. He's spreading the word to his brother, who'll go set it up with his cousins in three other rooms. That should be enough."

"How can we be sure?"

"Because he's sure. And he makes his living here. He's been working here for nine years."

"Did you say 'working' here?"

"Figure of speech."

"Nine years? He's what, twenty-two, twenty-three?"

"They start young. Children can get away with a lot more because we automatically assume they're innocent. They're very effective tools."

"Children are *tools*. Another figure of speech?"

"Shut up. We need to go get ready. When he signals us, we have to be in position."

As they made their way toward the elevator, Vail said, "What's the signal?"

"A smiley face texted to my throwaway. That and we'll hear the fire alarm."

"Fire alarm? That was my idea."

"And it was a good one, so I used it. They know how to set it off. That way we'll clear the lab."

"Maybe the entire museum."

"Works for me." DeSantos led the way into the empty car. "Now where are the cameras? We still need to avoid them because if they get a sense it was intentional, we don't want our faces on a recording going into a restricted area."

"The only ones I saw were in the corridor outside the lab."

"Nothing inside?"

"Unless they were well concealed, no."

As they exited the elevator on level B1, DeSantos pulled out his phone. "That's it. Got the text."

Before Vail could acknowledge, the fire alarm started blaring. It was shrill and high-pitched.

"Standard fire evacuation protocol for a building is using the stairs," DeSantos said over the din. "Know where they are?"

"End of the hall on the right."

"Let's give it a minute, then we'll make sure the hallway's clear."

A moment later, they moved up the corridor, keeping their heads down to avoid the cameras as best they could.

"We can't be sure everyone's evacuated."

"It's a fire alarm," DeSantos said. "Most people are gonna get out. And if there's one or two who don't, we'll deal with it."

I was afraid you were going to say that.

They approached the door and Vail entered the four digit code as DeSantos discretely wrapped his fingers around the grip of his handgun.

The lock clicked and she pushed on the metal handle. As it swung open she saw a red ceiling light blinking in the corner of the room.

They gave a quick look around, then signaled each other: all clear.

Except that it wasn't.

49

Uzi rubbernecked his head. Fahad was nowhere in sight. First objective was to get out of the building safely and the second was to get to the Arc de Triomphe. Third was to find Fahad.

Bypassing the elevator, he saved time by running toward the stairwell. He pushed through—and saw Fahad standing over the bodies of two unconscious men.

"What the hell happened?"

"French counterterrorism officers. We've gotta get the hell out of here."

They fled down the steps and hit the ground floor in seconds. After making sure there were no other cops in the immediate vicinity, they walked out, headed back to their car in a falling rain.

"Anything?"

"I think we're good." He handed Fahad the keys. "You drive. We're headed to the Arc de Triomphe."

As they navigated the streets en route to the monument, Uzi told Fahad of the email that had come through.

"Not sure we're gonna make it. Gonna be very close."

"Police," Uzi said.

Fahad hung a left and sped up to the next intersection and turned right on Rue de Londres.

Uzi lowered his chin. "Another two cops. And a soldier with a rifle."

He turned again and accelerated. "These detours are slowing us down."

"And if we get pulled over, our entire mission could be blown."

Fahad swung right onto Rue Le Champs Elysées, the equivalent of New York's Fifth Avenue: a wide, upscale shopping and residential district lined with patisseries, designer chocolatiers, and specialty stores such as a Bang & Olufsen audio showroom.

"How close?"

"Up ahead. Half a mile, give or take."

"Counterterrorism officers," Uzi said. "Either they were watching us or they were watching the same guys we were watching. That van we saw parked at the curb."

"Yeah, they were probably doing surveillance, waiting for the assholes to come home. Instead, it was us."

"We were pretty careful. You think they had bugs inside the flat?"

"That's what the Agency would've done. I think it's likely."

They had not used each other's names, so all the French authorities had on them were voiceprints.

Their tires made a sizzling sound against the rain-soaked asphalt as they swerved in and out of the slower-moving traffic.

Uzi consulted his watch. "Four minutes."

Ahead of them, in the center of a busy traffic circle, was their destination. Built in the same design as its smaller cousin, the Arc de Triomphe du Carrousel, which stood just outside the Louvre, the Arc de Triomphe de l'Étoile was almost three times its height at nearly seventeen stories and proffered an unimpeded 360 degree view of downtown Paris.

"Ever been here?" Fahad asked.

"To the arch? No."

"Carved marble's beautiful. And the thing's so big someone once flew a biplane through the center."

"I'll enjoy it some other time."

As they approached, Uzi was on the lookout for a place they could leave their vehicle where it would not get towed—or attract the attention of law enforcement. Problem was, as in any metropolitan area, parking was scarce.

They passed a building that featured a massive outcropping of large glass panes mounted on a metal skeleton that protruded at odd angles and directions, as if the facing had been twisted by an earthquake.

"We're gonna have to leave the car at the nearest curb space and hope it's here when we get out."

"It's got a clean title," Fahad said. "The Agency made sure it won't be traced back to them. If we have to abandon it, if it's towed, so be it."

He pulled to the right side of the street and they got out, walking briskly, and separately, toward the entrance.

Uzi cursed under his breath as they approached four police officers wearing dark jackets and large black-on-white POLICE placards on their backs with white, red, and blue patches on their arms.

"They have no idea what's about to go down right under their noses," Uzi said as they descended the marble steps to a long tunnel that ran beneath the street and up into the massive monument. A curved ceiling with up-lighting from the sides gave the passageway a contemporary feel.

"We have to buy tickets," Fahad said, pointing to a booth up a few marble steps off to the left.

"You're shitting me. We don't have time."

"Path of least resistance. We don't want those cops to come running when we force our way through security."

"Fine." As Uzi paid, he glanced at his watch. The meet was starting in one minute, assuming they were punctual.

"Shit," Fahad said, gesturing at the posted sign. "Elevator's out."

They began running up the cement stairs, its metal facing worn-through to its substructure—evidence of the number of tourists who had visited the monument during the past 190 years.

They ran up the tightly winding stairwell, using the iron railing as leverage after they passed the first two hundred steps. They wove past the occasional person walking down and finally stopped for a breath around number 250. Chests heaving, they glanced down at the spiral they had just ascended, then continued upward.

They hit the roof—or terrace, according to the sign—and exited through a glass-enclosed covering.

The view was spectacular despite the low-hanging charcoal clouds and constant drizzle. Off in the near distance stood the Eiffel Tower, unimpeded by the low buildings of downtown Paris.

Uzi scanned the area, which featured an elaborate smooth marble floor that stepped up in multiple tiered levels amid a network of metal drain grates. A continuous row of five foot tall steel rods ringed the perimeter to prevent people from falling, or jumping, off the edge to the street below.

The center of the roof was consumed by a raised section that divided the top into a narrow passageway along the length of the monument and a wider area on the short dimension, where the exit/entrance staircase was located. A glass-enclosed security booth sat empty.

They split up, Uzi going left and Fahad right. They were looking for anyone fitting the description of an Islamic extremist—which meant the pool was too great to accurately characterize. It could be a Frenchman, an Englishman, an American—along with a host of other nationalities including Chechen, Syrian, African, Moroccan. Because of the universal nature of the threat, it was difficult to put a physical face on the enemy.

There were only a handful of people on the terrace. A few were milling about, taking in the view of the Parisian streets and buildings, others walking along the slick marble toward another vantage point.

Uzi turned the corner of the short end and headed down the narrower pathway. A young couple was standing about thirty yards away, leaning against the railing, kissing.

So where was this meet occurring? He checked his watch: they were a few minutes late, but he was certain any discussion these men were supposedly having would last more than 180 seconds. Unless it was a simple handoff. Uzi cursed under his breath. Had they really missed them by two or three minutes?

As Uzi swung his head left to glance over his shoulder he was slammed in the back by two men who grabbed him by his arms and launched him off the ground and up against the spikes. The force knocked the air from his lungs.

Uzi fought to get hold of something to keep his body from being thrown over the edge—but the metal was smooth and slick. And wet.

He kicked backward, landed a couple of good blows.

But his attackers did not yield.

He wedged his knee between the rods and reached back with his left hand and grabbed a fistful of hair. The man twisted and pulled, trying to free himself, but there was no way Uzi was going to let go.

If only he could gain some space and pull his Glock or his knife.

That was not going to happen. He continued gyrating and kicking, then realized he did not have to *pull* his handgun.

He squirmed and got his right hand free, wedged it between his belt and abdomen, and grasped the hand of the pistol. It was a crazy move but he had no other choice—and nothing to lose.

His 5.11 tactical pants had some elasticity and they yielded as he pushed the Glock down into his groin, angled the barrel between his legs and pulled the trigger twice.

The recoil slammed into his groin and the pain was instant—but either he hit one of his targets or the gunshots got their attention and they loosened their grasp—long enough for Uzi to swing a vicious right elbow backward into the perp's head. The stunned man jerked back and dropped his hold on Uzi.

Uzi fell off to that side and took the other man down with him, his left fist still grasping clumps of hair. From his back he swung his right foot into the side of the tango's head, then drew his knee back and smashed the perp squarely in the nose with a Timberland boot. The man fell to the pavement.

Uzi struggled to his feet, trying to shake off the pain. He turned slowly to get a look at the other attacker. But he was nowhere in sight. A blood trail, however, indicated that he had been struck by at least one of the rounds and had staggered off, by the looks of the jagged red-tinged droplets.

Uzi knelt on the chest of the unconscious man and reached a hand down his tactical pants to move the Glock back up to his waist.

Fahad appeared on the far side and ran toward him.

"What happened?"

"Another guy—go see if you can catch up to him—follow the blood." He gestured over his left shoulder.

"That one dead?"

"Unconscious."

"Kill him."

"Mo, just go!"

"Do it," he said, and took off.

Quick glance up—the couple that had been near the other end of the railing was now gone—no surprise there. The area was otherwise empty. No surprise there, either.

Off in the near distance, below him somewhere, came the scream of sirens. And he knew the cops he saw down below would be on their way up. He had maybe sixty seconds to get the hell away or face certain detention and questioning—which he had to avoid at all costs.

He reseated the Glock and debated wiping it down and ditching it here but because he had it so close against his body he did not know if any of his DNA was in the slide. It would not take much: a sliver of skin from his leg during the recoil, a drop of blood.

He did an efficient pat down of the unconscious man and found nothing. He rooted out his phone and took a photo of the face—and that's when he realized it was one of the snipers from London: Samir Mohammed al Razi. That meant the one that escaped might be Rahmatullah Nasrullah.

The urgent sirens grew louder.

Fahad's voice echoed in his head: "Kill him." He was right; al Razi was a terrorist and his flat would eventually be discovered. In an effort to win his freedom he would describe Uzi to the authorities. How much did al Razi know about him? About all of them?

Uzi now knew the so-called meet was an ambush—which meant the tangos had known he and Fahad were in that flat. But how? What else did they know?

He could not take a chance. And he was out of time.

He pulled the Glock from his waistband and took aim.

50

Who are you?" Lufti Raboud asked.

DeSantos smirked. "I was going to ask you the same question."

"This," Vail said, "is the director of ancient documents. Lufti Raboud."

"Didn't think I'd be seeing you again, Miss Vega," Raboud said disdainfully. "Let alone with an armed thug."

DeSantos tilted his head. "Thug?"

Vail's phone buzzed. She glanced at the display: Tim Meadows. She reluctantly pulled the cell from her belt and answered the call. "Now's not a good time."

"Well excuse me for interrupting, Karen, but I thought you'd like an answer on some of those prints and photos you people have been bombarding me with."

"What about the last one I sent? Anything?"

"Yeah. And as a matter of fact, it wasn't easy because makeup powder is not an ideal medium—"

"Sorry, I didn't have access to proper equipment. I improvised."

"Go to a drugstore and get a plastic cup, a pipe cleaner, and superglue. Poke a hole in the cup, put the pipe cleaner through the hole, put superglue on the pipe cleaner and set the cup over the latent. The superglue reacts with the pipe cleaner, which heats up and creates fumes. The fumes adhere to—"

"Tim—Tim. When I said 'now's not a good time,' I really meant it. Do you have an ID?"

"You *are* impatient. And ungrateful." He paused a second. "Is that an alarm going off?"

"Which is why I don't have a lot of time."

"The man's Borz Ramazanov, a Chechen national wanted for—wait for it—terrorism, identity theft, and forgery."

"Really."

"No, I called you in France to bullshit you, just to yank your chain."

"That was rhetorical."

"Of course it was. Sorry."

Vail glanced at DeSantos, who was not so patiently waiting for her to finish the call.

"You want the other IDs? Yes or no?"

"Call you back." She clicked off and came up alongside DeSantos and faced Raboud. "So, Borz, you've got something we want and we've got something you want."

His eyes flickered at the mention of his real name. "And what do I want? Your gun, perhaps?"

"Your freedom. All we're interested in is the codex. Give it to us and you're free to go."

His eyes flicked between them.

C'mon, dipshit. We're running out of time.

"Now," DeSantos said, "or the deal's off. You've got five seconds."

Ramazanov firmed his lips in anger, then stepped over to a large, floor-to-ceiling wall safe and twirled the tumbler. Several turns and reverse rotations later, following a yank on the chrome handle and a loud metallic clunk, he pulled open the thick steel door.

Vail peered inside and held Ramazanov at gunpoint as he reached in and set aside a number of items before extracting a worn brown leather portfolio approximately three by four feet. He stepped back and handed it to Vail, who took it in one hand and grabbed his wrist with the other, then twisted it and pushed him into a desk. He yielded from the pain and bent over at the waist, his face pressed against the worktop.

"What are you doing?" he groaned.

Vail took a flexcuff from DeSantos and secured Ramazanov's wrists to the nearest immovable object.

"He looks uncomfortable," DeSantos said as he did a pat down of the man's body. He pulled a smartphone from Ramazanov's suit pocket and began thumbing through it.

"Let me go!"

Vail placed the portfolio atop a worktable and removed a couple of gloves from a dispenser to her far right. "As soon as we verify the document." She pulled it from the leather case and carefully set the sheaf of large papers on the flat surface.

"Who do you work for?" DeSantos asked.

"The Musée du Louvre. Not to state the obvious."

"How about the truth?" DeSantos said. "We know who you are. Who are you giving the codex to?"

"I don't know what you're talking about."

"See, the funny thing is, I don't believe you. And trust me on this—you don't want to piss me off. Last guy who did that—well, let's just say no one's heard from him since."

Ramazanov considered this, then said, "I don't know the guy's name. He paid me to authenticate the codex and then create a forgery. I didn't have time to do it because he suddenly called and said he needed the original immediately."

"When was this?"

"This morning."

"Why did he need it right away?"

Ramazanov tugged on the flexcuffs, which prevented him from standing erect. "Didn't say. And I didn't care. All that mattered is that I wasn't getting paid. No forgery, no payment. I told him these things take a lot of time."

DeSantos frowned, clearly dissatisfied with Ramazanov's answers, and moved to Vail's side, keeping an angle on their prisoner. He looked at the yellowed parchment, which contained Hebrew lettering. Some areas were faded while others were still dark and distinct.

"What do you think?" Vail asked.

"It's the codex," Ramazanov said.

Vail snorted. "A little while ago you insisted you didn't have it. Were you lying then or are you lying now?"

DeSantos pulled out his phone, made a call, and waited. He disconnected it a moment later. "Our friend's not answering," he said, referring to Uzi. "Must be busy. But we need that contact."

"He already gave it to me," Vail said of Uzi's acquaintance who used to work at the Israel Antiquities Authority—the contingency plan Uzi had arranged to determine if the item they recovered—*if* they recovered something—was in fact the codex.

Vail pulled out her Samsung to take photos. She made sure the halogen desk lamp was angled toward the ceiling, then turned it on. Next she disabled the phone's flash, but left the camera's infrared focus assist beam on, since she had been told it would not damage the fragile parchment and ancient ink.

She snapped some pictures of the flesh side of the parchment and then, handling it carefully, turned it over and shot some of the hairy side, where the ink was darker and in better condition.

She emailed the images to Uzi's friend and followed with a text message asking him to look them over ASAP.

"When do you think we'll hear?"

DeSantos shrugged. "I don't know how he's authenticating it. If he's even near his phone or PC."

"We've gotta get out of here. How long before they review the security tape and realize the alarm was bogus?"

DeSantos shifted his jaw. "Wish I had answers. But every second we stay here we're increasing our risk."

"Who do you work for?" Ramazanov asked.

Vail turned to him. "I told you. The Museum of Middle Eastern Affairs."

"Something tells me a document expert for the Museum of Middle Eastern Affairs doesn't break into the Louvre with a thug—" he shot a glance at DeSantos—"and steal rare manuscripts."

"And a terrorist and forger shouldn't be working as the director of ancient documents at an esteemed world-class institution," DeSantos said. "Obviously, the Louvre doesn't know who you really are. Not sure how you got through their security check. They're very thorough."

"Nice setup, though," Vail said. "A lot of valuable lesser known antiquities come through here. You siphon off a few—after you've created an expert forgery that you authenticate yourself and leave in the museum—then sell the real one on the black market."

"You have an understanding of the rare manuscript market."

"Unfortunately," Vail said. "How much is the codex worth?"

"Some would say it's priceless. But if you were to *try* to put a price on it, millions. Tens of millions. Maybe more."

"Even on the black market?"

"It's not unusual for Hebrew manuscripts to be sold covertly among dealers and collectors who are not above board. Even a stolen antiquity, which can't be sold on a legitimate market, the price can get quite high. A manuscript as old as this almost never changes hands. But the codex is unique. And with something that's one of a kind, the price sets itself.

"You only need one person who wants it bad enough, someone with the wherewithal to afford it. If you know about rare manuscripts, you know this is true." Ramazanov bent over, then flexed his knees, trying to find a comfortable position. "And here you are, trying to take it away from me. I'm obviously not the only thief here."

"Actually, you are," Vail said. "We're French intelligence."

"And we're running out of time," DeSantos said.

Ramazanov laughed. "French intelligence with American accents?"

"We're normally stationed overseas," Vail said dismissively. "So I get the forgery. Simple motive there—money. But how'd you get hooked up with terrorists? Did they offer you—"

"Katherine," DeSantos said firmly. "This isn't important."

"I need to underst—" Her phone vibrated. "Yeah."

"You sent me photos," the Israeli-accented voice said.

"I did. Can you verify?"

"There are three columns of Hebrew writing, and the words don't end in a straight line along the right margin—in other words, in today's terminology, it's not justified text. The line ends wherever the last word ends. That was the style of the codex scribe, Ben Buya. But it's not the codex. The writing is too irregular, with size variations of some of the letters. Ben Buya's penmanship was perfect. This is not even close."

"Are you sure?"

"Were you not listening to what I just said? Did our friend tell you who I am?"

"I don't have a lot of time. Straight answers, please."

"I'm sure."

"Then what am I looking at here?"

"There are a lot of ancient Hebrew manuscripts. Assuming it's not a forgery, you've got one there. They're all unique in their own ways with historic and archaeological significance. If I had it here I could probably tell you which it was. But there's only one codex. Because of what it is, when, how, and why it was created, and who wrote it, it's in a league all by itself."

"Appreciate it. We'll be in touch."

"Not it," DeSantos said.

"Nope."

"You're wrong," Ramazanov said. "That *is* the Aleppo Codex!"

"Was he sure?" DeSantos asked.

"Yes."

"Then let's get the hell out of here."

"What do we do with him?"

"We'll call, leave an anonymous tip with Paris police, give them his real identity."

"Bastards," Ramazanov said. "Why are you doing this to me? I can get you money. Lots—"

"Save it, asshole," DeSantos said as he shoved the Glock in his waistband. "Be thankful we're letting you live."

Vail was sure Ramazanov was confused as to who they were—they were clearly not law enforcement, but they weren't thieves either. And if she were him, she would not believe the French intelligence subterfuge.

Vail came up close to DeSantos's ear. "There's a bathroom in here with ventilation ducts."

"Where do they lead?"

"No idea."

"Too risky. We're better off trying to get out of here through an evacuated museum without getting seen. If we hit a dead end in the duct work and they reopen the place, there'll be hundreds of people who'll see us climbing out of a duct. And then we'll definitely get caught."

Hey, no argument from me. I was not looking forward to living through another claustrophobic's nightmare.

They checked the corridor, then walked out and headed up the staircase. The alarm was louder in the hallway, the high-pitched piercing whine stinging her ears.

"You sure that's the right move?" Vail asked. "Letting him live."

DeSantos glanced over his left shoulder at Vail. "I only kill when it's necessary—if it endangers our mission or my ability to operate now or in the future."

"What if he IDs us?"

"I didn't think you'd be in favor of killing someone in cold blood. You're surprising me. Or is this Katherine Vega talking?"

"I'm just trying to make sense of what we're doing—and how we're supposed to do it."

They were nearing the door to the public area of the Louvre. DeSantos put his fingers on the handle. "Look, he's not a guy with a lot of integrity. What's he got to sell? The identity of two people who did not steal anything, did not break any laws, and turned a known fugitive and terrorist into the authorities? And even if he's got something to sell and bargain with, what's he got—a physical description and no clear video images? I'm not saying there's no risk, but we should be fine."

"Okay."

"There's more, but I'll explain later. We've gotta get out of the museum. You go first, make sure it's clear. If you come across security or staff, act hysterical, like you got lost and couldn't find your way out and you were scared because the alarm was going off and you have anxiety—"

"Claustrophobia."

"Don't remind me." He cracked the door and peaked outside. "Looks good. Ready?"

"Ready."

He pulled out his phone and started dialing. "Answer this call and leave the line open. When you get a couple hundred yards, let me know and I'll leave. In case there are cameras we won't be seen together. Keep your chin down."

Vail did as instructed and headed out, through the museum exhibits, the Levant and Antique Iran, down the halls and past white and gray-toned, intricately carved marble statues as she made her way toward the exit.

"Approaching the Sully. No one's here."

"Keep going."

"Shit." Off in the distance, coming through the reception area and heading her way, were a dozen or more men dressed in silver helmets, dark bulky jackets, and yellow striped pants. She ducked behind a column and brought the handset to her ear. "Fire brigade's headed my way. Along with a bunch of cops. Get out of there now."

"Copy that. Already on my way."

"Hé! Que faites-vous là?"

Vail swung around and saw two security guards running toward her, yelling, pointing.

Oh, shit. If they search me, if they think I stole something during the commotion— She glanced around. *No good place to ditch the Glock and Tanto. No time to wipe them down.*

Vail turned toward the police and firefighters, then back to the guards. She needed to defuse the situation before the approaching first responders got within earshot. She figured she had about ten to fifteen seconds.

Thirty or so feet behind the guards, DeSantos was approaching on the run.

Vail headed toward the men, then threw her hands up to her ears. "How do I get out? The alarm's so loud, I can't stand it anymore! Help me get out of here, please."

"Down," one of them said, obviously unimpressed with her acting abilities. "Get down on the ground now!"

51

Uzi descended the stairs and realized that, with the elevator broken, this was the only way in and out. That meant any second now he could come face-to-face with the Paris police. And unlike their brethren in England, these guys were armed.

After forty or fifty steps he turned into a dimly lit room that looked like a small museum: there was a sizable scaled mockup of the arch, a vending machine that dispensed Medaille Souvenir from Monnaie de Paris—collector's coins stamped with the arch's image—and sculptures that appeared to commemorate French military victories.

Had Fahad found the other tango? Was the guy lying in wait? Or bleeding out somewhere?

Uzi pushed those thoughts aside. He had to concentrate on evasion and escape. There was no place to hide—at least, not effectively. But he had to figure something out because he heard the boots of men rapidly ascending the stairs.

He swiveled, saw a restroom, and knew it was his only option. He ducked inside and pulled the Glock from his waist band. He looked at it a long moment and again debated what he should do. Even if he hid the weapon in here, it would be discovered sooner rather than later. If he kept it with him at least he had a chance that it would not be found.

Uzi shoved the pistol back in his pants, then set his ear against the door, listening for when it might be safe to emerge.

A moment later, the voices and boot steps subsided. If they thought their suspect had fled, one or more officers might be standing on the other side of the door, checking the museum—and that meant clearing the restroom.

But he heard nothing. No bustle of equipment belts, no footfalls, no communication between two partners or the chirp of a radio.

Uzi drew in a breath and pulled open the door. He peered out—the area looked clear. He moved across the room, walking on his toes to prevent the click of heels against the floor.

He got to the steps and knew he had about two hundred to descend. And he had no idea who, or what, awaited him below.

He made his way down the spiral staircase, moving at a fairly rapid clip, getting into a rhythm as his feet clomped down the stone slabs.

When he hit the landing, three police officers were standing in a triangle, handguns drawn. Uzi immediately raised his hands and said, "I was in the museum and people came running down the stairs saying they heard gunshots. I thought it was a car backfiring, but the police came running up and told me to go down, not to go to the terrace. But I'm leaving for Chicago tomorrow morning and I won't have another chance to see—"

"Move along," the cop said with a heavy French accent. "Outside. If everything okay, you go back up. Keep your ticket."

"Any idea how long it might be?"

The cop's brow hardened. "Long time if you keep talking. Go wait outside."

"Right," Uzi said, backing away. "Sorry."

He walked through the tunnel and up the stairs, past another two cops at the entrance. Uzi nodded at them—a quick dip of his chin in acknowledgment—and started walking at a normal pace, wanting to run but exercising restraint.

The arch was at the center of a twelve-spoked wheel; a dozen streets radiated out in a 360 degree arc. He could not spend much time here—he would either see Fahad right away or he would move on.

He thought of grabbing a cab, but those in the vicinity had passengers and he did not want to stand around in sight of the police. Ahead was a Métro station, which would give him a decent chance of getting away from the vicinity and putting distance between himself and the victim.

He walked up Avenue de Friedland to get the train at the Charles de Gaulle de Etoile station when an ivory-colored Citroën pulled up in front of him.

"Get in," Fahad said through the passenger window.

Uzi pulled open the door and hit the seat the same second Fahad accelerated.

"So what was that?" Fahad asked. "Where the hell was the meet?"

"There was no meet," Uzi said as he buckled his belt.

"But you said—"

"It was an ambush, a setup."

"That's impossible. How could they know we were headed there? Unless—"

"They sent us there."

"You think those counterterrorism officers were invol—"

"No. The tangos probably had some kind of incursion detection system.

Either when we entered the flat or when I turned on the computer monitor, it started transmitting our conversation or—" he slapped his right thigh. "The webcam. When I started the PC it must've notified them and activated the camera. They saw what I was doing on the computer and they sent me a bogus email about a meet. They knew we'd take the bait. It's like dangling a flourless tort in front of a chocoholic. He has to take a bite. That's exactly what I did. And that's why they only gave us just enough time to get there. They knew how long it'd take to drive there, and they had people in the area ready to execute us. Or me. Maybe they didn't know about you."

Fahad turned left on Rue de Longchamp.

"Where we going?"

"How about back toward their flat. To get even."

Uzi bit down on his molars. He did not know if he should feel incensed or pleased that he and Fahad had beaten back their plans to kill him. In truth, he felt both.

Uzi pushed his buttocks back into the seat and sat up straight. "Let's go find the bastards."

52

DeSantos came up behind the two guards and rendered one unconscious with a vicious blow to the back of his cranium with the handle of his Glock. As the other turned, DeSantos struck him with an equally violent backhand. He went down but was still moving, moaning and writhing. DeSantos stuck his knee in the man's mid back then slammed him again in the head.

He would have a hell of a headache, a couple of nasty welts, a concussion, and some memory loss, but he would recover. And he would be alive. He would never know how lucky he and his partner were.

DeSantos grabbed the arms of the first man and started pulling him along the slick floor. Vail did likewise with the second guard, but struggled to move his mass, even though he was fairly slight. They got both bodies against one of the display cabinets, out of the direct view of the approaching officers.

"Cops must've gone in one of the other entrances," Vail said, peering out into the near distance at the sortie of the Sully access.

"There's a Denon access," DeSantos said. "I saw it on the map when we first came in. I think that's one of the places where the Roma were going to set off the alarm."

"So you want to just walk right out?"

"Something like that."

Vail gave him a dubious look.

"Best I've got. If we can get outside, we've got a shot."

"You want to split up?"

"Normally I'd say yes. But I think we'd look less suspicious if we were a husband and wife who got lost during the commotion of an emergency evacuation."

They walked straight out and then took the escalator down. Ahead was the mall—and several police officers and military personnel deployed at strategic points, no doubt there to prevent looting of the abandoned shops.

"What do you want to do?" she asked as they approached the cops.

"You'll think of something."

"Stop right there," yelled one of the officers, his right hand held up in front of him. "What are you two doing in here?"

"My husband was in the bathroom, he's got a bad case of the runs and he was stuck on the toilet when the alarm—"

"Honey!" DeSantos feigned surprise. "Really? That's too much information. Embarrassing."

Vail shrugged and turned back to the cop. "I couldn't leave him alone. I wanted to make sure he was okay."

"Oh." DeSantos bent over. "There it is again."

"You need a bathroom?" she asked, placing a hand on his shoulder.

"No, just—just some fresh air."

"Go on," the man said. "Up the stairs. Through the pyramid." He grabbed his radio and spoke rapid-fire French into it, hopefully telling the cops at the top that they were cool to let through. Either that or he was saying, "Arrest these jokers and throw them in the slammer. They tried to pull the old 'stuck on the shitter' ruse on me."

They emerged on the plaza, where hundreds of people were gathered, impatiently awaiting readmittance into the museum. DeSantos pulled his phone, read the display, then looked up. "C'mon. We've got a debt to pay."

"Now?"

"Got a rep to protect."

He led Vail ahead, toward the Tuileries Gardens and Arc de Triomphe du Carrousel. He made eye contact with a Roma Vail remembered seeing in the Mona Lisa Room then reached into his pocket and pulled something out. He shook the man's hand, deposited the euros in his palm, and kept walking down the path.

"You think we got out of there without getting captured on video?" Vail asked as they walked briskly, but normally, along the finely graveled, damp path. A drizzle had apparently been falling for some time as small puddles had formed on the walkway's decomposed granite.

"Not a chance," DeSantos said, head moving from side to side, surveilling the park. "But the only thing they'll have on us—if there were cameras there—is me attacking two security guards. Simple assault."

"You hit them with your *Glock*."

"Yeah, there's that. Guess it's not so 'simple.'"

After passing the Grand Bassin Rond—a large fountain and surrounding pond—sirens started up again and police cars whizzed by.

"Bad sign?" Vail asked.

"Definitely. I guess they found the guards—or the video of me doing my 'Glock karate chop.' Just keep walking. No panic, no undue attention."

They passed a couple of outdoor cafés featuring tables with red umbrellas poking up below intricately pruned medium-size trees. One eatery displayed a chalkboard wood-framed sign offering *vin chaud a la cannelle*—for the English tourists, "hot red wine with cinnamon"—that made Vail's mouth water.

They walked on and she glanced to her right, in the vicinity of a Métro station. But police were milling about, making that route of exit unappealing if not downright dangerous.

DeSantos took Vail's hand and gave it a squeeze. "I don't want you to be alarmed, but there are several French policemen behind us and two approaching from the south. Keep walking straight."

"You did say, 'Don't be alarmed,' right?"

"We can't outrun them because there are too many. And more in cars along the periphery."

"Are you sure?"

"Pretty much."

"You're not joking, are you?"

"Not now, no. Not this time."

Jesus.

"You think they ID'd us?"

"Let's not stick around to find out. Have you ever ridden a Segway?"

"Those things we saw the tourists riding this morning? The two-wheeled things with the pole you put between your legs?"

"Another time, I'd have some sexual comeback. But yeah, that's what I'm talking about. There are a bunch of 'em ahead of us. Tour group standing by the Luxor Obelisk."

Vail peered into the misty rain. "I see them."

"They're taking a break. The Segways are about twenty yards behind them. We're gonna borrow two."

"You want to try to outrun the police?"

DeSantos snorted. "They only go about thirteen miles per hour, Karen. We might be able to outrun most of the cops who are in boots and weighed down with utility belts. And they'll take us farther than someone on foot. But that's not the point. They give us mobility—we'd be able to go places cars can't. We need angles and distance."

They approached a dozen Segways parked in a line at a curb. A couple of the tourists were late leaving their vehicles, but the others were still at the obelisk, snapping photos.

"We just gonna walk up to them and steal them?"

"Pretty much."

"What about keys?"

"No keys. They've got controllers that have chips inside that keep track of that Segway's vital stats. There are security settings to prevent you from doing what we're about to do, but most tour companies don't bother with them unless the vehicles are going to be out of sight."

"So we're hoping to get far enough away that we'll be out of the controller's range before they realize two are missing."

"Put your helmet on and move it away from the curb. And be careful of how you lean because it responds to your body movements."

"How I lean?

"It uses gyroscopes to sense your body weight. Lean forward, it goes forward. Lean backward, it goes backward. Steer with the handlebars. Move them to the right side, you turn right. It takes some getting used to, but once you get the hang of it, it's very natural."

"Do I have time to practice?"

DeSantos glanced at her as they neared the vehicles.

"Just saying. This might not be pretty."

"It won't be. But I have confidence in you."

"Since when?"

"Since right now."

They walked the line of Segways, going for the two farthest from the tour group.

"And what if they see us and yell?"

"We'll worry about that if and when it happens. Once we get the helmets on, hopefully we'll look like two people from their group. These tours are put together on a first-come first-served basis, so other than your companion or friend, you don't know any of the other people. It's a group of strangers."

As they approached, Vail saw the black hard shell helmets hanging from the handles. She took one and quickly seated it on her head. It was a too big, but she knew that would be the least of her problems.

She climbed aboard and placed a foot on either side of the raised center panel, on the ridged rubber pads. On the outside of each of her ankles was a large air-inflated tire, partially covered by a mud guard.

Vail watched as DeSantos guided the vehicle with the movement of his body. Vail did the same—but overcorrected and nearly fell when she straightened her knees and the Segway jerked backward. She recovered and leaned forward, moving alongside DeSantos, listening for yelling—expecting someone to notice that they were stealing two very expensive vehicles.

She wasn't disappointed, because they had gotten a half block when she heard a female voice call out, "Hé, arrêter!" Vail interpreted it as, "Hey, stop!"

"Keep going, "DeSantos said over his shoulder, looking back at Vail, who was moving in a herky-jerky, start-stop fashion, generally forward—but too slowly. "Just lean toward the handlebars. She won't be able to catch us."

And hopefully she won't turn the damn things off with the remote.

Vail canted forward and her speed increased: a smooth acceleration. The rain beat against her face and prickled her eyes, but—she had to admit—the ride was exhilarating, much like she felt when she drove a car for the first time.

She wanted to sneak a look behind her, to make sure they were not being followed, but she did not dare shift her weight.

They moved down the asphalt street, which was worn to the original cobblestone, making for a bumpy ride. She came up alongside DeSantos, who had slowed to let her catch up. "We have to call the police, tell them about Raboud, that he's really Ramazanov. And where to find him."

"We're not gonna do that."

"What are you talking about? Why the hell not?"

"I left a pair of scissors on the desk next to him so he could cut the cuffs. I assume he'd be smart enough to look for a way out as soon as we left. It'll take him a while with scissors, but—"

"Why'd you do that?"

"He's worth more to us as a free man than one put through the French legal system."

She turned to him, her face hot against the wet, cold rain—and nearly lost her balance. "Hector, you're not making any sense."

"I rigged his cell phone."

"Rigged, how?"

"Something Uzi taught me. He called it a cross between Bluebugging and some other techno-hack stuff I didn't understand. He built some kind of app that looks to exploit weaknesses in Bluetooth and cellular signal technology. I took care of it while you were looking over that ancient manuscript. Bottom line is that if what I did worked, we'll be able to read the data on Ramazanov's phone—and eavesdrop on his calls. Supposedly we can even send texts from his phone to people in his contact list."

"Without him knowing?"

"Uzi's the one to ask, but I think so. He made it as dumb-shit proof as possible because when it comes to tech, I'm—"

"A dumb-shit?"

"Challenged." DeSantos looked around and appeared indecisive as he led her down the Rue Le Champs Elysées, past a large government-looking building, the tire tread channeling away the rain water that had settled on the pavement and making a swishing sound as the vehicle moved along the roadway. A white and charcoal chiaroscuro choked the expansive sky before them. A hazy misty pall hung over the city and partially obscured the Eiffel Tower, which rose above all buildings in the vicinity.

"Where to?"

"Good question," DeSantos said. "I screwed up."

"What?"

"Too open here. I'd wanted to get us into an area with alleys and narrow streets. That's our main advantage on these things."

"So far so good. No one's chasing us. No cops, no sirens."

As soon as she said that, a police car appeared, a blue striped white Citroën Jumper minivan that bore a red crest labeled "Police Nationale." Its two blue lights were swirling as the vehicle slowed half a block away.

"So much for 'no one's chasing us.'"

"They're turning right. Keep going, don't panic. We're just tourists taking a glide on a Segway."

On cue, another cruiser's siren wound up and the vehicle started moving in their direction.

"We need to get off these things."

"Not yet."

"No," Vail said, "Now. Someone probably put out a stolen vehicle code, and the police put it together with what they've now realized was a ruse at the Louvre. Not hard to add it up to a man and a woman on a couple of stolen Segways."

"Fine. There's a Métro station up ahead." He slowed and nodded at a red sign mounted on an antique light post. "Oh, shit. Métro Champs Elysées Clemenceau."

"Why's that bad?"

DeSantos glanced around. "Because on your left is the Grand Palais. And down that street to your right is the Élysée Palace, where the president of France lives."

"Nice work, Hector." White police cars were stationed up and down the streets in all directions. "It's like we rode right into a hornet's nest."

"Let's not get stung. We're already on the cameras. Let's ditch these and split up, head into the station and catch the next train. Wherever it goes doesn't matter. As long as it's away from here."

Vail leaned back to slow the vehicle and brought it to a stop in front of a parked car, partially hidden from view of many of the police vehicles and about thirty feet from the Métro entrance. She yanked off the helmet and set it on the Segway's foot pads and crossed the street. Keeping her head down, she approached the station and descended the steps. As if she had any doubt where she was, the word METRO was literally set in stone, carved into the decorative concrete bannister that faced commuters as they headed down toward the subterranean platform.

She purchased a ticket, trying to appear calm and casual in case she was under surveillance, keeping her chin down as much as possible while she waited for the train to arrive.

Where's Hector?

There were two dozen or so people in the area chattering with one another or reading iPads. A few sat on white chairs that were shaped like shallow ice cream cones.

As the seconds ticked by, she grew concerned. Had the police arrested him before he had a chance to get down into the station?

She heard a whistle, which sounded like a bird call. She glanced left and saw DeSantos standing about thirty or forty feet away, pretending to type on his smartphone.

The train pulled in and stopped and they got into different cars. As Vail took a seat, two men walked on carrying an accordion and a portable speaker. The taller one began playing an upbeat French tune while the younger musician shifted the amplifier to his left hand, pulled off his hat, and held it out for commuters to toss in euros. Several obliged.

DeSantos worked his way toward her, walking through the long train that lacked doors between cars but instead had rubberized connectors that bent, contracting and expanding when the Métro negotiated curves in the track. He came up beside her, facing the opposite direction. He said, gazing forward, "Our eavesdropping plan just paid off. The guy made a call."

"To who?"

"Arabic. Don't know. Well, I know a little but not enough to stake lives on it. But Uzi built the app so it records all tapped calls. I emailed the audio file to him."

"Hopefully it's a lead." After a moment, she realized DeSantos was distracted by something. "What's up?"

He tilted his head slightly to the right.

Far down, approximately two car lengths away, were three police-types dressed in SWAT-style riot gear with articulated shoulder pads extending down to their elbows. Their dark-colored, rain-slick jackets bore large white alphanumerical designations: 1A, 4C, 2B.

"Apparently there are several teams out looking for us," DeSantos said.

Several teams with submachine guns slung across their bulletproof vests. "Forgive me for stating the obvious, but this is not good."

DeSantos turned back toward the window ahead of her. "As our friend Clive Reid is fond of saying, shite."

53

Uzi was tapping his foot as Fahad drove toward the terrorists' flat. He did not know what to expect—if there would be Paris counterterrorism officers combing the building and neighborhood—or if the tangos had booby-trapped the apartment, fully expecting the two of them to return to exact revenge or to finish what they had started when the bogus email came through.

As he pondered those questions, his Lumia vibrated. He read DeSantos's email and then put the handset on speaker. "Listen to this. Hacked call from a forger, a known associate of al Humat. Santa tapped his smartphone."

The recording started—a conversation in Arabic between a man DeSantos identified as Borz Ramadazov and an unknown accomplice:

"We've got a problem."

"You didn't lose the codex—"

"It's safe. I showed them a different book from a few hundred years later and insisted it was the codex. Their expert knew it wasn't but they didn't think to search the safe."

"So you got lucky."

"I got lucky. But we need to get it out of the country. They said they were French intelligence, but they weren't government people, I could tell. All I know is that they were Americans. No idea who they work for."

"Where are you now?"

"They tied me up and were going to tell the police who I am but I cut myself free and I took the codex with me."

"Listen to me. Sit tight and await instructions. I'll talk with—"

"Can't. The museum's on lockdown so I had to get out. If those people figure out what I did, they'll come after me. Can't take a chance."

"So you're no longer in the museum?"

"I needed to get out of there, to a safe place. I had to assume my cover's blown so I couldn't stay. And I can't go home. The police will be looking for me, if they're not already. And I have a feeling those Americans will be too."

"He's not going to be happy if this is going to cause problems with your ability to—"

"I'll get it done."

"Who were these Americans?"

"Woman said her name was Katherine Vega, but that's bullshit. No idea about the male. But there was something about him. Not sure what it was. But he's dangerous."

"Bring the document to the safe house. Not the one on Rue Muller. It's been compromised. Go to the one in Montparnasse. Be there at seven."

Uzi disconnected the call and shared a look with Fahad, who pulled the car over to the nearest available parking spot.

"So forget about Rue Muller. How the hell are we gonna find a flat somewhere in Montparnasse?"

"How far is that from here?"

"Ten minutes, maybe fifteen. Depends on lights, traffic."

The rain picked up and began pelting the windshield in a rhythmic patter.

"Let's head over there. I can get us a location. I built the app so that it coordinates with the phone's GPS. If the wireless was off on the target phone, it turns it on. It picks up Wi-Fi signals along the way—a café, a company, a business, a residence—and the GPS puts the phone on a map. I'll get the location from Santa."

"That's a nice little app you designed."

"Santa, call me. I need GPS info on that phone." Uzi hung up and leaned back in his seat. "We've got plenty of time to get the address and get over there, scope the place out. See who comes and goes." He started dialing again.

"Who you calling?"

"Tim Meadows. He's gotta have an ID on some of those prints from London by now. Assuming the lifts were good enough. Makeup powder is far from ideal." He listened a second then let out a sigh. "Hey Tim. Uzi. Call me as soon as you get anything on those prints we emailed."

He hung up and put his phone away. "You think we're close?"

Fahad looked out at the dreary Parisian rain storm, the dark sky, and the angry clouds. "Just when I think we catch a break and cut off a tentacle, new ones appear. It's like a sea monster."

"The Loch Ness. We catch glimpses, and sometimes we even feel like we've seen it."

"But catching it proves elusive."

"Yeah." Uzi balled his fist. "A monster, all right. One we're going to slay."

54

Vail exited the RER station, followed a minute later by DeSantos. The RER, or Réseau Express Régional, was a modern underground rail that supplemented the century-old Métro subway. It featured fewer stops and faster arrival times—which served Vail and DeSantos well.

After seeing the officers who were on the first train, they switched lines to the RER and then quickly emerged from the subterranean system, hoping they had kept their faces off whatever security cameras the Paris police had access to.

They stood outside the Saint Michel Notre Dame station, a light rain falling steadily. As large tour buses passed, their wheels whooshed along the wet pavement, making a sound like steaks being grilled over a high flame.

Vail squinted against the precipitation and ventured forward along the sidewalk, using the canopy of mature trees to give her some cover. Being barren this time of year, they were of minimal benefit.

They bought a couple of nondescript tourist baseball hats lettered with "Paris" on the front. They considered buying umbrellas to shield them further, but the wind would almost certainly pull them inside out.

A block later they came upon a brasserie that had an outdoor take away stand for boissons, sandwiches, and crepes. "Think we've got time to eat? I'm starving."

DeSantos glanced around. "Now is as good a time as any. Go ahead."

Vail told the Frenchman behind the permanent stainless steel stand what they wanted while DeSantos kept watch. The cook spread the crepe batter on the griddle, pulled the top down and then brought it up and spooned on some butter. The wind whipped up and blew in their direction, ruffling the overhanging red canvas canopies.

As the griddle sizzled, loud bells began to ring. DeSantos came up beside her, facing away, keeping an eye on the landscape for trouble. "Notre Dame Cathedral. In case you're interested."

Vail turned and saw the imposing Gothic structure directly across the small side street from them. She craned her neck to the top, at the spires and gargoyles and chimeras and columns that stretched toward the sky.

There was a modest line of people along the side of the building preparing for a tour of the tower, according to the sign.

As she turned to check on the food, she saw three police cars converge on the plaza. But before she could say anything, DeSantos grabbed her hand and pulled her away.

Her stomach contracted in disappointment as they abandoned the crepes and crossed the street toward the church.

"They may not be here looking for us," she said.

"No, but they probably have our description. And once they see us, we're in the shit."

He pulled her toward the entrance of the cathedral. They got in line, but DeSantos pushed his way closer to the entrance, saying something about their lost child inside and they had to find him. No one objected.

"Keep your hat on and don't look up. I'm sure there are cameras in here."

Seconds later they entered the cathedral and followed the flow of people as they shuffled into the dark church.

Whoa. Vail craned her neck up and around, taking in the enormity of the space—and the intricacy of the sculptured stonework.

"What happened to keep your head down?"

"Sorry." She pulled her gaze lower as they moved deeper into the nave before turning left toward the exit. A low murmur filled the vast chamber. "I've seen pictures, but they don't do it justice. The scale is hard to appreciate."

DeSantos took her hand and picked his way past the slow-moving tourists. "Between this and the Louvre, you're having your arts and culture fill for the year. All in one day."

"What are we doing in here?"

"The police were outside, so we're inside. Soon as it's clear we can leave."

"Kind of like taking sanctuary in a church."

"Kind of not."

"You don't think they'll check in here?"

"We'd have to be fools to come in here. No way to maneuver, few places to hide, and no easy, quick exit."

Vail looked at him. "So what does that make us?"

"Very smart."

"You feeling okay? Because you seem to be confused."

"We'd be so stupid to come in here that they won't bother checking. Reverse psychology."

"That's not reverse psychology. But I'll accept your point—only because we're not being swarmed by teams of gun-toting, pissed off cops."

DeSantos stationed himself by the large doors that led to the plaza out front.

After five minutes of people pushing past them and leaving the cathedral, Vail tugged on his arm.

"How we doing?"

"Not sure. Getting dark, harder to see. We're gonna have to chance it."

"This is a stupid problem to have," she said. "We're the good guys and we're here to catch the bad guys."

Another tourist pushed by and went out the door. DeSantos shifted left and right to get a look. "I'll go first, scout things out. Count to thirty then follow. Stay within view of each other, walk deliberate but don't look rushed. We'll grab a cab or take the Métro—whichever's closest."

DeSantos walked straight ahead into the plaza while Vail hung back and did as instructed, passing the seconds as she looked into the busy square. She did not see any police vehicles parked along the curb. Because they were white, spotting them was easier than the officers' dark uniforms.

Although they had been inside no more than ten minutes, the dense cloud cover and bad weather had conspired to bring nightfall a bit earlier than usual—which Vail considered a benefit. If it was harder for them to see law enforcement, it would be more difficult for law enforcement to see them.

The rain was still falling steadily but had slowed to a drizzle. She ventured out into the plaza and turned right, toward the tree-covered sidewalk of Rue du Cloître, not far from where they had attempted to purchase crepes.

Before she could step off the curb, however, a man grabbed her forearm firmly and said, "Se il vous plaît venez avec moi. Je me pose des questions pour vous."

Vail turned and saw the navy windbreaker of a Paris police officer, his matching baseball hat sporting large white lettering that read, POLICE.

"I—I don't speak French. In English?" But she had a pretty good idea of what he wanted.

"We have some questions for you."

"About what? I'm here on vacation, I didn't do anything wrong. Well, I crossed the street outside the crosswalk, but a lot of people were. It wasn't just me. I didn't know. Is there a fine in France for jaywalking?"

Come on, Hector. Where the hell are you?

The man—who looked to be in his twenties—loosened his grip and squinted. "Just come with me," he said in heavily accented English. "I'll explain."

"But I'm supposed to meet my girlfriend for dinner. She's gonna wor—"

"You can call her from the police station." He tugged again, pulling her toward the curb—where, dammit, now she saw it. A white police cruiser.

The cop's hands were large and they had a good grip around her forearm.

"Police station? Whoa, wait a minute. What'd I do? In America, you have to tell someone why you're arresting them."

"We are not in America, no?"

Smartass.

"But—"

"Also, mademoiselle, you are not under arrest. Yet."

Vail used her body weight to stop their forward progress. "If I'm not under arrest, I'm not going anywhere except to that restaurant to meet my girlfriend."

"I do not think you understand."

"No," DeSantos said, behind the officer and pressing something into the back of the man. "*You* don't understand. The lady said she doesn't want to go with you. Take your hands off her." He gestured at Vail—a look that told her to take the handgun from the cop's holster.

Vail did so surreptitiously and placed it in her jacket pocket.

"Now, DeSantos said, "back up slowly. No fast moves."

He guided the officer a few feet toward his compact Peugeot sedan and opened the back door. "Get in."

Vail looked around, hoping the cop's partner was not in the vicinity—if he had a partner—and saw a commotion half a block away, in the plaza, near a trash bin. People were drawing close to it, trying to see what the fuss was about.

"Don't worry about it," DeSantos said, clearly noticing Vail's concern.

He was right—and she refocused her attention on the officer, who was now in the sedan. She knew the Paris police had budgetary issues, so perhaps patrols were done solo. *I sure hope that's the case here.*

"Hey," DeSantos said, taking care not to use her name. "Cuff him."

She pulled a flexcuff from her pocket and strapped his wrists together. Another one secured him to the headrest of the front seat, which would prevent him from moving or leaving the car.

DeSantos slammed the door and turned to survey the street.

"You started the fire?"

"A diversion. I needed to get as many eyes off you as possible. Let's get out of here."

They moved quickly down the block, outside the grouping of locals and tourists, who were watching the flames lick higher and wider in the plaza. The fire brigade's sirens were approaching in the distance.

"There's an RER station," Vail said, indicating directly ahead.

DeSantos suddenly diverted left. "Negative. LE approaching, near the entrance," he said, using the abbreviation for law enforcement.

They walked against traffic on the sidewalk, along a concrete retaining wall.

And that's when things got dicey.

55

Uzi's phone vibrated—and jolted him and Fahad to attention. He dug it out and answered Tim Meadows's call.

"The first set of prints Mr. DeSantos sent me, which looked like they were pulled off the screen of a cell phone, belong to Amin Qamari, a Moroccan assassin who's wanted for several murders in Amsterdam."

"We'll have to tell our Dutch friends at the General Intelligence and Security Service Mr. Qamari can be removed from their most wanted list. He's dead."

"Well, that's a damn shame."

"Notify Director Knox," Uzi said. "He'll take care of the notification when the time is right. What else you got?"

"One of the other prints matches Doka Michel, the leader of the French Islamic movement, Sharia Law for France Now. Its goal—as the group's name implies—is to oversee the transition from traditional French government to traditional Islamic Sharia law using rapid population expansion and voter mobilization to transform the country."

"Sounds so innocuous and official. Like the mission of a real diplomatic envoy."

"He's also suspected in planning several terrorist attacks, including the one on the Lyon police station last year that killed nine officers. According to what I was able to dig up, with Hoshi Koh's assistance—and by the way, she's a wasted talent in your office, Uzi. You really—"

"Tim, back on track. What'd you dig up?"

"Michel has colleagues in Belgium and the Netherlands, all focused on that one goal: taking over their respective countries by instituting Sharia law."

"Michel . . . why do I know that name?"

"I was wondering how long it'd take you to clue in on that. He's the son of Alberi Michel—"

"The man who stole the Jesus Scroll from the Qumran caves in the late 1950s."

"Give that man a gold star. Well, let's make it a silver because you took—"

"Anything else?"

"Still working on the others."

"Thanks, Tim. Let me know when you've got something." He disconnected the call and sat there, wondering what it meant. He related Meadows's findings to Fahad, who nodded.

"The Agency has been monitoring these Sharia movements for a while."

"So what will Parisians do in twenty years when the Muslim majority votes in Sharia law?"

Fahad thought a long moment and said, "A lot can happen in twenty years."

"So you don't think it'll come to pass."

"Our Agency analysts don't see anything that'll stop it. The French culture will disappear. There'll be some radical shifts pretty much immediately. As you'd expect. There'll be a purge of nonbelievers. A civil struggle, riots, maybe a civil war." He chuckled. "The Agency will probably get involved, agitate some of it themselves. We're good at that. But the bottom line is that the popular majority will be Muslim. This is the extremists' plan, we know this. They've told us for years now that this is a war that they're waging with population overbreeding. They're outbreeding the native Parisians six to one? Something like that. And their plan is to do this throughout Europe."

"Seems like an incredibly effective strategy," Uzi said.

Fahad nodded. "I have nothing against Islam. I'm a Muslim myself. But the system of governing is archaic. It'll set women's rights back centuries. It'll set everything back. Not just here. Lots of cities in Europe will lose their culture. You saw what happened in Iraq with Islamic State. Wherever they could they obliterated entire civilizations, cultures that were different from theirs. They were 'infidels' who did not believe. According to a literal interpretation of the Koran, which is what the extremists follow, if you don't believe, you're supposed to be killed."

"I guess it's a part of the natural course of political evolution. Every culture, every civilization falls eventually. That's been one of history's lessons. Everything eventually comes to an end."

"That's kind of dark."

Uzi bit his lip. "As much as I don't want to admit it, it's just the way it is. Futurists have been predicting the end of American society for years. Let's hope their future is not ours."

Uzi dialed DeSantos again, and again it went to voicemail. "C'mon, Santa . . ."

His phone vibrated almost immediately: a text from Hoshi Koh.

“DeSantos?” Fahad asked.

“My colleague. She got an address for Doka Michel.”

“How the hell did she get that?”

Uzi smiled. “She’s been paying attention to my hacking lessons. And she’s really, really good.”

“Hacking lessons?”

“Start the car. Until or unless we get something better from Santa, this is our priority.”

56

The voice came from behind them: the unmistakable bark of a law enforcement officer ordering them to stop.

And like most criminals who did not want to be caught, Vail and DeSantos did like all the perps they despised: they ran.

"Split up," DeSantos said, pushing her away from him. "I'll call you," he yelled, holding his hand up to his ear, mimicking a phone call, as he headed away from her.

Vail ran left and DeSantos right. She did not know how many cops were behind her, but she was not going to look. She needed to escape—without landing a bullet between the shoulder blades.

The drizzle had stopped, but she took extra care not to take a header on the slick pavement. She slowed to a brisk walk, ducking in between cars that were stopped in traffic and around tourists and locals who were out for an early dinner.

She thought of the foot pursuits she had engaged in during her career. In each case it became a race in which she or her partner outflanked the perp. She was in unknown territory now, where the next turn she took could mean coming face-to-face with armed officers.

Vail crossed the street and headed back toward the cathedral, into a lush greenbelt with small trees, tall hedges, and dense shrubbery. It would give her some cover where she could change direction outside the view of the police.

Except that when she reached the bushes she nearly ran into the retaining wall—beyond which lay the Seine, the five-hundred-mile river that coursed through the heart of Paris.

Vail flashed on her escapades with London's River Thames. *I don't have good luck with these.*

Still, she was out of options—and, apparently, out of room. She turned right and ran along the Premenade Maurice Carême, which paralleled the

Seine, using the wall of greenery as cover. She shed her jacket and pulled it inside out as she ran. The charcoal gray coat became azure. She pulled off her hat and glasses and fluffed her red mane as she emerged from the promenade.

Up ahead was a narrow span that crossed the Seine, the Petit Pont-Cardinal Lustiger, or "Cardinal Lustiger's small bridge." Several people were seated on a stone wall along the adjacent roadway, a few chatting, some reading, one on her phone.

Vail hopped on top, pulled out a Métro map from her 5.11 cargo pocket and quickly unfolded it. She dropped her chin and pretended to study it.

"Avez-vous besoin d'aide?"

Vail reluctantly turned to the man beside her. He was in his thirties, square jaw, pleasing Parisian face. She laughed, disarming and warm. Playful even. Robby flashed through her thoughts and she felt dirty. "English?"

"I do," he said, displaying a broad white smile. "Do you need help?"

Another time, another place. Five years ago would've worked. Stop it, Karen. Focus.

"I'm trying to get to the Eiffel Tower," she said, picking the first thing that came to her mind. *Can I sound more inept?*

"I'm Jean-Claude. Where are you from?"

"I'm . . . Roxxann," she said, shaking his hand, holding it a second longer than normal. "From Canada."

"And you don't speak French?" He put his index and thumb together. "Not even a little?" He squinted, friendly disbelief.

"I live on the west coast."

She was suddenly aware of the police officers no more than fifteen feet away—she saw their boots and navy pants. But she did not dare look their way. Her goal was to hide in plain sight. And it didn't get much plainer than fifteen feet away.

She lifted the Métro map. "Which line do I get on?" she said, flirting a bit with her eyes. "It's all so confusing."

"Here, let me show you." He leaned in closer, no doubt noticing that she did not have a ring on her finger. "Are you in Paris alone?"

"I'm here with a friend. But we went our own way today. And it's been a challenge getting around. I had no idea. I didn't know big cities could be so confusing."

"Well. Here we are," Jean-Claude said, pushing slightly into her left shoulder. "And this is Tour Eiffel. You want to take this line, right here, the—"

"You know, Jean-Claude, would you mind walking me to the right station?"

He sat up straight—as if this conversation might lead to something more than just a chance encounter on a bridge by the Seine.

"Of course. I could take you to the tower, if you would like." He glanced at his watch. "It's a little after six. Have you eaten dinner?"

Vail lifted her brow—as if the thought had not occurred to her. Her stomach rumbled at the mention of food. "I haven't. Do you know a good restaurant?"

"I know many." He slid off the retaining wall and held out a bent elbow, helping her off. They turned right, and Jean-Claude, who was a good six foot two, gave her some cover as he led her in the direction of the Métro.

They had just crossed the street when her phone rang. It was DeSantos. "Excuse me, Jean-Claude. My friend." She put the handset to her face. "Maggie, hi."

DeSantos hesitated. "You in trouble?"

"I should be able to manage. Where are you?"

"On the edge of the Seine, the Quai du Marché Neuf, right below the Pont Saint-Michel, alongside a dinner boat. Cross street Boulevard du Palais. Meet me there now. Boat's leaving in five minutes and we need to be on it."

"A dinner—" She stopped herself, realizing Jean-Claude was listening. "Okay, no, I understand. I'll be right there." She looked up—and realized she did not know which way to go.

"So sorry, Jean-Claude. My friend—she's, she's booked us a place for dinner and it's our last night, I didn't want to say no. Can you point me to the Pont Saint-Michel? That's a bridge, right?"

Jean-Claude smiled—disappointment evident on his face, but ever the gentleman, he was going to help her. "You're very close, five minutes at most."

Five minutes? How can I run without running?

He pointed her in the right direction and she gave him a hug and a peck on the cheek. "Again, I'm sorry. I was looking forward to dinner."

He handed her his card. "Call me next time you're in town."

She smiled. "I will." Over his shoulder, she saw a cop—so she turned abruptly, headed toward DeSantos.

Vail walked briskly, trying to appear casual while attempting to figure out how she was going to get there before the boat sailed. *A dinner boat? What's he thinking?*

She passed the line of cars that were parked at the curb, staying as close to the vehicles as possible. After a cluster of motorcycles she came upon a shop called Souvenir's Factory; if she had more time she would've bought a cheap Parisian pullover sweatshirt and a different hat. But she could now see the bridge up ahead on her left, which she was certain was Pont Saint-Michel.

As she approached, she saw two officers—and whipped her head to the side, trying not to make eye contact as she crossed the street and approached the sign that displayed both English and French:

Diners – Croisière

Dinner – Cruise

Embarquement

Boarding

An arrow pointed down toward the river.

She saw one of the officers looking directly at her as a large two-car articulated bus crossed in front of her, forming a screen. She used the cover to run toward the stone staircase, then descended the steps to the water's edge, where a long glass-ceilinged blue and white boat was docked. DeSantos was standing on the ramp talking with a uniformed man who looked the part of a ship's captain.

"I'm here," Vail said as she approached the vessel. She wanted to glance up, to see if the officers had realized where she had gone once the bus had cleared their line of sight, but DeSantos had her hand and was literally pulling her aboard—and into the cabin.

"When I said five minutes, I wasn't kidding. I had to give the captain some dinero to wait."

"We're in France and you're speaking Spanish?"

"Money's the universal language, no matter what you call it."

They walked into the dining room, glass comprising a majority of the ceiling and walls, with a wood floor down the center and red carpeting along the periphery. Sunken tables and built-in chairs ran in two rows along the sides of the boat. Passengers were busy snapping photos of one another.

Up above, on street level, Vail saw the two police officers standing on the Quai du Marché Neuf with their backs against the retaining wall, rotating their heads left and right, looking as if they were wondering where she had gone. One was chattering on his radio.

DeSantos, clearly clued in to her concern, said, "Idea is for people to see out, not for people to see in."

"Not sure I'm willing to stake my life on that."

As soon as she said that, another cop ran over to the officers. *Don't look down. Don't look down.* Vail rubbed her forehead with a hand. "When the hell are we gonna start moving?"

"Shhh," DeSantos said. "Relax. You look like you're under extreme duress. People are going to wonder what the hell's the matter with you."

"I'm a New Yorker. I'm a stressed out aggressive bitch."

DeSantos looked at her.

She cracked a broad smile. "That better?"

He squinted and said, hesitantly, "I think so."

The boat started moving, slowly, the landscape above them sliding by.

"Thank god." She looked up at the cops and watched them recede into the distance, her shoulders dropping in relief—only to see a dozen others standing on the Petit Pont-Cardinal Lustiger as they neared the cathedral. "Poor Jean-Claude."

"What?"

"Nothing." She sighed deeply as they glided under the bridge, putting distance between them and the police. "Now what?"

"'Now what?' Karen, I thought you were resourceful. We haven't eaten. This is a dinner cruise. We'll chow down, have a glass of wine, clear our heads and think."

Vail looked at him in disbelief. "You're amazing."

"I know. And thanks."

"I didn't mean that in a nice way."

"Then choose your adjectives better."

"How about infuriating? Or ridicul—"

"Welcome aboard, I'm Dominique," said a young hostess dressed in a black formfitting tux. "Would you like to take your seats?"

"We would," DeSantos said. "Can you wrap them to go?"

Dominique giggled. "I'm sorry, Monsieur, you are funny."

"That's what my wife says." He smiled at Vail. "All kidding aside, Dominique, how about a window seat?"

The woman giggled again. "But Monsieur, they're *all* window seats."

DeSantos made a point of looking around. "Indeed, you're right, my dear. Window seat it is." He turned to Vail and offered his bent elbow. "Honey?"

Are you kidding me? He's flirting? Vail rolled her eyes. *Ridiculous. Infuriating. Unbelievable. Insufferable. And damn good at what he does.*

The waitress brought two glasses and a bottle of Coeur de Méditerranée merlot and set it down in front of them. She pulled out a corkscrew, opened the wine, and poured it.

Vail was focused on the passing landscape above. When the waitress left, she turned to DeSantos, who was shoulder to shoulder with her in the romantic booth. "Seriously, Hector. How smart do you think this . . . dinner cruise is?"

"It was my idea, so naturally I think it was very smart."

"You know what I mean."

"I don't."

In a low voice, she said, "We're being pursued by the police and we're sitting in a boat made of windows riding through the heart of Paris. With no way to get off."

"Like I started to explain before, it's a sightseeing boat. The idea is that the tourists—that'd be us—get to see the city. That's why it's so dark in here. We can see out, but it's tough to see in. And we're moving at a pretty good pace. We'll be fine."

"Does this boat stop anywhere?"

"Only when it returns to port. It'll hit the end, then they hang a U-turn and head back."

She thought about that a moment. "If I'm Paris PD, I'd be looking at all avenues of escape in the vicinity we were last seen. And that includes this boat. They could be radioing the captain right now to prepare for our capture when we get back. Or he could be arranging for the boat to do an emergency docking at a low risk place where they've moved a tac team into position."

"Must you always think like a cop?" DeSantos asked as he poured the wine.

"Can't help myself. It's in my DNA."

He lifted his glass and handed the other one to Vail. "It's why we keep you around, my dear."

"'My dear.' Is that a new saying for you?"

"I'm growing kind of fond of it."

DeSantos clinked his glass against Vail's, then took a sip. He leaned back in his seat, staring out at the passing vista of older buildings. "How likely do you think it is that the cops are onto us?"

So he is *taking me seriously*. Vail examined her merlot. "The Paris police are generally pretty efficient. The chances are too high for us to risk it."

DeSantos chewed on that. "So they've got a couple of hours to figure it out and get their counterterrorism police in position to take us in. Unless they decide to force us to stop somewhere along the way."

The waitress stepped in front of them and set down plates of sear-roasted wild salmon with leek and artichoke ragù, according to the menu card on the table. An assistant followed with pear-shaped rolls and two cans of Coke.

They waited till the serving staff walked off before Vail leaned in close. "But if there's a fire in the kitchen, they have to dock immediately, right?"

DeSantos tilted his head back and eyed her. "Again with fire? Are you some closet pyromaniac or something?"

Vail looked at him. "I seem to recall a certain bonfire-type diversion outside the cathedral that was *your* doing."

"It did the trick, didn't it?" DeSantos dug into the salmon, turning serious. "I don't know what the ship's protocols are for an emergency docking. Gotta be something they can't put out with fire extinguishers."

She watched him chew and stab another bite. "How can you just eat?"

"Spec Ops 101. You eat when you have the chance to eat, you shit when you have a chance to shit. Besides, it's really good. You should try it."

Vail was starving so she lifted a big bite of the fish to her mouth. It did taste good—but she couldn't enjoy it. "Unless you have a better plan, the kitchen fire's our best shot. It'll create a commotion, and if they don't start heading toward the nearest port, we can jump and swim."

DeSantos scooped up another bit of salmon and wiped his mouth with the napkin. "I could call the police and tell them I planted a bomb in the Musée d'Orsay. After what's happened in DC, New York, and London, they'll overreact and divert everything they've got to the museum."

Vail looked at him a long moment. "You're right. Not about this, about what you said before about why you have me on the team."

"They *wouldn't* overreact and divert everything they've got?"

"No. Because of what's happened, they've got more police on the streets. They'd mobilize their bomb squad and a counterterrorism unit to handle the threat. Won't do us any good."

DeSantos absorbed that a moment. "Fine. But there's a problem with your plan. A ship's galley only has electric cooking equipment, for obvious safety reasons."

So obvious I didn't think of it. "So what the hell are we gonna do?"

"I didn't say they never use open flames. They use a torch to caramelize sugar, make crème brûlée, or a flambé dish like crêpe suzette or cherries jubilee."

"Crêpe suzette is on the menu."

DeSantos grinned. "Yes it is, my dear."

"Stop saying that."

"My guess is they're going to do it in the living room for the spectacle—it's very dramatic in a dimly lit interior. So once the flame crests, I'll tip the cooking pan over. The liquid will burn anything it touches."

"I'm worried about collateral damage."

"I'll set it off in a way that will minimize injury, okay?"

Vail studied his face in the candlelight. "Are you just saying that to make me feel better?"

"Of course."

Asshole. Vail's gaze roamed the interior. Despite all the predicaments she had found herself in since her unwanted affiliation with OPSIG, she never thought she would be resorting to arson to accomplish a mission. She hated to have to do this, but she could not think of another way out.

Sometimes the greater picture had to be considered, DeSantos told her. "The needs of the many outweigh the needs of the few."

"Is that some sort of OPSIG mantra?"

"Nope. *Star Trek*."

Vail shook her head. "I would've felt better if it was some moral principle the black ops world had developed in situations like this."

She had already taken an inventory of the interior and determined that there were no security cameras on board. DeSantos paid with cash so there was no traceable means back to them other than public identification. And most people were focused on the windows and the sights of downtown Paris, their meals and wine—certainly not their fellow passengers.

"Let me ask you again," he said. "Given your intimate knowledge of police procedure, how certain are you that Paris PD will be searching this boat when we get back to port?"

"Count on it. They'd have to be pretty incompetent to miss that detail. Someone's going to think of it. This is Detective 101 stuff."

He checked his watch then motioned to her plate. "Then I suggest you finish up. Because the crêpe suzette is next—and that means we're going to be evacuating this boat in the next few minutes." He pulled out his phone and consulted Google Maps, then looked out the window. "Pont de l'Alma is coming up. Now would be a good time." He rose from the chair and looked toward the setup in the middle of the dining room where the staff was prepping the dessert. "Food was delicious," he said, tossing his napkin aside. I think I'll go give my compliments to the chef. She's very hot, you know. Or—she will be in a couple of minutes."

"Be careful."

DeSantos winked at her. "Thanks for the concern. But I'll be fine."

"I was talking about the others in the dining room. No collateral damage, remember?"

After DeSantos rose from his seat, Vail pulled out her cell and saw that she had missed Uzi's text message. She turned toward DeSantos, who had disappeared somewhere into the dimly lit interior.

She texted Uzi back, apologizing for the late response and letting him know they had to "manage a situation with LE" and that her unnamed partner would be back in a few minutes. He replied a moment later.

> tim came thru
> prints match doka michel
> leader of islamic movement sharia law for france now
> could be lead on scroll b/c michel is son of man who stole it in 1957
> need gps location on that phone i hacked asap

The Eiffel Tower swung into view and all heads turned in unison, a number of people pointing at the iconic structure, brilliant amber-gold lighting enhancing its profile against the dark nightscape.

There was a loud clang as something hit the wood floor, followed by a whoosh and a draft of warm air. An alarm began ringing. The serving staff froze for a second, then rushed inward from wherever they were stationed—and seconds later Vail saw DeSantos, making his way along the periphery toward their table. When he arrived, he said, "Now we see what their emergency protocol is."

Vail screamed, then yelled, "Fire!" DeSantos did the same, followed by a couple off to their right. People scattered away from the flames, regardless of their proximity.

An announcement blared over the ship wide intercom—first in French, then in English:

"Ladies and gentlemen, this is your captain. Please move toward the stern, the back of the boat, where you boarded. We have a minor fire in the dining room and we're working to put it out as quickly as possible. I will keep you posted."

"Minor?" Vail asked.

"Sounds better than, 'We're fucked. But don't jump overboard just yet,' doesn't it?"

DeSantos and Vail joined the crowd, which was moving steadily but haphazardly toward the exit—many pushing, screams and gasps coming from a variety of distraught people.

DeSantos glanced back, concern evident on his face, assessing how efficient the staff's firefighting methods were. "In five seconds we better start moving toward Port de Suffren. It should be right there, ahead on the left."

Vail looked, but it was hard to see because the bright light from the building fire had illuminated the interior and reversed the effect of the windows: it was now easier to see in than see out.

Add in the heat and thickening smoke and everyone was pushing toward the exit, attempting to get outside into the fresh air.

As she turned back toward the exit, the boat shifted direction.

"Mesdames et Messieurs . . . Ladies and Gentlemen . . ."

"Here we go," DeSantos said in her left ear. "Soon as we get off, we need to put as much distance between us and the group as fast as possible. Without making it obvious."

The staff helped corral everyone in an orderly fashion toward the exit. They continued to work the fire with extinguishers, and the ceiling sprinklers clicked on and began dispensing water, dousing the passengers—which made them push forward faster toward the stern.

As they debarked, Vail glanced over her shoulder and saw thick smoke billowing from the boat's upper cabin into the dark gray sky. "Jesus, Hector . . ."

"More smoke, less fire. Looks worse than it is. And no major casualties. Thought you'd be happy."

"I am. And since we're off the ship and not in handcuffs, I'd say you did well. By the way, did you see Uzi's text, about the location he needs?"

"I gave him what I had. Safe house is the same place as the address Hoshi found for Doka Michel."

They stopped on the quay and looked in all directions, casually searching for a police presence. Seeing nothing in the immediate vicinity, they shuffled with the group toward the sidewalk, just outside an RER station. Off to their left and a hundred yards or so away, the Eiffel Tower rose into the sky.

"Everyone, please stay together," Dominique shouted. "We'll arrange for refunds and transportation . . ."

But what interested Vail more were the sirens blaring in the distance. "I think this is where we make our exit. Into the RER?"

DeSantos glanced around then said, "Yeah. Now."

They started down the stairs when they heard a voice from behind: "You two. Just a minute!"

57

Uzi and Fahad pulled up to the apartment building in Montparnasse in the heart of Paris's Left Bank, once the haunt of artists, writers, philosophers, and counterculture intellectuals such as Chagall, Picasso, Degas, Hemingway, James Joyce, and Ezra Pound.

After a postwar decline, the area had taken on a cosmopolitan character but had lost its avant-garde spark.

And now it harbored a safe house for some of the most virulent and scheming terrorists outside the Middle East.

Uzi and Fahad sat in their car on Boulevard de Vaugirard, across the street on the other side of a traffic median, the mature, though barren trees offering a modest canopy of cover from the apartment where their targets were supposedly gathering.

"Just us," Fahad said. "Frontal assault?"

"Only if we want to get our asses handed to us. We know what Aziz and Yaseen look like but we've got no idea how many men they have or what kind of weapons or booby traps they've got. We need a covert approach."

"Makes sense," Fahad said with a quick nod.

"What do a group of guys want, whether they're Islamic terrorists or bachelors getting together for poker?"

"Pizza?"

"Exactly. I'm sure they're getting hungry plotting murder and mayhem."

"So let me get this straight: you want to buy these assholes—who've killed countless numbers of people—dinner? How about some fine Bordeaux while we're at it?"

"A bit over the top." Uzi pulled out his phone, did a search, and found Pizza Pino a few blocks away. He ordered a large margherita pizza, then started the car. "I'll pick it up and you'll deliver it."

Nineteen minutes later, they were entering the building, the aroma of mozzarella cheese, basil, and tomato sauce wafting behind them.

"Wish we had the time and equipment to do this right," Uzi said. "A full-on SWAT team with MP5s, snaking optical cameras, flash bangs—"

"And stun grenades." Fahad shook his head. "Instead, we've got a dozen slices of pizza."

"Remember, we want these guys alive. We shoot to wound, not kill."

Fahad balanced the box on his left outstretched hand and used his right to check the Glock, which was perched in the small of his back with a round chambered. "Ready."

They walked up the two flights and down the corridor, then Uzi flattened himself against the wall, out of the sightline of the door. Fahad knocked, then waited. A moment later, he rapped again.

"What?" came a terse voice from inside.

"Delivery from Pizza Pino," Fahad said in French. "Large margherita pizza, extra cheese."

"Not ours," the man said.

"Yeah, yeah. Some guy called it in and told me to deliver it at 7:00. I'm fifteen minutes late so the pizza's free, along with our apologies."

The door swung open and the man said, "Give it to me."

Fahad moved his right hand beneath the box and took a half step forward while extending the pizza. As soon as he took it, Fahad grabbed his wrist and gave him a quick hard yank into the hallway. Uzi swung around and jammed his Glock against the perp's head while Fahad clamped a palm over his mouth.

"Name?" Uzi asked in Arabic into his ear.

"Abdul."

"How many others in there?"

"Four."

Uzi did not need to ask if they were armed; he knew they were. He twisted the barrel of the Glock into the loose skin of Abdul's temple.

"How many bedrooms?"

Abdul winced and tried to pull his head away from the handgun, but he was wedged against the wall. "One."

"Only one?"

"It's a small flat."

That was all he needed to know, and all he had time to ask. He reached back and cracked Abdul across the forehead with the Glock's handle. Abdul crumpled to his knees and Uzi hit him one more time on the base of the skull to make sure he was unconscious.

Uzi pulled a flexcuff around his wrists and quickly dragged him half a dozen feet down the hall while Fahad picked the pizza box off the floor and moved it aside.

"Yo, Abdul!" A voice from the apartment, approaching. "Where are you, man? Why do I smell pizza?"

The second man stepped into the corridor and Fahad shoved the barrel of his Glock against the man's temple while covering his mouth and pulling him backward down the hall.

Uzi went through the same routine: three men left inside; his name was Hijaz—not one of their major targets—so Fahad likewise rendered him unconscious, followed by a flexcuff around the wrists, affixed to Abdul's restraint. Even if they regained their wits, it would be difficult for them to get to their feet and maneuver effectively.

Three left, Uzi said to Fahad using hand signals. He hoped they were named Aziz, Yaseen, and Michel. Along with two ancient, extremely important Hebrew documents.

Two against three were odds they could manage, particularly considering the added benefit of a surprise incursion.

Uzi looked into the flat: there were no lights above the narrow wood entryway that could cast shadows and alert the tangos of their approach. He stepped inside and led the way, making no effort to quiet his Timberlands. He was considerably larger than both Abdul and Hijaz, but he doubted the other men would notice the weight differential during the course of a dozen footsteps.

He made a quick assessment of the floorplan as he went: the voices of men speaking Arabic echoed in the room at the far end of the hall, which he suspected was a den—and must lead into the bedroom, bathroom, and kitchen—because there were no other doors he could see.

Uzi stopped a few feet from the end of the corridor and waited for Fahad to inch up next to him. He whispered in Uzi's ear:

"On three. One, two, three—"

They swung into the den and instantly sized up the situation: two men, sitting on a couch huddled over a laptop, arguing. Third one not visible.

Tahir Aziz on the left. Other had to be Michel.

Kitchen clear, bathroom door open. Empty.

Aziz reached for his handgun sitting beside the PC on the coffee table.

"Don't move," Uzi barked in Arabic, anger permeating his voice—a "fuck you" attitude in his demeanor, his gun in line with his eyes, aimed at Aziz and clearly ready to fire. "Don't make me splatter your goddamn guts all over the flat. Landlord would be really pissed."

Fahad moved behind Uzi, headed for the bedroom to clear it. Since one man was missing—assuming they were given accurate information—the likelihood of Yaseen being in there was high.

Uzi stepped forward, angling away from the bedroom in case he needed to pivot and fire in that direction. "Get down on the floor, now!"

He approached carefully and stuck his boot into the back of the man he thought was Michel and ratcheted a flexcuff around his wrists. Another went around the man's ankles. Next he secured Aziz, pat them both down, and pocketed their handguns—.22 Berettas. Easy and quiet to fire. Good for silent kills.

Uzi looked up at the bedroom. He had not heard anything and Fahad had been in there too long. "Mo! What's going on?"

No response.

Uzi cursed under his breath.

"Come out, Yaseen." He said this in English because he knew the man had no difficulties with the language. "You have till three. One. Two."

"I'm not coming out. But you can come in or I will kill your friend. So now it is my turn to count. One."

"I'm coming."

But Uzi knew that if he approached the doorway, Yaseen would open fire. Game over. Uzi was not wearing a vest.

He also did not have any flash bangs or concussion grenades. No strobing lights to disorient him or other high-tech means to disable the tango without putting himself or Fahad in danger.

But he did have a low-tech method. Would it work?

"Two," Yaseen yelled.

He ejected the magazine from one of the Berettas and with it in his left hand, approached the door in a crouch.

In one motion, he yelled, "Mo, get down!" and threw the loaded magazine into the room, backhanded, as hard as he could. He swung left, into the open doorway, his Glock in ready-to-fire position.

Yaseen was focused on an area a few feet away where the magazine had struck. Uzi squeezed off a round and struck the tango in the right shoulder. He jerked back and sprayed the far wall wildly with automatic rounds.

Uzi fired again, taking care to avoid striking vital organs. This time Yaseen dropped his weapon, an MP7 submachine gun.

Uzi stepped into the modest sized bedroom, which featured a folded futon bed and a dresser. Boxes were stacked along one of the walls.

Fahad was picking himself—and the MP7—up from the floor.

Uzi noted three missing fingers on Yaseen's left hand. If there was any doubt as to the man's profession, that helped confirm it.

"You okay?"

Fahad hit Yaseen with a right cross and sent the man backward into the corner.

"*Now* I'm okay."

"What the hell happened?"

"He got the drop on me when I walked in. My fault."

Fahad pulled out a flexcuff and yanked his prisoner's arms back to fasten the restraint.

"Ahh! Son of a bitch. You did that on purpose."

"He's losing blood," Uzi said. Using his knife, he sliced off a long strip from the bed sheet. With Yaseen's arm abducted, Uzi saw that the wounds were not in the shoulder but were lodged a few inches above the elbow. He tied the tourniquet around the upper limb to stem the potential arterial bleeding. "Check on our friends, see if they're in any mood to talk."

"I'll make sure they are."

"This means nothing," Yaseen said. "You think that by capturing us you've won?"

"It's a start. But I'm not so naive to think that one victory will win the war."

"The war's over," he said disdainfully, resting his head against the wall. "You people just don't know it."

Uzi had a hard time arguing with that—but he had an equally difficult time accepting it. He was not waving the white flag and he didn't know any of his colleagues who were, either.

"You're Uziel," Yaseen said. "The Jew FBI agent."

"In the flesh."

"Kadir Abu Sahmoud has an order out to kill you."

"Yeah, how's that working out for him?" Uzi stood up and walked around the futon to the wall of corrugated boxes. He stabbed at one with his Puma and ripped open the front panel of the cardboard.

He moved to the next one, and then the next, tearing them open with angry vigor. They all contained the same item: suicide bomber vests.

Fahad walked in and surveyed the contraband. "Gotta be dozens."

Yaseen grinned. "We've got a whole army waiting to die for Allah."

"You fucking brainwash people," Fahad said. "I should shoot you right here, put you out of our misery."

"I believe your Constitution would prevent that. Of all our weapons, that one is maybe our most potent."

Fahad glanced at Uzi. That comment was truer than either of them wanted to admit.

"What about those jokers out there?"

"Aziz is not talking. The other one—"

"Michel?"

"Yeah, that's the thing. It's not Michel. Claims his name is Noori. I sent Richard Prati and Tim Meadows his photo to see if they could run him through the database, get an ID."

"So where's Doka Michel?"

Yaseen's lips broadened. "You missed him. He left twenty minutes before you got here."

"With the Jesus Scroll?"

Yaseen laughed.

Uzi ground his jaw. "Believe him?"

Fahad shrugged. "Let's tear the place apart. It's small, a few minutes should do it."

"Police are gonna be on the way. With all that gunfire—"

"You're not going to find anything," Yaseen said.

They ignored him and went about looking under, on top of, in the middle of, and behind everything in the flat. Other than the suicide vests, it was clean, just as Yaseen had claimed. Uzi figured the place was a secondary safe house used to store bombs, not for operational planning. When the Rue Muller location was compromised, they came here.

Understanding did not lessen the disappointment. But it was short-lived because sirens blared in the distance. Uzi ran to the window and listened. "We've gotta get out of here."

Fahad reached over to one of the open boxes and pulled out a vest. He unfolded it and found it fully equipped with explosives. He did a quick check, seemed satisfied, and rolled it back up. He pulled a second one from the carton and placed it with the first.

Uzi started to back out of the room. "I'll get Abdul and Hijaz and leave them with Noori. Get Yaseen ready. We'll take him and Aziz with us."

They stuffed socks into the mouths of their two hostages and tied a long strip of material around their heads, keeping the gags in place. They dragged the still-unconscious bodies of Abdul and Hijaz into the living room beside Noori and headed down the stairs.

Two minutes later, with the sirens getting louder, Uzi found an unmarked, rusted fire door at the end of the hall. He pulled it open and they stepped inside, keeping the two men in front of them. Uzi turned on his phone's flashlight to scout out the interior: a set of stairs led down to what looked like a basement, perhaps with a boiler or furnace. The building was several decades old and the room had a strong musty smell. Whatever this place was, it was likely only frequented by maintenance staff.

After descending the steps, they saw, through street-level half windows above their heads, the swirling lights of police cars. From the looks of the constellation of colors flickering off windows in the surrounding buildings, there were several of them.

"I'll go take a look," Fahad said.

Uzi moved the men into a corner against the far wall and explored the remainder of the room. He found another set of stairs that led to a different metal door.

When Fahad returned, Uzi showed him the exit he had discovered.

"They're deploying tac teams. Any minute now, they'll start infiltrating the building and setting up a perimeter."

"My bet is your door leads up to the street," Fahad said. "If I'm right about where it'll let us out, we may be able to get down the block without being seen."

"I'm sure the tac team hasn't had time to review the building's blueprints. They probably don't know about this exit."

They grabbed Yaseen and Aziz and shoved them up the steps. When they reached the top, Uzi shined his light on the door. It had warning stickers and other decals that had been painted over and rusted through in spots. Fahad pushed his Glock against Yaseen's temple as Uzi grasped the handle and pulled it open. He peered out and indicated that they were good to go.

Fahad closed the door behind him and helped usher the two men down the dark side street. Behind them, swirling lights painted the buildings.

"I'll get the car," Fahad said. "Meet you right here."

Thirty seconds later they were loading their hostages into the backseat, Uzi wedged up against them. In the small vehicle, the pressure against Yaseen's arm made him whimper. He started rocking back and forth, trying to head-butt Uzi, so Uzi elbowed him in the stomach, hard enough to send a message.

Aziz was comparatively docile, perhaps content to let Yaseen bear the brunt of their anger.

"Where we going?" Uzi asked.

Fahad looked up, his eyes gazing at Uzi in the rearview mirror. "Someplace quiet. We're gonna have a little chat with our guests."

58

Vail glanced over her shoulder at the person who had called after them. It was a man, standing alongside Dominique.

"We're arranging refunds and transportation," he said.

"No worries," Vail said, forcing a smile. "We already have alternate plans." She lifted her Samsung. "A friend phoned us, asked if we wanted to meet them for drinks."

And then the device vibrated. She looked down and saw DeSantos reach for his.

Vail turned back toward the cruise staff. "Thanks for your help. It was a lovely dinner while it lasted."

"Would you like a credit for a future—"

"We're flying out tomorrow. Thanks anyway."

"Honey," DeSantos said. "It's the Joneses. They have a question and I don't know what to tell them." He craned his neck around Vail and waved at Dominique. "Thanks again." He took Vail's hand and gave it a tug and they headed down into the Métro.

"The Joneses?"

"There *are* people named Jones, you know."

Vail stopped at the bottom of the stairs. "We can't take the train." If they were under suspicion, their last known location would be reported as this particular Métro line, she explained. "That'd narrow down their search."

"That cop mentality is handy to have around, you know?"

"Don't get too used to it."

He led the way to the nearest exit and they ascended to street level.

Vail wanted to read the message that had come through but it was more important to remain attentive to their surroundings in case something was amiss. Four eyes were better than two. "Did you happen to see who the text was from?"

"Uzi. He and Fahad have Yaseen and Aziz. He wants us to meet them at a building to be determined."

"How can we meet them at a place when we don't know where it is?"

"Because we're going to find it and tell them where to go."

"And how are we going to do that?"

"I'm calling our CIA buddy."

"Creepy Claude?"

"He's a spook, Karen. Most of the ones I've known over the years are a bit off. If you think about it, there has to be something wrong with them to do the work they do. You know?"

"I could say the same about you."

"And I wouldn't deny it." DeSantos pressed the phone to his ear and waited for it to connect. They emerged near the Eiffel Tower and started walking along Quai Branly, where every ten yards men were thrusting miniature blinking light mockups of the monument at them as they passed.

"No," DeSantos said, pushing the hucksters back as he waited for Claude to answer. He rotated the handset toward his lips. "Yeah, it's me. I need a place where we can do some Q&A with a couple of guys . . . exactly." DeSantos listened a second then said, "Perfect. Text it to all of us." He lowered the phone and checked the street sign, then brought it back up and gave Claude their twenty.

Vail's cell vibrated seconds later. She consulted the screen and realized they now had a location. She pulled it up on her GPS and made a quick assessment. "Only about three miles from here."

"Tell Uzi and Mo we're on our way."

"And how are we getting there? You want to risk a cab?"

"No need. Creepy Claude is sending someone to pick us up."

59

Uzi pushed open the rusted door and entered the pitch-black building. According to Claude, a fire had gutted it two months ago and it was tagged to be demolished. It still had the mildewed, carbon stench of burned timbers, fried electrical circuits, and fire brigade water.

Uzi pulled Yaseen, who was doing his best to resist, inside and yanked the door closed behind him. Aziz struggled as well, but it was not a serious effort and Fahad had no difficulty controlling him.

Claude was already there and locked the door behind them. He led them to the far end of the room with a powerful lantern. He stopped opposite two folding chairs.

The interior was high ceilinged and vast—at least seventy-five yards in length and width. Uzi turned on his phone's flashlight and craned his neck up and around, checking out the charred rafters to make sure nothing was going to come crashing down on them. Satisfied that it was safe enough, he joined Claude, Fahad, and the two terrorists along the wall, which was made of brick and concrete.

There was also a medium-size gray metal toolbox on the ground that did not belong.

Uzi knew what it was. He hoped their guests would cooperate, tell them what they needed to know, then stand trial for mass murder under various terrorism statutes. Uzi figured there was little likelihood of that happening.

When Fahad pushed Aziz into one of the chairs—or threw him into it—the handcuffed terrorist fell backward and tipped it over. They watched him struggle to right himself, but he ultimately did and found the seat.

Uzi brought Yaseen over and stood by his side while the man sat down. Fahad pulled a couple of flexcuffs from his pocket and fastened Yaseen's ankles to the chair legs. He ratcheted them tight, forcing Yaseen to lean forward. He then did the same with Aziz.

"So now what?" Yaseen said.

Uzi stepped in front of him. "You know what. We're going to ask you some questions and you're going to answer them. It can be very simple if you let it be. Or it can be painfully difficult if you make it that way."

"How's your arm doing?" Fahad asked. He walked over and squeezed it, feigning concern. Yaseen let out a loud growl. "You're going to need to get that looked at pretty soon. Or they might have to cut it off at the shoulder." He shrugged. "Sooner we get this over with, sooner we'll get you over to a hospital."

"Who's that back there?" Aziz asked, gesturing with his chin.

"Oh, him?" Uzi said. "That's just Claude. He's here to observe. He's an expert on . . ." He turned to Claude. "What is it that you call it?"

"Enhanced interrogation," Claude said.

"Right," Uzi said.

"How many young men and women did you strap bombs to?" Fahad asked. "How many did you incite to violence?"

Yaseen smiled. "That's important to you, I can tell."

"Answer the question."

"Who keeps track of such things?"

With a broad stance and arms folded across his chest, Uzi said, "You do. It's not about innocent children, it's not about what you think an intifada, or a jihad movement, will do for the Palestinians. It's what it will do for *you*. You're a killer."

Fahad drew back a boot and kicked Yaseen in the knee, sending the chair backward against the cement.

"How many of our people did you kill?" Fahad yelled.

Yaseen groaned as Claude and Uzi pulled him upright.

"Mo, I really think we should—"

"Answer me," Fahad said.

Yaseen narrowed his eyes and locked gazes with Fahad. "Seventy-nine."

"Seventy-nine. Dead because you brainwashed them into being an army designed to kill others under the guise of religious jihad. My nephew, Akil El-Fahad, was one of them."

"Akil." Yaseen laughed. "I remember him. So innocent, so committed to the cause. He knew you were working for the Israelis, informing on Hamas. That's why he sought me out. Why he wanted to become a jihadist. He thought what you were doing was wrong, betraying your people."

"You're lying. You didn't know my nephew."

"Tall for his age. A limp he got chasing a ball into the street in front of a car."

Fahad stared at Yaseen.

"Oh, I knew him all right. I took him under my wing, personally tutored him in jihad techniques. He was my star pupil."

Fahad ground his molars so hard Uzi heard it. He put a hand on Fahad's shoulder. "Ignore him, Mo. There's nothing to be gained by listening to this bullshit. He's a killer, that's it."

"I'm the one who built the vest he used," Yaseen said. "I'm the one who strapped it to his body."

"Bullshit."

"I'm the one who chose him for that mission. I gave him the courage to do it. And I'm the one who detonated the bomb."

"Son of a bitch!"

"Mo," Uzi said, stepping in front of his colleague. "Walk away."

Fahad pushed Uzi aside. "Walk away? Is that what you did when you came face-to-face with Batula Hakim?"

Uzi felt the bile rise in his throat, his blood pressure rising. "I wanted to strangle her with my bare hands, to feel the life drain from her body."

"You see," Yaseen said, "we are not all that different. Jew, Muslim—we all enjoy killing."

"We value life," Uzi said. "That's the biggest difference. Nothing is more sacred. To you, and those like you, a boy is just a tool for fighting your cause, a means to an end. An object that can be bought. Like when you pay a family for their son's death after he blows himself up and kills innocent civilians. You're a cancer, Yaseen."

"And now you're going to get some justice," Fahad said. He nodded at Claude, who opened the toolbox. Knives, pliers, hammers, ice picks, and other assorted gadgets were visible.

Uzi leaned forward, both hands on his knees, making direct eye contact with Yaseen. "We can avoid all that unpleasant stuff. It's up to you. We'll start with some simple questions. All you have to do is answer them truthfully. Like, what attacks do you have planned for the United States?"

"I'm not involved in the planning," Yaseen said. "I just build the bombs and help recruit the soldiers."

"The soldiers," Fahad said. "Like my nephew."

"Yes," Yaseen said matter-of-factly, without much emotion. "Like Akil. Allahu Akbar."

Fahad stepped forward and grabbed a fistful of Yaseen's hair. "Bastard. Don't use Allah's name in conjunction with murder. That's not what Allah is about. It's not what Islam is about."

"Isn't it? Strike down all infidels! Nonbelievers must be killed. What am I missing?"

"I'm not convinced you're just a bomb maker, an engineer, and a recruiter,"

Uzi said. "But I'll let you slide on that. For the moment. If you're not the guy planning the attacks, who is?"

Yaseen turned away.

Uzi stood up. "Look, asshole. We know how this is going to go, right? I'm going to ask you a question, you're going to refuse to answer, we'll spar a bit, and then Claude here will go to work." He walked over, closed the toolbox, and set it down at Yaseen's feet. It was heavy and the metal instruments shifted inside, rattling loudly. "I think we can both agree that you don't want to see Claude open it again. Because if he does . . ." Uzi shrugged. "Maybe he'll cut off a finger. Or two. Or an entire hand."

"Or I'll gouge out an eye. Or two." This from Claude, who seemed to say it with satisfaction. Uzi thought it was a bit disturbing. The way he saw it, torture of any sort was best avoided. At the very least, the more severe forms of enhanced interrogation, whether waterboarding, permanent physical harm, or overt pain, were a last resort, when lives were on the line. And even at that, it was a means to an end. Not a source of enjoyment.

His cell buzzed. He checked the display and read the text from Vail: she and DeSantos were en route. Uzi rested both hands on his hips. "I don't like you, Yaseen. And yet I'm willing to spare you pain and suffering. By the looks of things, I'm the only one here interested in treating you like a human being. The others are like sharks in a pool of water. And you're the chum. They can't wait for me to turn you over to them."

"Bad cop/good cop, is that it?"

Uzi blew air through his lips. "I don't think you get it, asshole. I'm trying to do the right thing here. Problem is, I'm more concerned for your well-being than you are. Tell us what we want to know."

Yaseen looked away again.

"I don't think he believes you," Fahad said.

Uzi turned to Aziz. His face was moist with perspiration despite the fact that the temperature was no more than fifty. "Your turn. Who's the one calling the shots for al Humat?"

"Kadir Abu Sahmoud. And Nazir al Dosari."

Uzi drew his chin back. "Who's Dosari?"

"Sahmoud's—"

"Shut your mouth!" Yaseen said.

Fahad pulled his Glock and shoved it between Yaseen's lips and into his mouth—taking a few teeth with it. The man's eyes widened—either from the loss of his pearly whites or because a powerful handgun was now a trigger squeeze away from ending his life. Hard to say.

Uzi took a deep breath. He had crossed the line as far as Bureau procedure went: if he was witness or party to any type of interrogation tactics that involved torture, he had to report it. But he was not here as an FBI agent; quite the opposite. "You were about to tell me who Dosari is."

"Sahmoud's protégé," Aziz said. "Anything happens to Sahmoud, Dosari takes over al Humat."

"Second in command," Uzi said with a nod. "Very good, Tahir." He walked over to Aziz and gave him full attention. "So tell me what *your* role is in the organization."

"I'm a member of the cabinet, the council of elders."

"But you were involved in the Madrid bombing. Were you the engineer?"

"That mission was mine. I planned it, executed it. And I was rewarded for it."

Uzi sucked on his upper lip. "You worked your way up. Congratulations on the promotion. Obviously in the minds of the council, you earned it. So being someone so high up in the organization, you know what targets are going to be hit. Tell me."

Aziz's eyes swung right, toward Yaseen. The Glock was still in his mouth. Fahad looked angry, just about daring either of them to refuse to answer.

"Tahir," Uzi said evenly, "I'm running out of patience. I'm going to give you one more chance. What targets have you selected?"

Aziz licked his lips. His entire body was now drenched in sweat, his shirt sticking to his chest. "If I—if I tell you, I'd be throwing away years of planning. Dishonoring many who died." He shook his head. "No. I will take the knowledge to the grave with me. To heaven, as a martyr in the holy jihad."

Uzi's shoulders slumped; he could not hide his disappointment. He did not question Aziz's resolve. Religious zealots put their beliefs ahead of their personal well-being. He had gotten all he was going to get for that line of questioning. "Then tell me something that won't betray your faith. Where are the Aleppo Codex and Jesus Scroll?"

Yaseen whined and shook his head as best he could with the Glock in his mouth. Fahad grabbed his hair and steadied him, yanked back, and shoved the gun barrel in farther. Yaseen started to gag.

"Tell me!" Uzi said as his phone buzzed. He straightened up, glanced at the display, and gestured to Claude to get the door. Vail and DeSantos had arrived. While Claude's shoes slapped against the dirt-strewn cement floor, Uzi faced Aziz. "Where are they? And don't tell me you don't know."

"The codex is on its way to the West Bank, Sahmoud's office. Or it will be." He turned away. "Doka Michel's the only one who knows the address."

"And the scroll?"

"I don't know."

"Best guess."

Aziz's eyes moved up, left, and right as he pondered the question. "Knowing Sahmoud, he'd keep it somewhere close."

Uzi nodded at Fahad, who extracted the Glock from Yaseen's mouth.

"You idiot," Yaseen shouted. He spit out broken pieces of tooth material. "You've betrayed all you are."

"Who cares about some old book and parchment?" Aziz asked. "It has no meaning to us. It's just a tool, a leverage point."

The door opened and closed and Uzi's head snapped up. Vail and DeSantos were headed toward him.

THE MILDEW IRRITATED VAIL'S NOSE. The building's interior was dark except for a high-lumen lantern resting on the ground, pointed toward the ceiling. Uzi, Fahad, and Claude stood in front of two chairs. And in those chairs—

"Give me a few minutes," Claude said. "I'll get the information."

Vail sensed that something was not right with Claude the night they met him. She hadn't expended much energy thinking about it, but now she knew. He was a psychopath, possibly an assassin who used his need-driven behavior to "legally" kill—and get paid doing it.

Uzi hesitated.

"Trust me," Claude said. "I'll get the info we need."

"No." Fahad walked over to the nearby wall and picked up what looked like two tactical vests. "We'll do it my way." He handed one to Claude and carried the other to Yaseen.

"What are you doing?" Yaseen asked.

Fahad made a show of admiring the workmanship. "Nicely made. I see the pride you put into each one." He held it up. "This is what you strapped to my nephew's body? His *fifteen-year-old* body?"

Uh, not tactical vests. Suicide *vests.*

Yaseen did not respond.

Fahad unfurled the garment, slipped it behind Yaseen, and turned to DeSantos. "Cut his hands loose."

DeSantos looked at Uzi—and Uzi nodded agreement. DeSantos sliced the flexcuffs, moved Yaseen's hands through the vest's cutaway shoulders, and resecured his wrists. Yaseen winced away the pain of having his arm twisted.

They followed the same procedure for Aziz, but Fahad and DeSantos moved him to the opposite end of the cavernous room and set him down.

Vail hurried to Uzi's side and whispered in his ear. "What the hell are they doing?"

"Fahad's nephew, the suicide bomber? Qadir Yaseen recruited him, turned him into a jihadi. Yaseen's the kind of guy you chase, Karen. A psychopath, a serial offender who uses religious extremism to get his kills."

Vail considered this a moment. "Psychopaths need the connection to the kill. Giving someone a bomb to wear is too removed for their needs. It doesn't fulfill the hunger. It's like eating a chocolate bar that has no taste. It's just not enjoyable."

"I get that. But here's the thing. He detonates the bombs remotely. His finger is literally on the trigger. And he watches."

"Okay," Vail said. "But what makes you think he's a psychopath?"

"He's got a vacant look in his eyes, the pupils are—I don't know, strange. Cold, empty, pinpoints of darkness. He killed Mo's nephew and has no remorse, no guilt. He's dispassionate, coldhearted, has no empathy for the pain Mo feels." He recounted the key points of their interrogation thus far.

Vail nodded. "You may be right. But there's more to it than—"

"Does it really matter?" Claude asked.

Vail turned; she was not aware he had been listening in. *In fact, we might have more than one psychopath in the room.* "It could. In terms of determining the right way to question him."

Claude looked past her shoulder at Yaseen. "He's done talking. And so are we."

"No we're not." She walked over to Yaseen and stopped a foot from his chair. "Give me some space."

"No." Fahad broadened his stance. "We gave him every chance to cooperate. Whatever happens now is his fault."

Vail clenched her jaw. "Move. Aside."

A moment passed. He finally yielded and backed away.

Vail tilted her head and observed their prisoner. He defiantly spit tooth fragments at her. She did not move. "When that bomb explodes, the ground shakes, smoke rises, body parts go flying. It's quite an extraordinary moment for you, isn't it?"

His right eye twitched.

"The fear, the pain on the faces of your victims. Their screams, their moans. Their shrieking when a limb is blown off. You're aroused by it. Seeing your victims' response to the pain you inflict . . . it's exhilarating. Deeply exciting."

Yaseen's lips parted. She had his attention.

"When you press that button and watch your bomb explode . . ." She waited for that image to fill his thoughts. "When you hear the women and children wail and cry . . ." She leaned in close and whispered. "You're sexually aroused. Aren't you?"

His eyes, riveted to Vail's, narrowed. His head tilted. "Yes." Barely audible.

"You're a sexual sadist, Yaseen. People are just objects to you. Things to be used, manipulated. You've got no emotional connection to them. Their agony, their suffering are inconsequential."

He drew back and licked his lips.

She stood up straight. "You get off on risk taking and thrill seeking. And let's face it. There's no job on the planet that's more dangerous than a bomb maker. You've obviously lost fingers from an explosion or two, and yet you keep on doing it. Because taking greater and greater risks excites you."

Yaseen laughed, exposing a row of jagged front teeth. "You know me better than I know myself."

"Karen," Uzi said. She turned and headed back toward him, where Fahad and DeSantos were now standing with Claude.

"How does that help us?" Fahad asked.

"To determine the most effective way to question him, I had to find out if you were right. You are. And I can tell you that his psychopathy governs who he is. He's not going to talk here, no matter what you guys do to him."

"We'll see about that." Fahad stepped to his right and held up two remotes. "Do you know what these are?" He looked at Yaseen, then turned ninety degrees and showed them to Aziz. "I know you recognize them," Fahad said to Yaseen, "since you built them."

"So here's how it's going to work," DeSantos said. "We're gonna ask you again what we want to know. Whichever one of you gives us the answers gets to live. The other one will not."

Vail nudged Uzi.

"Just a scare tactic," Uzi said under his breath.

"It's not gonna work."

"Mo insisted on trying."

"What targets have you selected for the US?" Fahad asked.

"Chicago," Aziz said. "O'Hare."

Yaseen jostled his chair, scraping it an inch along the cement. "Shut up, you idiot! They're not going to kill us. Their Constitution prevents it. They have no proof of anything our lawyer can't twist into a pretzel. *We* are in control, Tahir. Don't let them fool you."

"I'm going to give you one last chance, Yaseen," Fahad said. "Tahir gave us some answers. Now it's your turn."

"I've been through worse than anything you can do to me, preparing for a day like this. I'm at peace with what must be done. I'll be martyred. I'll have my virgins. And my family will be well compensated."

"Now what?" Uzi asked near DeSantos's ear.

"Last chance," Fahad said. He lifted the remote and turned it on, showed the red blinking light to Yaseen.

Uzi placed a hand on Vail's shoulder. "I think Santa's right. We should turn him over to Claude and have the Agency get him to Guantanamo to stand trial."

Fahad began counting. "Five . . . four . . . three . . ."

"I'm fine with that," Vail said. "Except how are we going to explain—"

A thundering blast blew debris into Vail, Uzi, DeSantos, Fahad, and Claude. Vail drew her Glock and swiveled on the balls of her feet, her ears ringing and her heart pounding in her head. *What the hell happened?*

She wasn't sure if she said it aloud—and her hearing was so muffled that she would not have heard it if she had verbalized the thought. One thing was certain, however: the chair occupied by Yaseen was now an empty, twisted hunk of metal.

"You out of your mind?" DeSantos said. He had Fahad by the lapels of his jacket, pushing him backwards into the brick wall.

"Get the fuck off me." He shoved DeSantos away and shrugged his coat into place. He faced Aziz, who was in shock. His mouth was agape, his eyes wide.

"Tell us what we want to know!" Fahad said. He was hyperventilating.

"Mo," Uzi said. He waited till Fahad looked at him, then set his jaw and said slowly, "Dial it down."

"I want answers!" He pointed at Aziz as he advanced on him. "Where are the attacks planned?"

"I told you," Aziz said, recoiling, shrinking into himself. "Chicago."

"Where else?"

"I—I don't know."

Vail wanted to intercede. But if there was a chance of getting Aziz to reveal the information, it was this very moment, when he believed that Fahad would press that button. Objecting, attempting to rein in Fahad, would undermine him, make him impotent. She only hoped he had not completely lost it. Fahad's brutal murder of Yaseen was unexpected, and yet it was not: one of the oldest motives in humanity's long, bloody history was revenge. While their orders were to eliminate Yaseen, it was best done quietly, efficiently, without malice. And without leaving evidence behind.

Fahad stopped a safe distance from Aziz.

"Last chance. You saw what I did to Yaseen. Now it's your turn. Five. Four—"

"Los Angeles, the defense contractors. We have someone on the inside."

"Which one?" Vail asked. "Look at me, Tahir. Which one?"

He turned to face her. "I don't know. One of the major ones."

"Man? Woman?"

"I don't know."

"What about nukes?"

"We had plans. A dirty bomb. I told them no, it was crossing a line."

"How were they going to do it? Where'd the nuclear material come from?"

"Iran, we got the material from Iran. We had two plans. We'd bring some in through South America. The drug cartel—Cortez—was going to take it from Mexico into the US, through their tunnels. The other way was through Canada. I don't know which Sahmoud chose, or if he did both."

"When?"

"Soon. I don't know exactly."

"And?" Vail asked. "You talked them out of it?"

Aziz hesitated.

"Answer her," Fahad said firmly.

"I thought so. But Yaseen said he was told to expect the delivery. He was in charge of coordinating the movement of the material once it got into the US. Two cities were being discussed."

"Which two?"

"Yaseen insisted on New York. Sahmoud and Dosari wanted Washington."

Vail turned to the chair that once held Yaseen. It was now a pile of rubble, blood spatter, and, no doubt, flesh.

"We need to get out of here," Uzi said. "The explosion. Police and fire will be here soon."

"They won't know where to look," DeSantos said. "The building's already condemned. The walls are intact. We've got another minute or two." He swung toward Aziz. "Chicago, Los Angeles, New York, DC. Where else?"

"I can only tell you the places we discussed. Abu Sahmoud and Dosari, they're the ones who make the final decision."

"We know about New York," Vail said. "When are the others going down?"

"Next week. That's all I know."

"Okay," Uzi said, advancing on Aziz. "Claude, call your people and have them meet us somewhere to pick him up. We've gotta get out of here."

"Then what?" Vail asked.

DeSantos and Uzi cut Aziz free of the chair. "Then we'll figure it out."

Vail lifted the lantern and toolbox; they had to get rid of any trace that could be tracked back to them. She noticed Fahad standing in the dark, staring ahead at the spot where Yaseen had been sitting.

"You okay?"

"I thought it would make me feel better." He faced her. "Revenge. But you know what? It doesn't change anything. Akil is still dead."

She gave his shoulder a squeeze. "I know."

60

Claude spent the entire drive on the phone, jabbering in French to several people. The first call, he explained, was to the man who had brought Vail and DeSantos to the abandoned building. They met him a mile south, passing two police cars that Vail surmised had been dispatched to the general area in response to what sounded like an explosion—even if no one could pinpoint its location.

The handoff went smoothly in the parking garage of a building that Claude identified as one that did not have security cameras. Uzi and DeSantos removed Aziz, blindfolded and bound, from the trunk and transferred him to the other vehicle and then both left the garage, thirty seconds after arrival, with no words spoken. Aziz apparently understood what was happening, as he did not resist. He was probably relieved to have survived being blown to bits and was accepting his legal fate in the hands of Americans—an infinitely better disposition than his colleague had received.

The second phone call, now that they were free of their prisoner's ability to hear, was to a man who was to arrange safe passage out of France. After hanging up, Claude explained they would be leaving from Le Bourget Airport, about nine miles from downtown.

The plane was parked at a secluded gate and they were ushered to the tarmac in darkness. It was late and the airport was ready to close for the night, but they were able to file a flight plan and keep the control tower personnel dialed in until they went wheels up.

"Headed where?" Vail asked.

"Ben Gurion airport," Uzi said. "You'll like it. Very modern."

I may like the airport. Not so sure about what will follow.

While en route, DeSantos called Knox to update him and tell him they were headed to Israel to secure the documents and apprehend Sahmoud. They talked in coded language to neutralize eavesdroppers, but DeSantos felt like he got the message through and Knox understood the major points.

Shortly after ending the call, Uzi's phone rang. "It's Prati." He pushed the speaker button. "Tell me you've got good news, Richard."

"You were spot on with that intel. The barge came through Canadian waters, right where you said. They offloaded onto a cabover van. We had a squad there but they couldn't intercept because of the terrain. We've got surveillance teams in unmarked vehicles lined up along the interstate, passing the eye."

Vail knew that "passing the eye" meant that a tailing law enforcement vehicle dropped off the suspect as another one, down the road, picked him up. It prevented the target from realizing he was being shadowed.

"We've identified a stretch of roadway," Prati continued, "two hundred miles outside the city that's thinly populated. It's being evacuated right now and state troopers are getting ready to deploy a tire deflation device in front of the van."

"What if there really is a nuclear device onboard?" DeSantos asked.

"There is," Prati said. "We've got mobile sensors picking up higher than normal background radiation. Enough to raise the alarm."

"And you still think blowing out the tires is the way to go?" Vail asked.

"Obviously there's risk," Prati said. "But we've been over it and that's our best option."

"We just got some other information," Vail said, "about al Humat bringing in Iranian nuclear material through the Cortez tunnels."

"When? Where?"

"All we know is Mexico. No idea when. Probably soon."

"And," DeSantos said, "they've apparently got an operative at a defense contractor in Los Angeles. Which one, we have no idea."

"Does Knox or Bolten—"

"No one knows yet."

"I'll bring them up to speed," Prati said. "We'll check it all out."

Ten minutes later they arrived at Le Bourget Airport. Claude led them to the tarmac and onto a set of self-deploying stairs that led to the hatch of the Boeing business jet.

They followed him inside—as Vail tried to keep her jaw from dropping open. It did anyway.

"A modified 737," Claude said. "It's got the range to take you where you need to go. Master bedroom, showers, dining area, living room."

Four plush ivory leather seats were arranged around a polished walnut table opposite a matching couch that stretched half the length of the room.

Claude looked around, seemed satisfied, then shook DeSantos's hand. "Bon voyage."

They thanked him for his help and he left the cabin, heading back down the steps.

Despite her misgivings about him, Vail appreciated his dependability and assistance. *Don't ever let me find out that you're a serial killer, Claude. Because then I'll have to track you down and arrest you.*

The captain left the cockpit and introduced himself. "I've filed a false flight plan that'll use a specially outfitted transponder to make us appear to be traveling half our air speed and heading toward Germany. On the return flight I'll pick up that flight plan and return here. No one will know where we really went." He nodded at a satchel sitting on the table. "It's all we could put together on short notice."

DeSantos peered inside. Vail saw what looked like satellite phones—and money in Israeli notes—shekels.

"We'll make do," DeSantos said. "Thanks."

"The phones have one special feature you should know about: RF fibers on a microchip. Pop the chip out and you've got a tracking device."

"How long in the air?" Vail asked as she sat down on one of the plush leather seats.

"Five hours. There's food, drink, beds, showers. My orders are to get you out of French airspace ASAP. We'll be pushing back in two minutes." He returned to the cockpit, where it looked like he was joined by a copilot—which Vail assumed was another Agency employee or contractor.

"I suggest we grab three hours of sleep," DeSantos said, glancing at his watch. "Then we'll meet back here for a mission briefing."

PART 3

"Blessed be he who preserves it and cursed be he who steals it, and cursed be he who sells it, and cursed be he who pawns it. It may not be sold and it may not be defiled forever."

—*Aleppo Codex* preamble, 930 CE

"It is the Holy Land. It's called that for a reason. It's holy to the three great monotheistic religions. That's two billion Christians, one billion and a half Muslims, and 14 million Jews. That's almost half the world. So what happens there matters."

—ETHAN BRONNER,
NEW YORK TIMES DEPUTY NATIONAL EDITOR,
WNYC ON THE MEDIA PODCAST, OCTOBER 9, 2014

61

Approach to Ben Gurion International Airport
Tel Aviv, Israel

Three hours passed too quickly. When Vail's phone alarm went off, she did not want to open her eyes, let alone get out of bed. It took her a moment to orient herself—but a short bump of turbulence was enough to shake her mind back to the present. They had given her the master bedroom, which, with a pillow-topped mattress, provided the most comfortable experience she had ever had on an airplane.

This is the way to travel.

They convened in the main cabin in leather chairs that surrounded the table. Large mugs of coffee were at each seat, black and steaming.

"Caffeine," DeSantos said, setting a carafe of milk next to Uzi. "Drink up, get your heads in order."

Uzi rubbed his eyes and did a couple neck rotations. "Let's get started."

"Some information's come in while we were sleeping," DeSantos said. "First, Prati said they took down that van without a fight. They found the same radiological material that was packed into the truck in New York City. The tangos were arrested and are being questioned. All the defense contractors in LA are in lockdown. All incoming and outgoing communications for the past year are being checked. Hard drives and servers are being examined. It's a friggin' mess, but they'll find him. Or her."

"And the Cortez tunnels?" Fahad asked.

"They're working on it."

Vail suddenly did not need the java to wake up.

"Second," DeSantos said, "Knox is en route. And we've got new orders."

They waited for him to elaborate. Instead, he took a drink from his cup.

"The president does not want us to apprehend Sahmoud," he said after

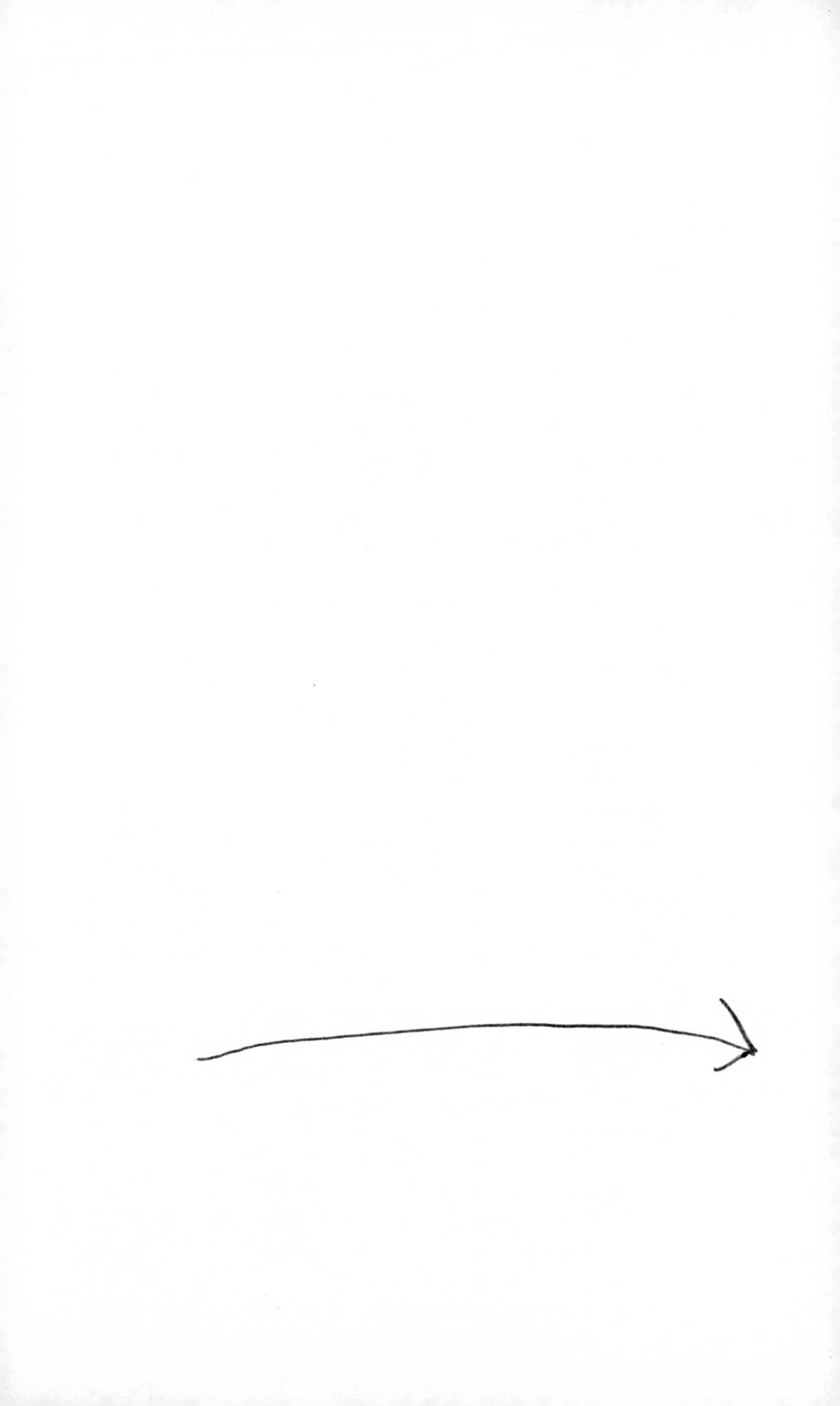

another swallow. He's concerned it'd send the wrong message while he's trying to negotiate peace."

Vail slammed her hand on the table. "Arresting a notorious terrorist, number three most wanted, who's launched attacks on the US and killed scores of people—that's sending the wrong message?" She turned to Uzi. "You have a relationship with the president. Why don't you talk some sense into him?"

Uzi broke a smile. "We don't have a relationship. I was at his inauguration."

DeSantos took another drink. "Doesn't matter. We're not going to obey those orders."

"We're not?" Fahad said, eyebrows arched. He tilted his head. "Shouldn't we put this to a vote?"

DeSantos stared him down. "No, Knox and Secretary McNamara are on board."

Fahad squirmed in his seat. "You're sure. The director told you this."

"In so many words. He used a passphrase."

"A passphrase." Fahad glanced at Uzi, then back at DeSantos. "I think we need to be absolutely clear on this."

"Let *me* be clear," DeSantos said. "You can accept what I'm telling you, or you can stay on this plane when we land. Or you're welcome to parachute out at any time during the next ninety minutes."

"Okay, let's all just take a breath," Vail said slowly. "Hector. Knox gave you new orders but then told you not to follow them. Is that what you're saying?"

"Right. Maybe someone was there with him, so he had to be appearing to tell me one thing when in fact he was telling me the opposite. Bottom line, nothing's changed. But I wanted you to be aware of what was going on."

That'd be great if I really knew what's going on.

"Boychick, you got us set up with wheels?"

"A friend's going to pick us up at Ben Gurion. Raphael Zemro. Former Shin Bet—Israel's security agency—which is where I met him. He's now a contractor. He may still do stuff for Shin Bet or Mossad, I'm not sure. But he understands what we're doing. He speaks our language. We'll be able to rely on him."

They talked strategy for the next thirty minutes then DeSantos left them to their own thoughts during the approach to Israel.

Vail watched as the landscape took shape, darkness enveloping the region for as far as the eye could see, except for brilliant pinpricks of light in one particular area, which she was fairly certain was Israel.

They were on the ground ten minutes later. It was a quiet arrival—the airport was, for all intents and purposes, still closed. Jumbo jets, mostly 747s emblazoned with the El Al Israeli flag logo, sat on the tarmac awaiting the morning's travelers.

They were met at the gate by an Israel Defense Forces colonel, which had been arranged by Knox with cooperation from his counterpart at the Shin Bet.

Vail, Uzi, DeSantos, and Fahad were ushered through Ben Gurion airport. They strode along the strongly sloped arrivals hall beside a divider made of tall, thick panes of glass. On the other side was another walkway sloped in the opposite direction, bounded by large bricks constructed to look like the Kotel, or Western Wall, one of the last vestiges of the ancient temple in Jerusalem and Judaism's holiest site.

They hit the main terminal, a spherical room that featured a two-story, circular waterfall that cascaded down from the ceiling to a shallow trough in the center of the floor.

The area was ringed by shops that were dark. The quiet of the airport was a bit unnerving.

The colonel led them through customs, stopping briefly to speak Hebrew to another soldier who had an MTAR-21 "Micro Tavor" assault rifle strapped across his shoulder. Minutes later, they were at the arrivals curb outside baggage. A dark-skinned man in his forties was leaning his buttocks against his black Chevrolet SUV, smoking a cigarette. When he saw Uzi, he tossed the butt to the ground and advanced rapidly, a smile on his face and his arms spread wide.

"Raph. Great to see you."

The two men embraced, then Zemro leaned back to appraise his friend. "You look like shit. See, you never should have left Israel."

"I had to, you know that. And you—a little less hair, but you're looking good. Still smoking, though."

"Old habits, you know?"

Vail snorted. *Yeah. I know.*

Uzi introduced everyone and they shook hands.

"Call me Raph." Zemro's accent was thick but his speech clear and easy to understand.

Zemro was an Ethiopian Israeli, Uzi explained, having been one of the many who were rescued in Operation Solomon, a covert military operation in 1991 that airlifted over 14,000 Ethiopian Jews to safety in a space of thirty-six hours when the Ethiopian government was on the verge of falling.

As they piled into Zemro's vehicle he looked around and said, "No bags?"

"Packed light," Vail said. In fact, they had left their belongings behind at the Relais Bosquet. Claude and his team had already picked them up and, by now, had disposed of them.

Zemro made a quick assessment and nodded his understanding. "Anything you need, I'll do my best to get it for you. Shower, clothes, food—"

"We could use some information," DeSantos said. "We're looking for Kadir Abu Sahmoud and Doka Michel. Sahmoud's office and a safe house Michel's using."

Zemro laughed, then reached forward and turned over the engine. "My friends, you realize these are—what do you say, a tall order?"

Vail chuckled as well. *I'd like to change my order, if you don't mind. Something on the safer side.*

"You know what's gone down in the US," Uzi said. "And England."

"I understand what's at stake. I'm just reminding you of what things are like here. I think you should be realistic."

"Being realistic isn't part of this op," DeSantos said.

Zemro shrugged. "I can take you to see a guy, one of my informants. I don't know if he'll be able to help you. This is more than anything we've ever asked of him."

"Something's better than nothing," Vail said. "Maybe he can point us in the right direction. Informants sometimes know more than they think. If they're given the right enticements."

Zemro grinned and he winked at Vail. "I like the way you think. This is true. But Hamas, al Humat, Islamic Jihad, these are bad people, you know? The worst of the worst. Very dangerous. They profit from the terrorism. Very much."

"Profit?" Vail asked. "What do you mean?"

Zemro accelerated and merged onto Highway 1 headed for Jerusalem. "Things are not like you know in America. The PLO—you know what PLO is, right? Palestinian Liberation Organization, they run the PA, the Palestinian Authority."

"Yeah," Vail said. "Got that. I read the news."

Zemro laughed again. "Then you know nothing. The news, the journalists, they are tools of the PLO and Hamas propaganda. Most of them, the media doesn't know they're being manipulated. Some don't care. But back to your question. The Palestinian Authority's taken money, billions of dollars from international donors—including your country—to build out its government, to make jobs, a police force and other institutions for the people. But most of that money never got spent on any of that. It went to corrupt politicians, their personal bank accounts."

"And no one knows about this?"

"*Everyone* knows."

Vail turned around to Fahad, who was seated behind Zemro. "Mo, you know about this?"

"Like Raph said, it's not a secret. Arafat was the worst. His personal estate is worth billions, holed away in foreign countries. He skimmed, he stole, he diverted. I wish I could tell you things are different now. But—"

"Why don't we do something to stop it?" Vail asked.

Fahad grinned sardonically. "We've got a saying at Langley: the devil you know is better than the one you don't. We're in no rush to push anyone out the door."

"Last year," Zemro said, "a senior security officer for Fatah sued a top Palestinian Authority official, claiming he stole over a billion dollars from Palestinian coffers."

"It's a lot worse than that," Fahad said. "Hamas and al Humat leadership control the smuggling tunnels they've built from Egypt into Gaza. The stuff that's brought through—food, cement, oil and gas, medical supplies, you name it—it's all highly taxed with the graft going to their personal bank accounts. In the US we call it organized crime. In *any* civilized country, it's called a damn shame. The people need that money."

"You said they profit from the terrorism."

"Oh yes," Zemro said. "If there is no uprising, no 'resistance' fight with Israel as the bad guy, the money does not flow in from Qatar, Kuwait, Iran, Saudi Arabia. Big fund-raising is done for the welfare and relief of the Palestinian people. But the people do not get the money. Or welfare or relief. The terrorist leaders and their families, *they* get rich."

An hour later Zemro was navigating the surface streets outside the walls of the Old City. He found a curb spot on King David Street and they walked through the modern Alrov Mamilla Avenue, an outdoor shopping center with upscale retailers and restaurants on both sides of a central walkway. Constructed of masonry block designed to mimic the Western Wall, it incorporated open air arches above the pedestrian promenade to help the mall blend with the adjacent Old City's architecture.

"I'm going ahead," Fahad said. "Best that I'm not seen with you. I run into someone I know, or if your CI knows I'm with the Agency—or if he even associates me with law enforcement because of you guys, I'll blow my cover."

"Where you headed?" Uzi asked.

"I'll see if I can find some people I know, ask around, get some intel. Let me know when you're done with your meeting."

The rest of them continued through the mall, but most of the stores were still dark.

"We're early," Zemro said as he led them to a contemporary-looking coffee shop. "The place I'm taking you to isn't open yet. We'll get something to eat, kill some time."

Vail was both tired and hungry, so she welcomed the caffeine and muffin. They sat in the sleek café nursing their drinks, Vail examining the chocolate brown cup with Hebrew lettering. "What does this say?"

Uzi, who seemed preoccupied, glanced over. "Aroma. It's a chain of cafés in Israel. Like Starbucks, much smaller scale."

A few employees from nearby shops filtered in to get their coffee as stores across the pedestrian walkway began opening for business.

"Probably best if I wander about on my own too," DeSantos said. "There are people in the biz I could run into. Not worth taking the chance being seen with a former Shin Bet operative. Don't know who you can trust to keep their traps shut. Let me know how your meet goes."

As DeSantos headed out the door, Zemro gestured at the wall clock. "We should go. It'll take us a little while to get there."

THEY WALKED THROUGH THE PROMENADE and exited the mall, crossing Yafo Street. The sun had risen about ninety minutes earlier and the developing morning light cast an orange-yellow glow on the sand-colored rock of the ancient stone fortifications that bordered the Old City. Its ridged castle-like teeth along the top gave it the appearance of a garrison—which it had to become millennia ago because of invading armies that repeatedly attacked, and sacked, Jerusalem.

As they approached the Jaffa Gate, one of eight entrances to the walled-off city, Vail pointed at something in the stone facing. "Is that?" She stepped closer. "Are those bullet holes?"

"From the War of Independence," Uzi said. "It's always been a place under siege, even in modern times."

They followed Zemro through the Christian Quarter, past the Church of the Holy Sepulcher—which Vail would have liked to see, regardless of the Jesus Scroll's revelations—and into the Muslim Quarter.

They moved down the myriad streets and alleys of the Arab souk, a long, narrow flea market comprising stalls where vendors sold a variety of items from shawls, hats, trinkets, and Holy Land postcards to cured meats and costume jewelry.

Uzi stopped at one and bought Vail a black scarf, which he told her to wrap over her hair. "You'll blend in better. It's a good idea for where we're going."

They came to an area that contained traditional storefront businesses, including one that bore a large sign in both English and Arabic that read:

Khaleel's Antiquities

Wholesale & Retail
Artifacts & Numismatics

A gray-bearded man was sitting on a chair in the front. Zemro shook hands with him—and Vail was fairly certain he had deposited a monetary note of some sort in the elder's palm as he passed.

They walked into the shop, which was large and filled with backlit display cases of antique oil lamps, coins, jars—dozens of shelves around the entire room, including a central showcase that was, likewise, full of ancient items, all bearing a written explanation of what they were, when they were found and where, and their purported age.

"I know this place," Uzi said as he and Vail followed Zemro to the rear of the store. "Been here once."

Zemro knocked three times on a door and a tall man answered it. He stepped aside to let Zemro pass, but froze when he saw Vail and Uzi.

"Friends," Zemro said.

The bodyguard hesitated, gave them a once over, then waved them all in.

The room was large and packed with books, papers, and items similar to the ones on display but still in the process of being categorized. Behind a large metal desk was a heavyset man of about fifty, a rank-smelling Turkish cigarette burning in an ashtray and a cup of dark coffee steaming by his left elbow.

"Mr. Zemro, my friend. What brings you here? And so early in the day." He turned to Vail, his gaze traveling the curves of her body as if negotiating a slalom course.

She let him look. *If it helps us get the information we need, I'll open the top three buttons of my blouse. And lean over your desk.*

"Friends of mine," Zemro said with a jerk of his head in their direction. He did not bother to provide any more details as he took the lone empty chair. Aside from the bodyguard who had answered the door, two other men were in the room. "Khaleel. I need some information."

"I did not think you were here for a drink. But you are certainly welcome to have one."

"I never pass up a Turkish coffee."

Khaleel gestured to one of the men. "Cup for Zemro." His assistant walked to the side of the room, where the brewer sat on a cabinet. He busied himself and returned a moment later with a small mug of what looked like thick black liquid.

Vail thought of asking for some—she was curious and it smelled good—but since Khaleel had thus far ignored them, other than undressing her with his eyes, she and Uzi were obviously unwelcome guests.

"You sell antiquities," Vail said.

Khaleel jumped backward as if he had stuck his finger in a light socket. He recovered quickly and forced a smile. "Is it that obvious?" He coughed a raspy laugh then reached for his cigarette and took a long drag.

"I'm known for my ability to point out the obvious. And for being blunt." She set her hands on the back of Zemro's chair. "What do you know about the Aleppo Codex?"

Khaleel locked gazes with Zemro. "Who is she?"

"She is *me*," Vail said. "My name's not important. But I'm curious if you've heard anything about where the codex is being kept."

Khaleel tore his eyes away and looked at Vail's face for the first time. "No one knows where it is. Half of it is missing."

"Yeah, the 'important' half. But a man like you, doing what you do, you know where it is."

Khaleel lifted his cigarette from the metal tray and took another drag. He blew the air toward the ceiling and leaned back in his chair. "And if I do?"

"Tell us."

Khaleel gestured to the two assistants, a quick flick of his fingers and wrist to send them on their way.

"I'd prefer if they stayed," Uzi said.

Khaleel seemed to suddenly become aware of Uzi's presence. He looked at him with disdain as he tipped his coffee back and drained the mug. "More," he said and held the cup out to one of his men.

Vail figured Uzi wanted to prevent them from making a call to someone who would follow her and Uzi when they left the store. When dealing with the grime of terrorism you could not be too careful. It was easy to disappear in the busy backstreets of the souk, only to emerge a year later on a desolate strip of desert in an orange jumpsuit with a machete at your throat.

It was a fine balance, she was sure, as Khaleel might be less inclined to talk with witnesses present. It depended on how much he trusted his men.

Khaleel considered Uzi's request, then nodded.

That settled, Uzi shoved his hands into his front pockets. "The codex," he reminded Khaleel.

Khaleel snorted and turned to Zemro.

Zemro reached into his jacket and pulled out a roll of bills—shekels. He peeled off a few and placed them on the desk.

Khaleel looked at them. Without lifting his eyes, he said, "It's in Gaza. A man by the name of Kadir Abu Sahmoud has—"

"We know who Sahmoud is," Vail said. "And we already knew he has it."

Another drag. "Then you know it's not there yet." Exhale, smoke directed toward the ceiling. "But it will be soon."

"When?"

"This I do not know. I only know what I hear."

"Where does Sahmoud live?" Uzi asked.

Khaleel laughed. "That I do not know either. But I have some photos if you want to try to figure it out."

"How'd you get pictures?" Zemro asked.

Khaleel took the refilled mug from his assistant. "Everything is for sale, is it not?" He took a sip then set it down and faced his laptop. He banged away at the keyboard, struck a final key with a flourish, and then appraised the photo he had called up. "I can get places the Mossad and Shabak cannot," he said, using the acronym for the Shin Bet. "I take pictures, I get money. Sometimes I buy pictures, sell for *more* money. I'm a businessman."

A businessman who may not live long enough to enjoy his riches.

Uzi swung the laptop toward him and Zemro. "What do you think?"

Zemro squinted at the screen, then zoomed in on the picture. "Hard to say." He stared at it a long moment then moved the image around, taking in the buildings in the vicinity. "I think I might know where it is. You sure this is Sahmoud's house?"

"That's what I'm told."

As Zemro scrolled left, Uzi pointed at the monitor. "Hold it. Zoom out a little."

Zemro did as asked. Uzi placed his fingers on the touchscreen and moved the photo to the right.

"That's Sahmoud, right?"

"Yeah," Zemro said.

"That guy," Uzi said, poking at a grainy image beside Sahmoud. "I recognize him."

"From where?" Vail asked.

"I don't know. It was—it wasn't that long ago."

"New York? London? Paris?"

"Not sure." He turned to Khaleel, then angled the laptop toward him. "Who is this?"

Khaleel tilted his head. "I've seen him but I don't have a name. He's important. He's in a lot of my Sahmoud photos." He paged through the others, but all were shot with a telephoto lens in suboptimal light.

Uzi found the best image and took a picture of the screen with his phone. Vail watched as he sent it off to Richard Prati and Hoshi and asked them to scour their servers, including the DEA narcoterrorism database, for an identity and background sheet.

"What about the Jesus Scroll?" Vail asked. "Where is that?"

"If I knew, I would not tell you." He laughed, exposing nicotine tarred teeth. "More coffee!" He pulled out a marijuana joint and ignited the tip with a lighter from his drawer. After taking a long toke, he leaned back in his chair. His large belly stretched his nylon shirt. "I do not know where the scroll is. I have asked, sent out feelers. But there are a lot of dealers, wealthier than me, willing to bid just about anything for that. And the codex pages."

"Do you know Doka Michel?" Uzi asked.

Khaleel took another puff. "I know him because of his father. I have heard rumors that he has the scroll. But he is someone I cannot get near." He squinted at Uzi then leaned forward in his chair. "You need something. A coin from the Maccabean times? Excavated by your Western Wall. A necklace." He grinned. "Bring you luck."

Uzi frowned but humored the man. He reached down his shirt and pulled up a gold chain, the bottom of which contained a small coin. It was worn beyond recognition. "Already got one. Bought it here, in fact." He winked.

That seemed to make Khaleel uncomfortable as the smile disappeared from his face. Uzi peeled off some shekels and set them in the top of an oil lamp that sat on the man's desk. "Thanks for your information. You hear anything, let Raph know."

As they left the store, Uzi and Zemro scanned the area to make sure they were not being surveilled—or targeted. They melted into the souk when Uzi suddenly stopped.

"What's the matter?" Vail asked.

"That guy in the photo. Trying to figure out where I know him from." Uzi glanced up, left, right . . . and then snapped his fingers. "It's the guy—" He physically shivered. "It's the guy Fahad met with in New York. His CI."

"You sure?"

Uzi pulled up the photo and studied the screen. "No doubt whatsoever. Unless he's got a twin."

"Your friend's CI is a terrorist?" Zemro asked.

"He certainly seems to be associating with one. One who happens to have a huge bull's-eye on his forehead at the moment." Uzi tapped out an email and then started dialing the satphone.

"Who are you calling?" Vail asked.

"Richard Prati." A moment later, Prati answered. "Richard, listen. Can you look into something for me? . . . No, it can't wait. You're gonna be late to your meeting. I need you to look into a guy named Amer Madari. He was in Manhattan several days ago. I was told he's a CI. He supposedly doesn't have a criminal history, but we need to rethink that. Run the photo I just emailed you through the facial recognition database, see if you get a hit for a terrorist with any of the known organizations. Start with al Humat, Hamas, Hezbollah, Islamic Jihad, Muslim Brotherhood."

"And the narcoterrorism database," Vail said.

"And the narco—right." Uzi listened a second, then said, "Yeah. I think this could be a bad dude. A real bad dude."

62

This was the day Mo went AWOL?" Vail asked.

Uzi leaned his buttocks against a wall. "Yeah." He brought the handset back to his mouth. "I need this info ASAP, Richard. I saw him meeting with my partner. We may have a real problem. Call me as soon as you've got something." He dropped the phone from his face and craned his head up to the sky.

Zemro scratched the back of his head. "So you talked with this Madari when Fahad met with him?"

"No." Uzi licked his lips—but his face displayed a pained expression, wrinkles, and jowls. Tension. "Fahad went off the grid for the better part of a day and didn't have a real good explanation for what he was doing. I had some surveillance done—I didn't know him back then and, well, being Palestinian, after what happened with Dena and Maya, I—I didn't trust him. He met with the man we just saw in the photo back at Khaleel's. I had my people run the image and I got a name—Madari—but he was clean."

Vail stepped closer, the three of them forming a tight huddle against the side of the building. "And now, we see this Madari hanging around with Kadir Abu Sahmoud, the number three most wanted terrorist in the world."

Zemro seemed to be thinking it through. "No good explanation for this, Uzi. He wasn't delivering pizza."

"No."

Vail's satphone rang. It was DeSantos's number. "Do we tell Hector?"

"He's had it out for Mo since London. I—maybe we should get confirmation, if that's possible, before we say anything."

"You're afraid he'll overreact."

Uzi looked up at the cloudless blue sky. "I don't know what to think. Maybe Santa's been right all along. But back in Paris—" Uzi lowered his voice, which was soft to begin with—"what Mo did to Yaseen. That wasn't an act, was it? I mean, was his nephew really killed?"

"You should tell your partner," Zemro said. "He needs to know."

Vail answered the call.

"You still in your meeting?"

"No, we're done. Come find us."

Zemro suggested a location to meet—in the Jewish Quarter, at the Western Wall.

Ten minutes later, they descended a series of steps that led to Kotel Square, a plaza dominated by the ancient but well preserved ruins of the fortification wall where the Jewish Second Temple once stood.

The gold topped Dome of the Rock rose from above the top of the five-story Western Wall, an area also known as the Temple Mount—where the First and Second Temples once stood, Uzi explained. "The Kotel—which is another name for the Western Wall—is two thousand years old and extends another ten stories underground. It's pretty cool. They give tours but you'd never be able to go down there."

"Yeah, no kidding." She took in the length of the wall. "Much bigger than what I imagined from the pictures I've seen."

"I think it's three football fields long."

"This is the holiest place on earth to Jews," Zemro said. "People from all over the world come here to pray, just like they came thousands of years ago to make pilgrimages to the Temple and sacrifices to God."

As they approached, Vail could see different strata to the masonry—large blocks at the bottom and middle, with smaller bricks toward the top. "What are those plants growing out from between the rocks?"

"There are different kinds," Zemro said. "Most common is Shikaron. It's poisonous, some kind of hallucinogenic. The ancient Jews used it as an anesthetic. The Egyptians and Greeks used it for pain relief. The Germans used it in the Middle Ages to make beer. It's still used nowadays in some medications."

They stopped at a low wall that stood a few dozen feet in front of the Kotel. A man standing by a tall bin on a ramp that led down to the Kotel handed Uzi and Zemro a couple of white beanies.

"Kippot," Zemro said to Vail. "Yarmulkas. We wear them on our heads as a sign of respect for God, to remind us that He's always above us."

Vail looked out at the Kotel, which dwarfed a number of men in black coats and hats standing with prayer books inches from its surface.

"We can talk here," Zemro said, moving a few feet to his right, in front of a three-foot wall.

"Hey." They turned and saw DeSantos approaching. The man at the Kippot bin handed him a yarmulke, and he placed it atop his head. "When in Rome, right?"

Uzi squinted. "Bad analogy."

"Good point. So was the CI helpful?"

"In more ways than one," Vail said.

DeSantos tilted his head as he studied Uzi's face. "Something's fucked up, isn't it? I can tell."

Vail told him about the Amer Madari discovery.

"I knew it!" DeSantos balled a fist and started pacing. "Goddamn it."

"Let's not jump to conclusions," Uzi said. "Something's not adding up. We've got some gaps. Mo was meeting with a guy who was seen with Sahmoud. I mean, yeah, it doesn't look good. But we need to know more."

"Bullshit. Give me one good explanation."

"I don't have one. I just think, for now we . . . monitor it. And watch our backs."

"We still have our mission," Vail said.

"And we might have a mole on our team," DeSantos said, "working against us. Until I know what the hell's going on I won't be trusting him with anything even remotely significant."

"I asked Hoshi to look into Madari. And Richard Prati at DEA in case they've got something on him in the narcoterrorism database." He leaned on the railing that faced the Kotel. "Raph?"

"Until you hear otherwise, you have to treat him as a hostile. You know the saying. Better safe than sorry. Or my interpretation: better alive than dead."

Uzi pulled out his satphone and started dialing.

"Who are you calling?" Vail asked.

"Gideon." He pressed SEND. "Raph, call Shin Bet. Talk to someone there you trust. See if they've got anything on Madari. I already sent you the photo." As Zemro walked off, Uzi waited for his call to connect. When Aksel answered, he glanced around to make sure no one was in earshot, then put it on speaker. "Gideon, it's Uzi. I need whatever you've got on Amer Madari."

"Am I supposed to know who Amer Madari is?"

"Short answer is yes. I'll send you a photo. We have him talking with Kadir Abu Sahmoud. And I have Mahmoud El-Fahad meeting with Amer Madari in New York City last week."

"Hmm." Aksel was quiet a moment. "Let me talk with some people. Is this a good number for you?"

"I'm actually in Jerusalem."

There was silence. Then: "Are you doing something I need to know about?"

Uzi's eyes flicked over to DeSantos, who shook his head no.

"I think it's best if I don't answer that."

"That in and of itself is an answer. Is your colleague Hector DeSantos with you?"

"Yes."

"That's all I need to know. And I have to tell you that I'm not happy that—"

"Gideon, if you were anyone else, this conversation would never be happening. I will give you what I have. We're on the same side here."

"Are we?"

Vail nudged Uzi's elbow. She whispered in his ear, "Your father."

"I guess it's my turn to ask you: is there something I need to know?"

"This is a game I do not want to play with you," Aksel said.

"Fine. I know you've been looking for the missing codex pages. And the Jesus Scroll."

There was silence before Aksel spoke. "Unfortunately, they've become chess pieces in a very dangerous game. And your government is on the wrong end of this one."

"How so?"

"A conversation for another time. One that can only happen in person."

"Fine. I'll accept that. But I need an address for Kadir Abu Sahmoud."

Aksel laughed.

Uzi pictured his firm but ample belly shuttering. "I wouldn't ask if it wasn't important. Do you have a location?"

"Take me off speaker." Uzi did, then listened intently for a moment. "Yeah, I got it . . . No, I'm not happy. We intend to apprehend or kill him . . . No, I get it . . . Be right there." He hung up, then huddled with DeSantos and Vail. "He said they're monitoring Sahmoud, tracking his movements. Watching to see who he's meeting with. He feels this is more valuable at the moment. And he's worried that if we were to kill him it'd only aggravate an already shitty situation. Everyone will think Israel was behind it and there'd be no way for him to prove otherwise. Unless we take credit, which is possible but not likely because officially this mission was scrubbed. President Nunn will state he hasn't sanctioned any such operation and deny the United States had anything to do with it. And he'd be telling the truth."

Zemro joined their cabal. "Aksel tell you anything?"

"Just that he couldn't tell me anything. You?"

"I've got a couple friends looking into it. They knew of Madari but don't have a file on him. I asked them to look into Fahad too. Just in case."

"They'll have stuff." He told Zemro what Aksel had related to him back when Fahad was added to their OPSIG team.

"Maybe it's like an iceberg. We see the tip but there's more beneath the surface."

"No doubt." Uzi rubbed his face with a hand. "Aksel's on his way over from the Antiquities Authority. We're meeting him at the Ramban Synagogue. A few minutes away, back the way we came."

"A synagogue?"

"It's safe. We can talk freely."

Uzi led the way, telling Vail and DeSantos that the congregation was founded in the 1200s after Jerusalem was destroyed by the Crusades. "It's now one of the oldest active synagogues in the Old City."

They arrived on Ha-Yehudim Street in the Jewish Quarter, a pedestrian square paved with cobblestones and planted with mature shade trees. The stone building they were looking for had a central dome and a plaque on the wall describing its history.

Inside, its columns and vaulted ceilings reminded Vail of the larger barrel rooms that she had seen in the Napa Valley—specifically the one in the castle winery where Vail had pursued the Crush Killer.

Worn wood pews filled the small sanctuary. Tablets with Hebrew writing sat at the front, above one of the columns. To Vail it looked like a representation of the Ten Commandments.

The door swung open and Gideon Aksel entered. Vail had never met the man, but Uzi's reaction gave away his identity. They exchanged nods—no hand shaking and no small talk. It was clear that Zemro and Aksel knew each other.

"Raph," Uzi said, "would you watch the front door, make sure no one approaches who shouldn't?"

Zemro nodded, then walked off.

Aksel unbuttoned his suit coat. "You sure you want to talk with . . . your friends here? I'm not sure this is a conversation for other ears."

"I trust them all with my life."

Aksel pursed his lips and gave a tight nod. "As it should be."

"What did you want to tell me?"

Aksel sighed. "We have conflicting missions, Uzi. This is a problem."

Uzi folded his arms across his chest. "We already discussed Sahmoud and—"

"That's not what I'm talking about. The security services are working to secure the codex pages and the scroll to prevent them from being used against us."

"Against—what are you talking about?"

"I suspect you already know the documents are in the hands of al Humat. Or its agents."

Uzi nodded.

"If you are successful in retrieving them, it'll be no different from the terrorists having them."

Uzi dropped his hands to his sides. "How can you say that?"

"It's no secret President Nunn and the prime minister don't like each other. There's been tension since Nunn was elected. He's made his feelings very clear."

"Not true," DeSantos said. "The two of them may not like each other, but the administration has done things behind the scenes that've supported Israel's interests. Like helping to fund the last stages of Iron Dome's development."

The left corner of Aksel's mouth lifted. "And you think that was for our benefit? Come on, Mr. DeSantos. You're a smart guy. Why do you think the US loaned Israel the last two hundred million dollars to finish development?"

DeSantos thought a second then titled his chin back. "Because we get to share the technology."

"Remember your Star Wars missile defense system? It never worked as promised. The Patriot system? Marginal at best. But the technology behind Iron Dome showed promise even in its earlier, flawed developmental state. It's a smart system that tracks a missile's trajectory and determines if it's worth shooting down—and then calculates the exact spot in its trajectory it should intercept it so the missile doesn't go down in a populated area. And it does it all in the blink of an eye. After Iron Dome proved its worth by shooting down over a thousand rockets Hamas shot at us from Gaza, the US had a potent antimissile system as a defensive measure—and deterrent—to thug countries like Russia and North Korea."

"So what does this have to do with the documents?" Vail asked.

"We've heard that there are factions in your government working to secure them so they can be used as leverage in negotiations. Your president wants a peace deal. He wants to do what no other US president has been able to do: broker a comprehensive, final two-state solution."

Uzi shook his head. "I don't know, Gideon."

"Indeed, my friend. There are a *lot* of things you don't know. Your secretary of state has worked against us in several key negotiating sessions the past few weeks. This is not how an ally behaves. But it is the way you leverage an enemy to do things they don't want to do. You twist their arm using whatever means you have at your disposal, no matter what the fallout."

DeSantos squinted. "Do you really believe your government would agree to impossible concessions just to secure the Aleppo Codex and Jesus Scroll?"

Aksel looked away. "This is not a cold calculus, Mr. DeSantos. It's not A plus B equals C. This is an emotional question, a religious issue, one that involves faith. And truths. The reality is that the government is a coalition of diverse agendas, needs, constituents. Add religion to the mix and it's an unwieldy group."

"And a significant part of that group," Uzi said, "is ultra-Orthodox."

"Meaning what?" Vail asked. "I don't know a thing about Israeli politics."

"It's a democracy, you know that much. But instead of two parties, we have thirty-eight, thirteen who currently hold seats in the coalition. You know how hard it is to get Democrats and Republicans to work together? Try adding eleven more. Point is, the ultra-Orthodox are an important voting bloc for the prime minister. Without them his government crumbles. And the ultra-Orthodox desperately want those ancient documents—especially the codex. In fact, these documents may be the *only* thing that could make them give up their claims to Judea and Samaria. Don't underestimate their importance."

"Judea and Samaria?" Vail asked.

"The part of Israel now called the West Bank," Uzi said. "It was known as Judea and Samaria for thousands of years. Jordan coined the phrase 'West Bank' sixty-five years ago."

Aksel buttoned his coat. "Remember this, Mr. DeSantos, Agent Vail. This conflict is not about giving the Palestinians land for their own country. They want *all* the land, all of Israel. This two-state solution is a political invention, an attempt to compromise, to appease the Palestinians. Because that's what politicians and negotiators and mediators do. But the Palestinians can't be appeased. Even if they're given the West Bank, they will not stop until they have it all. Make no mistake. This is about Israel's survival." He pointed at Uzi. "You know I'm right. And that's why any negotiations—however they're resolved—have to be done without a gun to our head. We *are* going to find those documents."

There was a knock on the door to the sanctuary.

"Coming!" Aksel said, then turned to leave. "I will let you know if I find anything about Amer Madari. In the meantime, please don't cause any trouble in my country. Better yet, go home and get out of our way. Catch the next flight out. I believe that's this evening at 6:00 PM."

63

Uzi waited until the door clicked shut before pulling out his satphone and moving closer to the window. "You don't mind if I disregard Gideon's recommended travel arrangements, do you?"

"Who are you calling?" DeSantos asked.

"An old friend who owes me. Big. Tell Raph—no one comes in."

As DeSantos walked off, Uzi brought the handset to his face. "Reuben, it's Uzi. I need an address." He listened a few seconds, then said, "Aksel can't know. . . . I'm serious . . . Yes, I'm on a satphone. It's fairly secure. . . . Kadir Abu Sahmoud." Uzi held the phone away from his ear, waited a second for Reuben to stop yelling, then said, "I need this. And now you know why Aksel can't know. . . . Make it look like it wasn't you, like it came from the outside . . . Fine, leave an identifier pointing back to me. I'll take the heat . . . Yeah. It's that important."

Uzi hung up, then faced Vail and DeSantos, who had returned. "Reuben was knifed by an al Humat operative in the West Bank. His phone had been destroyed but I figured out a way of tracking him through his vehicle. Everyone else had given up but I found him, dumped in a field, left for dead." Uzi took a deep breath. "Like I said, he owes me. He's going to give us Sahmoud's address. But they've got an ongoing op and he doesn't want to ruin it. Same thing Gideon told me."

"And it doesn't bother you that you're going to do just that?"

"I work for the United States government and Sahmoud is the architect of the terror attacks in DC and New York. Our job is to get those ancient documents and bring Sahmoud in—dead or alive."

Vail shook her head. "This is not going to end well. You heard what the director general just told you about tensions between the two countries. You may even be persona non grata in Israel."

Uzi tightened his jaw and turned toward the window. "Can't think about that. We have our orders. That's all that matters right now."

"Orders that were sent to us in code?"

DeSantos rolled his eyes. "Don't start with that, Karen. I know what Knox was saying. This is what we're supposed to do. Let's go do it."

64

They had gotten back to Zemro's car outside the Old City when Uzi's phone rang. It was Richard Prati. Zemro went to the rear hatch of the SUV while the rest of them climbed into the vehicle.

Uzi took the front passenger seat and answered the call as his buttocks hit the fabric. "Talk to me, Richard."

"It was coming up zeroes until your colleague, Agent Rodman, broadened the algorithm and included Interpol. Then we got a hit—a big one. This Amer Madari joker is Nazir al Dosari."

It took a second for Uzi to find his voice. "What?"

"Nazir al Dosari. He's rumored to be a rising star in al Humat, but everything we've got on him is several years old—"

"Are you sure? I mean, really sure?"

Vail and DeSantos leaned forward in their seats.

"Hundred percent, Uzi. He had facial reconstruction in Germany, at that ex-Stasi facial surgery clinic. We didn't know what he looked like but one of my guys got hold of a photo from a file the CIA bought three weeks ago. There was a meeting between Carlos Cortez and Dosari in Beirut. Money and weapons exchanged hands. The Agency had someone with a long lens snapping photos. I'll send you what we've got. There's something in the file that's classified and encrypted, but I'll give you what I have and let you run with it."

"Copy Hoshi Koh in my office. And thanks for digging into this, Richard. Sorry you missed your meeting."

"No you're not."

"You're right, I'm not. Talk soon."

He hung up as Zemro got into the SUV, his arms filled with tactical vests. "I have a feeling we're going to be needing these." He handed two back to Vail and DeSantos and the other to Uzi.

Uzi dialed Hoshi and secured the Kevlar with the Velcro straps while the call connected.

"Uzi. Where the heck have you been? Shepard's been on my c—"

"Listen to me—Richard Prati at DEA is sending you a file. The person of interest has a classified file at Interpol. I need to know what's in it."

"Well how am I—you want me to hack Interpol?"

"Now that you mention it, yeah. Good idea. Call me on my satphone. I'll text you the number."

"You have a satphone? Where are you?"

"I need this info ASAP, Hoshi." He clicked off and let his head rest against the side window.

DeSantos leaned back in his seat and waited for Uzi to explain. Finally he said, "So this is not getting any better, is it?"

Uzi sighed. "Nope. The guy Mo met with in New York is the number two in command at al Humat. Nazir al Dosari."

"We need to find Fahad," DeSantos said. "And bash his head in."

"No," Uzi said. "There's an encrypted file. I want to know what's in it before we jump to conclusions."

"Jump to conclusions?" DeSantos looked at Vail, his brow raised. "Boychick, I know you don't want to hear this, but read the writing on the goddam wall."

"I'm reading between the lines." Uzi's phone rang. It was Fahad. He held up his phone for Vail and DeSantos to see the Caller ID.

"Answer it," DeSantos said. "Tell him to meet us. We'll bag him as soon as he shows his face."

The phone buzzed. Uzi hesitated, then finally brought it to his face. "Mo. What's up?"

"You done meeting with Raph's CI?"

"Yeah, we're good with that."

"Was he helpful?"

"Was he helpful . . . not sure. We'll probably find out very soon." He ground his jaw. That was true in more ways than one. "Where are you?"

"Muslim Quarter. You?"

"Meet us where we parked. We just got back to the car."

"Be right there."

Uzi dropped the phone into his lap. "Now what?"

DeSantos snorted. "Now? We get him in here and—"

"Karen," Uzi said firmly. "What do you suggest?"

They all faced Vail.

She thought a moment, then said, "This is a tough one. If we accept the info and background we've been given on Mo as accurate and complete, I'd say this doesn't add up. He's got legitimate motivation to do what he did to Yaseen. I'm not condoning it, but it's understandable. I'd want to do the same thing. And if that's the case, there's no way he's working with al Humat. But if there's more to his story that we don't know, it's impossible for us to know what's really going on."

"And that's why we need to cuff him and take him somewhere," DeSantos said.

"Wrong," Vail said.

"Wrong?"

"Wrong. Despite their differences, Uzi has built a rapport with Mo." She turned to Uzi, who was still leaning against the window, staring straight ahead. "Am I right?"

"Yeah."

"That kind of rapport takes us weeks to achieve with a prisoner, with any hostile, suspect, or known killer. And Uzi's got it. He needs to use it, leverage it. In fact, the only person who Mo has a problem with is you, Hector. So you're the last person who should be interrogating him. He'll shut down. You won't get anything."

"You're sure of that."

"Yes. He's CIA. He's trained in the stuff you'd be doing to him—psychological or physical—he knows what'd be coming and how to resist it."

"I'll get more with a carrot than a stick," Uzi said, turning around.

"Exactly. When the time's right you need to confront him with these allegations. But gently, as if you're just chatting and it's no big deal. Do it at a time and a place where you can observe his facial tics and body language. It might be subtle, but you'll know if he's being straight with you. You with me?"

Uzi nodded.

"Eat the friggin' carrots," DeSantos said, turning away. "Give me a nice thick stick."

"Not this time, Hector."

Zemro, who had been observing the interplay, appraised Vail. "You want a job? Shin Bet, Mossad, they both use behavioral analysts."

Vail managed a smile. "Without me, these two goons would be in serious trouble."

Zemro laughed. "I agree."

Uzi's satphone vibrated. He glanced at the screen and blew some air through his lips. "Reuben came through. He's sending us Sahmoud's address."

"Because of all the terror attacks," Zemro said, "the checkpoints are active. My plates will get us in. Just let me do the talking."

A knock on the window made them all flinch. It was Fahad. Uzi unlocked the doors and he got in next to DeSantos, who shifted to the middle seat.

Fahad chuckled. "Man, you guys are on edge."

"Being around terrorists gets the adrenaline flowing," DeSantos said, his gaze out the front windshield remaining steady.

Fahad squinted and glanced at Uzi.

He held up his phone. "Just got Sahmoud's address."

DeSantos moved the phone to face him. "Those are GPS coordinates."

"A lot of the Arab neighborhoods in the West Bank don't have street names, so no addresses," Zemro said.

"Do you know where this place is?"

"From GPS coordinates?" Zemro laughed as he pulled away from the curb. "I'll have a better idea when we get close."

"So we don't really know what we're getting ourselves into," Vail said.

"Wrong." Uzi pulled out his Glock and checked the chamber. "We know exactly what we're getting ourselves into."

65

They followed the GPS, navigating the streets of downtown Nablus, driving through the town center and past electronics stores and groceries. Open-air bazaars with rainbow colored umbrellas shielded the markets' vendors against the sun—or today, against the threat of rain.

Zemro craned his neck to get a view of the area. "Looks like we're pretty close."

"I know some people here," Fahad said.

Uzi kept his gaze ahead on the metropolitan landscape. "Maybe we should let you off, see what you can learn."

"I think we should all stick together," DeSantos said.

He wants to keep his eye on him, make sure he doesn't blow our op.

"That woman we just passed," Fahad said, twisting his torso and watching out the rear windows. "I went to school with her. She's a real pain in the ass. Knows everyone's business."

"Pull over," Uzi said.

Zemro brought the car to a stop at a break in the car-lined curb.

"I think this is a bad idea," DeSantos said.

Uzi swung around to face Fahad. "Keep in touch. Don't go off the grid. We may need you once we scout out Sahmoud's office."

"Right." Fahad swung the door open and got out.

DeSantos studied Uzi's face. "I know you don't want to believe he's part of the problem. But it's not worth the risk. You're overcompensating for all the pent-up anger you've had toward Palestinians for murdering your family. But your *emotional need* to like the guy could get us all killed."

"You think that's what's going on here?"

"I do."

"Drive," Uzi said, gesturing to Zemro, who nodded and then pulled out into the traffic.

Hector may not be too far off in his assessment.

The streets were packed with yellow cabs bearing green and white license plates—a key designator for vehicles that entered Israel. The soldiers guarding the checkpoints knew to be extra careful when examining these cars and trucks, scanning the under chassis with long-poled mirrors and, during times of inflamed violence, bomb-sniffing dogs.

Vail wiped her sweaty palms on the thighs of her 5.11s. She checked her Glock and then the Tanto to make sure both were in place. She had not had to draw either one in a while, but she had a feeling that was going to change very shortly. Her heart was racing, beating against her chest wall as the tenths of a mile ticked off the odometer.

Zemro made several turns into secondary areas of the city, past apartment buildings and a number of hollow facades, structures that had been destroyed—either by bombs that went off while they were being constructed or by Israeli bulldozers in retaliation for a terror attack in Jerusalem or Tel Aviv.

The secondary roads were potholed and the houses were a mix of well maintained homes and rundown hovels.

The GPS took them down a side street that fronted a series of older structures. A block later, Zemro brought the SUV to a stop against the curb.

Uzi looked out the window at the surrounding neighborhood: they were in a light industrial area with tile factories, automobile repair depots, and carpet warehouses, by the look of the signs. He gave a final glance around and checked his mirror. "We go on foot from here."

Vail's breathing got tight as she popped open the door and they poured out of the vehicle.

Zemro led the way down the cement path between buildings constructed of large, pale yellow block masonry, a style Vail had grown accustomed to seeing on this trip.

"Are you armed?" Uzi asked Zemro by his ear.

"Don't worry about me, my friend. What's the saying? This isn't my first show?"

"Rodeo. This isn't my first rodeo."

"Good. It's not mine, either."

They continued through the wide alleyway, which doglegged right. Zemro slowed, glanced down at the GPS, and stopped. Vail, at his side now, was jerked back by his grip on her wrist. Before he had pulled her away, she had seen, ahead and slightly around the bend, two men standing guard on either side of a large brown metal door.

Zemro pressed his upper body against the masonry wall and reported on what he had seen. "They're armed. Assault rifles, maybe AKs. They had the al

Humat patch on their left shoulder. There's a double metal door set back in a stone archway. The entrance to Sahmoud's office, I'm sure of it."

"Here's our play," DeSantos said. "Karen, use your charm. Walk right by them, make eye contact as you pass. Maintain their gaze and, you know, do your thing."

"My thing?"

"Wink, smile at them seductively. Lick your lips. Something to get their blood pressure rising. But don't oversell it."

"And then what?"

"Then we'll take care of the rest."

Vail glanced at Uzi and Zemro and they both seemed to be on board with the plan. "Okay." She removed the scarf and tousled her hair, giving it a playful and sexy look. Then she walked off, her arms swinging and her butt rocking up and down.

"I TOLD HER TO GET *their* blood pressure up," DeSantos said, "not mine." He took a breath and followed several steps behind her.

Vail did as instructed, slowing as she made eye contact with the two guards, showing genuine interest in their appearance, undressing them with her gaze. She looked at them over her shoulder as she passed and then swung around, walking backward and holding their attention.

DeSantos ran up on their blindside, his Boker knife drawn. He sliced viciously and quickly at the carotid of the man closest to him, then drew it forward and blocked the other guard's attempt to raise his AK-47 and stabbed backhanded at his abdomen—once, twice, three times in rapid succession. Both men dropped to the ground as if gravity had increased exponentially in a split second, arterial blood spurting out from the first guard's neck.

Uzi and Zemro, handguns at the ready, came up behind them and moved the bodies aside. They took the AK-47s and slung them over their own shoulders as DeSantos checked the front door. It was unlocked.

He nodded to them, then turned the knob and pushed it open. It swung inward, squeaking softly.

Vail pivoted into the building. It was dark and dungeon-like, with only a few visible windows that were obscured by solid wood shutters on metal hinges. Light leaked in along their periphery.

She nodded at Uzi and Zemro, who dragged the two bloody bodies into the entryway, followed by DeSantos.

They stood there, backs against the wall, allowing their eyes to accommodate to the darkness. There were no guards there, which was a good thing—because at the moment, Vail could not see much, and she was sure her colleagues had the same problem.

Seconds later, she started to get a sense of the layout of the room: it was an old factory of some sort that had been cleared of all the machinery that had once been there. The walls were cinderblock and unfinished cement covered with spider cracks emanating in all directions. Puke green wood walls, with glazed windows, apportioned the space into separate offices.

They moved from the front of the factory to the back, clearing the rooms as they went, using hand signals to avoid giving away their presence in case someone was in the deeper reaches of the building.

Seconds later, Uzi called out. "Found something!"

They joined him at the rear of the facility. The smell was distinct and rancid. Vail brought a forearm up to her nose as she made her way over to the wall on the left, where she found a window. She pulled open the shutters, flooding the area with light. "What the hell is that?"

Seated on a chair in front of a portable table with folding metal legs was a body. A burned body.

"Not what," DeSantos said. "*Who*."

66

Exactly," Vail said. "Who is this?"

"I'd ask the two guys who were out front, but they're a little under the weather," DeSantos said.

Zemro used the tip of his Beretta to move the bones of the body's incinerated hand. "This was a really odd fire."

DeSantos took a step back and tilted his head, taking in the scene. "Judging by the condition of the body, it almost looks like a controlled burn. The table is intact, as if the intent was just to kill and burn the person but not anything else in the room."

"Raph, would you keep a lookout, make sure no one drops in on us?"

"Sure thing." He adjusted the submachine gun strap and moved off, toward the front door.

"He's only partially burned," Vail said. "Mostly from the waist up." She crouched behind the body, reached into the rear pocket of the still-intact jeans, and extracted a leather wallet. She set it on the melamine surface in front of the deceased and splayed it open. "This is Sahmoud?"

Uzi moved beside her and looked it all over. "Appears that way."

Vail shook her head. "I'm not buying it."

"Me either," DeSantos said. "Can we get some DNA? Or was it destroyed in the fire?"

"Because his lower extremity's intact," Vail said, "we can get some cells. The problem is the timing. It'll take a while to get a profile."

"Three days," Uzi said. "But there may be another way. A buddy of mine told me he heard that life scientists at the Weizmann Institute have developed an experimental method that could get us an answer within twenty-four hours, but it's not 100 percent accurate. It can check for certain markers but not produce an entire profile." He pulled out his satphone and moved to the window. He put it on speaker, dialed, and waited while it connected.

"Gideon, it's Uzi."

"Tell me you're on your way to the airport."

"We found something and I need your help."

"That sounds like a 'No, we decided to ignore your warnings and do something stupid.'"

Uzi and Vail shared a look.

"We've got a body, badly burned."

"Where?"

"Nablus. Sahmoud's office."

"Dammit, Uzi. Did you not understand me when I said—"

"Gideon. You know me. Did you really think I'd leave?"

"How'd you find his place? From one of my people?"

"Not important. You want to help or not?"

There was a long pause. Then Aksel said, "I'm listening."

"This body appears to be Sahmoud—he had a wallet in his back pocket with ID, but we have doubts."

"As you should."

"Weizmann," Uzi continued, "has that experimental DNA—"

"That was a rumor. But we've got something else. And yes, the test is already in progress."

Uzi looked at DeSantos, whose mouth slipped open.

"You know about the body?"

"Uzi, you know better than to ask that question, no? One of your ex-colleagues went in the back door at 4:30 this morning, took the cells, and left. The guards never heard a thing. At this point, I'll have the findings in about five hours, maybe sooner."

"Will you share them with us?"

"If you're on the next flight out of Ben Gurion, you have my word."

67

This doesn't make sense," Vail said.

Uzi stood there, phone in hand, staring at the body. "The burn pattern?"

"There's that, yeah. But also motive. Who'd do this? And why? And why just when we're about to close in on him?"

"First impression?" DeSantos said. "It's a decoy."

"Second impression?" Uzi asked.

DeSantos took a position in front of the corpse. "Someone had to know we were hot on Sahmoud's trail and left this body for us, hoping we'd take the bait."

Vail chuckled. "You mean hoping we were stupid."

"You think it was Khaleel?"

"That's probably a question for Raph," Vail said, "but just going by personality, he's someone who'd sell anything to anyone for money. So he could be a double agent of sorts. Informs for both sides."

DeSantos glanced around the room. "If this was a setup, there's no way Sahmoud would've left anything behind. But we're here, we should search the place just in case."

"I don't know how long we have," Uzi said, "before someone comes looking for the two missing guards. Not to mention there's a fair amount of blood out front."

"Just a few minutes, then we can go." DeSantos knelt in front of the body and examined it. He moved around the side of the table and then behind the corpse.

Vail turned and began along the adjacent wall, looking for hidden rooms or compartments. She had not gotten very far when DeSantos called out.

"Got something. Right here, the body."

Uzi stepped closer and shined his phone's flashlight where DeSantos had indicated. Three fine wires were visible protruding from the seat of the chair.

DeSantos took the phone and angled it closer to the area. "Looks like a pressure sensor. If we move the body, we'll be in a million pieces."

"If *that* was rigged," Uzi said, "other things might be too. Don't touch anything. We need to get out. Raph!"

"Yeah. Coming." They heard him walking down the hall—and then felt the walls shake as a loud blast filled the room. Dust clouds swarmed the air.

"Raph! Raph—you okay?"

But Vail already knew the answer without waiting for a response. "We need to get the hell out of here."

"You go. I need to find Raph."

"We're not leaving without you." DeSantos swatted away the fine debris that hung in the air and rode along the shaft of light that streamed in through the lone open window.

"Raph!"

Vail moved alongside them. Like car headlights in thick fog, the phone's illumination was both diffused and reflected back at them by the dense, relentless wall of dust.

Uzi suddenly stopped. DeSantos and Vail likewise froze in midstep. Ahead of them was a partial body. The skin was black—save for the chalky dust that covered his arms and close-cropped Afro.

Vail grabbed Uzi and hugged him, turned him away from Zemro's destroyed corpse. He squeezed her back and it was clear that he did not want to let go. "I'm sorry," she said by his ear.

He sniffled loudly, then pushed away. "No time. We need to get out."

"Which way?" Vail asked.

"We're closer to the back," DeSantos said. "But we don't know if the door's rigged. We've gotta go out the way we came in."

They moved an inch at a time, single file, DeSantos leading the way, clearing the space in front of him as they advanced.

When they reached the front, DeSantos brought the barrel of the AK-47 up and nodded at Vail, who pulled open the door.

DeSantos swung out into the alley. He indicated with a nod of his chin that it was clear and they retraced their steps back to Zemro's SUV.

When they got there, Uzi jammed the butt of his Puma knife into the corner of the small driver's side vent window and smashed the glass. He struggled to get his forearm through the narrow opening but was able to reach in and unlock the doors.

They got in and Uzi pulled out his satphone. He swiped and tapped, then handed it to Vail, who was riding shotgun. "Send Gideon a text. Tell him what happened and that they have to retrieve Raph's body. And to be careful because there are likely other bombs."

"We got lucky," DeSantos said. "That could've been us back there."

Uzi reached beneath the dashboard and fished around. A moment later he found the wires he was looking for and hotwired the car. He quickly pulled away from the curb and down the street, back into downtown Nablus.

Vail sent the message then felt the satphone vibrate. "It's Hoshi."

"Put her on speaker. And hand me that grease rag on the floor by your foot."

"Hoshi, you've got me, Uzi, and Hector."

Vail handed over the dirty towel and Uzi stuffed it into the hole created by the broken window.

"Where's Mr. Fahad?"

"That's a good question," DeSantos said.

I wonder if he knew the place was rigged and that's why he begged off going with us to Sahmoud's.

"So he's not with you?"

"No."

"I wish I had better news for you," Hoshi said.

Uzi leaned closer to the handset. "You couldn't break the encryption?"

"No, I did. But what I found isn't good."

"Just give it to us straight," Uzi said. "We're in no mood for riddles."

"So Nazir al Dosari's father, Uday, was a Shin Bet informant—Shin Bet's kind of like our FBI. Anyway, the Palestinians call these informants collaborators and Hamas and al Humat don't take kindly to it. In short, the collaborators are killed. When he was twenty years old, Dosari found out what his father was doing and turned him over to Hamas. That was in 1990. Uday was tortured and then killed by being dragged through the streets tied to the back of a motorcycle."

"Ratting out your own dad," Vail said. "Heartless. But given what these extremists are like, that's not surprising."

"This is depressing," Uzi said, "but it's not bad news regarding our case."

"Dosari has a half brother who's five years younger. And his name is Mahmoud El-Fahad."

Uzi stepped on the brakes and yanked the SUV over to the curb. "What did you just say?"

"Uzi," Vail said, "your window's broken. That rag definitely helps, but because of where we are, let's not shout this from the mountaintops, okay?"

He rubbed his forehead then let his head fall back against the headrest.

"You still there?" Hoshi asked.

Vail took the call off speaker and brought the satphone to her ear. "Still here. We need time to absorb this."

"I get it."

"Call us if you find out anything else." Vail hung up and leaned her back against the window, facing Uzi and DeSantos. Both were silent.

"Go ahead, Santa," Uzi said to the windshield. "Tell me you told me so."

"I'm not going to do that."

"Knox has to know this, right?" Vail said. "And Tasset?"

DeSantos rubbed his thighs. "You would think. That's a hard thing to keep secret, and if the Agency did their due diligence, which I'm sure they did, even if they missed it during their background checks, they would've seen that encrypted file. For all we know, that's why it's encrypted."

Uzi ran a hand through his hair. "Just like they knew about my work with Shin Bet and Mossad, I'm sure they know about Fahad. And yet they put him on our team. What does that say?"

"Text from Mo," Vail said, holding up Uzi's phone. "He's got a twenty for us." She turned around to DeSantos. "For what? Sahmoud? The codex? The scroll?" The phone buzzed again and she read the message. "He wants us to meet him where we parked outside the Old City on King David. He's getting a lift over there."

Uzi looked at Vail but did not say anything. He turned back to the windshield. She knew what he was thinking: could they trust him?

Uzi yanked the gearshift into drive and pulled back onto the road.

"Uzi," DeSantos said, "we need to discuss this."

"What's there to discuss? Mo's half brother is al Humat's second in command. His nephew blew himself to bits. And you're saying he's guilty by association."

DeSantos loosened his seatbelt and grabbed hold of Uzi's headrest, pulling himself forward, close to the back of his head. "Boychick, I'm saying we need to be careful. We don't have enough information. We don't understand the connections, the motivation. We have no clue what's going on in his head." He turned to Vail. "Am I right?"

"Yes."

"Everything that's happened," DeSantos continued, "everything *bad* that's happened, Mo's been away—meeting with an informant. Or trying to get intel. Or just plain AWOL. Coincidence? Yeah, maybe. Shit happens. Or maybe not. Maybe he's the one who's been tipping people off."

"Was he there when you were attacked at Arc De Triomphe?" Vail asked.

"No."

"What about that flat in Paris, when they sent you the email to go to the arch?"

"No."

DeSantos placed a hand on Uzi's shoulder. "He might be the one who gave the sniper your location at Times Square."

"He didn't know we were going to be there."

"He did," Vail said. "I texted him, hoping he'd meet us there."

Uzi sat tall in his seat. "I don't know what to say. I don't know what he's been up to or what he's thinking. He's CIA, he's taught to deceive, to have a cover story."

"He's taught to con you, to make you *believe* his cover story," DeSantos said. "So which is the real story? What's the truth?"

Uzi cut around a slow moving taxi. "What do you want to do?"

"I certainly don't want to walk into an ambush."

"Neither do I," Vail said.

Uzi thought a moment. "We'll go, hear him out, try to verify his intel."

"Okay." Vail nodded. "And if we can't?"

"Then we have an important decision to make."

68

Uzi pulled to the curb on King David Street. Fahad was standing there, talking to a woman wearing a burka. He excused himself and climbed into the backseat.

"I've got a location," Fahad said.

Vail shifted in her seat to face the three men. "For what?"

"Kadir Abu Sahmoud. His home, in Gaza."

No one spoke.

Finally Fahad looked at each of them. "Did I miss something? We've got Sahmoud's address—an actual address—and from what I could determine, he's there. This is awesome news. Let's go."

"We had a problem," Uzi said. "Raph's dead."

Fahad jerked back. "Dead? What happened?"

"The office was rigged with explosives. Raph tripped one."

Fahad's shoulders slumped. "Man, I'm sorry. I—I wish I was there. I—he was a good guy."

"He was," Uzi said.

Vail saw a liquid sparkle in his eyes, tears pooling in his lower lids.

An awkward moment of silence passed.

"Look," Fahad said. "I don't mean to sound insensitive, but we've got a line on Sahmoud—our objective from day one. What's the problem?"

"How do we know it's not another setup?" Vail asked. "We could walk into an ambush."

DeSantos turned to face Fahad, his expression hard. "Where'd you get this information?"

"From two of my informants. One in Nablus, a Palestinian Authority cop. He told me Sahmoud lives in Gaza near the resort beach community. He mentioned something that reminded me of another guy I know in East Jerusalem who works construction. I cabbed it over and made a couple of calls and found that they were paving roads near Silwan. He was a little dodgy, but bottom line is that his daughter and son-in-law live in a house down the block from someone who they're sure is Sahmoud."

"How can they be 'sure'?" DeSantos asked.

"His son-in-law owns a cell phone startup in Gaza City, but my CI has always thought their money comes from somewhere else—a stipend from the money Hamas gets from taxes on the goods smuggled into the strip through its four hundred tunnels—weapons, fuel, medicine, consumer goods, cars, appliances, drugs, cigarettes. Anyway, point is, his daughter and son-in-law are one of almost two thousand millionaires living in Gaza. And they've got a house that my CI described as gaudy."

"This is where Sahmoud lives?" Uzi asked.

"Down the street."

"Again," DeSantos said, "how do they know Sahmoud lives there?"

"His son-in-law told him one night when they'd had a lot to drink. They were sitting around the fire and he said he's seen Sahmoud. A few months later my CI and his wife spent the weekend there and saw guards escorting a man around that looked like Sahmoud. They drove him around in a town car that was heavy and fortified—as if it were bulletproof and blastproof."

"Anything else?" DeSantos asked.

Fahad shrugged. "That was enough for me—and it fit with what the cop in Nablus told me."

Vail took turns reading Uzi's and DeSantos's faces. They were processing the intel, running it through their bullshit meter. If she were plugged into this world, she would be doing the same.

Finally Uzi said, "I think we should go and take a look, maybe sit on the place for a few hours and watch."

DeSantos sucked on his bottom lip, then nodded. "I can live with that."

Hopefully we all can.

69

Gaza was everything Vail had expected—and *none* of what she expected when they first boarded the plane to Israel. She figured she would see what had been shown on news reports following the most recent war: total devastation, destroyed buildings, a landscape flattened by mortars and artillery and bombs, a poor and destitute population.

There were areas like that—shells of structures that once stood, piles of rubble still littering the scenery, residents in simple clothing and looking the worse for wear. But by and large, that was a fraction of what she saw as they drove toward the address that Fahad's informant had provided.

They entered Gaza from Israel through the Erez Crossing along the strip's northeastern border. As Uzi and Fahad explained to Vail, the sixty million dollar pedestrian and cargo portal was built by Israel when it withdrew all its settlers and soldiers from Gaza in what was envisioned by Israeli Prime Minister Ariel Sharon as a land-for-peace deal in 2005. If all went well, it would serve as the template for negotiating a similar pact for the West Bank, with the goal of establishing a Palestinian state.

But four months after the Erez terminal was completed, Hamas won the popular election for the territory, its reign of terror began, and all hopes of a negotiated peace deal were put on hold.

Blockades were put in place to stem the flow of weapons from Iran, and Egypt closed the southern border to prevent Hamas and al Humat terrorists from entering the Sinai and collaborating with the Muslim Brotherhood. Passage into Israel from Gaza was restricted to curtail suicide attacks and into Gaza from Israel to prevent the smuggling of contraband that could be used to build bombs.

Gaza became isolated and the people became a society controlled, manipulated, and intimidated by their elected government.

"I remember when my mom and I would take a bus into Gaza once a week to buy vegetables and fish," Uzi said. "No checkpoints. No problems." He glanced around. "That was before the intifada, before the suicide bombings."

"A lot of things changed," Fahad said. "If only we could turn back the clock, start again. Maybe things would be different."

Vail glanced at Fahad. *Is this an act, or is he sincere?*

With a scarf again covering her face, Vail took in Gaza City's high-rises and businesses, hotels, museums and bustling avenues. Apartment buildings and homes. Fahad told her there were theaters and several universities as well as beautiful beaches along the Mediterranean coastline with resorts and sophisticated restaurants.

The sun was starting its descent as the winter afternoon passed. Despite the gathering clouds, there was still considerable light left to the day.

DeSantos's phone rang and he dug it out of his pocket. "Hot Rod, talk to me . . . Yeah . . . Okay." He pressed a button and said, "You're on speaker."

"I got a hit on something. Not sure if it means anything, but I haven't seen any recent sit-reps from you guys, so I'm a bit in the dark. In case it's significant you should know that Hussein Rudenko's back on the grid. And he's in your area."

Holy shit. Rudenko!

"I knew we hadn't heard the last of him," DeSantos said.

"Hussein Rudenko, the arms dealer?" Fahad asked.

"Weapons trafficker wasn't bad enough," Uzi said. "He added terrorist to his resume. Karen, Hector, Hot Rod, and I got into it with him in London a couple of years ago."

"As soon as we heard there were rare manuscripts and antiquities in play," Vail said, "I should've known Rudenko was involved."

"Hang on," Uzi said. "We don't know for sure he's got anything to do with the codex or the scroll. Hot Rod, exactly what do you have?"

"I asked NSA to point their ears to Gaza and the West Bank in case anything came up that'd be important to you guys," Rodman said. "They trapped a cell call ten minutes ago and got a voice match to Hussein Rudenko."

"We're in Gaza right now," DeSantos said. "We need to know if Rudenko just happens to be in the area or if he's selling weapons or planning an attack with al Humat."

"I'll see if NSA can track the phone's GPS. Give me a few minutes."

DeSantos ended the call and set his phone down on his thigh. "This is no coincidence."

"If we look at this logically," Vail said, "the most obvious reason for Rudenko to be here, now, is that he has possession of the scroll."

"We know that al Humat—or one of their representatives—has the codex," Uzi said. "That phone conversation we intercepted in Paris from Borz

Ramadazov after he left the Louvre—he said he had it and was bringing it to the safe house. He had no reason to lie because he had no idea we'd tapped his phone."

DeSantos swung around in his seat, taking in the city streets, no doubt doing some surveillance due diligence. "But we just missed Doka Michel, who supposedly was transporting the codex to Sahmoud's office. Someone tipped Sahmoud, so when we got there, there was no codex and no Sahmoud, and the place was rigged. He knew we were coming." DeSantos glanced at Fahad. It was subtle, and Fahad was looking out the window, so he probably did not notice.

"Rudenko could be buying it," Uzi said. "Or the scroll."

"Does this change anything?" Fahad asked.

"Yeah," Uzi said. "I doubt Rudenko's going to be alone. He's going to have a small, well trained security detail with him."

Vail curled some hair behind her right ear. "What do you make of the fact that he's come to Sahmoud rather than the other way around?"

"Sahmoud's ability to move in and out of the territory is restricted," Uzi said. "And he's at the top, or near the top, of just about every intelligence agency's most wanted list. Much safer for Rudenko to come to him. Into Egypt, through the Sinai, then the tunnels into Gaza."

Fahad pointed at the road ahead. "Slow down, we're getting close. Turn left."

Uzi followed the instructions and decelerated. Ahead, about seventy-five yards away, was a guard booth and two metal pillars that rose from the roadway. "Gated community." He pulled the car to the curb.

DeSantos leaned forward to study the uniformed security officer, who appeared to be alone in the small brick structure. "We should hang out here till we hear back from Hot Rod."

Rodman's assessment came in a moment later:

> he's in gaza blocks from you
> will send address

"That goes with what my CI told me," Fahad said. "We've got the right place."

A second later, it came through on DeSantos's phone. "This doesn't match the one your CI gave you."

Fahad consulted the screen, then leaned back, his face twisted in confusion. "That's easily two blocks away."

"We go with Hot Rod's intel," DeSantos said. "Agreed?"

"Agreed," Uzi said. "We can always double back to Mo's house if we don't find anything."

"The numbers are transposed," Fahad said. "Two digits are reversed. Maybe that's it."

And maybe not.

Vail looked out at the street. Large houses with adobe tile roofs and solar panels were set back from the road. None of them had perimeter walls or metal gates. "If we know Rudenko's there now, we shouldn't wait. We've got no idea how long he's going to stick around."

DeSantos tapped away at his phone. "Operationally, it'd be better to wait till it's completely dark. I just asked Hot Rod to let us know if Rudenko moves."

"How are we tracking him?" Uzi asked.

"NSA and NGA," he said, referring to the National Geospatial Intelligence Agency. "Combination of cell phone intercepts, GPS data, and infrared heat signatures from a drone equipped with FLIR sensors."

"Those sensors can be defeated."

"So far we've got a fix." DeSantos's phone vibrated. He took a few seconds to read the text, then paraphrased it: "Apparently there's a bunker-like room that's hardened and shielded to some extent. They can see four men along the building's perimeter and outside that room, but the others are less distinct. They think there are a total of eleven in and around the house. Rudenko's one of them and, presumably, Sahmoud."

"Wife and kids?" Vail asked.

DeSantos looked long and hard at her, then texted Rodman back. The response was near-immediate, despite the ten thousand miles separating them. "He wants to know if we're serious. And he wanted to know who asked."

Vail shook her head. "Yes, I'm serious. And I want an answer."

Six minutes later they had a response. "Best they can tell, his wife and two boys are out of town in Italy at their villa."

"Any backup?" Fahad asked. "Or just us?"

DeSantos glanced down at his phone. "Just got blueprints. And real-time images with infrared signatures. Check your satphones. Let's make sure we all have the same feed."

Uzi and Vail pivoted in their seats, pulled out their devices, and called it up on their small screens.

"Can't really see inside that room," Vail said.

"That's the shielding," DeSantos said. "Probably layers of concrete, maybe metal. We know men are in there but they look like blobs rather than well defined human outlines."

Great. We're not quite blind, but close to it. Kind of like being severely near-sighted and having your glasses smashed.

Fifteen minutes later, they had devised an operational approach to infiltrate the house, and although they had the layout and location of the tangos, they were guessing about who and what was inside the hardened room. They also did not know al Humat's security protocols and what obstacles they were going to face.

They had one advantage: the element of surprise—at least for the moment—so the idea was to maintain it for as long as possible.

They assumed there would be motion sensors that would set off perimeter lighting and video cameras linked to a hard drive recording mechanism. That was a reasonable supposition, though by no means guaranteed.

"If it's cloud-based," Uzi said, "it could be a huge problem."

"Odds?" DeSantos asked.

Uzi considered the question. "Al Humat isn't known to be tech savvy—and a lot of the extremist groups take al Qaeda's lead and avoid tech whenever possible because they know it can be tracked by the good guys. So I'd gamble that their video is, at best, recorded on a local hard drive. More likely it's just live feeds with no archival storage. They're not worried about catching or prosecuting intruders by identifying their mugs from a recording. They just want to prevent someone from doing what we're going to do. But since camera feeds can be hacked, they may avoid them altogether and rely only on security personnel."

"I'm more concerned with how we're going to coordinate with each other once we leave the car," Vail said. "We don't have comms devices."

DeSantos nodded. "As we work our way toward Sahmoud, if something goes south, text will be our quietest and quickest way of communicating."

After walking through the plan a final time, they initiated their first line of attack: removing the security booth guard from the equation.

Fahad was the logical candidate to approach the man given his native appearance and language skills. Uzi would follow a moment later as backup and support in case there was someone else nearby.

A minute after Fahad left the SUV, DeSantos's satphone rang.

"It's Knox. Text Fahad, tell him to wait."

Uzi yanked his phone out and started typing as DeSantos answered and placed the call on speaker. "Yes sir."

"Are we secure?"

DeSantos looked around and made sure no one was in earshot. "You've got me, Uzi, and Karen. We're in a car."

"I'll be landing in a matter of minutes. Status?"

DeSantos gave him a quick update. "We're getting ready to go in."

"Getting those docs is job one. Sahmoud is a secondary priority, but a priority nonetheless."

DeSantos glanced at Vail and Uzi. "We'll take care of both."

"Just make sure you secure those documents," Knox said. "Keep your emotions in check, temper your desire for justice. I want that fucker to pay for the American lives he's taken too. But the codex and the scroll . . . while their strategic and historic value is obvious, there are other considerations. And because of that, after taking possession of them, you're to turn them over to Mossad."

Vail kinked her neck. "If we're going to give them to the Israelis, why not just have *them* infiltrate Sahmoud's compound. They're much better equipped—"

"Because you've got your mission and you'll carry it out. And because if I thought that pulling out now would work, I'd call the director general and tell him what we've got and let him deal with it. But there's no time for that. You're down the street from two prime targets. You bug out now, we may never find those docs again."

Uzi ran the back of a hand across his beard stubble. "Why are we giving the codex and scroll a higher priority than capturing the number three most wanted terrorist?"

There was a prolonged pause. Just when Vail thought they had lost him, Knox began speaking.

"President Nunn wants to control the documents for his own strategic reasons. My sources tell me he plans to use them to force concessions from Israel to win the peace."

"I thought that's what the Palestinians are doing," DeSantos said.

"It carries a great deal more weight with the president as the driving force behind it. And to Nunn, being the only president who successfully brokered a peace agreement between the Israelis and Palestinians would cement his legacy. But you know what? I don't give a shit about a president's legacy. If there's peace it should be a negotiated agreement, not some leveraged form of blackmail. Despite best intentions, negotiated agreements sometimes fail. But extortion *never* works."

"Take the documents out of the equation for a minute," Uzi said. "The administration could just withhold military aid loans to Israel and leverage them that way. Wouldn't that have the same effect?"

"Not that simple," Knox said. "Those military loans are required to be spent in the US, so taking that money out of the US economy, and the jobs it would cost, would not be very popular at home. Congress would never go for it, anyway. No, this is Nunn's only shot. They're secret negotiations, which means no one's supposed to know what he's planning to do with these documents. So if you repeat what I've just told you, it'll be clear who leaked the information. I'm the only one who knows what's really going on outside a very small, well controlled circle."

Apparently not as well controlled as you think. And now not as small a circle as it was before.

"Secretary McNamara and I don't buy into this strategy. It's the wrong approach and won't lead to a healthy peace."

Vail squirmed in her seat. Defying—and undermining—the president? *This feels dangerously close to treason.*

"That's why you're not going to bring the codex and scroll home," Knox said. "Give them to the Israelis. Bring them to the Shrine of the Book building at the National Museum. We have to ensure that this leverage—this undue influence that these documents provide—is taken out of the equation."

DeSantos signed off and Vail texted Fahad to tell him to resume the operation.

"Showtime," Uzi said.

DeSantos gave him a fist bump. "Good luck."

UZI LEFT THE SUV and followed the path that Fahad took to the guard booth along the sidewalk, using the cover of bushes and hedges where possible. From fifteen feet away, he watched through the window in the front of the small brick structure as Fahad greeted the officer.

From what Uzi could tell in the descending darkness, there was some discussion between the two men. A moment later, Fahad was the only one visible.

Uzi advanced and found the militant seated in a chair, dressed in an al Humat uniform, his head resting on his forearms. He looked like he was asleep. But Uzi knew better.

Conspicuously absent was an array of video screens for surveillance monitoring—a good sign and hopefully an indicator of whether or not the residents of the neighborhood felt the added level of paranoia was necessary.

Fahad began searching the small desk drawers while Uzi examined a spiral bound log book that contained Arabic writing. Visitors were required to sign in. Their license plate numbers were recorded along with their names and addresses. "Looks like they have regularly scheduled check-ins with someone—someone on Sahmoud's personal detail. Probably one of the guys in that house."

"Makes sense. What's the interval?"

"Every thirty minutes. Last one was . . . eighteen minutes ago." Uzi checked his watch. "So we've got twelve minutes. That's cutting it close." He texted DeSantos and Vail and gave one last look around. "Let's go. We don't have a lot of time."

70

Rudenko is our third priority," DeSantos said, "and only because he may have the scroll. If it's clear he doesn't, we let him go unless taking him down won't jeopardize our primary objectives: the two documents first and Sahmoud second. You okay with that?"

Vail frowned. "You mean because I'd like to put a bullet behind Rudenko's ear?"

"Because of that, yeah."

"I understand the mission priorities, Hector. But forget about Rudenko. What if it comes down to the two docs or Sahmoud?"

"You heard our orders," DeSantos said. "Codex and scroll are number one. That said, I'm betting Sahmoud is in the bunker—the most secure room in the house. Which means he'll have the docs there too. Assuming I'm right, we should be able to grab *both* the docs and Sahmoud."

I hope you're right.

DeSantos looked out at the guard booth. From what he could see in the failing light, he told her, Fahad and Uzi had been successful. "Let's take a minute for a dose of reality."

"I kind of assumed I was living a nightmare."

"Most of the time," he said, ignoring her, "a Special Forces operator aims to get in and out. He avoids contact with the enemy. We don't have that luxury. We've got vests but no head gear. We have guns but no suppressors. No comms and limited intel. So to keep the advantage of surprise, the Glocks stay in our waistbands until we don't have any choice. This is close quarters combat. Use your knife. And your hands."

"We've already gone over this."

He twisted his body to face her. "I need to know if you can handle yourself. This isn't going to be yelling at some perp a block away to stop while sighting him with a .40-caliber. This is in your face, kill or be killed."

She looked into DeSantos's eyes and absorbed what he was saying. There could be no doubt. No hesitation.

"I've been involved in close quarters combat. You know that."

"Al Humat chooses its guards from its best fighters, Karen, those who've proven themselves by killing innocents—which shows their commitment to the cause. These aren't rent-a-cops."

Sahmoud and Rudenko are two of the worst offenders I've come up against. I want them. Badly. But can I do it?

She had the training. She had the weapon. She had gone hand to hand with serial killers and deadly assassins. But would she have the killer instinct in a situation where *she* was the intruder?

She had crossed the line in the past, sometimes purposely and sometimes inadvertently. This felt different. There wasn't a question of *if* she would encounter tangos. They were going in to purposely engage them.

Vail realized DeSantos was waiting for an answer. She held his gaze and said, "We're taking down one of the world's worst. Two of them if we're lucky. I'm in."

DeSantos nodded slowly. "Let's do it, then."

71

Ten minutes passed and the light was fading rapidly. Over the Mediterranean, the sky still had some life to it. But to DeSantos's right, the death of cloud-covered darkness had settled in.

Most importantly, he had difficulty seeing the landscape around him: just how he wanted it.

He moved slowly to keep from tripping motion sensors, a painstaking process but one he had perfected during years of similar missions.

Waves crashed in the distance but his auditory sense was focused on those noises that would mean the difference between life and death. His field of vision had narrowed, his concentration was deep.

He had one objective at the moment: the man on the other side of the door. According to his screen, the guard was two and a half feet away, only a one inch slab of wood separating them.

He had little choice but to permit Fahad's participation: although he had strong suspicions, he had no proof. With a force of four against eleven, they had a chance of success. With three the odds dropped significantly. DeSantos had to trust him.

But not completely. He had texted Rodman and asked him to make sure Fahad's regular cell phone and satphone were monitored. If he made a call to anyone other than the three members of his team, they were to be notified immediately.

It was enough fighting eleven men; he did not need one of his own working against them.

DeSantos knew from the infrared imagery that the guards were armed with what looked to be AK-47s. They probably also had small arms and even bladed weapons. The objective was for him, and his team, to strike unexpectedly. And fast. It took time and effort to move a heavy submachine gun toward an enemy. Too much time in close quarters combat—which is what this would be. Plus, they were likely not expecting an incursion and, despite what he told Vail, even if they were their best fighters, he did not know their specific level of training. They might shoot well at fifty yards, but did they practice weekly? Did they practice home invasion scenarios? Using his SOG SEAL seven-inch knife, he scraped the exterior surface of the door. Lightly, at first.

No response.

Again, a little more deeply.

Footstep. Hand on the knob. Creak of the hinge as it opened.

DeSantos tossed a small rock to his right. It rustled the leaves of a bush and the guard stepped out onto the cement stoop. The AK-47 was slung across the man's shoulder, gripped sloppily in his right hand, pointed at the ground.

DeSantos swung the double-serrated blade backhanded through the moist, cool air and struck the man in the left kidney. He stiffened and opened his mouth to scream but DeSantos slapped his fingers over his lips.

He yanked the knife out and stabbed again, this time a vicious, fast jab to the right side of the man's spine. He struck bone and went through it. The man's legs went limp and DeSantos put him down with a final strike to the throat so he would not make a noise that would give away his position.

DeSantos yanked him into the foliage, stepped over the bloodied concrete, and into the house.

VAIL MADE HER WAY to the southeast side of the house. She had approached as DeSantos advised her, along the plant line and staying clear of gravel, keeping on grass wherever possible to avoid making unwanted noise. She moved slowly but deliberately and was successful in not setting off the motion sensors.

She stood at the front door for a moment and heard only the crashing rumble of ocean waves. It was unnerving. The satellite imagery showed her mark—a soldier standing rock-still, a foot away, guarding the entrance to the home. Adrenaline flooded her bloodstream and her hands felt unsteady. She wiped her palms on the back of her pants and took a long, cleansing breath.

DeSantos's face flashed through her thoughts as he leaned forward and looked her in the eye. "I need to know if you can handle yourself."

I've stormed buildings, jumped out of helicopters, and parachuted from the back of a military jet. I can do this too.

Vail shoved the phone in her pocket and brought a fist up to knock.

This man is a killer. Kill or be killed. Kill or be killed.

She rapped lightly on the wood surface. The door immediately swung open and a large male stood there, angular face with close-cropped dark hair and wearing a uniform with the unmistakable green/yellow/black logo of al Humat.

A submachine gun was balanced against his right forearm. His hand relaxed and the barrel dipped slightly when he saw a woman standing at the door. Not much of a threat.

Vail did not hesitate: she spoke the words Uzi coached her to say in Arabic—"I have an urgent message for Kadir from Doka"—and handed him a note. When he reached out to take it she stepped forward and thrust her long Tanto blade into his midsection, an uppercut designed to miss the ribcage. It sliced through as if she had cut into Jell-O. She yanked the handle left and right, severing the abdominal aorta.

The fighter's eyes bulged wide and his torso bent forward in shock. Or pain. He dropped the AK-47 as his head jerked back. He grabbed her throat with a broad, thick hand and squeezed with surprising strength.

Don't panic, Karen. He's bleeding out.

Kill or be killed.

She gave the Tanto a final jerk back and forth and then grabbed it with both hands and yanked it up and down, sawing in and out.

Three long seconds later the man's eyelids fluttered closed and he collapsed into her, releasing his hold on her neck. She stepped aside and helped him down to the shiny granite entryway.

Vail used her left Timberland boot to roll him over. She stuck her foot on his abdomen and extracted the Tanto, then gave it a quick wipe on his pants—her black 5.11s were now smeared maroon with blood.

She moved to her right into an expansive living room whose walls featured a large representation of the al Aqsa mosque in relief, alongside the Dome of the Rock, which was covered with what looked like real gold leaf—just like the actual building. She knelt behind a needlepoint upholstered chair to consult the drone's infrared imagery. Four men were down, which meant that Uzi, DeSantos, and Fahad were also successful. That still left an unspecified number of security personnel—two outside the room and maybe three guards and two tangos inside the room.

Vail slipped the Tanto back into its sheath and removed her Glock. A round was chambered, so it was ready to go. At this point stealth was no longer an option—nor was it necessary. All the men were on the same floor: the basement.

Judging by her team's movement—they were all closing in on the room—she was the last to dispose of her assigned target. But she resisted the urge to move too quickly. Although she had only seventy-five seconds until the guard's scheduled check-in, the last thing they needed was for any of them to be discovered now, before they were all in position.

A minute later, with time winding down, she had descended two floors and stood on the landing, a few feet from the mouth of a long hallway.

Approximately thirty feet down the cement corridor was another al Humat officer. He was likely keeping watch at the door to the large room behind him, where an important business transaction was occurring.

Vail leaned her back against the wall and waited for the text from DeSantos. It came seconds later:

count to ten then go

She shoved the satphone in her front pocket and took a breath, hands wrapped around the Glock's polymer handle. *Seven, six, five, four . . .*

72

Uzi and DeSantos faced the second door to the basement bunker, where Sahmoud and Rudenko were likely located. They were ninety degrees from the main entrance, where Vail's target was stationed.

"I like your new uniform," DeSantos said of Uzi's al Humat black shirt with embroidered patches depicting the organization's logo.

"He wasn't all that bad for a terrorist. He gave me the shirt off his back."

This was by design—Uzi would engage the guard with his hands rather than his knife—in case they needed an intact uniform.

They had thirty seconds before the scheduled check-in with the security booth officer was due—assuming they kept to their schedule. According to the logbook Uzi had seen, they were punctual.

Fahad remained upstairs, ensuring guards did not enter the house once the shooting began. That they were in the basement, two levels down, lessened the likelihood the gunfire would be heard.

DeSantos tried the knob carefully, slowly, quietly, and determined it was locked. The door appeared to be solid metal—which meant it was heavy, likely reinforced, and impervious to being kicked in.

If this had been another time and place, Uzi would've set a charge of C4, taken cover, and blown it off its hinges.

They had reviewed the file photos of each wanted man. They would have milliseconds to identify them and shoot the others. How many were there? Impossible to be sure.

One mistake and they would lose the ability to detain and question two of the most dangerous criminals in the civilized world. However, Knox had made the overriding objective clear.

"We can't shoot through this," DeSantos whispered.

"Agreed. We should knock."

DeSantos gave Uzi a look.

"I'm serious. Sometimes the simplest solutions are right in front of you."

"I've got nothing better. Go for it." DeSantos texted Vail and then moved out of sight.

Uzi lifted his balled fist toward the door and rapped on the cold steel surface.

"What," someone shouted in Arabic from the other side.

"Message from Doka," Uzi replied. "Important."

The countless hours Uzi had spent in Shin Bet's academy, then Mossad's training facilities during ops preparation, and in the FBI Academy's shooting house, flashed through his thoughts. His heart was pounding and his pulse was racing. He took a breath. The knob turned and the door swung in a second before Vail's first gunshot rang out.

Uzi shouldered the door open. DeSantos swiveled into the room, took aim, and drilled a number of suited men in the chest.

Yelling

Chairs toppling

Frantic bursts of return gunfire

Uzi located his target and squeezed off several rounds, the sound deafening, the smell of cordite suffocating, obscuring visibility.

"Where is he?" Uzi yelled. "Where's Sahmoud?"

Another two gunshots, then Vail burst in, crouched low with her Glock in the ready position.

Uzi moved deeper into the room and surveyed the carnage. Neither Sahmoud nor Rudenko was there. He pulled an AK-47 off the dead body of one of the downed security guards and tossed it to DeSantos.

He rooted out his satphone and saw an amorphous, unaccounted for heat mass behind the large desk near the far wall. Uzi hand signaled Vail as he moved cautiously toward the man.

A middle-aged male with a salt-and-pepper beard was seated on the floor, his back against a vertical row of wood file drawers. His right hand was pressed against his abdomen.

Assessing the threat and determining there was none, Uzi shoved the Glock in his waistband and knelt in front of the man.

"Kadir Abu Sahmoud, you're a prisoner of the United States government."

73

Vail came around the edge of the desk and studied Sahmoud. He was leaking blood from an abdominal wound and was in a great deal of pain. Given their covert status, there was no way to get him the kind of medical attention he needed to save his life. How long he had she did not know. Because of their training, Uzi or DeSantos could make a more accurate assessment.

"Get me to a hospital and I will make sure you are well compensated," Sahmoud said through clenched teeth.

"Call Mo," Uzi said. "Tell him we've got Sahmoud but not Rudenko."

"Copy that," DeSantos said as he removed his phone.

"The dumbwaiter," Sahmoud said. "He's . . . gone."

Vail moved across the room and examined the small elevator. She craned her neck and looked up the shaft and saw that the car was on a level maybe twenty feet above her. *Is Sahmoud telling the truth or is Rudenko hiding somewhere?* As Vail turned to face the room, a group text arrived from Fahad:

> infrared shows man moving away from
> back of house on foot. cant pursue

Rudenko! Son of a bitch.

She glanced at DeSantos and shook her head. She replied and told Fahad to make sure there were no surveillance cameras—and if there were, to erase any recordings.

While DeSantos patted down the dead guards, Vail turned her attention to the primary objective and began a systematic search of the room. She did not have far to look: a walk-in safe behind the desk, a few feet from Uzi, was ajar. She pulled the six-foot-tall metal door open enough for her to enter and turned on her phone's flashlight.

On the left side were a number of flat cases and assorted cardboard rolls, stacks of money of various denominations—shekels, dollars, pounds, euros. A large velvet pouch of uncut diamonds. Several canvases of what looked like Renaissance era paintings.

As she sifted through the contents of the shelves, she heard Uzi and DeSantos begin to interrogate Sahmoud.

Off to the right she saw a portfolio that was strikingly similar to the leather cases she had seen in the Louvre restoration vault. She set it on a small table in the center of the vault and carefully unzipped it.

Whoa. So this is the Aleppo Codex.

It was as the rabbis in Brooklyn had described: once bound, now mostly loose pages of about 10x13, dark brown ink on tan parchment, roughly thirty lines to a column, three columns to a page. The handwriting was so perfect it could have been typeset on a computer.

Her palms were sweaty, her heart still racing—but it was not just the residual adrenaline. She was holding one of the most important documents produced by mankind. It brought back memories of her first trip to the Metropolitan Museum of Art as a young art history major and seeing Diego Velazquez's oil on canvas, *Juan Pareja*.

The scroll?

Vail closed the portfolio and pulled off the metal endcap of a spiral wound cardboard shipping tube. She peered inside: another parchment, this one looking a good deal more fragile. She did not want to risk pulling it out for fear of damaging it. Vail opened three others—and while each contained what appeared to be valuable documents, none matched the description of a Dead Sea Scroll.

"How's he doing?" Vail asked, poking her head out of the vault.

"Not very cooperative," Uzi said. "He confirmed that Rudenko sold him the scroll. Rudenko bought it twenty-some-odd years ago from someone who smuggled it out of the Vatican."

"So the Vatican got its hands on it?" Vail asked.

"They offered nineteen million dollars to get it back. Sahmoud made a better offer. No one knew who had it. He felt now was the time to sell because of what he'd been told about the peace negotiations."

"He was right," DeSantos said. He was standing beside the kneeling Uzi, the pilfered AK-47 in his grasp, legs spread. A position of readiness.

Vail whispered in DeSantos's ear, "With the gunshots, even down here, there's gotta be others on their way. And someone may discover the dead guard at the gate. Don't know about you, but I don't want any part of that."

"Especially with Fahad watching the shop. What about the codex and the scr—"

"Got both."

DeSantos nudged Uzi in the shoulder. "Boychick, we gotta go."

"Take me with you," Sahmoud said through a tight jaw. "I'll pay you . . . Two million each."

Uzi laughed.

Sahmoud winced. "Diamonds in the vault . . . worth twenty-five million. Take them . . . they're yours."

"They're ours anyway," DeSantos said. He lifted his phone and took a snapshot of their prisoner's face. "We should leave him here."

Sahmoud began to laugh—a rough chuckle that had a raspy edge to it.

"What's so funny?" Uzi asked.

"The man who made all this possible. One of your own." Laugh. Wince.

"What are you talking about? Who made what possible?"

Sahmoud's head fell back against the wood desk. "He . . . helped us locate the bank. He . . . made it possible . . . to buy the scroll." His eyes closed.

C'mon asshole, don't die on us now.

Uzi and Vail shared a concerned look—but he started talking again.

"His idea to use it . . . to leverage . . . the Israelis. Knew they'd give in . . . Not many weaknesses . . . but their holy books . . . their holy land . . . can't help themselves." He laughed again, brought his knees up to his chest. "He found out . . . FBI director coming . . . to make sure . . . I was sent to . . . America . . . for trial. Warned me."

Uzi got in his face. "Who? Who warned you?"

He opened one eye. "Take me . . ."

Uzi hesitated, then said, "Fine. We'll take you with us." He turned to DeSantos and said, as convincingly as possible, "Get something to use as a stretcher." Back to Sahmoud: "*Who* warned you?"

He swallowed, licked his lips. "Ward . . . Connerly."

74

"The president's chief of staff?" Uzi glanced at DeSantos, the look saying, "So it wasn't Mo."

"That's why you planted the burned body," Vail said.

Sahmoud managed a crooked grin, his eyes closed, his voice weak. "You weren't . . . smart enough . . . to get the . . . clue."

"Clue?" DeSantos asked.

The note pinned to the Times Square vic. The first ward. Ward Connerly. "First" applies to the president, like the First Lady, the first dog. The president's chief of staff.

She explained it to Uzi and DeSantos.

"Nothing . . . you can do . . ." Sahmoud said. "Never . . . find . . . evidence . . ." His voice tailed off, his arms went limp, and his head dropped to his chest.

DeSantos pressed two fingers against Sahmoud's neck, then straightened up. "Looks like he's reached his end of days."

"WHAT ARE WE GOING TO do about this?" Vail asked.

"Nothing," DeSantos said, feeling for hidden compartments in the desk. "Our job's done. We'll give it to Knox, let him run with it. Right now we grab what we can, get the hell out of here."

"Sahmoud could've been telling the truth," Vail said. "Guys like Ward Connerly know how to cover their tracks, they use straw men to do the dirty work. If there's nothing out there linking him to this—"

Uzi walked into the vault and started rummaging around. "There's more than one way to build a case. It may take a while, but we'll get him." He pulled out his phone, put it on speaker, and set it on the table.

"Rodman."

"Hot Rod, it's Uzi. Sorry to wake you."

"Wake me? Been at the ops center pulling double shifts. What do you need?"

"Ward Connerly. Get what you can on him."

"The president's chief of staff?"

Uzi explained what Sahmoud had told them. "Any connections to Middle Eastern types that look suspicious, dig deep. Speed matters."

"We'll get a team on it right now. Hodges," he shouted away from the phone, "get your ass over here." Back into the handset, he said, "If there's something to find, we'll find it."

"We'll be on the move. Anything comes up, tell Knox and Hoshi Koh at my office."

"Got something," DeSantos said. He handed it to Vail, who brought it to Uzi.

"Hang on a sec," he said to Rodman. Uzi studied the two-page printout for a moment, then said, "Looks like a list of al Humat cells in the US, with contact numbers for what could be the leader of each one. Hot Rod, I'll send it over to you. You'll need an Arabic translator."

"We're on it. Check six."

Uzi hung up, then took a photo of the spreadsheet and emailed it to Rodman.

"If that's what you think it is," DeSantos said, "that's a huge win."

Uzi opened a cabinet in the vault and rifled through its contents. "We'll see. No idea how up-to-date it is—assuming I'm right." His back to DeSantos, he said, "But I don't share your optimism about bringing Connerly to justice."

"I think we should be happy with our score and call it a damn fine job."

Vail checked her watch, then pulled open another desk drawer. "Assholes getting away with a crime doesn't sit well with me. Especially when those assholes are in positions of power." She found a booklet made of clear plastic sleeves containing maps. Although she could not read the Arabic, it had GPS coordinates and was marked up meticulously with bold blue and red lines crisscrossing the pages.

Vail walked back into the vault and showed it to Uzi. "What is this?"

He flipped through the pages and paused to read the Arabic. "A diagram of their tunnels. Red for the ones that go into Israel. Blue for the ones coming from Egypt into Gaza. That's gold. Take it with us, we'll turn it over to the IDF."

As Vail shoved the booklet into the back of her waistband, she noticed that Uzi was slowly unrolling a parchment.

He stooped over the document as he read the Hebrew. "This is it."

"The Jesus Scroll?"

Uzi brought his gaze up to hers. She saw wonderment in his eyes, nothing short of amazement.

"I'm actually holding one of the Dead Sea Scrolls. The same one that my zayde—my grandfather—held." He gestured to the thick stack of pages at his right elbow. "And the Aleppo Codex. We found it. We *really* found the codex." He shivered. "Sorry. I just . . . I feel like I'm touching my history. My cultural *essence*." He shook his head. "I'm babbling."

"I understand." Vail inched closer for a better look. "It *is* extraordinary."

A moment later, Uzi straightened up suddenly. "We've gotta get going. Go help Santa finish our search. I'm gonna pack this stuff up. All we have to do now is get it to the Antiquities Authority."

UZI EMERGED with four containers. "I've divided up the documents into these cases. Safer that way. Something happens, one or two of us is more likely to make it through. Avoids the all eggs in one basket thing." He kept a mailing tube for himself, handed another one to Vail, and gave the portfolio to DeSantos, who also took Fahad's satchel.

"We've been here too long," DeSantos said as he consulted his satphone. "We need to go. Call Fahad, get a status."

Vail did so and headed for the stairs. Fahad answered immediately. "Mo, we're coming upst—"

"We got a problem."

Vail stopped at the bottom of the steps, phone pressed against her ear. "What kind of problem?"

"Vehicles approaching. Army vehicles. Shit, Karen. It's al Humat. And they're armed. We've gotta get out of here, now!"

They ran up to the main level, where Fahad was waiting. DeSantos handed him the satchel as they all moved to the back of the house. "We've divided up the docs, each of us has a part."

"Good idea," Fahad said as he slung the bag over his shoulder.

Uzi pulled the back door open. "Split up, meet at the Shrine of the Book. Go!"

75

Vail ran through the yard in a northerly direction, scaled a masonry wall, and ended up in a lightly landscaped greenbelt. She fastened her scarf as she continued on past palm trees and meticulously pruned hedges, then made her way back to the street.

Fifteen minutes later, after finding a dark, well shielded area, she stopped to try to get a bearing on where she was. She knew that Google Earth and Bing Maps did not provide clear satellite imagery of Israel and the Palestinian territories, so she had to rely on regular street maps and general topography. Unless—

Is the drone still overhead? She pulled out her satphone and tried to call up the real-time imagery. It was no longer online—but then she remembered she had the booklet tucked in her waistband.

That it was written in a foreign language was challenging, but she was able to get a sense of the area using the coastline and beach as a reference point. There were a couple of tunnels into Israel that appeared to be nearby.

She plugged in the GPS coordinates of the closest one and followed the screen to set off in the right direction. By her estimate, she was about three miles away. What would the entrance look like? She had seen CNN videos during the war, but those were mostly the openings on the Israeli side, holes that emerged from rock outcroppings in rural areas.

For now, her main concerns were finding a way to traverse the distance and arriving safely. Not knowing who she could trust and not speaking Arabic, she could not pass for anything other than what she was: an American, or at best, a westerner. Who was working with al Humat or Hamas or Islamic Jihad? It would be impossible for her to tell.

She had to think like a Special Forces operator, not an FBI agent. *When I get back, if Knox insists on keeping me in OPSIG, I want more training. I need to know what the hell I'm doing. Enough of this on-the-job bullshit.*

The air had grown chilled, the sky overcast. A light drizzle had begun falling.

Vail came to a suburban neighborhood, not nearly as well kept or affluent as the area of Gaza City and resort community she had seen. Plain-faced concrete apartment buildings rose all around her. Graffiti marked the sides of most structures in all directions. The streets were illuminated, but not well lit, which both played to her advantage and placed her in greater danger.

She perused the parked cars and tried the driver's doors as she passed. All were locked. Even if she got into one, it might take her a while to remember how to hotwire it. The last thing she wanted to do was get caught trying to steal someone's vehicle in Gaza—especially since her clothing was soaked in blood.

She placed a hand on her Glock and walked down the street. A moment later, a dark sedan turned the corner, headed toward her. Engage or not? She stepped in front of it and held up a hand. *A woman standing in the rain. In distress, with blood on her clothes. How could he ignore that?*

As anticipated, the driver stopped. Vail smiled broadly and moved around to the window, which cranked open, revealing a male who looked to be in his mid-twenties. He said something in Arabic, then flashed a grin of his own. It did not last long, however, as Vail brought the Glock up and shoved it into his temple.

"Get out," she said firmly by his ear. Vail did not know if he spoke English, but he seemed to understand the language of aggression because he put the car in park and opened the door. Vail kept her handgun trained on him as he got out.

"Sorry," she said. "Very sorry. I'll take good care of it." She pulled the beat-up Honda into gear and accelerated away from him. After making a few quick turns, she pulled out the satphone and checked the display to see if she was pointed in the right direction. The receiver was having a difficult time getting a signal.

Shit, the clouds. The weather, it can't get a lock on the satellite.

It flashed a blinking red warning across the display: NO SATELLITES. Five intolerable seconds passed—during which Vail held her breath—before a green message appeared: RETRIEVING SATELLITE DATA. The mapping image populated the screen and she sighed relief.

One left turn later and she was on track, headed for the tunnel.

FAHAD MADE IT SAFELY AWAY from Sahmoud's house, but not without a brush with a trailing al Humat SUV. He felt it was best to make a non-stealth exit, moving through the adjacent yards before emerging on the side of a home and appearing to be coming from the garage. He had examined his clothing for blood earlier, while standing guard, and reversed his jacket to hide the lone blood spatter.

The satchel was in his right hand as he walked along the sidewalk, glancing over his shoulder at the military vehicles bearing the familiar al Humat window sticker.

He had hoped to avoid contact but was almost inviting it by strolling past their convoy. When the militant stopped his car and whistled at Fahad to approach, he pointed at his chest and asked in Arabic, "Me?"

The man extended his hand out the window and wiggled his fingers. "Come here."

Fahad stepped off the curb and had started toward the SUV when shouting down the street caught the driver's attention. He swung his head toward the disturbance, then accelerated hard, burning rubber.

Fahad figured they had discovered one or more of the dead guards. He continued on down the street, casually glancing left and right, counting the seconds until he was out of their view.

He passed the security booth where another al Humat officer was examining the guard. His neck was broken, so there were no overt signs of death like a gunshot or knife wound. It would take him a bit to determine why the man was not responsive.

Fahad picked up his pace and covered at least half a mile before turning right down a side street.

CIA Director Tasset had put him on the OPSIG team to deliver the codex and scroll to one of several safe houses the Agency maintained throughout the world—including one on the outskirts of Jerusalem.

But Knox had directed them to turn the artifacts over to the Israelis.

His course of action should be clear. He was a CIA officer and he was given orders—his sole reason for being on this operation was to secure the documents for the Agency. He answered to the director. But he only had a portion of them. Was his role, his covert mission within a black op, still significant?

He pivoted 360 degrees. The apartment building he was looking for was nowhere to be seen. In its place was a vast lot and an enormous pile of concrete rubble—likely one of the many Hamas structures destroyed during the recent Gaza war. An Agency informant claimed that a lot of the money donated to Hamas for rebuilding had been stolen and diverted—which could explain why the debris was still sitting there.

He stopped a woman coming down the street with her young son and asked if she knew where his friends had moved. She turned and pointed. "It's an apartment building, on the corner, two blocks away. Second floor, I think."

Fahad slung the satchel over his left shoulder and proceeded down the street. He turned onto the broken cement path that led to the front door and consulted the listing of names posted at the foot of the stairs. He ascended a couple of flights, and a moment later a middle-aged woman came to the door.

"Mahmoud!" Karima stepped forward and gave him a hearty embrace, then leaned back and appraised his face. "What are you doing here?"

"In for a visit, to see my family. Pay my brother a visit."

Her bright expression sagged. "Your brother?"

"We've patched things up."

Karima stepped back. "Good. That's good." She took his hand and turned, leading him toward the kitchen. "When did you get in?"

"This morning."

Karima let go of his hand, turned around, and smiled. "It's wonderful to see you. You look good. What have you been doing with yourself?"

"I've still got that job in Virginia. Things have been busy. And you?"

Her smile faded. "Things are not so good with Hamid. He—" She stopped, glanced around, found Fahad's eyes and said, "he's mixed up with al Humat. I told him it would only bring bad things to our family. But the money is . . ." She shook her head. "He said he wants to do this."

Hamid's involvement with al Humat introduced a variable Fahad had not anticipated. He rubbed at his temple. "Hamid's always had a rebellious streak."

"So have you." She grinned again, tried to lighten the sudden tension in the air. "Sit down, stay awhile. Coffee? Hamid will be home soon. Maybe you can talk some sense into him."

"Hamid and I didn't exactly leave things in a good place." Fahad's forehead sprouted perspiration. The last thing he needed was to confront Hamid. Was he merely a sympathizer? Soldier? Official? Knowing his friend, it was all three: he was not someone who followed; he led.

With what Fahad was holding in the satchel, and the fresh news that Kadir Abu Sahmoud had been killed, running into Hamid could be disastrous. He took a step back out of the kitchen. "Besides, I can't stay. I just wanted to stop by and see how you two were doing." He had come to ask a favor, but now his sole focus was to get out of the apartment.

Before Karima could reply, a key slipped into the front door and the lock turned. Fahad's head whipped around as his free hand slid toward his Glock. A second later, a man walked in wearing a black shirt. With an embroidered al Humat patch.

76

DeSantos was huddled in an alley behind two cars and a dumpster. He pulled out his cell and called a friend of his who lived in Sderot, a town bordering Gaza that had borne the brunt of Hamas rocket fire—until those rockets became more powerful and were able to reach deep into major Israeli cities dozens of miles away.

The psychological trauma of living in a constant state of readiness, of having mere seconds to flee to a bomb shelter, of having your young children grow up playing in indoor schoolyards and "parks" because it was unsafe for them to be outside, was far-reaching and had damaged an entire generation.

DeSantos met Inbar Ramon during an op in Moscow in the 1990s. She had been working for Mossad as a *swallow*, a female sexpionage operative whose mission was to seduce a finance official to get a line on corruption payments that they surmised were finding their way to an Iranian proxy in Lebanon. Both Israel and the US Department of Defense had an interest in stopping the flow of money.

After the mission, Inbar and DeSantos had a brief romance that ended when he left Russia and she went back to Sderot. Two months later he met his wife Maggie. A year later Inbar got married.

After quickly dispensing with small talk, DeSantos explained that he was in Gaza and needed to get through the security barrier.

"You're not serious."

"I wouldn't joke about something like that."

"Hector, what you ask . . . as you can probably guess, the border is very tightly monitored, for obvious reasons. Where are you?"

"I saw a sign for Sheikh Za'id. Know where that is?"

"Let me see what I can do. I know someone at the Erez border crossing. You're a few miles away. I'll text you directions. What name are you using?"

"DeSantos. Mossad knows I'm here, no point in trying to use a cover."

"While waiting to hear from me, make your way over to the border. Call you back in ten."

UZI HAD HITCHHIKED to within two miles of the Erez crossing. The youth who had given him the ride—for twenty shekels—made small talk with his passenger when the young man touched on the news that Kadir Abu Sahmoud had been found murdered.

Uzi had figured they would drive through the checkpoint after their operation. But news of Sahmoud's demise traveled faster than he had anticipated and touched off what he expected to be a severely escalated alert level among both Palestinian and Israeli forces. He imagined that Israel was denying a role in the murder—or at the very least was refusing to comment, as Israelis often did, regardless of whether or not they were involved.

At times like these, with the border locked down tighter than usual, each individual was highly scrutinized. But he did not see an option.

He was a quarter of a mile away when five masked men approached, armed with submachine guns. "What are you doing here?" one yelled at him in Arabic.

"Headed to the crossing. I have to visit my father in Nablus. He's ill."

"Past curfew. They won't let you through."

"I know," Uzi said, "I need to try."

"What's in there?" the taller militant asked, nodding at the tube.

"Some blueprints of a house I designed for my boss. I wanted to show my dad. He's a retired architect."

"Bullshit," the man in front said. "Get down on the ground."

"Why?"

"Because I said so. Because Kadir Abu Sahmoud was killed. Because there's a curfew. Because you look suspicious walking around out here in the rain. And we're searching everyone."

As a general rule it was smart to submit to law enforcement when you were told to do so. But these men were not law enforcement—and Uzi was not in an area where the rule of law was respected.

"Okay," he said.

They were not well trained, as they had approached him casually, overly confident, cocky, and ill prepared to take action. Their weapons were not in a position of readiness and they did not have good spacing. Two were stacked behind their colleagues.

They stood only about fifteen feet away, but with the poor illumination and their ski masks on it was impossible to tell how old they were.

"Get down now!"

Even with a balky knee, Uzi was still plenty fast. Could he outrun them before they got their submachine guns into firing position?

Uzi slowly crouched down while shielding his right hand from the men. He pulled his Glock and started firing. He hit two—but because of the way they were closely aligned, his shots were more efficient, and three of the militants hit the pavement.

He turned and ran, the roll tucked under his left arm as he put the trunks of nearby palm trees between him and the pursuing tangos. He had gotten about thirty yards when he felt the burn of a gunshot wound sting his arm. He recoiled and dropped the tube. Rounds struck the pavement at his feet and a metal pole near his head, so he ducked and spun around and began running a zigzag route, his Timberlands slapping puddles and mud as he passed the Erez Industrial Park ruins.

Ahead was the caged screening corridor, a three hundred yard cement-walled passageway featuring a blue and white sign that read, "Welcome to Erez Crossing" written in Hebrew, English, and Arabic, along with the following warning—in Arabic only: *Continuing with violence results in the withholding of ease of access and luxury for the people.*

The border control pavilion was a secure facility that consisted of passageways, gates, turnstiles, doors, high-tech body scanners, and identity checks. The army and Israel police monitored each phase remotely behind blast proof concrete-and-glass enclosures.

Uzi knew that for security reasons, there were no direct human contacts with Israeli personnel until the very end. And there were delays at each phase of the crossing. As a result, if his pursuers followed him into the complex, he would be leaving it in a pine box.

He ran into the corridor made of tall concrete blast walls. Behind him he heard the footfalls of at least two men. Then, shouting in Arabic for him to stop. Were they serious?

About a hundred yards ahead he saw the remote-controlled turnstile bounded by a tall chain-link fence. He started flapping his uninjured arm, gesticulating, turning and pointing behind him as he continued toward the gate. He knew the police were watching through surveillance cameras. The only question was, were they paying attention? And if so, would they get there in time?

If he drew his Glock, there was no way the police would approach him. He hoped they also saw the al Humat men pursuing him and understood that he was the good guy in this scenario.

The area was brightly illuminated, though another thirty yards later a spotlight hit him in the face and a blaring klaxon sounded. Several police officers in blue uniforms came through a thick metal door, clad in tactical vests and helmets.

"Stop! Get down," they yelled in Arabic.

Uzi stumbled to a jog, then pulled up and dropped to his knees. "I'm American," he said as they surrounded him. "Being pursued by two or three armed al Humat—"

"Check it," the lead officer said. Four of the men headed down the corridor the way Uzi had come. The cop then pulled his two-way and barked orders in Hebrew. He lowered his radio and knelt in front of Uzi. "What are you doing in Gaza?"

"I have an appointment with Director General Aksel."

The man shared a glance with one of his underlings as if to say, "Did I just hear right?"

"We need to search you," one of the others said. "Don't move."

Uzi glanced up and saw the three-bar insignia on the senior officer's shoulder: a sergeant major. Peretz, by his nametag.

"You'll find a Glock and a Tanto," Uzi said, "and a satphone and a Lumia."

"Call it in," Peretz said to one of his men. "And get a medic over here."

The cops emptied the pockets of his 5.11s and backed away from their detainee, showing Peretz the cache—which was exactly as Uzi had described—except his satphone's screen was shattered and his Lumia was missing.

"Get up," Peretz said. "Name?"

Uzi got to his feet. "Aaron Uziel."

Peretz pulled an Israeli bandage from the backpack of one of his men and began applying the compression dressing to Uzi's arm. "Mind telling us what you were doing in Gaza? And why you have an appointment with the director general of Mossad? You're no ordinary American."

Uzi chuckled. "Trust me, Sergeant Major. You wouldn't believe me even if I told you."

Peretz frowned. "Actually, if your friend is Hector DeSantos, I might, in fact, believe you."

VAIL ARRIVED AT THE LOCATION of the tunnel entrance. But the sky was now completely black save for a sliver of moonlight that was fighting to be seen through the otherwise dense cloud cover.

There was barely enough illumination to keep her from stepping in a hole as she navigated the hard, rocky soil.

With the satphone in her left hand and the Glock in her right, she stumbled her way to the coordinates. She hoped no one engaged her, because staring at the backlit screen destroyed her night vision. If someone approached she would not be able to see him.

After five minutes of searching—and the phone losing its satellite signal, then regaining it—she stopped at a rock outcropping, where the tunnel's mouth was supposedly located. *You've gotta be kidding. It better be here.*

She turned on her Samsung's flashlight and found the entrance behind a large boulder. Then it hit her: she was headed underground into a tunnel. How long it was, how tight it would be, she had no idea.

Claustrophobia or not, she had no choice but to push forward. Safety resided on the other side of the border.

She wrapped her left arm around the tube and looked into the abyss: there was a metal ladder bolted to the wall that led straight down, perhaps thirty feet. *Holy shit.*

Vail took a deep breath and started descending, one rung at a time. As she neared the bottom, her right foot slipped on the next to last step and she hit the ground hard. A jolt of pain shot through both ankles.

Shake it off. Keep going.

She held up the flashlight. Ahead of her the tunnel stretched as far as she could see, with a bend near the end. *Was* it the end, or merely a turn?

Standing there and debating it was fruitless. Vail turned off the satphone to conserve the battery—there was no reception down here—and trudged forward, keeping the light in front of her. There was electrical conduit mounted along the left wall and bare bulbs every thirty feet or so. But she did not see a switch.

The spherical tunnel was constructed of formed concrete bunker-style sections and stood about six feet across at its widest point and about six feet tall at its apex. At five foot seven, as long as Vail remained in the center, she would be able to stand straight.

Another hundred yards—and she heard a noise. She stopped, painted the area with her flashlight. Nothing.

She reached for her Glock—but it was gone. *Shit. Shit!*

Vail spun around and peered into the darkness behind her. *Might've fallen when I fell off the ladder. Go back? No. Could've also dropped it up top. I may never find it. It'd totally suck if I got captured looking for my gun.*

As it was, she did not expect to find anyone else down here. And once she reached the end, she would no longer need it.

Vail rested her palm on the handle of her Tanto and continued forward. She kicked something made of glass and it bounced repeatedly ahead of her, ultimately striking the concrete wall.

Her heart, already beating hard, felt like it skipped a beat. Perspiration blanketed her body and she felt clammy. Between the anxiety of claustrophobia and the stress of not knowing what lie ahead in the darkness, she would not be surprised if she had a coronary.

Stop it, Karen. Nothing's lurking in the darkness and you're not gonna have a heart attack.

Vail reached the bend but was dismayed to see that it continued on. That, however, was not the problem. The road forked—and the two options led in opposite directions.

She stood there trying to reason it through based on which direction she was headed on the surface and where the satphone image had indicated Israel was located. It was a nearly impossible equation because she did not know which direction she had been walking when she entered the tunnel.

Vail turned left to see if there was any indication as to which way she needed to go. But as she took a step forward someone grabbed her from behind.

77

The man's forearm was locked across her neck, cutting off the blood flow to her brain. She would lose consciousness in a matter of seconds.

His other arm was around her torso, pinning her limbs to her body. Vail dropped her phone and the tube and tried to raise her arms up—but she could not pry them loose.

As he dragged her backward she dug her heels into the dirt, hoping to throw him off balance. But he maintained his center of gravity.

The darkness was disorienting, the only light coming from her cell lying somewhere on the ground. And even that was fading as he squeezed harder and she started to lose consciousness.

Using her legs, she pushed herself side to side—and drove them both into the concrete wall. His grip loosened, enough for her to get some oxygen, enough to free a hand.

She reached back to grab him—and felt cold metal. *A gun!* She got her fingers on it and pulled, but he jerked her back and it went flying somewhere into the darkness.

Fuck. She swung her left foot out, hoping to kick the weapon away to prevent him from getting to it. She hit it once but could not tell if it traveled any distance.

He jerked her hard to the right—and she was able to reach down low enough to touch the handle of her Tanto.

But he rocked her back the other way and then yanked her toward him, arching her spine and regaining control over her free hand.

Her head struck the ceiling of the tunnel and her fingers slipped off the knife's grip.

He shouted something in Arabic and she screamed something in English.

She began rocking on the balls of her feet, bucking left and right—and again his grip weakened enough for her to pull a hand from his grasp. She grabbed the Tanto and jerked it from its sheath, then fought to draw her forearm forward.

He pulled. She pushed.

She yelled long and loud to summon her strength—and then slammed her heel onto the top of his foot.

He recoiled and she drew the blade back hard, toward his body. And stabbed him in the thigh.

He screamed.

Now there's a language I understand—

She jabbed at his body again and again, blindly using him as a pin cushion. But none of the thrusts were deep enough to do life-threatening damage.

He tugged back on her neck, compressing her larynx, but she kept stabbing, hoping the pain would eventually force him to try to get the knife away from her—which meant he would have to loosen his grip on her throat. And once he did that he would no longer have control.

A few seconds, that's all she needed.

She continued thrusting and he continued yelping—until Vail got the window she was waiting for. He reached for her arm and grabbed her wrist, but she had already transferred the knife to her other hand.

Vail twisted out of his grip, spun, and started slashing, left, right, left, as if the Tanto were a sword and she were a swashbuckler. She struck something soft, but in the darkness it was hard to know if she did any damage.

She couldn't blindly thrust because if he got hold of her arm, he could take the knife from her. And then he would surely make her pay for treating him like a cooked Thanksgiving turkey.

Get away from him!

Vail backed down the tunnel, running the palm of her left hand along the wall to give her some bearing.

She stopped suddenly and listened, doing her best to slow her respiration, to keep noise at a minimum. She could no longer see the light from her phone but she could hear the tango breathing loudly.

Let him come for you.

Vail stood there, back flat against the cement. One minute. Two.

She slowly reached into her pocket and rooted out her spare magazine. She tossed it away, about ten feet to her right, hoping to hit the wall. It did—and seconds later he advanced.

Vail waited a beat, then stuck out her leg and he ran right into it, then struck the ground with a thud. She pounced on his back and jabbed the Tanto into his neck, then grabbed his hair and pulled his head back. A final slice across the front of his throat and all movement stopped.

She slid off his body and fell onto her side, her heart thudding, her hands shaking. Hyperventilating.

VAIL PUSHED HERSELF UP and stumbled away, slamming her back into the wall and her head into the curved ceiling.

Focus, Karen. Calm down.

She took some deep breaths, slowed her pulse, then licked her lips and pushed forward, back the way she had come, hoping to find the pistol she had dislodged—and the tube Uzi had given her. A couple of minutes later she had both in hand.

She chambered a round and sheathed the Tanto.

Continuing a few paces farther, she came upon the fork in the tunnel—which she recognized only because of the slight breeze she felt coming from the other shaft she had taken from the surface. She felt around—hoping to find something that the tango had—a drawing, a diagram of some sort—that could show her the way out of here, one that would take her into Israel.

Wait, the booklet I found at Sahmoud's.

She reached back—and it was still there, wedged into her waistband.

If only I could see it.

Then she remembered the satphone. Its screen should throw off enough of a glow to read the map.

She powered it up and held it over the page, traced her tunnel with a finger and determined she needed to take the path where the dead militant lay. She moved forward and found her Samsung and reactivated the flashlight.

As she gave a final sweep of the area, she saw what appeared to be a cot against the wall along the other corridor. She jogged over and took a quick look: the tango had been sleeping down here. Why? To guard what? She moved a bit farther in and saw wood crates stacked along the wall with Arabic writing on them. She pulled one down and used her Tanto to pry off the top. Grenades, assault and sniper rifles were nestled among Styrofoam popcorn bits. She thought of taking one of the rifles with her, but the ammo must have been in a different box.

She headed down the tunnel, stepped past the bloody al Humat militant, and continued on. If the map was to scale, she had another ten minutes of brisk walking to reach the exit.

When she climbed the ladder to the surface, she found a metal covering and a fair amount of brush obscuring its opening. Upon emerging, she dropped to her knees and breathed in the fresh, damp air. While crouched there, at the edge of what looked like farmland, a light drizzle prickled her cheeks.

Seconds later two headlights struck her face. She shielded her eyes and got to her feet. The driver pulled up alongside her and rolled down the window.

"I need some help. Do you speak English?"

"Of course I speak English." He squinted, leaned closer and said, "You're bleeding!" He got out of the car and came around to walk her over to the passenger seat.

"I'm fine, it's not my blood. I got into a fight with an al Humat soldier."

"Al Humat? Where?"

"In a tunnel. There's an opening a few feet from where you found me. They've got a cache of weapons down there."

The man pulled out his phone, made a call and jabbered Hebrew at someone on the other end. He hung up, then thanked her for the information.

"During the war, they came out of the tunnels, attacked the kibbutzim—our communities—then disappeared back inside."

"I heard."

"I have to ask. What were you doing down there?"

"You don't have to ask and you don't really want to know."

He looked her over, his eyes resting on her blood-soaked shirt. "What can I do for you? To repay the favor."

"I need a ride to the Israel Museum."

His brow rose. "In Jerusalem?"

Vail tilted her head.

"Okay, okay. It'll take us a bit. You need something to eat? Drink?"

"No time. Just get me there as soon as possible."

He laughed. "You know how Israelis drive?"

"Not a clue."

"Crazy. Fast. Hang on." He accelerated hard and Vail was slammed back into the seat.

78

The man was telling the truth. He drove like a demon, zipping around cars and getting Vail to Jerusalem in just over an hour. By the time he pulled into the Israel Museum's parking lot at 8:00 PM, the rain had stopped.

A few vehicles were still there, likely staff and whoever else they were supposed to meet. A curator? Police? A Mossad officer? Vail realized that in the rush to get out of Sahmoud's house they had gotten no details as to what was going to transpire when they arrived.

As she neared the entrance, she passed through security barriers and walked by a rectangular reflecting pool. She saw a sign for the museum offices as well as those of the Israel Antiquities Authority.

If they knew what I had in this tube, they'd be out here with a red carpet.

A sign directed her to the gallery entrance, where she was met by two black-suited men with close-cropped hair and earbuds. If she had been in the US, she would have guessed they were Secret Service agents.

"Karen Vail?" one of them asked.

"I've been accused of worse."

He looked her up and down, lingering on the blood stains soaked into her shirt and pants.

The other agent gestured at the tube. "We'll take that."

"No, you won't."

He looked at her a long moment, his expression stern, as if he were deciding whether to challenge her. He finally said, "Come with me," and he led her through the admissions area and into the museum, up a long corridor with dark walls and a charcoal granite floor. Dramatic exterior spotlighting illuminated the frosted glass windows to her right.

They passed ancient floor-to-ceiling mosaics, which, according to the posted sign, were from sixth-century Beit She'an ruins.

First the Louvre, then the Israel Museum . . . someday I'm going to visit all these places with Robby. No guns, no bad guys. No killers. No terrorists with bombs or chemical weapons.

A girl can dream, right?

The agent led her outside, where they crossed a long, narrow cement promenade that stretched into the distance to her left. Ahead was a dark gray freestanding rectangular wall, and to her right a shiny white brick dome with a nipple on the top.

"What's that?" Vail asked.

The agent slowed, turned, and said, "The roof of the shrine. It's designed to look like the lid of the clay pots that contained the Dead Sea Scrolls." He swung back and continued on and Vail hustled up beside him. They entered an area designated "The Shrine of the Book," then descended a series of stone steps with a glass-sided railing that led into a small plaza.

Several suited men and women were standing there—which Vail immediately pegged as part of Knox's protection detail.

Her escort stopped at the door and said, "Inside. They're waiting for you."

Vail walked into a dark corridor with museum displays on each side. They appeared to deal with the discovery of the scrolls in the Qumran caves, but she did not stop for a look.

She proceeded straight ahead into a dramatic atrium that had a dome-shaped ceiling; she was underneath the white brick structure she had seen outside a minute ago. In the center sat a circular display case five steps up on a raised platform that contained a Dead Sea Scroll that had been unfurled.

On the main level, along the periphery, were wall-mounted exhibits featuring scroll sections and informational placards.

Vail ascended the stairs where two women and several men were standing—two of whom she knew: Gideon Aksel and Douglas Knox. Knox had been pacing. He stopped and looked up when she entered the room.

Vail swallowed deeply and suddenly became aware of the tube she had tucked under her left arm—and its significance.

"Agent Vail," Knox said. "You have something for us?"

"Yes sir." She stepped forward and handed it to a woman who reached out and took it from her with extreme care. *If you only knew what I just put it through.*

"I'm Tamar," the woman said. "Thank you. For bringing this to us." She and three of the other men descended to the main level where a temporary table and an assortment of magnifying lenses and tools were located.

Knox came up alongside Vail. "Glad you made it." He squinted in the dim light. "You've got blood spatter all over your clothing."

"You should see the other guy."

Knox tilted his head and a smile teased the corners of his mouth, a sign of approval.

"Agent Vail." Tamar's voice echoed in the empty room. She was holding her white-gloved hands vertically, like a surgeon in an operating room. "Other than some Arabic papers, this tube is empty."

"What?" Vail leapt down the steps. She lifted the container and peered inside, then looked at the table. *What the hell? Could they have fallen out when I dropped the tube? No. I would've seen them.*

"Where are the documents?" Askel asked.

"I—I don't understand." She brought her gaze up and looked at him. Then at Knox.

"Hector called me two hours ago," Knox said. "He told me each of you were bringing portions of the codex and scroll."

Footsteps drew their attention. They looked up in unison to see DeSantos walking in, a portfolio in his hand.

Vail could tell he was reading their faces as Tamar reached over and took the bag from him.

"My tube was empty," Vail said. "There's no way I lost the pages. I mean, I guess it's possible but I can't see how. I would've seen them."

A moment later, Tamar's stern voice echoed in the chamber. "This is empty as well." Even in the understated light, Vail could see that her jaw was firm, her eyes fiery.

What the hell is going on?

DeSantos rooted out his phone, started dialing.

"You're calling Uzi?"

DeSantos did not answer. He lowered the handset and cursed under his breath.

"Either of you hear from Fahad?" Knox asked.

Vail bit her lip. "Nothing."

DeSantos indicated likewise.

Seven minutes passed. Knox paced. Vail and DeSantos sat on the bottom steps of the shrine.

Vail was concerned about Uzi. Thinking about the two ancient documents they had been entrusted with. And starting to have doubts about Fahad's true intentions: were they as DeSantos claimed—nefarious—or beneficent, as Uzi claimed?

DeSantos rose up and began to stretch when Uzi walked in. Vail immediately noticed that he was not carrying anything.

Aksel was the first to question him. "Where's your—"

"Gone. I was intercepted by al Humat militants and I got away with a GSW to the arm. I lost the tube, but—"

"Our docs are missing," Vail said. "My tube and Hector's portfolio are empty."

"I know."

DeSantos stepped forward. "What do you mean, 'I know'?"

"I gave it all to Mo."

Knox descended the steps and stood face-to-face with Uzi. "You what?"

DeSantos's face shaded red. "Boychick, are you crazy? We've been worried about him since the day he joined our team. He may've been the one who almost got you killed."

"I don't think so."

Aksel came up beside Knox and folded his short, thick arms across his chest. "Let me get this straight. You gave two of the most ancient, most holy documents of the Jewish people, to a Palestinian? A CIA operative? After what I told you? And you expected him to bring it here, to turn it over to Israel?"

"Yes."

DeSantos shook his head and walked out of the chamber, heading for the shrine's exit.

Knox cleared his throat. "Agent Uziel, you should've consulted me on this."

"No time, sir. Al Humat was approaching Sahmoud's house. We had to get out right then—or we wouldn't have made it out alive."

That's not entirely true. You had to put everything in Mo's satchel before we knew they were coming.

"Given the situation, I felt he stood the best chance of getting back here safely, without being challenged and detained. Or killed."

"The situation?" Knox asked.

"He's Palestinian, sir. He speaks Arabic, he looks like them, he knows their culture, he's got friends in Gaza." Uzi swallowed. "And family."

Yeah, he's got family there, all right. A brother named Nazir al Dosari.

"Director Tasset was running a covert counter-op with him," Knox said, "which I only found out about a little while ago. He was working with the White House to secure the documents for the president. Had we known, Secretary McNamara and I never would've put him on this mission."

Uzi sat down on the step and bowed his head. A long moment passed. "I didn't know. I really thought we could trust him."

"Mo only thinks he has parts of the codex and the scroll," Vail said. "Even if he felt compelled to carry out his mission, it wouldn't do the president much good."

"But if he looked inside, he'd know he had everything," Aksel said. "Brilliant move, Uzi. You've managed to fuck things up again."

Vail expected Knox to say something in his operative's defense, but the director remained silent—in effect, endorsing Aksel's comment.

A moment later, the shrine door opened and closed. All heads swiveled in that direction, where DeSantos and Fahad were entering.

"Thank god," Knox said.

Amen to that.

"Sorry I'm late," Fahad said. "Stopped by a friend's to get a ride to the checkpoint. Turns out he's now with al Humat. Could've gone south real quick, but he got the call about Sahmoud and took off." He stopped and seemed to realize that everyone was staring at him.

"You have something for us?" Knox asked.

He pulled the satchel off his shoulder and handed it to the director, who gave it to Tamar. She regloved and immediately went to work with her team.

They huddled around Tamar's makeshift laboratory as the curator carefully unzipped the case and splayed it open. She pulled off a few layers of tissue paper and the pages of the Aleppo Codex stared back at them.

Aksel's lips parted, while Knox pushed his glasses up his nose with a finger and leaned over the table to get a better look.

"Extraordinary," Tamar said. The other conservationists concurred.

Tamar glanced at Fahad and gave him an appreciative nod, then moved on to the other item, a tubular shaped object similarly wrapped. She gently removed the paper and exposed a well preserved scroll. With gloved hands, she and two of the men carefully peeled back the first several inches.

Everyone leaned in for a glimpse. Tamar remained longer than the others, examining it with a jeweler's loupe before straightening up. "More tests are needed, but it does, in fact, look like the genuine article." She turned to the other woman, who was hunched over the codex.

She lifted her magnifying lens and spoke to Tamar. "I have to study this further in the lab, but I believe these are the missing pages of the Aleppo Codex."

Uzi tapped Vail on her shoulder and gestured to the others to follow. He led them outside to a raised lookout over a one acre scale model of ancient Jerusalem and the Second Temple, shortly before its destruction in 70 CE—the precise time documented in the Dead Sea Scrolls.

Uzi sought out Fahad, who was following a dozen feet behind. "Be right back," he told Vail.

"A MINUTE?" Uzi asked as he approached Fahad.

"Sure."

Uzi gave him a shoulder hug. "Thank you, man."

Fahad canted his head. "Hey, just doing my job."

"No, not for that. For renewing my faith that your people and my people can get along. After what happened with Batula Hakim and her brother and all that other bad shit with Hamas and al Humat, I've had my doubts."

"Believe me, I've had my moments too. I'm not without baggage."

"So there's hope."

Fahad rocked back on his heels. "Well, now that we've solved the Israeli-Palestinian issue, maybe we should become diplomats and tackle other world crises."

They both laughed.

"I've gotta go brief my boss," Fahad said. "Not gonna be an easy conversation. Tasset's going to be pissed." He paused, then deadpanned, "You think there are any job openings at the Bureau?"

Uzi chuckled. "You'll be fine."

"See you on the plane." He pulled out his phone and headed for a nearby bench.

UZI REJOINED VAIL AND DeSANTOS at the railing overlooking the Second Temple model.

Vail was slipping her phone back in her pocket. "Got an email from my boss. He just put a new file on my desk and wanted to know how soon I can get back to doing some important work—profiling serial killers."

"What'd you tell him?" Uzi asked.

Vail smiled wanly. "Told him I can't wait."

Uzi took a deep breath of damp, cool air. "I hope we're making headway against those cells back home. Santa—how long till you think we'll hear something?"

"Spoke to Hot Rod on the way over here. The list of cells we got from Sahmoud's was spot-on. We've got tac teams in eleven cities ready to strike simultaneously—FBI, marshals, local PD. Massive operation."

"You think we'll get 'em all?" Vail asked.

DeSantos considered that. "Eleven's pretty damn good. But no. I don't think we'll get them all." He stared into the darkness for a moment. "We dealt them some major blows. I think we'll be okay for now. Things will be quiet. A few months, a year, two years. Who knows."

"What about Connerly?" Uzi asked.

DeSantos shrugged. "NSA intercepted a call between his phone and a number the CIA had been tracking belonging to Hussein Rudenko. Don't know what was discussed, and we can't be sure it was Connerly, or Rudenko, on the line, but—"

"There'd be no reason for the president's chief of staff to have a phone call with an arms dealer and terrorist who's on the FBI most wanted list."

"Without having a recording of the conversation," Vail said, "you can't prove Rudenko and Connerly were talking."

"Not a smoking gun," Uzi said. "But we might be on to something."

"Or it might mean nothing," Vail said.

Uzi shook his head. "I don't believe in coincidences where things like this are concerned. I think Sahmoud was telling us the truth."

"Good luck with that," DeSantos said. "We can't put the president's chief of staff in a black site room and interrogate him. There'll be lawyers."

That's torture enough.

"It's now Knox's problem," DeSantos said. "And the attorney general's. When, and if, they find something, justice will be served. If not, Sahmoud is a really bad guy who did really bad things. He was a whole lot worse than Connerly. We take our wins where we can get them."

"Where have I heard that before?"

Uzi pursed his lips. "I believe it was on a naval carrier on the Atlantic Ocean somewhere off the coast of England."

They laughed again.

"You know," Vail said, "if I didn't know any better, it looked like you and Mo are in a good place."

Uzi turned to DeSantos. "Yeah, well, hate to say I told you so."

"But you're gonna say it anyway."

"No, no, no," Vail said with a shake of her head. "I'm not buying that whole 'I trusted him' line, Uzi. I know you better than that. You embedded some tracking chip in Mo's jacket, didn't you?"

"Nope. I knew we could trust him."

"Really," DeSantos said.

"Trust has to start somewhere, Santa, and, really, we were trusting him with far more important things—our lives. I had faith in human nature, in *Mo*, to do the right thing. He's a real person. True to himself. To who he is, who his family is. And was."

Vail looked at him. "Remember what the rabbi said about truth? That there may not be such a thing?"

"I still think there are some truths in life."

"And I still think you were at risk of being played a fool."

"I made sure he wasn't," DeSantos said.

Uzi tilted his head. "What are you talking about?"

"I hedged our bets. Sorry, Boychick. Too much at stake. I took the active tag chip out of my satphone and slipped it into Fahad's satchel right before we left the house. Need be, we could track it." DeSantos chuckled. "Of course, I wasn't anticipating cloud cover."

Uzi leaned back against the railing. "So you're saying that you didn't trust my judgment."

DeSantos considered that. "Faith is powerful, but at the end of the day, we're just people. And people approach things with their own biases."

Vail grunted. "Kind of like what the rabbi said about truth. We see things through our own lens. We think what we're doing is right."

"But others may not see it that way—and they may be wrong. So I needed an insurance policy that these historic treasures were not only placed in their rightful place but that they were not used as blackmail in peace negotiations. Those were our orders."

"If Mo figured out that you'd given him everything," Vail said, "and if he wanted to turn it all over to the Agency, and if he knew about the chip, he could've ditched your tech and disappeared."

DeSantos nodded slowly. "Then I guess in the end, it all came down to trust. And some luck."

Knox came up behind them as DeSantos's phone rang. He excused himself, pulled out his cell, and took a few steps away.

Knox placed a hand on Uzi's shoulder. "Thank you both for a job well done."

"What will come of the scroll?" Vail asked.

Knox looked out over the brightly lit model of ancient Jerusalem. "They're going to store it in the museum vault and keep it quiet. Their goal was always to bring it home. Disclosure of its contents was never part of the plan."

"Do you believe it's possible to keep it under wraps?" Vail asked.

"I know Prime Minister Wolff," Knox said. "Making it public, causing harm, that's not what he's about. The director general told me it wasn't their place to release any ancient text that would denigrate, in any way, Christianity's belief structure. No one would benefit from that. Looking at it pragmatically, it'd drive a wedge between Judaism and the Catholic Church, requiring decades, if not centuries, to heal. I'm sure the prime minister doesn't want that to happen. Neither does the Vatican. There's a lot going on here."

"That means we're sworn to secrecy as well."

"That goes for the entire mission, Agent Vail." Knox leaned both hands on the railing. "The president has been pushing construction of a new airport in the West Bank and a shipping port in Gaza. I'm told he's been riding the Israelis really hard. They've said that without a properly negotiated settlement and monitoring forces in place, and without the dismantling of Hamas, al Humat, Islamic Jihad, and Islamic State, the airport and shipping port would be significant threats to Israel's survival. Friends of mine in the military and intelligence community agree. That's what was at stake. That's why we did what we did. That's why we defied the White House."

They absorbed that for a moment.

"Why do you think we had to defy the president in the first place?" Vail asked.

Knox stared off into the distance. His jaw tightened. "Our work is done here. Thank you both again for a job well done."

As he walked off, Uzi gestured at the blood spatter on her clothes. "Tough time?"

Vail pulled the Tanto from its sheath. "Your gift saved my life tonight."

"You know," he said, "that knife is taking on legendary proportions: first it saved my life. And now yours. It's got its own built-in mojo."

"Should we do a *Game of Thrones* thing?"

Uzi tilted his head. "A what?"

"*Game of Thrones*. The TV show. HBO."

Uzi shrugged. "Don't watch much TV."

"Robby and Jonathan got me into it. A medieval soap opera. The knights name their swords. What do you say we name this knife, 'Tango slayer'?"

Uzi chuckled. "Hey, it's yours now. Name it whatever you like."

"I'll have to think on it."

After a moment, he said, "How about Tzedek?"

"Tzedek?"

"It's a Hebrew word. For justice."

Vail looked at the blade, spit on it, and wiped the dried blood from its surface with her blouse. "Tzedek. Justice. I like it." She angled it forward, catching the glow of a nearby spotlight against its black matte finish. "You familiar with the Bible?"

He cocked his head to the left. "I think I've heard of it."

"There's a verse . . . 'Never take revenge. Leave that to the righteous anger of God.'"

Uzi shrugged. "I think a little revenge is okay sometimes. As long as it's done with well reasoned moral intentions. To right a wrong. A tooth for a tooth."

I've definitely had those feelings. "One of the psalms says, 'Blessed are they who maintain justice, who constantly do what is right.'"

Uzi leaned back. "I never took you for a religious person. I learn something new about you every day, Karen. You're a very complex individual, you know that?"

"Complex? Yeah. Religious? Not so much. The psalm is just something my mother used to tell me when I was a kid. I wrote it on an index card and had it above my computer screen in my office. I thought it expressed what I do as a federal agent. We maintain justice, always striving to do what's right."

Uzi examined her face a moment. "You said you *had* it over your desk. Past tense."

Vail turned away. "After Robby disappeared . . . I—" She shook her head. "I did what I had to do. But I didn't do what was right, I didn't maintain justice. I stepped over the line."

"Sometimes things aren't black and white." The voice came from a few feet behind them: DeSantos. "You did what was right for the one you loved. It didn't meet the standards of the laws we strive to uphold. But if you—if *we*—hadn't done what we did, a lot of people would've died. Good people. People who've done a lot of good things for a lot of *other* people since then."

Vail played with some loose dirt by her left shoe. "You talking about back then, or this op? I did things tonight that—"

"Your moral compass is what matters, Karen. What's in your heart. You always mean well. You always try to do the right thing. Sometimes it takes a while to know what the right thing is—or was."

Vail smiled inwardly. DeSantos's comment was similar to something she had once told Robby. She looked out over the model of Jerusalem and tried to picture herself back thousands of years, standing where she was at this very moment . . . learning from the wise rabbis who roamed the streets, doling out wisdom and creating law for a population who was only beginning to learn how to conduct themselves, how to live for the benefit of the community. How to put their trust in a higher being. How to *believe*.

It was the birth of a religion that would spawn other religions, changing the world in ways no one could have ever predicted. Good, bad, indifferent—organized religion had its positives and negatives. But its effect on civilization was palpable.

Vail was not sure if she believed in God or some other entity that governed the souls on earth. In many cases she thought she did not—she had looked into the minds of countless killers and seen evil. No God would dare create that. Hitler, Stalin, Idi Amin, Pol Pot, Bundy, Chikatilo, Gacy, Dahmer. Yet these scourges of humanity existed. She was sure religious sages had an explanation, but at the moment it was unimportant.

Vail turned back to the Israel Museum's dome, where the Dead Sea Scrolls—and now the complete Aleppo Codex—were housed. She felt a sense of satisfaction that she had played a role in helping bring these ancient artifacts, these transformative documents—to their rightful resting place, back where they began millennia ago.

"You okay?" DeSantos asked.

"Huh?" Vail turned. "Yeah, fine. Just thinking. Waxing philosophical."

"I didn't know you had it in you."

Vail had to laugh. "I learn something new about myself every day."

ACKNOWLEDGMENTS

I approached this book with trepidation because any time you wade into religion and/or geopolitics there's potential for someone to get offended. That was not my intention. Any religious commentaries contained within are merely story points that evolved from ideas, discussions with experts, brainstorming "what if" sessions, character motivations, and dramatic potential. I was not attempting to discredit, support, proselytize, or convince. In other words, I was telling a fictitious story. That's the definition of a novel.

Those of you who have read my previous works know that I strive to construct a compelling tale while keeping true to the facts of the source material. Although I have done that in the *The Lost Codex*, there are times when I deviate from the truth. One of those times involves the Aleppo Codex's journey from Syria to Israel, which in reality was much more complex. While there are pieces of information—some verifiable and others based on witness accounts, statements, and court testimony—the current location of those two hundred missing pages remains unknown. A few books tackle the subject but one in particular is a standout read: *The Aleppo Codex: A True Story of Obsession, Faith, and the Pursuit of an Ancient Bible*, by journalist/author Matti Friedman. Using his skills as an investigative reporter, he peeled back multiple layers of subterfuge and deceit. Regardless, as my editor reminded me, I am writing fiction and my job is to tell the most entertaining story possible. Although I altered the facts of the codex's journey once it left Syria, everything up to that point regarding its history, relevance, and contents is accurate to the best of my knowledge.

Finally, the issues affecting peace between the Israelis and Palestinians are fluid; public opinion changes frequently, and not everyone believes that the "mind-set" presented in *The Lost Codex* will prevail. Some believe peace is still possible. What form that takes, and if or when it happens, remains a mystery.

Because of the sensitive nature of some of the information I've included in this novel, certain sources wished to remain anonymous. Where possible

I referenced the organization or agency, but in other cases I have remained silent.

With that in mind, thanks to the following individuals:

Steve Garrett, US Navy Hospital Corpsman Senior Chief (Diver/Free Fall Parachutist/Fleet Marine Force)—also known as HMCS (DV/FPJ/FMF) (ret.)—for his thorough review of the manuscript and for correcting my Special Operations Forces terminology and procedures, for his knife-related expertise, parachuting and skydiving instruction (I would never send Vail out the back of a C-17 without getting it right!), for details regarding RIBS, IBSs, and Zodiacs, as well as body disposal methods in bodies of water. I did not ask Steve how he knew the latter.

Mark Safarik, Supervisory Special Agent and Senior FBI Profiler with the FBI's Behavioral Analysis Unit (ret.) and principal of Forensic Behavioral Services International, for his review of the manuscript, for FBI and law enforcement procedural nuances, and for his assistance with details regarding behavioral analysis and fingerprint forensics.

Mary Ellen O'Toole, Supervisory Special Agent and Senior FBI Profiler with the FBI Behavioral Analysis Unit (ret.), and Program Director for the Forensic Science Program at George Mason University's College of Science, for her information and background on psychopathy, suicide bombers, and sniper attacks, and for reviewing the pertinent excerpts for accuracy.

Tómas Palmer, cryptographer (and technogeek first class), for once again saving the day. My initial email to Tómas carried the subject line, "Vail, Uzi, and DeSantos are in trouble again. Tómas to the rescue." Tómas helped me understand cloud bouncing (yes, this is real), as well as satellite internet transceivers (also real), BlueJacking (real), RFID chip tags (real), and more. In Tómas's lingo, he helps me "geekify" my novels and makes it possible for Vail and company to better the baddies.

Derek Maltz, Special Agent in Charge of the Special Operations Division (SOD), Drug Enforcement Administration (ret.), for his background, information, and stories regarding narcoterrorism and the collision—and collusion—of the drug cartels with Islamic terrorists. His framing of the issue helped immeasurably. Also, **Paul Knierim**, assistant Special Agent in Charge, Drug Enforcement Administration, **Dawn Dearden**, Chief of Public Affairs and **Joseph Moses**, Public Affairs Section Chief, Office of Congressional and Public Affairs, Drug Enforcement Administration.

Mark Spicer, Sergeant Major, British Army (ret.), sniper instructor/trainer, and counterterrorism expert, for his information regarding terrorist threats facing the US, the Hezbollah/Mexican drug cartel connection, law enforcement's approach to reining in these groups, and his experiences in England and Northern Ireland. **Rigo Durazo**, Director of Combative

Training, Craft International, for his knife-fighting expertise and close quarters combat instruction.

David Weis, rabbi, for background information and religious and philosophical discussions that helped me frame the issues, and for stimulating discussions regarding the *Dead Sea Scrolls*, *The Aleppo Codex*, and other ancient texts. His review of the manuscript helped ensure I didn't make any egregious errors. Any remaining errors are my responsibility—or artistic license.

Theresa Moraga, theologian, for her background information, theories, and discussions on a variety of religion-related topics and for her contacts with professional theologians. All of this was crucial in helping me understand, and construct, the issues triggered by the Jesus Scroll.

Matti Friedman, journalist and author, for his background and insight on the Israel-Palestinian issue, citizens' on-the-street sentiment, the Middle Eastern mind-set, the two-state construct, the *Aleppo Codex*, Gaza, and background on Islamic terror groups. Matti's review of pertinent sections of the manuscript were vital. As noted, I recommend Matti's nonfiction book, *The Aleppo Codex*, for a riveting nonfiction account of the codex's disposition. **David Pollock**, PhD, Kaufman Fellow, The Washington Institute for Near East Policy, for background information regarding Palestinian public opinion, Palestinian public opinion polling, the peace process, and West Bank security concerns in a two-state solution. **Avi Isaacharoff,** Middle East analyst for *The Times of Israel*, for background information regarding the two-state solution.

Lawrence Wein, squad detective, NYPD, for help with the New York City chapters and NYPD-related questions.

Mark Waldo, crime scene investigator, Santa Ana Police Department, Forensic Services Section, for his assistance with lifting fingerprints using makeup powder and Gun Bluing techniques.

Christopher Schneider, executive director, agency relations, 5.11 Tactical, and assistant SWAT team leader Anaheim Police Department (ret.), for assistance with the equipment and logistics regarding DeSantos's Desert Eagle and SWAT/tactical unit terminology.

Jason Rubin, captain, United States Marine Corps, for help with the chapter dealing with the F-22. **Richard Drapkin**, restaurateur, restaurant consultant, and attorney, for his assistance with staging the kitchen fire aboard the dinner cruise ship. **Valentin Robiliard**, for ensuring my French translations were accurate. **James Rollins**, *New York Times* best-selling author, for being my eyes and ears for the C-17 cargo hold (he's been there, done that). **Lauren Dellar** for her experiences living in Israel, for refreshing my memory regarding Ben Gurion Airport, and for her affiliated contacts at Palestinian rights organizations.

Steve Israel, congressman (D-NY), and **Gidi Weiss**, Lt. Colonel, Israeli

Air Force (ret), and International Marketing and Sales Manager, Raphael Advanced Defense Systems Ltd., for information regarding Iron Dome, its funding, and technology sharing between Israel and the United States. (The assertion that the program was funded by the US contingent on the premise of money for technology was my invention. For obvious reasons, I did not ask if it were true.)

Thank you to those who wished to remain nameless, who provided me with insight and perspective, and to those who gave me research and analysis regarding Congressional testimony pertaining to Iran and Islamic extremist groups.

The terrific team at Open Road Integrated Media. There are many individuals toiling behind the scenes in the publishing and promotion of my novels, but among those I've worked with closely, I'd like to specifically recognize **Megan Buckman**, **Lauren Chomiuk**, **Rachel Chou**, **Hannah Dudley**, **Nina Lassam**, **Emma Pulitzer**, and **Andrea Worthington**. It would be tough to find a finer group of publishing professionals in the industry.

John Hutchinson and **Virginia Lenneville** at Norwood Press, who produce those fine hardcovers that feel great in the hand and look wonderful on the shelf. Pride goes into every book they publish, and it shows. They are outside the box thinkers who never shy away from trying something new. It's always a pleasure working with them.

Few things are as important in publishing as having exceptional editors who know your genre and your style and who can help you make your work realize its maximum potential. *The Lost Codex* is the eighth novel on which I've had the fortune of working with **Kevin Smith** and, as always, his insight and feedback help me slather on the wax from which I go to work, polishing the manuscript. On the topic of polish, I can't say enough about my copyeditor, **Chrisona Schmidt**, whose elbow grease brings it all to a brilliant shine. Chrisona is the best of the best and she makes a tough task—navigating grammatical rules and style manuals—fun to tackle.

My agents, **Joel Gotler** and **Frank Curtis**, for their years of guidance and advisement. Publishing has become an ever-changing world and it's vital having a team with decades of experience under their belts. Their counsel is a tremendous asset.

Richard Prati and **Steven Johnson** for their support regarding Norwood Press's hardcover edition of *Spectrum*. Norwood could not have done it without them.

My fans and readers, without whom my novels would go unappreciated; my Facebook fan group administrators, **Sandra Soreano** and **Terri Landreth**, for keeping everyone engaged and plugged into what's happening in the "Alan Jacobson universe," and to all those who post and keep lively discussions going.

As a writer, I am easily distracted, always thinking, observing, brainstorming. My wife **Jill** shares me with my fans and readers, publisher, publicist, agent, attorney, subject matter experts—and laptop, which is often mistaken to be an extra human appendage. But when I'm able to disconnect from my fictional world and step back into reality, my soulmate is always there for me.

ABOUT THE AUTHOR

Alan Jacobson is the national bestselling author of ten thrillers, including the FBI profiler Karen Vail series and the OPSIG Team Black novels. His books have been translated internationally and several have been optioned by Hollywood.

Jacobson has spent twenty years working with the FBI's Behavioral Analysis Unit, the DEA, the US Marshals Service, SWAT, the NYPD, Scotland Yard, local law enforcement, and the US military. This research and the breadth of his contacts help bring depth and realism to his characters and stories.

For video interviews and a free personal safety eBook co-authored by Alan Jacobson and FBI Profiler Mark Safarik, please visit www.AlanJacobson.com.

Connect with Jacobson on Twitter (@JacobsonAlan) and on Facebook (www.Facebook.com/AlanJacobsonFans).

THE WORKS OF ALAN JACOBSON

Alan Jacobson has established a reputation as one of the most insightful suspense/thriller writers of our time. His exhaustive research, coupled with years of unprecedented access to law enforcement agencies, including the FBI's Behavioral Analysis Unit, bring realism and unique characters to his pages. Following are his current, and forthcoming, releases.

STAND ALONE NOVELS

False Accusations > Dr. Phillip Madison has everything: wealth, power, and an impeccable reputation. But in the predawn hours of a quiet suburb, the revered orthopedic surgeon is charged with double homicide—a cold-blooded hit-and-run that leaves an innocent couple dead. Blood evidence has brought the police to his door. An eyewitness has placed him at the crime scene, and Madison has no alibi. With his family torn apart, his career forever damaged, no way to prove his innocence and facing life in prison, Madison must find the person who has engineered the case against him. Years after reading it, people still talk about his shocking ending. *False Accusations* launched Jacobson's career and became a national bestseller, prompting CNN to call him, "One of the brightest stars in the publishing industry." Note: Detective Ryan Chandler reprises his role in *Spectrum* (Karen Vail #6).

FBI PROFILER KAREN VAIL SERIES

The 7th Victim (Karen Vail #1) > Literary giants Nelson DeMille and James Patterson describe Karen Vail, the first female FBI profiler, as "tough, smart, funny, very believable," and "compelling." In *The 7th Victim*, Vail—with a dry sense of humor and a closet full of skeletons—heads up a task force to find the Dead Eyes Killer, who is murdering young women in Virginia . . . the backyard of the famed FBI Behavioral Analysis Unit. The twists and turns that Karen Vail endures in this tense psychological suspense thriller build to a powerful ending no reader will see coming. Named one of the Top 5 Best Books of the Year (*Library Journal*).

Crush (Karen Vail #2) > In light of the traumatic events of *The 7th Victim*, FBI Profiler Karen Vail is sent to the Napa Valley for a mandatory vacation—but the Crush Killer has other plans. Vail partners with Inspector Roxxann Dixon to track down the architect of death who crushes his victims' windpipes and leaves their bodies in wine caves. However, the killer is unlike anything the profiling unit has ever encountered, and Vail's miscalculations have dire consequences for those she holds dear. *Publishers Weekly* describes *Crush* as "addicting" and *New York Times* bestselling author Steve Martini calls it a thriller that's "Crisply written and meticulously researched," and "rocks from the opening page to the jarring conclusion." (Note: the *Crush* storyline continues in *Velocity*.)

Velocity (Karen Vail #3) > *A missing detective. A bold serial killer. And evidence that makes FBI profiler Karen Vail question the loyalty of those she has entrusted her life to.* In the shocking conclusion to *Crush*, Karen Vail squares off against foes more dangerous than any she has yet encountered. In the process, shocking personal and professional truths emerge—truths that may be more than Vail can handle. *Velocity* was named to *The Strand Magazine*'s Top 10 Best Books for 2010, *Suspense Magazine*'s Top 4 Best Thrillers of 2010, *Library Journal*'s Top 5 Best Books of the Year, and the *Los Angeles Times*' top picks of the year. Michael Connelly said *Velocity* is "As relentless as a bullet. Karen Vail is my kind of hero and Alan Jacobson is my kind of writer!"

Inmate 1577 (Karen Vail #4) > When an elderly woman is found raped and murdered, Karen Vail heads west to team up with Inspector Lance Burden and Detective Roxxann Dixon. As they follow the killer's trail in and around San Francisco, the offender leaves behind clues that ultimately lead them to the most unlikely of places, a mysterious island ripped from city lore whose long-buried, decades-old secrets hold the key to their case: Alcatraz. The Rock. It's a case that has more twists and turns than the famed Lombard Street. The legendary Clive Cussler calls *Inmate 1577* "a powerful thriller, brilliantly conceived and written." Named one of *The Strand Magazine*'s Top 10 Best Books of the Year.

No Way Out (Karen Vail #5) > Renowned FBI profiler Karen Vail returns in *No Way Out*, a high-stakes thriller set in London. When a high profile art gallery is bombed, Vail is dispatched to England to assist with Scotland Yard's investigation. But what she finds there—a plot to destroy a controversial, recently unearthed 440-year-old manuscript—turns into something much larger, and a whole lot more dangerous, for the UK, the US—and herself. With his trademark spirited dialogue, page-turning scenes, and well drawn characters, National Bestselling author Alan Jacobson ("My kind of writer," per Michael Connelly) has crafted the thriller of the year. Named a top ten "Best thriller of 2013" by both *Suspense Magazine* and *The Strand Magazine.*

Spectrum (Karen Vail #6) > It's 1995 and the NYPD has just graduated a promising new patrol officer named Karen Vail. During the rookie's first day on the job, she finds herself at the crime scene of a woman murdered in an unusual manner. As the years pass and more victims are discovered, Vail's career takes unexpected twists and turns—as does the case that's come to be known as "Hades." Now a skilled FBI profiler, will Vail be in a better position to catch the offender? Or will Hades prove to be Karen Vail's hell on earth? #1 *New York Times* bestseller Richard North Patterson called *Spectrum*, "Compelling and crisp . . . A pleasure to read."

OPSIG TEAM BLACK SERIES

The Hunted (OPSIG Team Black Novel #1) > How well do you know the one you love? How far would you go to find out? When Lauren Chambers' husband Michael disappears, her search reveals his hidden past involving the FBI, international assassins—and government secrets that some will go to great lengths to keep hidden. As *The Hunted* hurtles toward a conclusion mined with turn-on-a-dime twists, no one is who he appears to be and nothing is as it seems. *The Hunted* introduces the dynamic Department of Defense covert operative Hector DeSantos and FBI Director Douglas Knox, characters who return in future OPSIG Team Black novels, as well as the Karen Vail series (*Velocity, No Way Out,* and *Spectrum*).

Hard Target (OPSIG Team Black Novel #2) > An explosion pulverizes the president-elect's helicopter on Election Night. The group behind the assassination attempt possesses far greater reach than anything the FBI has yet encountered—and a plot so deeply interwoven in the country's fabric that it threatens to upend America's political system. But as covert operative Hector DeSantos and FBI Agent Aaron "Uzi" Uziel sort out who is behind the bombings, Uzi's personal demons not only jeopardize the investigation but may sit at the heart of a tangle of lies that threaten to trigger an international terrorist attack. Lee Child called *Hard Target*, "Fast, hard, intelligent. A terrific thriller." Note: FBI Profiler Karen Vail plays a key role in the story.

The Lost Codex (OPSIG Team Black Novel #3) > *In a novel Jeffery Deaver called "brilliant," two ancient biblical documents reveal long-buried secrets that could change the world as we know it.* In 930 CE, a revered group of scholars pen the first sanctioned Bible, planting the seed from which other major religions will grow. But in 1953, half the manuscript goes missing while being transported from Syria. Around the same time, in the foothills of the Dead Sea, an ancient scroll is discovered—and promptly stolen. Six decades later, both parchments stand at the heart of a geopolitical battle between foreign governments and radical extremists, threatening the lives of millions. With the American homeland under siege, the president turns to a team of uniquely trained covert operatives that includes FBI profiler Karen Vail, Special Forces veteran Hector DeSantos, and FBI terrorism expert Aaron Uziel. Their mission: find the stolen documents and capture—or kill—those responsible for unleashing a coordinated and unprecedented attack on US soil. Set in Washington, DC, New York, Paris, England, and Israel, *The Lost Codex* is international historical intrigue at its heart-stopping best.

SHORT STORIES

"Fatal Twist" > The Park Rapist has murdered his first victim—and FBI profiler Karen Vail is on the case. As Vail races through the streets of Washington, DC to chase down a promising lead that may help her catch the killer, a military-trained sniper takes aim at his target, a wealthy businessman's son. But what brings these two unrelated offenders together is something the nation's capital has never before experienced. "Fatal Twist" provides a taste of Karen Vail that will whet your appetite.

"Double Take" > NYPD detective Ben Dyer awakens from cancer surgery to find his life turned upside down. His fiancée has disappeared and Dyer, determined to find her, embarks on a journey mined with potholes and startling revelations—revelations that have the potential to forever change his life. "Double Take" introduces NYPD Lieutenant Carmine Russo and Detective Ben Dyer, who return to play significant roles in *Spectrum* (Karen Vail #6).

More to come > For a peek at recently released Alan Jacobson novels, interviews, reading group guides, and more, visit www.AlanJacobson.com.

THE KAREN VAIL SERIES

FROM OPEN ROAD MEDIA

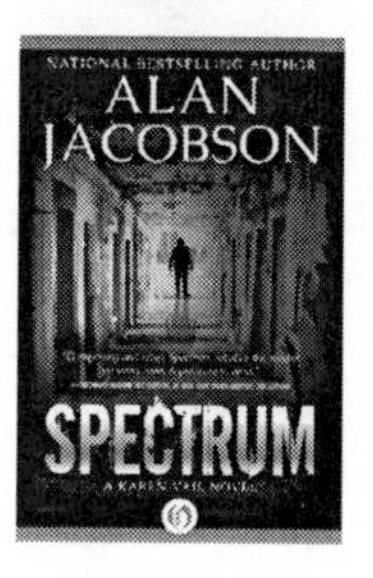

Available wherever ebooks are sold

OPEN ROAD
INTEGRATED MEDIA

CPSIA information can be obtained at www.ICGtesting.com
Printed in the USA
BVOW02s1915041015

420683BV00001B/1/P